AMAZON/Print VERSION ONLY

Ebook/Print Cover: Carol Marques Design
Editing & Formatting: Little Tailfeather Publishing
Cassandra's logos: Pretty in Ink Creations/Artlogo
Alphas: Kat Silver, Becky Ross, Erica Taryn
Arc Teams: Cassandra's claws
Sensitivity Readers: Brit Mason, Gail Jericho
Chapter Art in print: @spookacola
Translation Consultant: Mo Jacobs
Legal Services: Joshua Farley, esq.
Images/Fonts: Creative Fabrica, Depositphotos, Shutterstock, & Photoshop

No GenAI was used within this book. All errors and greatness are by an adhd muppet.

Little Tailfeather Publishing

APEX ACADEMY
CAPERS

IN PREY WE TRUST

INTERNATIONAL BESTSELLING AUTHOR
CASSANDRA FEATHERSTONE

STALK CASSANDRA FEATHERSTONE IN THE DARK CORNERS OF THE WEB

JOIN MY FACEBOOK GROUP AND FOLLOW ME EVERYWHERE!

WANT MORE?

SIGN UP FOR
MY BI-WEEKLY MANIFESTO FOR A
FREE SERIES SAMPLER:

Join my Ream as a FREE follower or exclusive subscriber to get access to cover reveals, WIPs, Serial Stories, and personal chats from me!

Content Information

This is a *paranormal whychoose romance with poly elements*—our FMC, Delores, will not have to choose between love interests.

There are many situations included that are intended for mature audiences (18+).

In this book/series, there may be instances/references (be they small or lengthy) that could trigger some individuals such as:

- liberal use of appropriate consent
- biting
- BDSM and intro to BDSM
- primal play
- raw sex
- shifted sex
- traumatic childhood
- MMF, MM, MFM, MF, MMFMM, and more
- super heinous puns (seriously, lots)
- underage drinking
- drug use

- unhealthy coping mechanisms
- body parts in jars
- neurospicy MMC
- death
- body modifications
- fancy genitalia
- mate knots/barbs
- slightly unhinged MMC
- bullying (in person and on social media)
- PTSD
- blood
- emotional abuse from parents and friends
- alcohol abuse
- domestic violence
- implied child abuse
- body dysmorphia
- bad language
- fight clubs
- emotional manipulation
- power play
- adorable nicknames
- physical intimidation
- coercive emotional abuse by authority figures (not in poly group)
- voyeurism
- rough sex
- biting
- masturbation play
- sex with wings and tails
- attempted/successful kidnappings
- therapeutic abuse (not sexual)
- marking
- lawyers (ugh.)
- professors/student (above 18+)
- age gap (from 17 yrs to almost 2000 yrs)

- use of sex toys
- family dysfunction
- suspension play
- rope play
- pegging
- betrayal (non-poly group)
- disabled side character
- absolute disrespect for shitty parents
- pop culture references (so many)
- brief mentions of non-body positive dieting culture
- brief mentions of parental death
- mention of drug sales and distribution
- very liberal re-imagining of history
- discussion of other species as lower
- official corruption
- name calling
- occasional misogyny
- inappropriate use of a library
- exhibitionism
- discussion of non-MC treating a side character with a disability poorly
- hand necklaces
- adult bullying
- magical kinks
- impact play
- sensory deprivation
- abusive bosses
- elitism
- bribery
- corpses
- fat shaming (not by MCs)
- drama
- physical threats to FMC and others
- species-ism
- discussion of shifter trafficking

- discussion of trafficking auctions
- suspicion of brainwashing

No sexual practices in this book should be taken as safe or appropriate for real life application.

Content information is important and I don't ever want to harm a reader with inaccurate information.

Author Ramblings

Readers,

I truly didn't think I'd ever get to this book, and I'm so very grateful to everyone who has supported me in doing so. It hurt my heart to think I'd have to give up a world I spent so much time crafting and a storyline I was so excited about because of some external trauma.

But here we are and I'm overjoyed.

Including fan requested scenes in the last book such as the snowball fight and the rave (and more) was a blast for me, and I strive to make sure I get to anything y'all missed in my bonus scenes. You can always message me with wishlists! I crave talking about my books with readers.

I consider myself lucky to do the thing I love so much and share it with all of you.

There's been a lot of drama in the book world lately and authors are struggling to survive the waves. I haven't escaped unscathed, but like a phoenix, I'm stepping out of the flames to be reborn.

I've let go of all the past pain and I'm moving on from the trauma to forge my path in a much healthier, more sustainable fashion.

This series is part of that growth and much like Dolly, I'm more myself without all the negative influences holding me back.

I'm very proud of the re-written versions of the previous books and the positive responses all of you amazing readers have shared with me. I appreciate all of you, especially my author friends and my alpha readers. All of you help me continue finding the joy on even the worst of days.

Unlike many, I actually read all the feedback and sometimes glean very useful information from it. I don't focus on unkind or unhelpful statements; that doesn't serve me or my readers. Like any book/series, there are folks who don't enjoy my brand of wacky humor, deep character development, and detailed world building—that's totally okay. If they prefer a different style or content, I absolutely support choosing authors who will fulfill that need.

We should all be reading what we love and I believe that with all my heart.

That said, I'm also aware a handful of readers were disappointed by the changes to the first two books. I knew when I was re-working them to better fit within my brand and the kind of story I always wanted to tell that focus on character development, world-building, and plot might not be what some previous fans were looking for. Regardless, I've brought the Apex world back into alignment with my values, my beliefs, and the quality I want to give my readers in my books.

My books always get spicier as the series continues, giving the characters time to grow into relationships and weather situations with a distinctly mature flair. Focusing on fleshing out those characters allowed me to dispense with some less desirable references readers didn't enjoy and add in things I was more comfortable with. The focus of the series is Dolly and her men finding one another, overcoming their pasts, solving the mysteries, and establishing a strong family together.

That's what I always wanted and I'm so happy it''s reflected in my words now.

As we progress through the series, Dolly is maturing and learning that holding onto the pain from those who have damaged you won't fix the hurt they caused. It also will not help you heal. There's a sage wisdom in that I've been slowly taking into my own heart.

If setting boundaries and refusing to allow people in your life to use and abuse you makes you the villain in someone's petty little story, then so be it.

You cannot control people who are determined to blame their shortcomings and flaws on you, nor can you stop them from flinging their toxic goo far and wide. All you can do is learn from the experience and move on—something Dolly and I have in common.

We've both had to tangle with groups of adult bullies (though hers are much younger) who simply will not take the hint and find something else to do with themselves. In *COP*, Dolly figured out that if your 'friend' spends their time tearing down others—even if they 'deserve it'—they are the problem. If you're afraid to say something because you could be next, that person is not your friend.

It doesn't matter if it's 'venting' among friends in a private chat or said in confidence—it's unlikely you're the only friend they spread these rumors to and if they do it to others, they will do it to you.

She's learned through the past two books that regardless of the beautiful presentation on the outside, some people are rotten to the core. The Heathers using their perceived power to hurt everyone they deem unworthy wasn't something to ignore; it was a boundary she should have set, and she paid for not doing so.

Much like her, I had a deeply painful learning experience and I know some of you will feel her despair in your bones. But I hope you enjoy watching her grow and develop as a person throughout this book. She's getting stronger and more confident because she's surrounded by people who love her and treat her well for once in her life. The changes in her were marvelous to write, and even her men grow as individuals as well.

Finding her peace and learning to love herself for who she is—rather than worry about who she is not—is a lesson we can all relate to.

Thank you for joining me on the journey.

Blood and guts,

Cassandra Featherstone

QUEEN OF SMART. SASSY SPICE

READER'S NOTE
A FEW THINGS YOU SHOULD KNOW…

Come Out & Prey and *Let Us Prey* should be read *before* this book. I also highly recommend reading the bonus scenes available here.

This is a multi-book series, so *everything will not be revealed in the first book*. Some plot lines will continue through series in a larger arc and not get resolved in the first or even the next book.

I write lengthy books with intricate world building, strong character development, and *lots* of tiny threads that stretch throughout a series that may not always seem important at first glance. However, I promise nothing I put to paper and leave in the book is unimportant; it may simply become *more* important later on. There is no 'throwaway' detail in my worlds, so every scene will mean something eventually.

I promise it will all get tied up and have a HEA; don't worry!

In Prey We Trust is a why choose/poly romance, which means our FMC will not have to choose.

I would consider it a medium burn, slow build family group. It will get spicier in the following books. If you're looking for porn with little to no plot, no judgment, but this isn't the series for you.

It's also not closed door or FTB, so I believe the spice will be worth the wait. I realize spice scales are subjective and everyone has different opinions on it, so forgive me if mine and yours aren't totally aligned.

There are some characters and creatures that speak in other languages. I made the *translations clickable end of chapter notes* to help.

Just an FYI:

There are a *lot of puns*—they are intentionally bad at times and writing them made me giggle. If you don't like silly, world-specific humor like that, it may annoy you.

There are some words that are slang, jargon, or foreign that may seem to be spelled wrong—*please email the author or find her on social media rather than report to Amazon* if you find a typo. This has been proofed and edited *several* times since release; if you believe you found errors, you may not be correct. It could be a stylistic choice or a dialect choice. Please do not assume the two ARC teams, betas, alphas, and several proofers missed everything you believe is incorrect.

Please do not email critical feedback that is not a simple typo or formatting issue—this book is written and released. It will not be changed after publication to suit personal editing opinions or requests.

If you see this book *anywhere besides Kindle Unlimited in ebook format,* please reach out to me via social media or email. Pirating kills my ability to write full time and I am so grateful for your help.

Contact my team for typos or to report piracy: teamcassandrafeatherstone@cassandrafeatherstone.com

In Prey We Trust Playlists

CHAPTER TITLE SONGS

In Prey We Trust Chapter Playlist

BONUS PLAYLIST

Pred Games Workout Jams Playlist

House
Aquatic
House
Feline
Savananda Kavrit
International
Library &
Diplomatic Archives
Shirdal
Arts
Complex
House
Reptilian

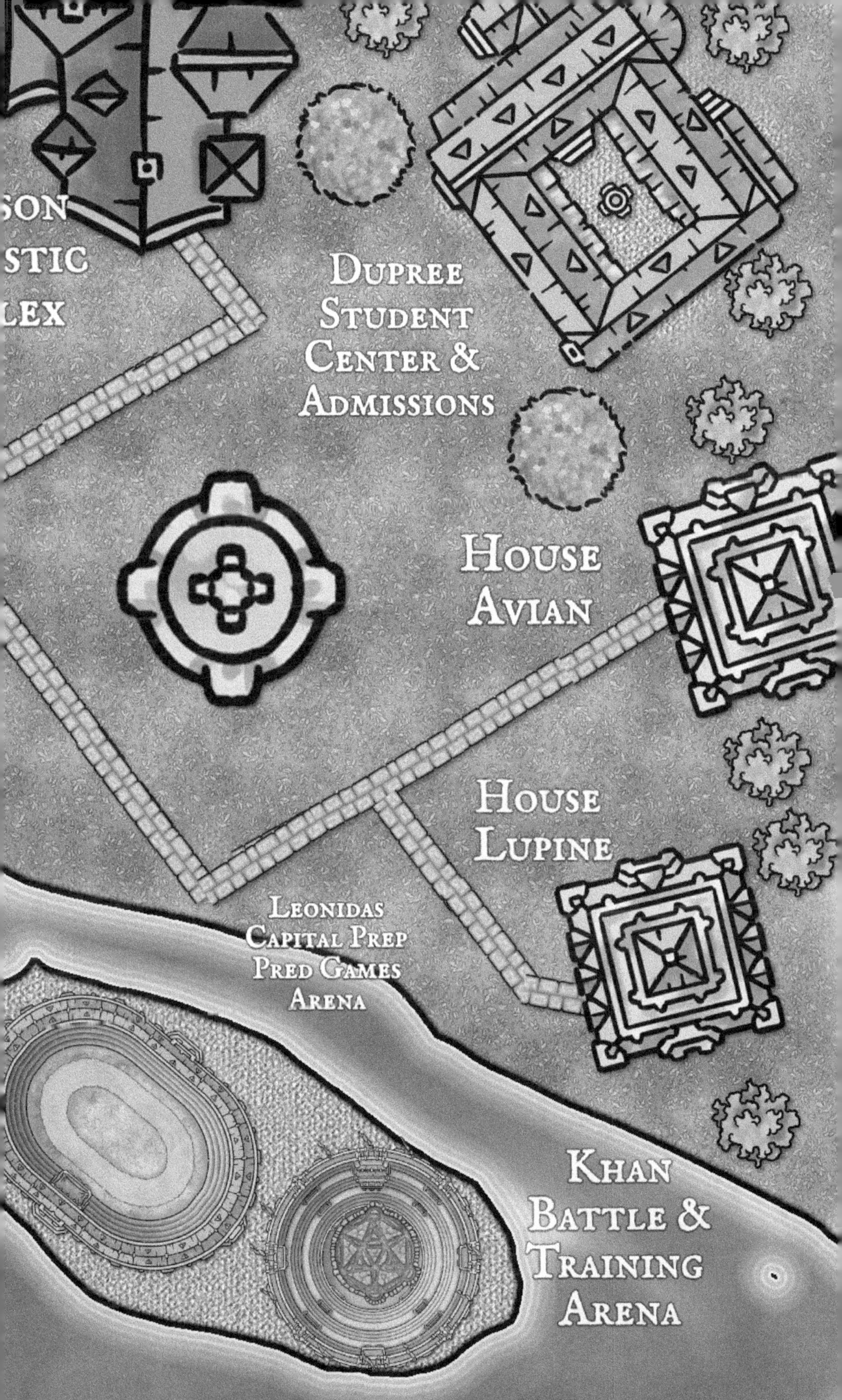

SON
STIC
LEX
DUPREE STUDENT CENTER & ADMISSIONS
HOUSE AVIAN
HOUSE LUPINE
LEONIDAS CAPITAL PREP PRED GAMES ARENA
KHAN BATTLE & TRAINING ARENA

Name:
Delores Diamond Drew
Semester: Fall 2023

CLASS SCHEDULE

All class schedules subject to administrative and professorial approval.

time	monday	tuesday	wednesday	thursday	friday
7:00 AM		SS 201 Shifter Studies Felix Khan	DANC 201 DANCE & MOVEMENT Natasha Blutarsky	SS 201 Shifter Studies Felix Khan	HDISR 100 Human Diplomacy & International Shifter Relations Kamara Rakoto
8:00 AM	COUNSELING CARINA ROCKLAND				
9:00 AM		SPE 201 Speech2 Adriatica los Feliz		CDES 201 Costuming Chester Khan	ENG 325 Shakespeare Renard Laveaux
10:00 AM	ACT 301 ACTING 3 Adriatica los Feliz		ACT 301 ACTING 3 Adriatica los Feliz	SDES 201 Set Design Chester Khan	
11:00 AM		MUS 201 Music Theory 2 Madame Solange de Bouvier			PGT 400 Pred Games Team Practice Zhenga Leonidas
12:00 PM	VOICE 201 Vocal Private Madame Solange de Bouvier			SHY 201 Shifter History Herr Helmut Blitzen	
1:00 PM			HDISR 100 Human Diplomacy & International Shifter Relations Kamara Rakoto		
2:00 PM					
3:00 PM	SHY 201 Shifter History Herr Helmut Blitzen	PIANO 201 Piano Private Madame Solange de Bouvier	PGT 400 Pred Games Team Practice Zhenga Leonidas	COUNSELING CARINA ROCKLAND	
4:00 PM					

VICTORI SPOILA IRE

To everyone in their final stage of healing…

Telling your bullies to fuck all the way

off is the best reward.

Know your worth…
then add tax.
~Anonymous

Previously On
Let Us Prey...

Our intrepid bunny shifter, Dolly, arrived at Apex Academy with a chip on her shoulder and revenge in her heart. She'd spent the summer learning to make it on her own, despite all the attempts at abuse thrown at her by her ex friends and douchebag Todd.

Unfortunately, even her first day turned out to be a trial when she discovered her dorm completely trashed. Luckily for her, Fitz the lovable psycho worked out a solution with the reclusive winged professors for her to take up residence in their Tower—as long as she stayed in her space.

Of course, that would never *happen, right?*

As school kicks into gear, Dolly joins the theater program with her new friends, Rufus and Cori, hoping to do something she truly loves for once in her life. Her mother continues to be a snarky, calculating sociopath, but our girl is handling it.

What she isn't handling is the intense attraction to five professors and the constant bullying from the mean girls who just won't die, the Heathers. They try to have her killed by dingoes, treat her like garbage, and cause trouble in every class they share. Much like a severe case of the clap, she just can't shake them without some serious doses of their own medicine.

Dolly and Fitz grow closer because she accepts him for who he is. Through all the interactions in their classes, she slowly worms her way into the hearts of Aubrey, Felix, Renard, and Chess. By the time Apex hosts a big Halloween bash, she's got their trust—mostly—but her efforts are for naught when the dead body of a student gets discovered nearby.

The mystery only deepens from there because not only has no one been able to explain the poisoning at the prom, but this dead student comes out of nowhere as well. Dolly and her men investigate when the administration and Council seem unconcerned with the increasing number of students disappearing after holiday breaks, but every clue they find leads to more questions.

After Yule, more kids from Apex don't make it back, so the guys form a circle around our bunny, trying their hardest to keep her safe. She muddles her ways through classes and the continued jabs from the Heathers, but the body count just keeps rising.

How's a girl supposed to concentrate on exams and hottie boyfriends when bodies appear in her home?

By the time midterms are over, everyone is on high alert and it's rough at Apex. The Heathers try to get her expelled for plagiarism, a dead student drops from the balcony at rehearsal, and the Council still refuses to help. Our makeshift family of shifters has a ton of leads and riddles solved, but they still don't know how everything connects—until Chess discovers a clue that sends everyone into the secret prey tunnels on the Blood Moon.

Mystery, magic, and mayhem blend as they discover their families and those in the Council have something to do with all of this—and Dolly shows she has more power than being simple prey. When they chase after shadowy figures and a lightning imbued bunny, the guys end up having to save one of their own…or so it seems.

In Prey We Trust picks up a few weeks after *Let Us Prey*. I recommend you read LUP Bonus Scene #2 here to find out more about what happened in between!

Lush Life

Delores

"They won't get finished in time for the start of school?"

My screech echoes off the walls of my room and my eyes fly open as I cover my mouth. Lucille and Bruno *should* be out with their latest flings still, but I hate risking their ire. Staying here during the summer wasn't my idea nor my choice. In a shocking turn of events that surprised no one, my bitchy mother demanded I come home after the explosions rocked Apex. She pretended it was out of concern, but she was covering her ass.

Lucille was the major vote for not adding security to the campus after the disappearances and deaths. Spinning it as if the violence escalating completely surprised her to the point of destroying most of the campus buildings was a PR move. Pink's family controlled the press, so the Barringtons made sure that was the story people heard. The news said they were confident Apex would get rebuilt and ready for students *with* additional security by the fall, but it looks like that didn't work out.

I don't know how the Council warded off the Sibbies, nor do I know why none of the missing students were found—not even bodies. All I know is that I was a prisoner here all summer, save for working at Luc's, and my asshole parents haven't been here more than a handful of days at a time. They've been traveling all over the world, leaving me to haunt the halls like I'm fucking Rapunzel. Each day, I get a little more stir crazy, but at least I've been able to keep in contact with my friends and my guys.

That's the only lifeline keeping me sane.

"Girl, my parents got the letter last week! How are you in the dark? Your egg donor is the one who pulls all the strings in this puppet show," Rufus says as he continues working on Cori's nails.

I sigh, watching them enviously through our Fangtime chat. "Lucille and Bruno barely speak to me unless it's threats or nasty comments about my 'trashy makeover.' And they're *never* here, which is a blessing and curse. Lucille has Mattie with her all the time and Bruno has Bruiser with him. So they hired an entire staff of imposing dickheads who patrol the house, follow me to work, and report back to them every time I take one step out of my room."

Cori clucks her tongue, her forehead wrinkling as she looks at me with concern. "They really want people to think they give a shit about all the people who died, huh?"

"Absolutely not. They want the masses to think they give a fuck about *me* because I'm an heir—despite being disowned—and that the Council takes the danger seriously. It doesn't; Lucille is just pissed someone pulled one over on her spies." I rub my hands over my face in annoyance, then look at them both seriously. "If Apex won't be ready, what the fuck are they going to do?"

"Having it ready was a *pipe dream*, Dollypop. Those fucking bombs took out half the main building, the Shird, the upper section of the library, the academic complex, two dorms, half the staff housing, and the entire gym. And since *we* know they weren't just spicy Playdoh like C-4, the area is full of some..." Rufus lowers his voice to a whisper, "... magical contaminant that's kept the workers dropping like flies. That's if you believe the rumors on the Prey-net and I do."

"Poor Aubrey," I murmur as I rub my chest. "His real treasures were all underground, but it has to be *killing* him. He can't get to the things he wants to save down there."

Cori snorts. "Man, your guys have definitely been trying to keep your spirits up, babe. The National Library sent a team, and the big lizard man was with them. His treasures are fine, as I assume everything in your precious Tower is. Interesting how whoever did this didn't have the *cajones* to piss off the two flying warlords by touching their space."

"How do you know all this? I've been searching everywhere for this kind of info, Cori." My eyes narrow and Rufus trills a knowing laugh. "What? Why are you laughing?"

"Oh, because our darling Coco has been chit-chatting with all the lovely prey friends of your rock man. She talks to Raina and the cranky nurses all the time. Apparently, the prey staff still live onsite because the magic doesn't affect them as badly. We get *all* the juicy tidbits." His expression is smug and I wrinkle my nose, wanting to reach through the screen and throttle my bestie.

"Ugh, fine, you bitches. Tell me what you know that my dickhead parents have failed to mention before one of my stupid body-guards comes in to do their checks." I look over my shoulder at the door, infuriated that no amount of strings the guys or Luc tried to pull could free me from this nonsense.

I'm nothing more than a set piece or an auction item, but they enjoyed taking my freedom.

"Apex has five years of students, as you know, and the classes always get smaller towards the end because people don't make it. So the Council split up the students and staff among the other four major academies for at least the first term, though it's likely going to be the entire year. Some of the staff are heading to Bloodstone, the fourth and fifth years are going to *Zhuǎn xīng*

U&M, the third years are headed to *Académie des crocs et des griffes*, and the second and first years are going to Capital Prep."

My heart leaps into my throat, and I swallow hard as tears spring to my eyes. *How is that fair?* There's no way Lucille didn't arrange this, so I'd get separated from the only friends I've ever had. That doesn't bode well for how they've divided the staff. "Guys, I can't… What will I do without you? What about the guys? Goddess, I *hate* my fucking mother!"

Rufus gives me a cagey grin. "Aw, Coco, she loves us!"

"Apparently," she teases with a soft smile. "Don't worry, Dolly. *Someone* pulled some very sketchy shit from the background. Both of us got letters separately from the general 'Welcome to your new reality' letters from Apex. They informed our parents we would *not* be attending *Académie des crocs et des griffes* like the other third years. It said they selected us for a mentoring program to help develop the arts programs at the brand new Shirdal Arts Center at Capital Prep."

I blink. *Holy shit.* "Who the hell convinced the Shirdals to create an entire program at another school? How did they get you two exceptions from what the Council decreed?"

"I can only assume a group of powerful men with deep pockets and strong connections to people who could sway our former headmistress to circumvent the edicts," Cori says. "Notice no students are being sent for a stay at Bloodstone; I'd bet they were involved in making sure that didn't happen, either."

Pulling an annoyed face, I mutter, "Would have been nice to ditch the fucking Heathers and my ex there, though."

They both laugh and it makes everything feel like it's going to be okay again. Being locked up here all summer has been soul crushing, but the few moments I get with the people I care about have helped me survive it. Despite not being able to see them in person, the few minutes on video chat or the times I've felt Fitz watching from afar kept me afloat. If my mother had them all scattered to the wind next year, it would have been devastating.

"Where are all the professors going?" I ask as Rufus applies Cori's polish to the nail form. "I hate thinking anyone I like is getting sentenced to that hellhole."

"Ha! Well, your guys obviously finagled their way to Cappie. Professor Balena is going to the *Académie* and Sarabhai requested U&M because it's close to her homeland. They scattered a bunch of the English department to the wind, but Cormac is coming with us, as are the saucy Professor Leonidas and our fearful leader. I don't know any of the ones who they say are going to Bloodstone, except Abel—which we *know* isn't true," Rufus says thoughtfully. "Maybe they all died in the explosions and this is a cover-up."

I ponder that for a moment and nod. "That makes sense. Lucille knows no one will confirm or deny anything that goes on there. Hiding any casualties as transfers would keep the death toll down in the press."

"Do we know for sure *any* of the professors supposedly being transferred survived? It hit the staff housing pretty hard. Maybe all of them are gone." Cori frowns as she looks at me. "They rushed us out of there so fast after the bombs that we only saw your guys because they wouldn't let anyone near you."

Remembering the limp form of Chess in Felix's arms makes me suck in a deep breath. I'm still not sleeping well since that night.

The vision of Clarice and Bettina haunts my dreams—the two of them working on him until he showed signs of life. Argyle bitched at the rest of us while tending to our wounds, but he was so still for so long that I was sure he was gone. Fitz nearly tore the place apart while we watched him in the coma. His drug tolerance made it impossible to sedate him, so I stayed with him while Felix watched the nurses check him over that night.

"Oh, Dolly…" Cori's voice cuts into my thoughts, rousing me from the pain. "If you could see your face, girl. It's okay; he's alive and we're all going to be together. We survived."

Licking my lips, I nod. "I know, Coco, but it's a trauma. It's not going away soon; I just have to work through it. Seeing people die has been a regular part of my life since I was little, but never anyone I care about. The acceptance I have for killing those who deserve it doesn't extend to you and my guys. And fuck knows Lucille wouldn't let me talk to anyone, so I'm internet therapy-ing the hell out of myself to work through the pain."

Rufus growls, baring his fangs for a minute. "Hermes on a pole dancing, Dollypop. Even my asshole gang member relatives had me sit with a headshrinker a couple of times when I got back. I may be crazy as a bedbug, but they'd prefer it not be white coat crazy."

"Yes, it'd be a shame if the future leader of a criminal organization were to be truly insane," Cori quips. I laugh and she shrugs. "My folks sent me, too, but we're hippie dippy for preds."

Uh, yeah, they are.

"I did my best, guys. I'm not sleeping great, but I don't cry at the slightest trigger anymore. And my bunny is talking to me again, which, as you know, was a problem for the first couple of weeks." That was scary as hell and I don't know if her silence was about fear of losing a fated mate or my separation or the weird blue shit the night Apex exploded. She's back, but it's with no sort of explanation for the absence, even in my gut.

"Good," Rufus says as someone yells in the background. "We were worried about that, especially with our new home next year. Apex is the most vicious school on a pred level, but Cappie is going to be a nightmare of politics and leverage and violence. They bred every motherfucker who goes to school there with the attitude of your exes, D. You need to have every bit of your strength."

"Why? I mean, I thought Apex was the cream of the crop where all the Council heirs go," I ask in confusion.

Cori chuckles. "It was. But now all of them are going to Cappie, which was full of the children of diplomats, international rich fucks, society mavens, and celebrities. You're headed to a place where the *entire* population has a minimum of several million, not just the chosen few. And they've *all* been raised to think their shit doesn't stink—Spiderella, The Sphinx, and the Real Housewolves all have kids who go there."

By Poseidon's salty balls, that's the worst news I've heard all day.

"So you're saying I won't just have my old enemies, I'll have to navigate a full student body of people who hate me either for what I am or who I'm related to?"

"Yup," they chorus.

Another yell sounds out, and Rufus rolls his eyes. "Okay, Dolly-pop, we gotta go. Aunt Brandine needs us in the salon again. Start packing up your shit. We'll send snaps of what we received tonight, so you know what to do to prepare."

"Thanks, guys. I miss you," I say as I blow a kiss at the screen.

"Ciao, bella!"

The screen goes black and I'm left alone again, hoping like hell everything will go as they said.

Because with my luck, it definitely won't.

I Feel Like I'm Drowning

Fitz

"I fucking hate this!"

Chess gives me a soft smile as I pace back and forth in our room in the spacious townhouse Felix acquired for us just down the lane from the campus of Capital Prep. "We know, baby. But it's not that much longer until school starts."

Whirling, I narrow my eyes at him as he lies on the giant bed. "All of you fuckers should have let me deal with her parents. No one would have batted a lash at a secret assassin."

A snort sounds from the doorway, and I see Felix looking at me in amusement. He's been a hell of a lot less tense since the night of the explosion, despite our separation from my baby girl. "It wouldn't have surprised anyone, Fitz, but it would have put an even bigger target on the princess' head."

"That's probably true," Chessie says as he holds his hand out to me. "Angel isn't ready to take their place on the Council—if she'll ever be—and it would have created a power vacuum. Her mother is an enemy best left to a more helpful time."

Raking my hand through my hair, I growl in frustration. "I can't stand her being so close and not be able to go near her."

"We *know*," my brothers chorus and I snarl again.

Felix tilts his head. "Why didn't you go help Ren and Aubrey set up their new fortress? You could have burnt off some of that nervous energy."

I glare at him. As if I had an interest in watching the flittering gargoyle decorate while our stodgy librarian meticulously catalogs everything they saved from the Tower. "Because I don't want to play Martha Stewart; I want to see my baby girl!"

"*Fitz*," my twin says in his 'no nonsense,' voice. It's not a Raj command, but it's laced with power just the same. "You've watched her every day, like you did last summer, and you survived. Stop throwing a tantrum."

Turning my head from side to side, I crack my neck as frustration zooms through my body. I know Felix is worried, too, but between nursing Chessie back to health and being unable to get within sniffing distance of my girl for weeks, my patience is shot. My consort insists he's a hundred percent now, but I notice how easily he tires after being active for a while. He's still on the mend, and I can't work out my aggravation in a fun way, either.

I'd never forgive myself if he relapsed because I'm too keyed up to hold my shit together.

"Why don't we call Dolly? If we hop through the perimeter exit we created, we can visit Aubrey and Renard in their new home and video call her. I bet they'd stop squabbling over throw pillows long enough to chat with her," Chess says with a grin. "I'd like to see her, too."

Felix rubs his hand over his jaw, thinking about it for a moment. "There's plenty of room in that fucking mausoleum. The gargoyle has a bell tower, the dragon has an underground lair again, and the third floor is completely theirs. I don't see why it can't be the new hangout on campus."

Huffing an annoyed sigh, I nod and stop pacing for a moment. "Fine. But those assholes better have set shit up for everyone, or I'm calling in favors to have a fucking tunnel built to this damn house."

They look at another, lips quirking in amusement, but I'm not fucking joking. I'll hire a goddamn squadron of moles if that's how get access to my baby girl twenty-four/seven.

What the hell is the use of being filthy rich if I can't make my life easier?

By the time we get to the sneaky entrance we had created at the back edge of the school, my veins are buzzing with energy. I don't know how Chess or the winged woe-is-me warrior are dealing with this shit. Felix and Señor Spicypants haven't slept with my baby girl yet, so I doubt they have this drive to be as close to her as possible. It's making me crazier than usual, and I have no outlets for my pent-up energy.

Well, except the continued torture of her ex friends and boyfriend, but that only lasts for a little while.

Since I found out the damn school might not be ready in time for the fall semester a month ago, I started diverting my fury to appropriate targets. I don't know if they realize who's been creeping them all out with random notes, gory gifts, and scary threats, but I'd bet my furry ass they haven't been sleeping. I haven't taken a trophy from the plastic blondes yet, but that's because I'm waiting for the right thing at the right moment. I know for a fact the two ancients we're visiting saved her jars when they packed up, so I'll add to the collection once she's settled in.

"No one's asked this yet, but where in the hell is our girl going to live?" Chess says as we slink along the river bank to the back entrance of the *Savananda Kavrit International Library and Diplomatic Archives.*

Unlike the library at Apex, the damn thing is a multi-level compound. It has a bell tower, complex underground facility, and a full fucking staff of prey working to assist the librarian. It pissed my fire breathing friend off that a Sphinx family founded this place. Its collection is rivaled only by the National Library in the city proper. The amount of threats and beatings it took to send their exiled family member on an extended sabbatical was exhausting.

You can't even beat the living shit out of a Sphinx without them droning on about their biology and internal medicine and whatever other fucking riddles pop into their head.

"This place doesn't separate the dorms by years," Felix says as we swipe the cards Renard made for us to get in after hours. "They do it by species and the princess isn't a major species, so she'll probably get stuck in House Reptilian. It's the smallest population of the five. According to the shit in the staff packets, takes in the amphibians and other preds who don't fall under Lupine, Feline, Avian, or Aquatic."

I blink, rounding on them in disbelief. "Does that seem like a bad fucking plan to anyone else? Who the hell trusts snakes with rabbits?"

Mt twin grimaces as we make our way through the maze of hallways that will lead to the archivist's quarters. "No one, but she'd be no better off than any of the others. In fact, she'd be worse off in most of them. House Aquatic might be safest, but half of that place is submerged, so we can't try to move her there."

This place is weird as fuck and I can't even imagine why fucking rock stars send their kids here.

"Calm down, Fitz," Chess says as he grabs my hand. "We'll work something out; we always do. You said Dolly took jujitsu this summer, right? She can hold her own for the first week until we work this shit out."

I grumble and squeeze his hand. "I know; I know. We don't have sway here yet because we haven't dominated the staff or administration, so we don't have the pull we need. I fucking hate waiting, though."

Felix pauses before he swipes us out of the library proper. "Oh, but I have plans, brother. Don't worry about how we'll fix things; worry about what we need to do in the first staff Pred Games to show everyone who's in charge at Capital Prep this year."

That makes my tiger roar inside of me, and I crack my knuckles. "At your command, big bro. Always."

We head down the short hallway to the double doors of the dragon's lair, and I frown at the plush carpeting beneath my feet. Classical music plays from hidden speakers. The paintings are original. This damn place is swanky as hell. Suddenly, I'm less worried about killing fuckers in the staff games as much as pissed these two wankers landed in the sweetest place on campus. Irritation ramps my energy up again, so I let go of Chess' hand and shoot to the front of the group.

Throwing open the heavy doors in agitation, I call out, "Oh, Lucy, I'm hooooome!"

After all, their casa is me casa, right? It's only fair.

"Holy shit," Felix mutters as we take in the scene before us. "How did these assholes hit the goddamn jackpot?"

"Better question: *where* are these assholes?" I retort as I stride into the vast dome ceilinged room that serves as their living area. They have a giant sitting area, a fully stocked bar, and a kitchen that's making Chess drool as he stares at it. The floor plan is completely open, rooms blending seamlessly into one luxurious space big enough to hold them even when they shift—including the damn dragon.

"This place is amazing," Chess says as he toddles like a zombie toward the huge professional grade kitchen.

Whatever. It's not like we haven't seen places even ritzier than this shit.

"I still want to know where poetry boy and Scaly Fried Chicken are," I mutter as Felix heads for the bar to pour himself something stupidly expensive.

Neither of my brothers is acting like they've ever seen a fancy fucking house before. I stride down the adjoining hallway, narrowing my eyes at the doors there. I suppose there's enough room for them to have guests, but why aren't they coming out to greet us? *Rude, that's what it is.* I throw open the door at the very end of the hall, hoping it's one of their bedrooms, as I grin like a lunatic.

"Heeeere's Fitzy!" I shout as I pop my head in.

The sight that greets me makes my jaw drop and, for the first time in a very long time, I have absolutely no words.

"Close the door, you psycho!"

Too shocked to answer, I just do as instructed, turning on my heel to head back into the living room. I plop down onto the couch, blinking as the information races through my head like some online meme full of equations and confused looking humans.

Did I just see….?

"Fitz, you look like you saw a ghost. What the hell is wrong with you?" Felix says as he drops onto a cushy armchair next to my seat. He sips his drink, looking pleased as hell at the amber liquid he chose. "One minute, you're here being hyper and pissy, now you're acting like your brain is broken. What gives, man?"

My eyes cut back and forth between my brother and my consort, unsure how to answer that question. I may be off my nut most of the time, but I know when I've stepped in some shit. This was definitely some major fucking shit, and I have no idea how to handle this.

I'm not made for moral quandaries, for fuck's sake.

Chess frowns as he joins me on the couch, scooting close until I wrap my arm around him. "Maybe we should call my angel. Talking to her always makes him feel better."

Swallowing, I nod at him, still not speaking for fear I'll lose my grip on my tongue and spill the damn beans about my discovery. Felix rolls his eyes, but he nods and Chess sets the DiePad up on the table so she can see all of us when she answers. The little ringing sound is mesmerizing, but the second she answers, the tightness in my chest recedes.

Baby Girl always knows what to do. She'll tell me.

"Fitz! Chess! Felix!" she cries out as she leans into the screen with a bright smile. "I'm so glad you called. I'm dying of boredom here. Where's Aubrey and Rennie?"

I feel the color drain out of my face and I cough. "Uh, we just got here and uh, I went looking, but I think they're busy…"

Felix rolls his eyes and Chess chuckles. "Busy fighting over wall sconces or some shit, I bet."

"No…"

That one word catches my girl's ear and she tilts her head, squinting at me. "I'm sure they'll be free soon. I know they'd be upset to miss the video chat, no matter what shenanigans they're getting up to."

"When are you leaving for campus?" I blurt, scratching my head sheepishly when the other two give me odd looks. "I miss you, baby girl."

Nope. Didn't seem suspicious at all. No one has a clue I know a big ass secret now.

"Well, funny story about that…"

Wish You Were Here

Delores

"…so I literally *just* found out from Cori and Rufus that we're not going back to Apex. I guess Lucille didn't feel the need to share anything with me until next week when I pack up? Shit, I don't know, maybe not even then. She'd find it funny if I showed up at the wrong fucking place and had to drive like a maniac to get to D.C. in time."

Every one of my guys is silent for a moment, but I can tell they're waiting for something. Then, as if planned, Fitz loses his shit. "I'm going to flay that bitch alive and serve her in the cafeteria."

Chess winces as my passionate tiger lets out a snarl of anger that only quiets when Felix gives him a stern look. "We all miss you, angel, but Fitz is antsy. His tiger is giving him fits with the forced distance."

My lips curve and I tilt my head. "Yeah?"

"Yeah, princess," Felix says as he leans in closer. "I've known this idiot since the womb, and I don't think he's ever been this edgy, even when he was on a bender. Though he's been even weirder since we got here today."

I frown, trying to work out what would bother Fitz when they agreed to video chat. Usually, it makes him bounce off the walls and threaten to flash us all, so I don't forget what his trouser snake looks like. "Fitz? Fitz? What's going on?"

The question stops his pacing, and he leaps back over the couch, eyes wide as he looks into the camera so closely it's jarring. "I've seen things. It's messing with me."

Felix and Chess shrug—or I think they do—behind him, so I smile encouragingly. "What things?"

"Can't say." His brow furrows, and he looks confused as he thinks for a moment. "Not bad, just surprised."

Now that is very interesting.

"Mmmm. Well, maybe you should talk to Aubrey? He's seen damn near everything over the years it feels like." I blink and narrow my eyes. "Unless it's a weird lump or something…in that case, go see a damn doctor."

His eyes widen in panic, and suddenly, I feel like I know *exactly* why Fitz is struggling. It's not a medical condition or a weird porn video that freaked him out. They're calling me from Rennie and Aubrey's new place—without the two of them present. Covering my mouth to keep from laughing, I squeeze my eyes closed as I let the humor roll over me.

Poor Fitz. He doesn't know what to do except keep his mouth shut—which is damn near impossible for him.

"Princess, do you have any idea how the hell to calm him down? If we have to deal with this all day, I swear to Bast…"

Focusing on the tiger looking at me from a much too close camera angle, I wink. "I understand, crazypants. Just… wait for me to get there, okay? Show me how well you control your urges, and maybe I'll give you a reward."

Fitz pulls back, snapping into his normal persona as he gives me a fangy grin. "A reward? Oh, baby girl. You have *no idea* what kind of depravity I've been thinking up this summer…"

"I do," Chess mutters with a smirk. "I'd set some boundaries, angel."

"Fitzy would never do anything I'm not comfortable with, Chessie. Though, if you'd like to chaperone…" I look at him through my lashes, feeling my face get hot as I say it out loud. "Or maybe Felix has instructions for us."

The elder twin huffs a laugh, his dark eyes dancing as he ponders my words. "I'm not sure you're ready for that, princess."

Jutting my chin out, I meet his eyes. "Try me, *sir*."

That answer draws a growly curse from Felix, a groan from his twin, and a sharp intake of breath from Chess. I grin broadly, feeling pretty damn good about my boldness as they stare at me. *Way to go, Dolly. You're a sexual badass.* Crossing my arms over my chest, I let them drool in silence until I see movement in the background.

"Hey! Is that Rennie and Aubrey?"

One by one, they blink out of their sex trance and turn to look at the last two members of my new family group as they stroll in. I have to hide my smirk as I take in Rennie's messy hair and Aubrey's rumpled looking shirt—especially since it's buttoned wrong. Fitz squirms in his seat, but the others don't seem to notice how out of character the appearances of their friends are.

Men wouldn't notice an alligator sneaking up on them until it bit them in the ass, I swear to Hera.

"Good afternoon, bento bunny," Aubrey rumbles with a soft smile. "It's good to see you smiling. You've been rather melancholy this summer."

Arching a brow at his casual tone, I tilt my head and smirk. "That's a new one. Feeling spry this afternoon, big guy?"

If he realizes I know Fitz barged in on one of their big secrets, he doesn't show it. "I'm taking great pleasure in my work here, yes."

"I'll bet," Fitz mutters, and I have to stifle a giggle.

Keeping this to himself for days is going to be almost impossible for him.

Rennie glares at the back of the hyper tiger's head as if he's trying to erase his memory through sheer willpower, but Aubrey shrugs. "Despite being run by a *Sphinx*, this collection is quite extensive and I believe it will aid us in finding the next pieces to our puzzle."

Felix rolls his eyes at the dragon's look of distaste. Apparently, dragons and Sphinxes get along as well as wolves and tigers, but it's less physical competition as much as intellectual. He mentioned how angry our grumpy book lover was to discover some texts and scrolls famous families donated here rather than Apex.

"At least you won't have to work as hard to get it up to speed?" I offer with a small smile. "That has to count for something."

He huffs and Rennie steps forward, giving me a mischievous look. "Our new home is quite luxurious. You'll enjoy the upgrade, *ma petite.* Plus, I've added my layer of security to their formidable set-up. No dead bodies will show up in our private sanctuary this year."

Of course, he can't promise no dead bodies *at all*, especially after the events at the end of last year. His suspicions about magic users and their connection to bad juju at the school were spot on. We had a story prepared by the time anyone reached us and we've all stuck to it without fail. If the Council won't call in the Sibbies, none of us wanted to end up in some rubber room because we suggested the magic they insisted was gone has returned.

And fuck if anyone of us know why I shot blue lightning out of my hands—that's on the 'to do' list for sure.

As if he can hear my thoughts, the gargoyle squints at me. "No… side effects to your shift now that your bunny is listening again?"

"Nope," I reply. We've been cautious as hell about referencing the secret shit while I'm home. Lucille and Bruno aren't here, but I'm not stupid enough to believe one of them hasn't bugged the entire place hoping to catch some info.

"No one has touched you, right, baby girl?" Fitz pushes his way back to the front, studying me as I shake my head. His frustration at being unable to protect me all day, every day, has been one of the hardest things to manage during this stupid break.

I cross my finger over my chest in an 'X.' "Nope. The body guards hover like flies, but they haven't done more than leer."

"Even the ugly mutt?" Felix growls low.

"Yes, even Lucius stays an acceptable distance when he looms threateningly. I promise, guys. I'm okay, and we'll be back together soon." The alarm on my dresser goes off and I groan. "It's time for my jujitsu lesson. This guy is hardcore, Felix. Where the hell did you find him?"

He grins smugly at me. "One of Fitz's former Pred Games competitors. He'll have you ready for Zhenga's boot camp, for sure."

I wrinkle my nose, pouting at him. "If by ready, you mean so tired I can barely move afterward, then you're right. Who decided I have to compete in these damn things, anyway? They're on my shit list."

Chess raises his hand, looking sheepish. "I mean, Felix mentioned it first, but once we knew we were being sent to a school with an established team? I knew it would put you in the spotlight looking formidable, not weak. It will help you avoid the attacks students arranged at Apex if people see you as strong."

Snorting, I give him an incredulous look. "Chessie, I beat Gold and Todd's asses in public and they still pulled shit."

"Only sneaky backroom politics, though. The physical threats died down once you showed your stuff," he says confidently. "I wouldn't have suggested this if I hadn't done research on this school, Angel. The sports angle will help keep you safe."

"Fine, fine. Rah, rah, I'm full of school spirit," I say with a grimace. My alarm goes off again and a loud, pounding knock on the door makes me jump. "Shit! I gotta go. That's one of the goons."

Blowing them a kiss, I swipe the screen off and run over to slip on my tennis shoes. Once I grab my gym bag and water bottle from my desk, I slip my phone in my pocket and head for the door. When I pull it open, the nasty wolf in charge of the security flares at me with his yellow flecked eyes.

"Madame Lucille detests tardiness. This will go in my report."

Instead of letting him intimidate me, I stick my nose in the air, putting on the affect of a true heir as I breeze past him. At the stairs, I grumble to myself, "You can stick your report directly up your ass, you fuck knuckle."

Pleased with myself, I jog downstairs and head for my car.

Everyone knows wolves have excellent hearing.

PIECE OF YOUR HEART

AUBREY

"He hasn't said a single word. Don't you find that strange?" I ask my companion as he flits about in the main bedroom. When we negotiated the positions at Capital Prep, Renard insisted on taking over the entire staff quarters for the library as part of our contract. I didn't find out why until he gave me the grand tour of the enormous room he declared as Dolly's. She's supposed to live in the reptile dorm across the way, and nothing I said would deter him from remodeling this place for her, so I let him have his project.

Between that and cultivating a garden put back, it's kept him from retreating to the bell tower to brood over her absence.

I'd be lying if I said he was wrong about commandeering the entire area for our family, though. They connected the annex to both my library and his mini tower. Plus, it's spacious enough to hold everyone once we can congregate. He put our theory boards in the sunroom with a view of the river and garden, so our work will be safe from visitors.

"It's puzzling to me as well, *mon ami*. But Fitzgerald is nothing if not a mystery only *ma petite* seems to be able to solve. Perhaps she's had her paws in his silence?"

My lips curve as raven curls fall out of the messy bun he's been wearing to keep the longer locks from getting in his face. Chess showed him how to scoop it all up in a hysterical lesson that our girl would have thoroughly enjoyed watching. He won't say why he's growing it out, but I noticed even straight laced Felix seems to forego his usual cropped look now and I assume it's because Dolly likes it.

Hmmph. I'll not be joining that little boy band soon.

The dragon inside of me flares up, disagreeing with my decision not to indulge his mate in any way she demands. Sending him the internal version of a middle finger, I roll my eyes and stroke my hand over the sand cat in my lap. If my animal thinks I'll roll over for every one of her whims, he's got a battle coming. Fitz and Chess spoil her enough as it is. I'm watching my oldest companion flit about like an interior decorator to make certain every single thing she could want is within her grasp.

Felix is right; she needs a firm hand or two so she doesn't get out of control.

That makes my dragon snort and I huff, scratching Jinx again to distract myself from the much more vocal behavior of my inner beast. "You're not the boss of me."

"What?" Rennie says as he looks over his shoulder in confusion. "Who said I was?"

"No one," I grumble. "At least, no one who wants to live has."

He grins, walking over to pick Jinx up and set her on the floor. Once she toddles over to a pile of pillows and curls up, he drops into my lap, lounging lazily. "That's not a game we play, *mon ami.* Is the thought of adding our *belle lapin* making you ponder new scenarios?"

Blinking, I consider that for a moment and shake my head. "That will probably be the bailiwick of our exiled Raj. I'm more interested in your favorite—the chase."

"Oh, she *likes* to be chased. Her scent fills with excitement, arousal, and this bit of fear from her animal that's delicious," Ren coos as he leans into me.

Wrapping my arms around him, I rub my cheek on his head, feeling my body respond to that picture. "I can't believe she asked you to hunt her—in public, no less. Snacksize surprises me like no one has in my long life, except for you."

The gargoyle shrugs with a mischievous grin. "Our girl calls us all in different ways, *mon fougueux*. You've kept her at arm's length long enough, I believe. Perhaps when she arrives, we might take flying again? Would that soothe the flames consuming you?"

Pulling back, I look at the shifter who became the center of my world despite every obstacle I put in his way. "I'd love to, even if it will piss Fitz the hell off. He definitely knows one of our secrets now, and he'll assume we're whisking her away for something sexier than eating."

"Who says we aren't?" His hand comes up to cradle my jaw as he kisses me thoroughly enough to leave us both breathless. "I find that idea very appealing, Lord Draconis."

Chuckling as I tug his shirt off, I arch a brow. "Do you, Monsieur Laveaux? Just what might we be doing on this *steamier* journey?"

"Oh, so many delectable things," he says as I tug on his nipple rings playfully. "We can chase her through the trees until one of us catches her. Loser takes bottom."

I laugh again, tickling my fingers down his abs to trace around his belly button. "Mmm. Is that a reward or a punishment? I can't decide."

"In this game, no one loses, *mon amour*. Everyone wins."

I can't argue with that.

Instead of responding, I unbutton his fly and lift his cock out, stroking it slowly. He shudders when I tighten my grip—my gargoyle loves a bite of pain with his pleasure. Leaning in, I scrape my slightly elongated fangs over his shoulder as my hand works his shaft. "Tell me more, Rennie. If you're the bottom, what else is happening?"

His breath comes out in a soft hiss, but he looks at me with electric blue eyes. "For me to be the bottom, our darling rabbit would have to make good on that pegging promise she made to Fitz at the rave."

My hand cups his balls, rolling them in my palm as I nod. "Mmm. She'll need a harness then."

"Fuck," he growls low. "Our girl would be *magnifique* trussed up in Domme leather and straps. Especially with you fucking her above me."

Merciful Ra, I'm going to lose control of myself *picturing this shit.*

"Oh, yes, babe. That primal urge in her will make her a rowdy one. She'll fuck the living shit out of you if we make sure there's a little surprise for her on that strap-on. Would you like that?" His ass is wiggling over me so I know the answer, but I want to see him come apart before I get relief. Renard is beautiful when he's pushed to let it all go and I want him to fall over the edge while we discuss sharing the lovely Delores.

"Ummm. Clit stim inside… got it," he pants raggedly as I continue jacking his cock roughly. "You'll wait until she's dripping and then take her from behind. Her screams are even musical."

Of course they fucking are.

Leaning down with a smirk, I suckle the tip of his pierced dick, swiping my tongue over the leaking moisture. His scent is all night time and mate, like a spicy aroma made to entice me by the Fates. I wonder if Dolly will be the same? Squeezing him, I rumble as I look into his hazy eyes. "Ren, *mon amour*, what does she smell like?"

"H-Honeysuckle…" His eyes roll back when I run a fingertip over his hole and he shudders again. "And it's intoxicating, like when I suck you off."

"Would she like it if we shifted and licked her together?" Lifting my head, I let go of his cock and nip his earlobe firmly. "That changes our anatomy significantly."

His hips buck, and he nods wildly. "I think she'd enjoy *all* of it shifted."

I blink, trying not to stop as that smacks me in the face and makes my dragon roar in approval. "Too big, babe. The dragon, at least. But maybe you…"

"Half shifted. Surrounded by our wings."

The image sends the beast inside of me into overdrive, and I shoot out of the chair with him draped in my arms. Walking over to the bed, I drop him on it before I tear my shirt off and free my aching cock from the confines of my slacks. "Where did you stash it?"

His lips curve as he splays out on the bed he picked for our sassy bunny, looking like the cat who ate the canary. "Bottom drawer in the nightstand on the right."

No one knows the broody gargoyle like me—he's already planted a stash of naughty shit for her. My dick throbs as I root through it, finding the cherry lube he favors and slathering it on quickly. By the time I approach, his skin has turned obsidian, and he's sporting fangs. I warm it in my palm, letting the heat from my dragon take over, then slip thick fingers into his ass. His gasp of pleasure pushes the primal part of me hard, and I know we're going to be cleaning up a hell of a mess afterward.

"Now, *mon amour*," he pleads as he writhes on the digits. "I need to feel you split me in two."

He doesn't have to ask me twice.

Lining up, I slam into my lover hard and fast. He grips me like a vise and I grunt when my dragon ripples over my skin. Our wings meet on either side of us, and I hold on to his hips as I set a punishing rhythm. I've almost forgotten what we were talking about as I fuck my original mate into the plush mattress, but he grins in satisfaction.

"Imagine once she's ready to be in the middle, taking us both."

My eyes roll back in my head, and this time, I shudder. Dolly for between us like they made her to be there and the thought of her writhing on our cocks makes me wild. Hips bucking, I pound into him even more roughly, lost in the web he's been weaving. When my orgasm gets close, I lean down and bare my fangs at him hungrily. His head tilts, and he reaches up to pull me down so we both have an angle.

The simultaneous bite knocks me into oblivion and he comes with me, spurting over my stomach as we reaffirm the bond we took on so many years ago. My cock jerks inside of him, coating his ass with an enormous load of hot cum until it leaks out.

Panting, he pulls his teeth out of the bite and looks at me with a hazy, satisfied smile. "I love when you get out of control, *mon fougueux.*"

"This is a mess," I murmur back as I lift my head to brush my lips on his. "Think she'll scent it even after we clean up?"

The slow grin on his face makes me chuckle. "I sure as fuck hope so. Call it... bait."

That motherfucker tempted me on purpose.

Good on him.

The Very First Night

Delores

The days following my call with the guys have been excruciatingly boring. I'm finishing up the last of my summer work for Luc and most of his college-aged prey left at the end of last week. It leaves me with Emile and the rest of the pangolins, half of whom are still terrified of me. The poor leader has tried a thousand times to get his people to realize I'm prey, but I think they sense the fierce parts of me, no matter how hard I suppress them.

My ridiculous bodyguard 'shadows' follow me everywhere. That means I can't go dancing or even visit with Clotilda because they scare everyone. I'm down to work, the gym, the mall, and home where I can go without one of those assholes telling me they 'need to confer with Madame Lucille' before I leave. The noose seems to tighten as it gets closer to the time I make my getaway to school, and I don't have a clue why.

What's Lucille's game, and why does she care?

I haven't been able to work out her angle beyond showing the world she's protecting her heir as much as possible while I'm home. That made sense right after the explosions, but now? It seems like she's doing it to spite me—which is possible—or there's some other machination for making sure I can't see anyone until I get back to school.

"She makes you paranoid, D," I mutter to myself. "Luckily, there's only two more sleeps until it's time to hit the road for the capital. Then you're away from this prison and at home with a family that actually gives a damn about you."

Yep, I've done a lot of talking to myself this summer.

The silence is deafening and I groan, wishing I could make time go faster. Without the chatter of my friends or my men, this place is like a damn crypt. Even the Tower had noise, whether it was music or echoes in the vents or even the sound of the Captain and his crew doing stuff. "Okay. You need to get food and a giant water bottle. Dehydration does weird shit to your mind and hunger makes you a snarly bunny. Then it's time to work on packing for a bit."

I sigh, opening the door to my room to find two bulky shifters in ill-fitting suits in my hallway. Neither of them looks familiar, but they smell like bears. My senses have improved *a lot* since the 'secret magic bunny' shit. Even though I don't recognize these particular assholes, I know they're part of the wolf leader's crew. They must be some kind of security company Bruno's using because all summer, I've been finding new fuckwits watching me at every turn.

No wonder I'm paranoid; they're all really out to get me.

As usual, I flip them off, trotting downstairs to the kitchen to toss together a light snack and my big ass water. Master César is a jaguar shifter, and he's had me on a strict training plan from the second I walked into the first class, so I have to follow the rules. Oddly, this doesn't feel like when Lucille tried forcing diets or surgery down my throat most of my life. Instead, his regimen requires a balance—as there is in all things, he says. I'm not sure how into the whole 'Zen' part of my training I am. However, structuring my intake to maximize my energy has helped me ward off my depression about not seeing the people I care about.

I open the fridge and pile my plate full of fruit, cheese, and the cold chicken breast bites, humming a little as I add from all the containers for variety. The other good thing about this clean living junk is not worrying about having to cook or order out a lot. César went shopping with me at the beginning of each month since the summer began. We spend entire days here creating prepared meals and snacks to last. It cut out the daily decision drag and also kept me from buying less healthy options on an extra trip to the store.

I'm probably in the best shape of my life, despite not losing a pound. Everything is toning, and it makes me look badass.

"Fitz is going to *love* that," I giggle to myself when I consider how much stronger my thighs are alone. "I could probably kill someone with my legs alone if I wanted to."

Grinning as I grab the stupidly large water bottle and my full plate, I head back to the stairs, ignoring the assholes outside my door yet again. Once inside, I kick the door closed and yell at my Alexa to engage the security. I ordered new locks and installed everything myself when I found out my parents were leaving me alone with unknown preds all summer. It might not hold forever, but it discourages them from interrupting my calls or spying on me while I sleep. Anything they do to get in without my permission will set off an alarm and I'll at least have enough time to grab my handy knife from under my pillow.

A predatory bunny can't be too careful, even in her own home.

"Play T. Swift mix," I call out before climbing into my big reading chair and curling up. I've got five new books on my Kindle, delicious food, and hours before anyone will look for me. If there's any upside to this confinement, it's definitely having an infinite amount of time to catch up on my favorite books and write songs.

If only my guys were here to snuggle in with me...

"HOLY SHIT!"

What sounds like something hitting the window by my chair wakes me from an unexpected nap and I blink in the dark. My Kindle is asleep, too, and the program that dims my lights at dusk did its job—despite me nodding off like a senior citizen well before dinnertime. It's definitely after eight p.m. and by the look of the landscape, it's probably closer to ten. I didn't even feel sleepy when I sat down, but I'm usually wiped the day after my lessons. They're designed to push me as far as possible without injury in the shortest time possible, so I'm barely hobbling home by the time César lets me leave.

My night vision isn't great, but when the object hits my window again, I know I didn't imagine it. Dropping to my knees to keep out of sight, I growl softly. There's a rotating guard crew outside at night, so whatever the hell they're doing, it's *not* their fucking job. I have to stay out of its sight line to make certain the damn thuds weren't a ploy to get me to give someone a better target. Crawling to my bed, I reach up with one hand, grasping both the knife and my damn phone before I head back to my chair.

Everyone is too far away in the capital. If this is dangerous, I'll have to defend myself until help arrives.

"It'd be super fucking cool if people would stop trying to kill me this year," I mumble as I click my phone screen open with the encrypted passcode. When I look at the open screen, the adrenaline coursing through me slows a bit. "Is he serious? What the hell is he *thinking*?"

> TigerWoody: Baby Girl!

> TigerWoody: Baby Girl!

> TigerWoody: Baby Girl!

> TigerWoody: Baby Girl!

TigerWoody: Baby Girl!

TigerWoody: Baby Girl, answer me, goddamnit! I'm outside your window and I don't have much time before those asswads wake up!

The noise that made me think a fricking *assassin* was trying to get into my *bedroom* while I was snoozing is my crazy ass boyfriend. The same crazy ass boyfriend who should be six hours away right now.

Another glance at my phone shows a big red dot with twelve messages on another chat, and I sigh as I look at it.

CSpot: Has anyone seen Fitz? He sort of disappeared after we called my angel this morning.

TigerKing: Don't worry. He probably just went to blow off steam at the gym or something.

CSpot: He was acting really weird.

TigerKing: How the hell could you tell?

CSpot: Felix, it's been two hours. Is he answering you?

TigerKing: No. Renard? Aubrey?

CSpot: They've been MIA, too. What is going on?

LustyLibrarian: Calm down, Chester. We're cleaning up a mess in the main room.

CSpot: What mess?

EmoBatman: Never you mind, nosey pants.

TigerKing: So no one knows where my brother is?

CSpot: Not good.

Of course, I know where the hell he is and if he gets caught by my parents' goons, I'll be in the shit knee-deep.

I stand, disengaging the locks on my window and peer out into the darkness. "Fitz! Fitz, what the shit, dude? Where are you?"

A grinning tiger shifter pops out of the gigantic tree outside my window with a slightly unhinged look in his eyes. "Right here, baby girl. I was hiding Delta Force style."

Rubbing my hand over my face quickly, I grab his arm with the other. "Get in here. If these douchewhistles on guard catch you, Lucille will lose her damn mind. Who knows what kind of shit she'll pull if she thinks my sentence got cut short?"

"Fire in the hole!" Fitz whisper-yells as he does a flip into the window, landing on the floor with a loud thump. When I shush him, he rolls his eyes and splays his body on the ground like a beached whale. "I'm ready for my closeup, Ms. DeMille."

I cover my mouth, trying not to laugh. "Has Chessie been making you watch old movies again?"

Fitz nods, his eyes sparkling up at me. "Ever since you told him I learn better by listening, they have subjected me to every movie, TV show, and play he can find on the Preynet. I think he's trying to cram thirty years of learning into, like, five months."

A noise outside my door spooks me and I put my finger to my lips as I creep over, listening to the wood for a moment. When it doesn't happen again, I let out a long breath. "The *jibrones* must be doing rounds in the house. I think we're safe."

His expression is still amused and I know it's because he wouldn't hesitate to take every single moron wandering this house out. "Good. I couldn't wait another fucking minute to see you, baby girl. I jumped on my bike the second you signed off this morning."

Oh, shit. The other guys are still looking for him.

"Fitz, you didn't tell anyone where you went and they're blowing up my phone." I pick it up, firing off a brief explanation before I put my hands on my hips. "You'd lose the damn plot if I took off on you guys like that."

Smirking, he shrugs. "That's because it's my job to help you stay safe and you've never told me to back off. Sneaking around me would mean you didn't like it and we know that's not true. Besides, I'm a big boy and I can take care of myself."

"I can take care of myself, too. Your sadist trainer is making sure of that," I mutter as I narrow my eyes at him. "That doesn't mean our family isn't worrying."

A bright smile splits his face, and he rushes over, grabbing me in his arms and spinning us around. "You said 'our family' and you can't take it back."

I blink, feeling a flush creep up my neck as he continues whirling us happily. "I did, you crazy fool. Now put me down before I barf my healthy snacks all over your face."

His eyes widen, and he stops, sitting me down slowly. "Uh, I can deal with a lot of shit, including entrails. But vomit is a hard limit since that prom, baby girl. I'll toss my cookies like a drunk chick at a frat party if I even catch a whiff. No chunky firehose action, you hear me?"

"Pissing on an enemy's head? Check. Vomit? Big red 'X.' Got it," I say playfully.

His expression turns dark as he looks down at me. "Snarky little brat."

"What are you going to do about it?"

"Oh, you'll see."

Bad Things

Fitz

My baby girl looks like every dream I've had since that stupid school got blown to smithereens by magic weirdos.

Okay, she's got more clothes on than my dreams, but that's fixable.

Running my eyes up and down her frame, I grin wickedly as I take in her attire. She's got on adorable pink tiger print silk shorts that barely cover her delectable ass and a matching bralette. Her rainbow sherbet hair is in twin ponytails and she has adorably pink polish on her fingers and toes. Her gorgeous tatts and shiny piercings contrast with it perfectly, adding a little dark to her shining light. My hands clench into fists at my waist while I try to figure out where she's hiding her fun drawer in her Pepto pink monster Mommy approved room.

Felix was right; our sexy bunny is definitely both a Barbie girl and a punk rock princess rolled into one.

"I give up, baby girl. Show me where you're hiding the good time and I'll reward you," I growl softly. My finger trails over her cheek and down her neck, stopping at a pink ribbon choker with a glowing amulet on it. "Oh, good. Monsieur Maudlin's trinket will make sure I don't have to shred this cute little outfit."

Her nose wrinkles, but she cocks her head at a nondescript looking pink file cabinet next to her desk. "Over there. And you'd better not tear up all my underwear this year, Fitz Khan, because there's no need for it."

Walking over to her sin bin, I open it and grin broadly before I respond. "Baby girl, I *enjoy* destroying your shit and you're free to replace anything you want—on us. I'll open a fucking charge at that fancy string and lace place."

She huffs, but I can *feel* the smile on her face. "Fine. You can *all* contribute. That way it's fair."

Turning back to her with a bottle of lube and a blindfold, I shrug. "Khan money is Khan, babe. But you're going to have to ride the scaly coaster before you ask Scrooge McDragon to pony up."

Her eyes widen as I approach with my selections, and she swallows hard. I can smell her excitement and the honeysuckle scent I've missed makes my tiger push hard against my skin. Stalking closer, I lean in, putting my forehead against hers for a minute. *Sweet Aphrodite, this girl makes me lose control.* When I pull back, I wink play-fully, tilting my head at the bed. Her tiny grin spreads as she scam-pers over, touching that damn stone and melting her damn clothes away without a word.

"That asshole," I mutter under my breath. Dolly laughs as I grumble, but I don't move to her bed yet. She's got some amateur hour restraint stuff in there, but I'm not using that on her. She doesn't know it's dangerous and I won't risk teaching her bad habits. Spotting something serviceable holding back her curtains, I deviate in that direction and whip the ties off her drapes.

Which, if you're wondering, the carpet matches, even if my girl's doesn't currently.

"Are you… sniggering at yourself?" she asks in amusement.

I shrug, making my way back to where she's reclining like a damn offering to the old gods—all smooth skin and pink nipples and magical hair. "Maybe. I'm here for my amusement, baby girl, even if no one else is laughing. Now, climb up there like a good girl and put your wrists by those iron posts."

"Fitz!" she hisses with wide eyes. "Bondage? I *have* handcuffs; you don't have to steal from the decor."

Shaking my head, I hold up the soft material. "This is better. Your stuff is… not regulation, let's say. And as someone new to this, plus a newer shifter, you'll end up bruising yourself. Felix would *murder* me if I taught you bad BDSM habits from the beginning."

Her features pinch in an expression I know means she's worried she'll screw up, but she nods. Biting her lower lip as she settles in against her enormous pile of pillows, my girl does exactly as I asked. "Okay. Now what?"

The trusting look in her eyes blows me the fuck away, and I will never *let her down.*

"I'm going to bind your wrists and put on the blindfold, then we'll play, baby girl. While I'm doing that, I want you to pick a safe word. Do you know what that is?" I smile when she nods, crossing to take her hand in mine before I start. "Tell me with words. I need words when we do this because consent is very important in this world."

"Yes. I mean, yes, I know. It should be a word I say that really means to stop—for whatever reason—and it has to be something I wouldn't normally say, so it doesn't slip out," she replies.

Pleased, I nip one of her fingertips, loving how she shivers. "Perfect. You think about that and I'll—"

"Oh, I know it," she cuts in with a mischievous smirk. "My safe word is Beetlejuice. If I have to say it three times, buddy—it's showtime."

She catches me so off-guard that I blurt out the first thing that comes to my mind. "Fuck, I love you, baby girl."

Uh-oh. Retreat, retreat!

Her expression wars between shock and fear, so I gently take her hand and place a kiss on her palm. "Don't have an eppy, D. It's trippy for it to come out that way and I've sure as fuck never said that anyone not Chess before, but it feels like I'm getting there, you know? So I'm not going to walk it back because it jumped out without a bunch of brain work. Got it?"

Nodding, she swallows hard before she murmurs, "I don't know what love feels like because I *thought* I felt it for Todd, but… I know that's not true now. It was a dream, but what I feel for you is real. But I don't know how to quantify it yet. Is that okay?"

I grin, sinking my teeth lightly into the meat of her thumb. She groans and my dick twitches. *Oh, yeah, I'm okay with you figuring it out, baby girl.* "Absolutely. We'll have a hell of a lot of fun along the way. Now, though, it's time for you to learn some new tricks."

Her lips curve and the look on her face returns to mischievous. "I *love* when you teach me, kitty cat."

Oh, that's how we're playing it now, hmmm? Game on, baby girl.

It only takes me a moment to tie a constrictor knot around the wrought iron post. I know it's an advanced level knot, but if she really wants out, her shift will give her plenty of strength to break this fabric. Tying a shifter up successfully, especially one with the raw power Dolly has, is almost impossible unless you have the right equipment. This is more about getting her used to the practice and allowing her to feel safe for the first time.

A deep inhale tells me my plan is working—the scent of her arousal is increasing and fuck if I can't wait to get my hands on her. I pat her hand and walk to the other side of the bed with my super-sized woody damn near busting out of my pants. Dolly giggles as she watches, and I squint at her, pretending to chastise her. I haven't put the blindfold on yet, but when I deprive her of her sight *and* her freedom, I know she's going to be like a live wire.

"Just be still while I finish. You're doing so well, baby girl," I murmur softly. I'm a much less stern taskmaster than my twin, so the contrast will be startling if he gets his furry head out of his ass. Her cheeks get pink at the praise and I grin broadly while I tie her other hand. When that's done, I lift the blindfold, and the fear flitters through her gaze again. "Do you trust me, Dolly?"

"Yes." Her answer is so quick I barely have time to breathe.

Holy shit. Only Felix and Chess have ever said that.

I lean in, placing the blindfold over her eyes and securing it carefully before I kiss her much more gently than my body wants me to. The surety in her voice hit me in places other than my cock, and she *definitely* deserves a reward now. "Good girl."

"*Why* is that so damn *hot* yet it makes me feel so bad for liking it?" she mutters against my mouth.

"Because you're becoming a badass, but you still want to be taken care of—and everyone has told you those have to be mutually exclusive." My hands wander to her nipples, twisting them lightly, loving the gasp that escapes against my mouth. "But they aren't, and it takes a powerful person to let go of their control."

It's quiet for a moment, then she whispers, "Ohhhhh. I get it."

Then a look of pure wickedness takes over the bottom half of her features and I'm a wee bit glad I'm the one with *her* tied up at the moment. "I don't know who that's for, baby girl, but I hope I'm there to see it."

Done with words, I lift myself up and tug off my shirt. I move off of the bed, standing at the foot of as I watch her adjust to the cool air and darkness under the blindfold. Her skin flushes from her face down her neck and continues to spread as I shuck my pants eagerly. Chessie's not wrong about the angel moniker, though her personality is swinging towards devilish in contrast.

Luckily, I'm an asshole who delights in extremes.

"Are you okay, D?"

Her teeth sink into her plump lower lip for a second and she nods, letting out a slow breath. "It's very different. Like my nerves are tingling everywhere and my bunny senses are trying to make up for not being able to see."

"Exactly," I reply. "Depriving you of a sense or senses makes everything else more intense, especially because you're not able to move."

"If my bunny didn't trust you, my heart would probably explode. It's beating pretty fast as it is."

Her admission is adorable, and my fangs drop hungrily. I shake my head, trying to push the big guy off, but he refuses to budge. I know she's not ready for mating, but he's a stubborn fucker about her. "Word on the street is that you let the Dark Kite hunt you sometimes, D. Your bunny has her own kinks, methinks."

That gets a giggle out of her and I watch her gorgeous tits shake as I work to calm my beast *and* my leaking cock.

Mine, my tiger growls inside of me and I shoo him.

Not yet, buddy.

My hands grasp her feet, massaging them slowly until she lets out a strangled sound of approval. I can feel calluses on her toes from dancing and her work with my ex-rival in the gym. She has to be aching here, too, so I continue digging my thumb into the arch of her foot, reading every twitch that makes her turn to jelly. Wringing each toe firmly, I lean in to plant soft kisses on her ankles while I work. It's obvious when the last bit of tension ebbs from her form, so I move upward to her muscled calves.

Sitting between her legs, I work my way past her knees to her thighs, loving the moans of pleasure spilling from her lips. The sounds are so husky and loud that I have to pause several times to get control of my response. I'm going to shoot my goddamn load on her comforter if I'm not careful, and Fitz Khan never does that. Dolly's hips writhe when I knead her thighs and the scent of her drenched pussy almost does me in.

"Fitzy… pleeeeeease," she whines as her back arches and her hips rock a little. "I need you."

My hips jerk and I rub my cock on the bed to get some much needed friction. Baby Girl isn't as experienced as me, but she's got a stranglehold on my cock even when she's *not* touching it. I give her mound a light tap, making her gasp and buck. "Shhh. Enjoy the sensations."

Her voice is ragged as she whispers, "Holy. Fucking. Shit."

Indeed, baby girl. Just you wait.

Once she settles, I spread her legs more, delighted when I'm able to push her thighs much farther apart than usual. *Score one for flexible dancers.* Starting at her knees, I pepper kisses and nips from her knee to her inner thigh, leaving a dark bite mark just shy of her heat before I move to the other leg. The trembling has started again, and it makes my tiger rumble happily inside. He likes my teeth marks on her, especially here, and I dig my fingers into her hips to lift them.

"You smell like a feast and I'm going to devour," I growl at her. "Don't you dare break those bindings or I'll stop."

Looking up from her flushed body to her face, I grin before I lower my mouth to her soaked pussy. My tongue slips over her folds, tracing the shape of her slowly. The teasing makes her whimper, but I continue lapping everywhere but where she wants me as I soak in the needy sounds she's making. When I finally suck her clit between my lips, her howl is ear-splitting and her entire body locks up with the orgasm crashing over her. I wait until the shivers lessen, then lift my face to look at her chest with a satisfied smirk.

"Holy Bridget in the bathwater," she breathes softly. "What the hell are you doing to me?"

"Worshiping you, baby girl." I slip two fingers inside of her, curling the tips to rub against the swollen spot inside of her gently until she pants again. "And I plan on doing it until the sun comes up, so pace yourself."

"Fuuuuuuuuuck," she groans as she rides my hand eagerly.

I chuckle as I slip another finger in, coating it in her juices before I tap the back entrance gently. Her body tenses under me, but she finally relaxes as I suckle on her clit. My pinky works its way into the tight hole, testing her reaction, but she only gasps my name and pushes into my tongue.

Our girl is fucking perfect.

It doesn't take long before Dolly is riding my fingers and face like a pro, her wetness coating my face as she gets closer to another climax. Lifting for one moment, I lick a line from my hand to her sensitive nerves, then blow cool air over her hot sex. "Give me one more, baby girl, then I'll fuck you into the mattress."

This time, I nip her lightly as my fingers slam into her. Her wail echoes off the walls of the ridiculously pink room as her walls squeeze my digits hard enough to hurt. My cock throbs, but I grit my teeth and hold off, not wanting to waste a single drop when I could be buried inside of her. When she goes limp, I withdraw and sit up on the bed, reaching up to take off the blindfold.

Her eyes burn with a red heat as she looks me over head to toe and within seconds, she's torn the bindings clean off the posts. With a victorious expression, she sits up, pushing my chest hard. "Time to saddle up, cowboy. I'm ready to ride."

Fuck. Yes.

Welcome to the Jungle
Delores

Stretching my ridiculously sore muscles, I yawn and open my eyes. I have no idea what time it is—Fitz kept his promise to make me scream until I damn near passed out around dawn. My foot hits something and I pop up immediately, looking over the gorgeous body snoozing on his stomach like the giant cat he is. I thought he would sneak out before the sun rose so my nasty guards wouldn't see him, but here he is, clinging to one of my stuffed animals like a barnacle.

This is bad. What am I going to do?

Before I can work it out, my phone buzzes from the nightstand and I roll over to grab it. The group chat is going absolutely bonkers and I have to squint to even make out the words. My body aches in all the best ways, but my brain still feels melted. Fitz explained this might happen if I fell asleep while he was cleaning me up. He called it 'subspace,' but we didn't get much further than that before I think I drifted off.

Can you have a hangover from too much awesome sex? Maybe that's what he meant, because that's how I feel.

This time the phone actually rings and I shake my head, hoping to clear it enough to speak to the guys. Gathering my sheet up around me like a towel, I push the video chat button and croak, "Hello?"

Four sets of dropped jaws greet me on screen and I feel my face turn red. *Do I really look that bad?* Touching my hair, I try to smooth the pieces down and force a smile as I watch them crowd into the frame.

"Princess, what are you doing?" Felix says with a stern look.

Wrinkling my nose, I huff at the question. "You're all looking at me like I have a big zit."

Chess puts his hand over his mouth, chuckling softly.

His Raj just rolls his eyes and smiles. "You look well and truly fucked, Princess. It's *not* a terrible sight at all. I assume my asshole twin is still there? He didn't call, so we took the liberty."

"If he's asleep like a lazy bum, kick his ass," Aubrey mutters. "We have better things to do than track down a grown adult running away from home like a kid."

I tilt my head at him. "Better than talking to me?"

Aubrey looks flabbergasted for a second, making a few fumbling sounds, and Rennie cuts in. "You got him, *ma petite*. He'll be disputing that all day. Which works out well because the tuckered tiger is going to escort you here when he drags his tail out of your sheets."

"What?!" I almost lose my sheet as I yell and they all snicker. "But it's two days early. Lucille will go nuclear. Her goons have *very* specific instructions and they *never* deviate. Trust me."

"Good thing we pulled a few more strings when that deadbeat turned up missing last night," Felix drawls lazily. "The coach sent a message to your mother, saying you need to be at team activities tomorrow."

I blink, then I look around my room. "I'm not nearly packed."

"Make Fitz help you get as much done as possible until the Captain and Raina arrive. This nervous motherfucker sent them at the crack of dawn this morning." Aubrey looks smug, as if his flub isn't as bad compared to Rennie worrying about me.

Chess sighs and smiles softly. "It will be good to have you back here, Angel. Dealing with all the bickering all summer has been a pain in my ass."

"I'll give you a pain in the ass!" Fitz yells, his voice muffled by the pillows he's buried in.

Sighing and rubbing his temple, Felix tries hard to look like he's not going to laugh, but he's failing. Finally, he lets out a small chuckle, then growls at his naked twin. "Get dressed, you lazy shit. Help Princess pack so you can get back before midnight."

"Can't we just buy her new stuff?" Fitz whines. "I'll take her shopping. The winged weenie can come if it makes him happy."

"Which one?" Chess and I speak at the same time.

The tiger rolls over, showing a glorious amount of hard tattooed muscles and shrugs. "Both of them. All of you. Fuck, who cares if I don't have to pack shit."

"We have to pack *some* stuff, you know," I mutter. "Not everything can be replaced at the drop of a black card."

"Then let's get on with it. I want you out of this mausoleum and into the new nest, baby girl."

With that, he does a barrel roll to the side of the bed, flashing his biteable ass at the camera as he goes looking for his clothes.

"Bast, save us from the constant view of Fitz's junk," Aubrey mutters. "Get your things together, bite size. We'll talk again when you're on the road."

"Got it, Smokey and the Bandits… over and out!" Fitz calls out.

I grin and wiggle my fingers at them with a fond expression. "Talk soon."

With that, I close the window and turn to find my tiger wearing one of my crop tops with his pants as he preens in the mirror.

Aubrey's right… Bast save us.

SINGING ALONG WITH MY EPIC AND COMPLETELY RANDOM 'TUNES to Rock the Road' playlist, I check my mirror to see if Fitz and the raccoons are still close by. My goofy boyfriend is weaving in and out of traffic like a daredevil. Occasionally, he drops back to stay even with me every once in a while so he can blow kisses and make inappropriate gestures. In contrast, The Captain and Raina are just behind me on their ride—a custom, raccoon-sized Harley with a sidecar painted with kraken tentacles and flames. I had to bite my tongue when they rolled up with pirate skull helmets and loud Gilbert & Sullivan playing because I didn't want to offend them.

But it was really, really hard not to laugh.

I didn't know Raina was the Captain's mate *and* his first mate, despite not working on the docs. Apparently, my food smuggling friend from the cafeteria has her own little prey based harem. It includes the Captain, an armadillo from the armory, a skunk from the laundry, and triplet quokkas from the cleaning staff. They didn't all join her, but I'd bet their motorcycle band would have been fucking *hysterical* to see.

We worked together to pack my car with the most essential shit. Despite the disdainful looks my mother's security dicks gave us, my guys were right: she'd informed them to allow me to leave early. I didn't even have to fight with the fuckface wolf to get my Mustang filled with my shit. Once it was done, we took off for the road to the Capital without so much as a middle finger to my captors and the weight on my chest has lifted substantially.

I can't wait to be back with my actual family, even if it means I have to do a bunch of sporty shit with Zhenga.

It's not the curvy lioness that aggravates me—at least, not after the explosions. She calmed her bullshit after she had me in class and honestly? One day, we might even be friends. *Okay, we might be friendly, if not friends.* But she's not the reason I'm making my 'yuck' face as I sing along to *The Proclaimers*. That's because I'm going to be involved in a sweaty, gross fight to the pain sport simply to raise my profile, so people quit trying to murder me for breathing.

Knowing Zhenga, she'll force me to take it super seriously and that's going to piss off my dance teachers. Anyone who wants to dance, even semi-professionally on stage, has to avoid things that might injure their money makers—their face and legs. The Pred Games are no-holds barred and at the college level, they don't allow killing, but maiming is on the table. Every time I step into a ring, I'll be risking one thing for the sake of another—all because I'm a goddamned bunny.

It feels like a curse when I say it that way and I don't mean for it to; I love my bunny—now.

The roar of an engine startles me out of my head and I squint as I see Fitz dropping back again. He waves at me, then points ahead, but all I see are the big ass semis that always seem to be in my way. A smaller engine creeps up on the other side of my car and I realize The Captain is now flanking me along with my tiger. I can't close my eyes, but I let my mind go still as I reach out with all of my senses, trying to figure out why they're suddenly in such a defensive posture.

A huge blast echoes off the hills around us and the aftershock rocks my car when it hits me. The sky darkens and even the air feels oppressive as I suck in shaky breaths. This isn't *exactly* like the scene at Apex where we almost lost Chess, but it's close enough to hit a trigger. Gritting my teeth, I allow the rabbit to fill me with rage for the people who got injured or killed in that nonsense. The

Council isn't releasing anything that gives true numbers, but I expect it's larger than what's being reported.

And whoever set off that explosion up ahead is in league with those hooded motherfuckers.

Tires squeal as the traffic all starts to swerve and brake to avoid the mess I can't quite see yet. Turning my wheel hard, I steer clear of my motorcycle riding friends until I've pulled over on the side of the highway. Fitz roars up, parking his bike and hopping off to stand in front of my car door. He pulls his helmet off, handing it to me to stow on the seat as he waves at the small prey animals coming around my back bumper.

"Baby Girl, I don't know what in the fuck is going on up there, but it looks really goddamn familiar," he says with a low snarl. "I don't want them anywhere *near* you."

My eyes narrow as I see the Captain and his mate brandishing their own weapons. "I'm not sitting in the car like I'm helpless. Hell, even Raina is armed."

"Mr. Renard warned us there could be trouble," Raina offers as she waves the miniature compound bow. "We would let no one hurt his mate, Dolly."

There's that word again. As if I'm not suppressing a panic attack already.

"Right. Of *course* he did," I mutter as I try to get my shit together. "Then we're *all* in this, got it? No one is putting me in a bubble—never again."

Fitz shakes his head, then runs his hands through his hair. "They're all going to fucking kill me when this gets back, but okay. Let's go find out what the Gregorian Monks up there are cooking today."

I hold up a finger, closing my eyes for a second as I let my half-shift emerge, then I take his hand. "Now I'm ready to kick some fake Sith Lord ass."

Raina and The Captain follow along as we creep up the shoulder, crouching behind cars and vehicles that are pulled over or stopped in the middle of the road. When we get to what I think is the epicenter, I see a flipped tractor trailer spilling liquid all over the pavement. Four shitty Ghostface wanna-bes are stalking through the mess like they're on a mission. I growl softly when the faint scent from that night catches the breeze. It's not as strong as the night my bunny went apeshit, so I don't think the source of it is here, but these fuckers are *definitely* working with whoever it was.

It reminds me how pissed I am that these frigging assmunches have ruined orchids and hydrangea for me.

They notice us and a wave of energy ripples through the air, making my fur stand on end. I don't know if this happened to all the disappearing students from last year or I'm just special, but I am done with playing with these psychos.

I stand up, letting go of Fitz's hand as my claws lengthen. "Oi, you faceless assholes! If you want me, come fucking get me."

Fitz's face drains of color and Raina gasps.

This year, I'm not staying on the defensive—it's the Year of the Rabbit and I'm ready to claim my crown.

Bad Feeling

Chess

I don't know how I know—my connection to Fitz has always been there, but not as active as they taught me mating bonds were. But when something is truly amiss, I get itchy, then anxious. It's almost as if his hyperactivity slides down the bond to me while he's focused on whatever it is. And right now, I feel like I'm going to jump out of my skin.

Walking over to the bar Ren and Aubrey set up, I pour myself a gin and tonic. I'm not as fond of straight liquor as the others, but I need a balm for the nerves firing within me. Felix and I have been here working on various shit Henny assigned to our group when we arranged to be at Capital Prep together. The flying duo is in the library proper, re-cataloguing at Aubrey's insistence. Apparently, dragons and sphinxes have *very* different ideas about how libraries are maintained, and he's been a beast about it since we all arrived.

"Chess, you don't normally partake at eleven a.m." Felix lifts his head from his files, his eyes cutting into me with the intuition of a leader. "What's going on?"

I pause, not wanting to overreact and seem too emotional. "I feel like there's something not right. It's got me on edge, that's all."

"What have I told you about trusting your instincts? They're as good as the rest of ours, and you don't need to doubt yourself. Tell me what has you drinking," he replies as he sits aside his work.

"A feeling. When Fitz has major emotions, there's a flood of energy that flows through our mating bond. It makes me jittery and I've been sensing it growing for about an hour. I'm sorry I didn't mention it, but it could just be him getting excited over a cool car." I smile crookedly. "We both know his temperament."

The tiger raises an eyebrow. "Have you ever felt this when it was something silly or unimportant?"

Blinking, I turn inward to think about that question. I don't recall getting the tingle of endorphins when Fitz was out carousing or even if he's just fighting. No, this is a specific thing that happens when he is in danger, and my eyes widen when I realize it. "I think he's in danger. That means…"

"The Princess is in danger," Felix says grimly. Turning back to his computer, he fires off a message in one of the open windows and within moments, the door to the private residence opens.

Renard and Aubrey look a bit disheveled, but I imagine moving all those heavy ass books is tiring even for shifters. There's an odd anxiety coming from them and I don't know if it's because Felix sent up a red flag or they sensed something off. Aubrey clears his throat after he sees my drink, then looks at my Raj.

"Felix, you said it was an emergency. No one's moving. What the bloody hell is going on?"

I walk over to the couch, taking a seat next to Felix. He's pulling up the GPS on Fitz's phone and bike. "We believe there's a problem with the convoy returning. I've got a *sense* that Fitz is in trouble."

"Through your bond?" Renard asks. When I nod, he hums softly. "We should take it seriously. The two of you keep quiet about how your particular bond works, but they teach gargoyles to pay very close attention to the warnings their bonds give them. If you feel Fitz is unsafe, you are likely correct."

That doesn't make me feel any better.

"They've stopped," my Raj interrupts. "Fitz's trackers are still and the system says they have been for about fifteen minutes."

Aubrey narrows his eyes at the tiger after he glances at the screen. "Would you like to share why you didn't use this to track him the other night, Felix? It would have saved a lot of worry."

My face heats and I raise my hand sheepishly. "That's my fault. I promised Fitz we wouldn't use the GPS we put in on everyone's tech and vehicles unless we were *certain* one of us was in danger. Agreeing to his terms was the only way I could get him to do it."

The other two roll their eyes, but Renard is the one who asks. "When did you two hatch this…very insightful… plan?"

He's not thrilled; I can tell by his tone. But honestly, once we started leaving campus with Dolly, it worried the hell out of me. *Looks like I was right.* "I asked him to do it when we started taking my angel off-campus for dates. I was worried about what might happen if one of us ran into trouble. It flags the system if we aren't within the given ranges set."

"You programmed our date locations?" Aubrey growls, the affront clear on his face. "By Ra's ears, Chess, you're getting as paranoid as Fitz."

"Obviously not," Felix says wryly as he smirks. "There's nothing about where they stopped and no one has communicated a rest break. They're still three hours away and I assume your prey friends haven't texted, either, Ren?"

The gargoyle reaches in his pocket, pulling out his phone and frowning. "No. The Captain would let me know if they'd stopped for a normal reason. Chess may have invaded our privacy, but his fears were not unwarranted."

"Fine. But Felix knew, and we didn't. That's poor communication —do better, both of you," the dragon grumbles as he and Ren join us on the sofa. "We could fly, but whatever is happening might be over by the time we arrive. This was carefully planned."

Studying the map, I tilt my head, considering all the options. This smacks of the abductions from last year—a student from a well-known family traveling to or from the school because of a break. The kidnappers are keeping track of break schedules and likely have spies to help monitor the coming and going of their targets. Dolly wasn't supposed to leave for two more days, yet they could ambush her in the perfect place to catch her vulnerable.

What they couldn't account for was Fitz and the pirates.

"She has people with her who would die before they allow her to be taken," I mumble. The frightened expressions on the faces of the most alpha members of our family are scaring me. "They're not without protection."

Aubrey is the one who snorts at me. "Rennie may be the only one who saw it, but I don't think you guys realize how dangerous our girl is on her own. She tore Abel limb from limb—all she left were blobs of flesh, blood, and gore. And his head, of course."

"But… she was infused with that blue stuff and terrified. I mean, do you think—"

My question isn't even finished before the gargoyle smirks at me knowingly. "Trust us, Chester. *Ma petite* is learning to take care of herself and when she develops fully, she'll give all of us a run for our money. I could not work out how a prey animal got imbued with magic *and* the spirit of a predator, but she is. It is both beautiful and terrifying in the best ways, *mon ami*."

"So we just sit here and hope for a phone call?" Felix shakes his head, looking like he needs a gallon of scotch. "That can't be the answer."

He can't stand not being in control and this is straining his ability to stay calm.

"Anyone else want a drink?" I stand, heading over to the bar to refill my glass. Felix grunts and the other two follow, so I pour my G&T first, then three generous single malts. Handing the rocks glasses out, I poke my brother's arm. "Perhaps we should see if Fitz has more surveillance than he told me? If you're logged into his system, you can access his shit. I wouldn't be surprised if he was doing more than watching Dolly in person."

The tiger blinks, then nods. "He was going crazy this summer, but not as much as I would have expected. He *has* to be hiding something."

"It might only be in her home," Ren says. "That might have been enough for him."

I shake my head. "No way. Last year, he was in town watching her and his access only increased at Apex. There's more than a pinhole cam in her room, for sure."

"You think she knows?" the dragon says curiously. "I mean, it didn't bother her when he trailed her like a puppy at Apex."

Felix looks up briefly and chuckles. "Whatever is there, I'm sure she expects, even if he didn't tell her directly. Princess knows my brother craves her like air. They have an interesting dynamic with that."

"I'll say." Aubrey shifts in his seat, then points at the screen. "There, Raj. Click that one. I don't know why, but it looks important."

Fitz's desktop is filled with icons, none of them labeled, and multiple screens running code that had to be minimized. Even I don't know why Aubrey picked the particular one he did, but when it opens, a full screen view of the school from satellite level. I blink, staring at it as Felix maneuvers the mouse to zoom in close enough to see people's faces outside the admin building.

"Holy shit, he hacked a Council satellite," I mutter. "He'll get in so much fucking trouble if anyone finds out."

Renard shrugs, his lips curved up wickedly. "I highly doubt anyone will catch our hyper friend. Look at the way he has things situated. We wouldn't even have known if there wasn't an emergency, Chess."

"Type coordinates in that tiny box," Aubrey interrupts, pointing a thick finger at a small window. "I think he can fucking move this thing. It won't be quick unless he's got the entire network."

The view inches a bit, then flips to another picture immediately and I groan. "Which he does. Ares above, Fitzy, you're completely insane."

"It's treason for certain, but our name provides more forgiveness than most realize," Felix sighs. "Our father would cover it up in a red hot second, then ask him to do it again to keep tabs on our enemies."

He's got us there. The current Raj would dance in glee if he knew.

"Pan the view," I murmur as I squint. "Then zoom in."

Felix does as I ask and we wait, knowing this isn't like turning a security camera. It won't move quickly and the view we had showed nothing of interest. But it's near where they stopped and a voice in my head is telling me we're on the right track. I don't know if it's intuition or my bond with Fitz, but we're close to figuring this shit out. My fingers tap on my leg rhythmically as we sit there, holding our breath as the view slowly moves. I started teaching myself piano this summer because I thought it would be fun to accompany Dolly and I'm nervous playing scales out of habit.

"Very nice, *mon ami*. You're getting better," Ren says as he nods at my right hand.

Of course, the Frenchman knew how to play well.

"Why haven't you told my angel you're classically trained, by the way?" I ask curiously. "She'd love it."

The sing-song voice of a snarky dragon is my answer. "He wants to *surprise* her with his musical gift. It's so *adorable.*"

Felix and I chuckle, and the tension in the room lifts slightly. We're all staring at the computer, but a weight has lifted. Normally Fitz and Ren are the comedians, but since my angel came into our lives, even Felix and Aubrey have loosened up. It amazes me every time I see it.

"I think I see something," Felix rumbles as he leans forward. He flicks the wheel of the mouse, pushing in closer, and the growls that fill the room come from every single one of us.

From a bird's-eye view, we can see a dozen hooded people engaged in a battle Royale with one tiger, two raccoons, and a *seriously* pissed off bunny.

This isn't good at all.

Fight Back

Delores

There *were* only three of them when I let out the battle cry.

Unfortunately, within seconds, nine more popped out of the goddamn aether and fanned out with their comrades. Each of them seems to wield some type of magic, but fuck me if I know what it is. All I know is my bunny is in rage mode and holding back to study these fuckers like Felix taught me almost hurts. Raina and The Captain spread out to cover the flanks, just in case, and Fitz went one-ton tiger the second their back-up arrived.

I'm the leader, somehow, and I have to show them I can do this.

"Who the fuck are you?" I growl as they chant. The colorful array of powers grows slightly when they begin, and I take a deep, calming breath. I have no idea if I can do anything like I did at Apex or if that was a fluke. Nothing I tried all summer brought about sketchy blue energy, so I'm inclined to believe it is the latter. But I won't go down without a fight—especially since I think these jackholes are part of the disappearing students problem. "I *said*, who the ass-reaming *fuck* are you guys?"

The tallest figure finally looks at me, but their face is in complete darkness inside of the hood. I don't know if it's a mask or a spell, but their identities are a mystery. A deep, melodic voice echoes in the air as it speaks, *"Impossibile, venimus domum. Genus nostrum per saecula cruorem quaesiverunt similem tuum.*[1]*"*

What is with *bad guys and fucking Latin?*

I turn to look at Raina and the Captain, unsure what to do. Tiger-Fitz definitely doesn't speak it and what little I know from music and pop culture will not help unless they want a folksy quote. "Any chance either of you knows what they're saying?"

"Aye," the Captain says as he nods at me. I look surprised, and he gives me a wily grin. "Treasure maps, lass. It sounded a wee bit like 'Impossible one.' We're here to bring ye home. We've been searching for ye for centuries or something close."

TigerFitz bats at my hand and I look down to see hunger glinting in his eyes. He's on #teamkillthemall and I can't blame him. *What would you do if masked magic nutters came to kidnap you?* I smile down at him, scratching his head lightly with razor-sharp claws. "My super hot psycho boyfriend has the right idea. If they will not give up, there's only one option."

"Walk the plank, ye scurvy dogs!" The Captain gives me a feral grin and Raina sets her crossbow with a deafening 'click.'

Fitz leaps forward with a roar that rattles the windows of the car behind us, not waiting for further directions. His target is the willowy leader, so I head for the acolytes on her left side. The distinct pop of bolts fills the air and the chanting stutters when they find their mark. My eyes catch the tiny pirate raccoon charging into the right flank of the circle while his mate picks off as many as she can. I don't know how the hell her ammo is made, but every time she hits someone, they jerk like they've been tased.

When I get to my group of hooded asswipes, I note which color magic they're using. Aubrey and Rennie will ask me this, and I have to remember every detail possible. The one furthest to the left is wielding something red that immediately turns into a whip of fire. Ducking quickly, I do a somersault across the ground, barreling into its legs like a damn bowling ball. It knocks the fiery wizard person over and before it can get up, I pounce. I know the others are watching and waiting for their turn to enter the melee, but I'm not sure why. I hear a pained snarl from Fitz and another round of bolts behind me, so I use this moment to pull the hood off.

Scooby-Doo reveal for the win!

But it won't budge, and when I go to poke my clawed fingers into the eyes of my captive, they disappear into nothingness. Realizing this isn't going how I imagined, I look over to see my tiger going for the throat of General BlankFace as they tumble over the ground. He's not playing and I don't have the luxury of being sentimental, either. My lips curve into a large, fangy grin as my bunny takes control, as my claws rake over the tender skin of its throat. The blood from slashing my flattened fire guy literally spurts into my face like a red glitter glue bomb, and I sputter as I push to my feet.

"What the actual *fuck?*"

I don't have time to consider what in the hell this shit means as contestant number two shoots green vines from their hands, grabbing my legs to yank them hard. Two more vines follow and I snarl at the earthy smell of the magic trying to hold me. Obviously, this dickwad is some Poison Ivy reject and if I don't keep my hands free, I'll get sucked in like that damn plant in the wizard movie. My eyes cut to the side and I consider my moves quickly.

The fire. Asshole number one set a bunch of brush on fire.

Twisting my body, I dive and roll to the right, using the force of my bunny leap to drag the idiot with me. The vines tighten on my ankles when it figures out where I'm army crawling, but I grit my teeth and pull him along with every ounce of strength I have.

More vines brush against me as I fight my way to the burning bush. If I can just reach it, I know I'll be able to get the plants to release and I can fight this fucker with head on.

A crossbow bolt whizzes past my head and a startled yelp of pain comes from the shithead holding onto me. Their grip loosens a fraction, and I use that to drag us both to my target. My hand grasps one of the burning branches and I hiss at the pain, but waving it towards my feet makes the fucking Audrey II like greenery let go of me. *Yes!* I shout in my head as I roll over and spring to my feet. The hood villain backs away as I wave the fiery stick, but I keep advancing. When I get close enough, I toss the distraction in the dirt before launching into a flying spin kick combo that drops him like a sack of potatoes.

Two down, I think to myself as I make quick work of my evil grass-type gym leader. *Now for the purple pussy watching us.*

"Your mother was a hamster," I yell as I charge toward my last opponent. Maybe not the most badass trash talk ever, but I'm new at this shit.

A weird boom echoes through the air and my head suddenly feels like it's going to explode. Dropping to my knees, I hold on to it, rocking as the pain thuds in my brain. *Shit. Purple bad. Purple is terrible.*

I gasp as tears well up in my eyes and suddenly, the entire world around me changes. Images of death and destruction flit past me in rapid succession, including the bodies of my friends and my men. There are so many shifters dead around them, and everything is dark in the sky. The tall hood Fitz is fighting is standing over the carnage, laughing in a musical tone that doesn't sound like what I heard earlier. Its laugh gets louder and higher pitched the longer it goes on until it feels like a full-on villain victory scene.

"Come with us or this is your future," a voice says in a low, hypnotic tone. *"Everyone you love will suffer."*

"Wait a minute. This is bullshit. It's like a kids' movie. I'm not falling for some dime store Mysterio B-Reel." The illusion shimmers, my recognition making the magic falter slightly. My eyes narrow and I look at the corpses with fury. "This *isn't real*. You can get fucked, you faceless Kadabra!"

Another pop and I'm back to the battle, panting as I look up at the figure who was fucking with my mind. Before it can respond, I do a backward roll, then kip up to a standing position. My fists clench and I stare at the asshole who dared to show me the only people who care about me in gruesome death masks with organs hanging out. Rage pumps through my veins and I hear my heart thumping in my tall rabbit's ears as the fury spreads through me.

Sparks dance over my raised dukes and my expression turns smug. "Clobbering time."

"*Redi domum, discipuli mei. Nunc lepus relinque.*[2]"

The loud command comes from behind me, and I know it must be the dick Fitz is battling. Raina and The Captain have gone quiet, so I can only assume they handled their rainbow magic cult people. My friend's bolt saved my bacon with the eco-wizard, so I'm grateful, but I wish they'd jumped in before that nightmare vision. Taking my eyes off the jerk in front of me, I watch the bodies disappear one by one. I grit my teeth and whip back to my opponent, hoping to get one final blow in before it's gone, but it's too late.

I'm about to shoot my mouth off at the leader despite my battered body when TigerFitz limps over. He's got a gash above his left eye that's bled all over him and I can tell by the way he's walking he'll need to heal when he gets home. General BlankFace snaps its fingers and disappears in a puff of black smoke, leaving me to look around at the scorched field tiredly.

"There's no way this is what those other spoiled kids encountered," I groan. "They must have popped in, grabbed their target, and skedaddled."

The Captain trudges over, his hat missing, and his sword covered in colorful glittery blood. "Aye. Ye were a special case, lass. Those scallywags were strong. Good thing our most gracious gargoyle provided me mate with special artillery."

"Fuck, yes," I reply with a gigantic sigh. "Taser bolts are pretty damn cool. Where'd he get that shit?"

"Liberated from the Apex armory during re-building," Raina chirps. "After we gathered everything needed from the Tower, Monsieur Renard had all the prey who he protects to search the grounds and tunnels for anything useful. We found so many wonderful things that it took four trips to move."

Well, I'll be damned.

"Good job, Raina." Looking down at TigerFitz, I smile as much as I can. "Come on, baby. You gotta shift so you can ride the rest of the way home. We don't have a trailer for your bike and you know we have to get back before someone sends out the fucking Sibbies to look for us."

The tiger rolls his eyes at me, but then quickly shifts to my slightly less vicious boyfriend. "Gonna be a bitch nursing this shit for four more hours. Healing would go faster as the tiger, but you're right, Baby Girl." His eyes roam over me for a second and he squints. "Are you okay? Looks mostly superficial. Good thing I took that leader fuck. Don't mess with the black ropes; they hurt like hell."

My expression is haunted for a second and I shake my head. "Not the purple, either. Trust me."

"You can tell me later." Fitz reaches out and despite both of us wincing as he tugs our bodies together, he kisses me firmly. "For now, we need to blow this joint like a sailor on shore leave."

"Gross," I mutter as I pull back. "But you're right. We don't want to be here if they regroup or law enforcement arrives."

"To the fleet!" The Captain says as he grabs Raina's hand.

Into the wild blue yonder we go.

---

1. Impossible one, we have come to bring you home.
2. Return home, my followers. Leave the rabbit for now.

FAMILY

FITZ

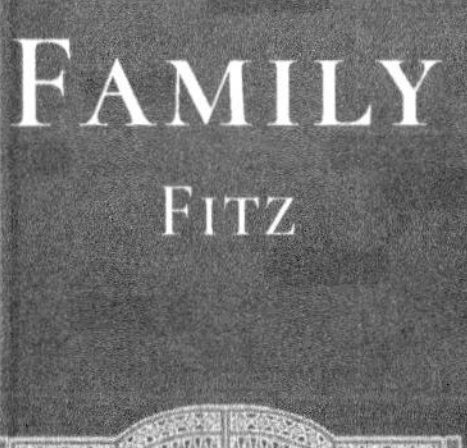

"Of fucking course we handled it. Give me a break, bro. Well, yeah, we're a bit banged up; we were in a ten on four free-for-all!"

My brother has been shouting in my ear—with the help of the others—for the better part of an hour. Baby Girl isn't on this call and thank fuck for that because she'd be pissed. Her form wasn't perfect, but from what I could tell while I was wailing on the lead fucker, she held her own. The ferocity our girl is claiming as her own is sexy as hell, and I will not stand in her way for a moment. My fellow boy band members need to hop on board and let her show them how brave and capable she is.

"Look, Felix… she took down three of the shitstains on her. I didn't see any of the light show, but I was focused on the main one. No, I don't know if they're men or women. If I could tell, I would know, wouldn't I? Odin's dry socket, bro, let us get home before you interrogate me."

He drones on for another moment or two before I let out a sigh of frustration. I know he can't stand being out of control and this shit happening while he was so far away is making him crazy. Truth is, I need to be focused on my surroundings, *not* his nitpicking. For all we know, another squadron of hooded fruitcakes will appear on the road to Capital Prep and I have to be ready.

"Bro, I'm hanging up. I have to be sharp in case we get hit again. Save the blistering lecture for when we're safely in the Weenie Nest."

That said, I click my headset off and go back to watching the road. Baby Girl is decompressing by singing along with her radio and the gargoyle's prey minions are on the other side. The pirate nods at me over the hood of her car, letting me know he's monitoring things, too. Their skill was surprising, but honestly? I don't have the foggiest fucking clue how prey shifters raise their cubs. Maybe having to worry about hungry dicks like me forces them to train their young to be fighters from the get-go?

I wonder if old granite balls knows? He probably does.

I blink, realizing there's something we need to consider in this new place. Renard's crew will be there, but our girl needs to get the prey shifters at this new place on her side, too. These pirate bandits can help with that and I'll have to ask Sriracha Shorts if the medical chicks are coming, too. If so, that's another way to increase my baby girl's profile on campus. The more shifters we get to support her, the more likely she'll have allies to help her navigate a new place full of enemies—new and old.

Grinning to myself, I push the accelerator harder. I want to get back to the stupid school as fast as possible. Even Felix's inevitable lecture is worth sharing this idea with everyone.

Fitz Khan—fighter, lover, and super genius—is on the job.

BY THE TIME WE PULL INTO THE WIDE, TREE-LINED DRIVE OF Capital Preparatory Academy, I'm ready to rock 'n roll. Ideas have been fluttering through my brain like butterflies the entire drive and I'm eager to share them. Baby Girl is going to be so proud of me for getting all my random threads in order so everyone can understand the connections like she does. My excitement only grows as we take the twists and turns until we hit the back road to cross over the river and enter the small back lot behind the fancy library.

I almost forgot she hasn't seen this set-up yet.

When we park, the raccoons hop out and get to work on unloading her stuff immediately. I know my girl hates having staff do everything for her, so I don't protest when she grabs some of her stuff despite her injuries. In fact, I join her in carrying a few bags because I'm respectful like that. Her smile is my reward, which is more than enough to compensate for the pain.

"Eager to see our new digs, baby girl?" I ask as we approach the newly installed reinforced door. Renard and Aubrey went all out to add to the already crazy levels of security the Cappie library had going and it included new doors at every entrance. "I know this seems like a damned fortress, but I swear, the Flying Fearmongers were on a tear. They would have made it bomb-proof if they'd had time."

Dolly gives me a tired smile, her eyes soft. "They want to keep all of us safe, Fitz. I can't argue with that and neither can you. Since our last school *exploded* from magic we thought didn't *exist*, I figure we have to prepare for everything, even the impossible."

"That will make my control freak twin *supremely* happy. He's mapped routes between buildings and every single thing that could happen out like he's in a wartime drama. It's driving the others batshit." Swiping my arm over the scanner, I see her surprise and shrug. "Cards and fobs get lost and stolen, baby girl. You'll get a chip, too."

Her nose wrinkles. "I'm not a fan of being chipped like a pet."

"Wait until Chessie uses the scanner I found to see if you are and don't know. Felix and I had to cut out ones our fucking father probably put in at *birth* because those scars were *old*."

"Just. Fucking. Great," she mutters. "Why the hell would she always have idiots following me, then?"

Before I can answer, we're greeted by our family storming down the hall like we're trying to raid an enemy camp. The simple answer would be because the chips aren't being actively monitored like a bodyguard can. It's the same reason I hacked into the Council satellites last year—in case we *needed* to find someone in danger. Tech like this is more for emergencies than it is continual surveillance, and my guess is almost every heir in the Council families have them, whether or not they know. But she's not ready to hear that, so I keep my trap shut while my family smothers her in attention.

We deserve a little lovin' after that damn ambush.

Chessie breaks from her embrace to let Aubrey in and heads for me, squeezing tightly enough to make me grunt in pain. "Oi, love. Be careful. We're both a little banged up, but nothing the healing won't fix after a few hours."

"Banged up?" Felix thunders as he pushes the growling dragon out of the way to look at our girl. "Where are you injured? Renard, call for our friends in the medical bay."

"I'm okay. Really," Dolly says in a tired voice. "Fitz is right; we'll heal."

"Absolutely not, *ma petite lapin*. The Raj is right. We will ask a nurse we know to come check you out. Fitzgerald, you will get examined as well. With the Pred Games starting not long after school resumes, we need you both in good shape."

Oh, shit. I forgot about that. Thank fuck Frenchie McPointyTail bargained for the staff he protects to be sent here.

"I agree. We won't allow anyone but our own medics to come near us because I don't trust the staff here yet. Fitz hasn't finished checking out any of the staff who aren't from Apex. It's dangerous to assume anything until we clear them fully." Aubrey finally stops glaring at Felix for cutting in line, then gives me a look that says 'hurry, the fuck up, asshole.' He gestures at the hallway. "Come see our new nest, snack size."

Baby Girl's grin brightens, and she reaches out to grab his huge hand. "That would be amazing! I'm excited to see what Chessie said you were all working on. I want to see the tiger den, too, and all the buildings. It's hard having to learn a whole new place again, but I'm also *dying* of curiosity. That folder didn't say shit about anything."

Renard wrinkles his nose, sniffing. "The perch isn't quite satisfactory, but everything else will do."

I roll my eyes and clap him on the back. "Come on, Dark Flight. You can complain about your lack of creepy old buildings while we show our girl the layout here. Eventually, she'll follow you up to your inadequate roost."

Dolly giggles and follows as we head to the main room. When we stop, she gasps softly. "Oh, this sunken couch area is *amazing*. I love how it's close to the kitchen and the bar. I think it's big enough for all of us without squeezing."

"Unless we *want* to squeeze," I mumble as I pinch Chess with a playful grin.

Felix gives me a narrow-eyed look, then shakes his head ruefully. "We tried to housebreak him while you were gone, but it obviously failed."

I'm about to snap back when our girl shrugs and gives me a *very* soft expression. She walks over and kisses my cheek lightly before she says, "I like him exactly how he is. That goes for all of you, by the way."

Where the hell did these butterflies in my chest come from?

"We like you just as you are, too, angel," Chess adds as he glances around the room. "Even if you give us heart attacks."

"Gives *you* heart attacks? Were any of you dicks there when she screamed 'come at me, bro' at a group of hooded magic fucks?" I shudder and shake my head. "Shaved five years off my life, baby girl."

"She *what*?" Felix shouts as his tiger rumbles loudly.

"They were attacking anyway. Why not throw them off guard by projecting confidence?" The smirk she flashes at my tightly wound twin is perfect.

He's going to lose it in three… two… one…

"Felix, perhaps it would be best if we save the lectures for after she and Fitz recount what happened?" Renard drops onto his favorite spot, sprawling out in a relaxed pose. "Chess, can you contact Bettina? We should have them checked out sooner rather than later."

The fight drops out of my twin as he nods. With all the greetings and fun, we forgot they wanted us looked at, ensuring there weren't any issues with healing on our own. His frightened rant will have to wait until we get everyone settled and checked out by the nurses.

If I'm very lucky, it might even be derailed entirely by debriefing our girl on this ridiculous school. Apex was a shark tank full of heirs and rich kids, but Cappie is the home of even worse assholes —it's filled with children of celebrities, diplomats, and international leaders. In some ways, they're worse than the kids of Council members or rich business tycoons. These little fuckers have been raised with the same entitlement and money, but they're *far* more media savvy than even that Barrington twit.

And someone's going to tell our girl those half-wit exes of hers are going to be here, too, if she hasn't figured it out yet.

"Not it!" I blurt out.

They all look at me in confusion and I growl when I realize I crossed from in my head to out loud. Dolly walks over, taking my hand and pulling me to the middle of the huge, recessed sofa nest. I follow her, but it doesn't keep me from squirming a little as everyone else settles in. Her big blue eyes meet mine and she chuckles. "What are you 'not it' for, Fitzy?"

Fuck me running.

"I didn't want to be the one to remind you all they sent here the second years, so your micropenis ex and the Bitch Squad will be here, too." Frowning, I cross my arms over my chest as I pout a little. I royally fucked that one up.

She sucks in a deep breath, then blows it out slowly. "Yeah, I figured. But here's the thing: I survived them once and I can do it again. With you guys on my side, as well as the back alley deal one of you worked to get Rufus and Cori here. I think I can handle whatever they throw at me. The Heathers don't get to rule my life anymore; I'm free."

I look over at Spicy Salamander with a wicked grin. "Does that mean we can rein hellfire and brimstone on them now?"

"Not if you'll get shitcanned for it. I definitely need you guys here more than I need to see them get their just desserts." Her eyes dance. "But that doesn't mean I'm saying you can't find creative ways to exercise your thirst for revenge."

"Evil. I *love* it," the gargoyle says happily. His tail flicks out behind him and I can see the wheels turning in his extremely mischievous mind. "I'll confer with the two of you about my thoughts."

"If you're all done fucking around, I'd love to hear what happened from the Princess. Can we manage that without getting distracted?" Felix asks with a smug look on his face.

"If you can manage to not be an overbearing *dick*," I mutter.

"Fitz!" My baby girl giggles, but dutifully turns to look at my brother with a prim smile. "I'm ready when you are, Sir."

Oh, she's clever.

I'm falling in love with this girl more every minute.

Falling in Love

Delores

Felix's rant wasn't as bad as I expected. It was obvious the shit with Chess shook him up as badly as the rest of us and he's struggling with wanting to keep everyone safe. Unfortunately, every single person in our family is headstrong, stubborn, and really fucking tired of being targeted by random baddies. It's constantly grating and seems to only get worse, even when we think we've made headway.

But that's what the real bad guys do, right? They keep chipping away at you until you surrender or put them in their place.

Now that my grumpy tiger has his fears off his chest, we're looking over the materials for Cappie while we eat the delicious Chinese food Chess whipped up. I'm watching Renard wield his chopsticks like a seasoned pro and when I look at Aubrey, he's holding his the same way. My lips quirk when I remember Fitz came flying to my house yesterday because he found out their secret. It's obvious he's forgotten that minute detail, but as soon as the adrenaline wears off from our fight, he'll be anxious again.

I can't believe the two of them hid it from the others for a decade and everyone else at Apex for much longer.

Once you know what to look for, it slaps you in the face. The way they kid one another gently or make accommodations without asking isn't just a friend thing. Their dedication to one another is noticeable when you see the ease between them as they move about their space. I've never seen Aubrey get his scotch without automatically grabbing a drink for Rennie. And the dragon definitely prefers his horde room, but alternated with the gargoyle's nest without complaint. My winged warriors don't flash it around like Fitz and Chess, but they're settled like an old married couple.

"What are we going to do about the dorm situation?" Chess asks around a mouthful of Udon noodles.

I groan, looking at the map again. "The only good thing about this is the damn Reptile house is across the way from the library. It's close to here, so if I end up with a roommate, I can sneak in and out."

Aubrey arches a brow. "My worry was the safety of your belongings and your privacy. We know reptilian shifters are quite sneaky and avaricious. They can be bought."

"Great. Here I thought having to use the tunnel from the mainland would stop the idiots because this thing says it requires a swipe card. Now you're telling me the killer is *in my house*," I grumble.

Would it be so hard for shit not to be complex while I'm adjusting to a whole new set of people and places?

"I think we scope out her dorm in the morning before more students arrive. If it appears her room is ill-suited, which it likely will be, *ma petite* can leave her things in the main room here where I had the Captain stow them."

Felix narrows his eyes at the gargoyle. "Had this planned out, did you?"

Rennie chomps a bite of broccoli with relish before he winks at me. He's talented at assessing all the angles from above, so he definitely saw this question coming. Fitz's plan to house me in the Tower last year did wonders for keeping me safe as I slept, dead body notwithstanding. I know he realized leaving me in a dorm full time would make my space far too accessible to all of my enemies—known and unknown.

"I like that idea," Fitz says, as he rolls over to hold a piece of beef up for me. "She can buy a spare set of shit to put there in case someone checks, but leave all her real things here. We're going shopping tomorrow night to replace what we didn't pack, anyway."

"Fitz!" The elder twin gives him a stern look. "Your orders were to pack everything she needed."

"Felix, we're all rich as fuck with nothing to do but spoil our girl. Why would I bother gathering up a bunch of shit to move it again later?"

Aubrey is the one who jumps in. "I agree with the lunatic. Rennie loves shopping and would enjoy tagging along. I have no qualms with splitting up the gifts."

Chess and Felix look dumbfounded, but my crazy tiger beams. "That's the spirit, you old penny pincher! We're going to give our girl the full *Pretty Woman* treatment—minus the snarky sales person. Otherwise, we'll be removing blood from the purchases."

My face heats and I look at them all shyly. "You don't have to. I mean, Luc pays me well enough to avoid using Lucille's blood money… and I'm not asking anyone to—"

"Angel, we're not offering. We're *insisting*." The cheetah scoots over and takes my hands as his eyes meet mine. "I know we didn't get to really discuss this last year because of all the chaos, but you are going to be our mate. That's how this works."

Annnnd now I can't look at any of them because the emotions running through me are so huge it feels like I'm going to burst.

"He's right, Princess. Protecting and taking care of you are our chief priorities, so stop worrying about whatever has you twisted up. None of us were raised to allow a mate to want for anything." Felix arches a brow at me, his lips curled in a smirk. "As my brother keeps saying, you're the queen of this ambush—start acting like it."

"Hell yeah!" Fitz whoops as he grabs me away from Chess to plant a smacking kiss on my lips. "I knew these assholes would all get on board eventually. Get ready to be pampered, baby girl."

I must look startled because Chess scoots close to both of us and smiles gently. "Let's start with shopping for her rooms and such first, love. I think an avalanche of presents is making our bunny nervous."

Nodding, I give him a grateful smile in return. "Yes. Starting with necessities and school stuff would be good. We can discuss other things…later." The word presents sticks in my mind for a moment and I gasp. "Speaking of that, where is Jinx?"

Aubrey harrumphs. "The little fuzzball is sleeping on a ridiculous bed in your room. Just wait until you see it—Rennie spent the last few weeks getting it ready."

"Can we go now?" I clap my hands, excitement filling me at the prospect of seeing what on earth the gargoyle thought a room specifically made for me should look like.

"Of course, *ma petite*. We'll show you, then we can come back to finish going over your schedule and the forms."

I cannot wait *to see this.*

OF ALL THE THINGS I COULD HAVE IMAGINED, *THIS* WAS NOT IN THE realm of possibility.

When they opened the door to what was obviously the largest room in their annex, my jaw dropped. They painted the walls a deep blue that stretches to the high ceilings, where tiny stars and a bright, luminescent moon have been painted in painstaking detail. It fades towards the floor, where soft grass meets matching plush carpet. All the furniture is handmade, carved to look like climbing trees with little hollows and painted moss as accents. And the bed… the bed is enormous, with a sprawling head and footboard designed to resemble my midnight dragon with his head at the top and tail curled around the end. Huge, fluffy white bedding with mounds of colorful pillows and stuffies in the shape of all of their animals rest, just waiting to be cuddled.

There's even a big, climbing treehouse with levels for Jinx in one corner and a shelf for my Fitz trophies over the bedside tables.

"Rennie… oh my goddess…" I don't have the words to describe how this is affecting me; my heart feels like it's going to burst out of my chest and run away. "This is… perfect."

His smile is brilliant as he reaches out and pulls me into his arms to drop a kiss on my temple. "Fitz told us your room at home doesn't look like it ever 'fit' you. I left space for your keyboard, music, and plenty of accouterments in the closet you can pull out to organize your girly things. He helped me choose the books to add to the ones you left in the Tower. We brought everything left over from last year and put it away to the best of our knowledge."

Tears fill my eyes as I look at Aubrey, knowing the big bookshelf and study area on the other side of the room were likely his doing. He smirks a little, winking before he ruffles my hair. Fitz leans in to kiss me despite being held by the gargoyle, then bounces into the room to leap onto the bed. Laughing at his antics, I turn to Felix and Chess.

"That bed is big enough for all of us, you know," I murmur as my cheeks heat. "Monsieur Laveaux has plans, it seems."

Felix chuckles, his eyes dark as he leans in to feather a kiss on my mouth. "Indeed, Princess. I think perhaps we should plan that date sooner rather than later, don't you?"

Excitement courses through my veins and I murmur, "Yes, sir."

His growl makes my thighs clench and Rennie squeezes me close. "We can *smell* that, *ma petite*."

"Goddamnit," I mutter as I bury my face in his chest. "A pox on all your sensitive noses. It's not fair."

"You can do it, too, bite size." Aubrey looks mightily amused as he tilts his head. "Train your nose as you did to identify species. Didn't Fitzgerald tell you?"

My eyes narrow as I glare at the lounging tiger on my dragon shaped and sized bed. "No, he absolutely *did not!*"

All of my men look amused and I frown, pulling out of Rennie's arms to playfully stomp to the bed. I know they want to laugh and I don't blame them. My asshole parents taught me not one fucking thing about being a predator outside of killing people who disobey. The longer I'm around other preds, the more I realize that it's like I was raised with no knowledge that would keep me alive or even help me understand who I am. I'm a literal tourist in the world I was supposedly raised to be a ruler of. It's infuriating as hell.

"I don't think we grasped just how little they taught you about being a pred until now," Felix says as he scratches his chin. "Everything you've done so far is based on instinct or what you've learned from Fitz and your friends, isn't it?"

Dropping onto the bed in an embarrassed slump, I nod. "Yep. And it's not like they offer a remedial class in basic predator shit. No one but me was raised like Rapunzel in a tower hoping to be used as a puppet."

Fitz rolls over, grabbing me and wrapping around me like a crazy spider monkey. "It's okay, baby girl. Now that we know, we can *all* be your teachers. I know how much you *love* that."

The chorus of growls that fills the air tells me they like that idea as well. *Methinks the big growly men all have a little 'being in charge' fetish; good to know.* The teasing glint in my eyes brings Chess over to join Fitz and me, and I sigh happily as he sandwiches me in with the tiger. A soft purr kicks up in his chest, and I wiggle in delight. It's my absolute favorite thing, and the cheetah knows it.

"He cheats with that all the time, you know," Fitz says, as he buries his face in the back of my neck. "Be strong—though I honestly can't resist it, so I don't know how to teach you that one."

Felix walks over, sitting down next to Chess and resting a hand on my hip. "He's not lying. Our cheetah is not above using it on me, either. It helps calm the rage for certain. I'm not as soft as my twin, but I won't claim I can tell you how to resist, either."

I feel the mattress dip again, this time more substantially, and I know Aubrey and Rennie have joined us. I tilt my head up to look at them as they recline against the headboard together. "Rennie uses his tail to cheat. It's like a big hug, too."

Aubrey laughs. "She's not wrong about that. His wings are a weapon as well."

My psycho tiger stiffens behind me and I know exactly when he remembers what he saw before he came to my house. I give the dragon and gargoyle a knowing look, then turn back to Fitz. "Something you need to discuss, crazypants?"

"Uh, no. Nope. Not a thing. Can't imagine why you'd ask," he blurts.

Rolling my eyes, I reach up and tug on Aubrey's pant leg. They need to come clean now or it's going to be a problem later. I get why they've kept it to themselves in the past, but now that we're a unit, secrets will only be weapons that can be used against us. "Out with it."

"Oh, for the love of…" Aubrey makes his signature stuffy librarian harrumph and shifts a bit.

Fortunately, Rennie isn't as stubborn as him. "*Ma petite* is trying to get Fitzgerald to admit he discovered our secret the other day."

Felix frowns. "What, the room surprise?"

I giggle and Aubrey snorts before saying, "And you wonder how we kept it a secret for centuries? People see what they want to see."

"Kept what a secret?" Chess says, as he looks at me in confusion.

"Holy shit," I mutter. "Men are totally obtuse. I knew something was up, but I figured it had to do with the sleeping space until I found out. I wasn't totally clueless like this. I don't feel so bad about not knowing the pred stuff now."

"Will someone just fucking say it before I explode?" Fitz pleads. "It's *killing* me."

Looking at Rennie, I wait, and he just grins mischievously. I heave a sigh. "They're not telling you they're a couple and have been for a very long time with no one knowing. I assume they're mates like Fitz and Chess, but I didn't ask, so I can't speak for them on that part."

"Oh, thank *fuck*," Fitz says, as he wriggles closer to me and nips my neck. "It was hot as hell, but I didn't want to be the one to spill the bean slapping."

The two cats who were in the dark are quiet for a moment and I think they're remembering all the little things that should have given them clues. Finally, Felix pats my hip again and nods. "Well, okay then. Now that you tell us, it makes perfect sense. You didn't have to hide it, you know. I don't give a fuck about Fitz and Chess; I certainly wouldn't have cared about you two."

"We didn't think you were prejudiced, Raj," Aubrey laughs, and I feel him shaking above me. "We're just private creatures by nature. Neither dragons nor gargoyles are as social as big cats or most of the surrounding shifters. We're more insular species and our relationship wouldn't be acceptable to dragons, much less others."

"Gargoyles wouldn't be thrilled, either, trust me." Rennie shrugs and mutters. "They exile you for outside of the clutch relations."

"Do you want to talk about it?" I whisper. "I know you don't normally…"

"Not today, *ma petite*, but maybe someday."

Aubrey leans over and kisses him lightly. "Then Fitz stumbling in on us was a gift rather than an annoyance." He looks at the rest of us and shrugs, his face a little red. "I don't know the complete story, either. Maybe with all of us supporting him, my mate can finally get the trauma out."

I'll be damned. Fitz's rambunctious lack of boundaries is saving someone else.

It's an Apex miracle.

I Would Do Anything For You

Chess

 living room and strategized our way through my angel's class schedule.

Unlike the staff at Cappie, the Apex exiles arrived not long after they shut the school down for renovations. Their professors aren't exiles but preds who chose to educate, so they have homes and families to see during the breaks. While that's a pleasant change from an entire staff of angry cast-offs, it means we couldn't tell if her new professors will be problems. They limited our knowledge to what we could scrape from the Preynet and social media.

Felix wasn't happy, but luckily, she still has most of us for various classes. She'll see me as adjunct with her new theater professors and she has Renard for British Plays & Poetry. Felix is running her Intermediate Shifting class, but Fitz will have to stalk her on his own. That pisses him off because the dragon finagled her for an aide period, but the rest of her classes are all with Cappie staff.

I'm worried about the two wildcard classes: Shifter History and Human Diplomacy. Neither of the professors have much presence online outside of official bios, and something feels intentionally concealed. It made Fitz swear for two hours while he tried to dig up dirt on the dark web, but we're stuck assessing on the fly. But we only have so much room to fiddle with things or we'll raise alarms we don't want blaring around Dolly.

Her personal infamy is enough, thanks.

After going over routes and check-in protocols, we let our girl climb into her giant lizard bed to get some sleep. She insisted everyone simply find a spot and stay with her—an offer absolutely no one could refuse after her being gone all summer. We stacked Aubrey and the gargoyle on one side, the twins on the other, and I got to curl up with my head on her stomach. It felt exactly right, and even Felix woke up with a less grouchy disposition.

We ate breakfast while Dolly told us about her summer working with the designer and groaned about the trainer. The twins shrugged unrepentantly, and Fitz crowed about how well she handled herself in the mini-battle with their attackers as proof he chose well. She begrudgingly admitted it helped before flinging a potato at him that started a small food war. Aubrey broke it up when he got nailed with a mushroom.

It was probably my favorite breakfast ever and I don't care how silly that sounds.

Now my Angel is getting ready for her first practice with Zhenga while Felix runs back to our place to grab the three of us a change of clothes. I stayed here to clean up while Fitz bothers Dolly, then make the list for our shopping excursion. The dragon is back in the library and Renard is working alongside me in a companionable silence.

"Do you really want to come get school supplies with us?" I ask as I hand him a pan to dry. "You can stay and work on lesson plans if you need to. I know you got handed a few lower-level classes along with your normal ones, and that's not your usual semester."

His lips curve, and he shakes his head. "*Mon ami,* I have forgotten more about literature than most of the people here ever learned. I don't need to prepare plans to talk about books or plants or even nocturnal shifters. It's the benefit of being nearly a millennium old."

"I forget how long you and Aubrey have been alive until you say shit like that," I admit ruefully. "Neither of you looks over your mid-thirties and, though you have your quirks, you adapt very well."

"My scaly friend was not always as flexible as he is now. When I first arrived, he barely spoke to anyone, and hadn't for decades. Did you know I learned sign language just in case he was deaf?" The gargoyle smiles fondly and shrugs. "After I wormed my way into his good graces, I could bring him out of his cave more often. It took patience and dedication, but he's definitely caught up with the times."

I blink, turning to look at him incredulously. "Uh, no, I did *not* know that. You two *never* talk about the past. I mean, occasional snarky references, but nothing substantial. Is that because you were keeping 'the big secret' or is being secretive in your nature?"

"A bit of both. Our species are reclusive—like most rare shifters— and they keep to themselves because of the exotic trade. I know Aubrey was taught similarly to me as a child; any information you share about us could lead to people being killed or captured. So you keep your counsel more often than not."

Nodding, I hand him another platter. "That makes sense. The Khans are pretty close lipped as well, but for different reasons. Can't have anyone knowing the extent of their reach and how many fingers they have in what pies," I reply. "We're technically still under oath, so we're not supposed to share a fraction of what we do, but I think the twins are past giving a shit. How much more could the Raj punish us without admitting what the true reason for Felix's exile is?"

"A power grab. It was obvious from the moment you arrived, though Felix took a long time to work through his anger and pain." Renard hums a little, then points at the hallway. "We are all here because people deemed our presence dangerous, Chester. Change is never easy and those who hold the reins dislike letting go if they believe their ways will end. Whether it's your ambush, my clutch, Aubrey's clash, or even the megalomaniacal Lucille Drew, they all fear what will happen when beings such as us are given the power to enact new beginnings."

"I suspect the factions we have buzzing around us are at opposite ends of that spectrum," I murmur. "The magic users have powerful support—otherwise, they wouldn't have been able to infiltrate Apex and get the information to abduct students. Whoever is moving chess pieces on the other side is aware of this gambit or simply acting to prevent Dolly from surviving this mess." Pausing as I put down the dish towel, I look over at him seriously. "Being in the Capital makes this so much worse, you know."

His snort tells me he knows exactly what I mean. "Yes, now we have to account for a third wildcard in this equation—humans."

"Capital Prep is hidden well enough to make campus life less stressful, but when we venture out, it won't be like the town outside of Apex. Hell, even the shifter areas of Cambridge are less exposed than a shared capital city."

"Indeed. The consequences for exposing things we should not are steep."

That quiets us both for a moment because the attack on our family occurred in the open. The magic users seem completely unconcerned with the shifter laws and we can't account for their behavior. Once we wipe down the counters, we move to the sunken living area where all the planning materials from last night are still spread out. I hand him the list of textbooks while I tackle the other materials.

"We need to go to the bookstore first, then we'll get the other supplies at a megastore." I wrinkle my nose when it occurs to me that we will have to make several stops to get everything. "Dolly said we have to find a dance house and a sporting goods store for her equipment. And Fitz is *dying* to take her clothes shopping, so that will not be an option."

Renard grins, his eyes dancing with merriment. "I think we should all go. This will drive Felix and *mon fogeaux ami* insane on many levels. Fitz's hyperactivity, *ma petite*, trying on clothes, and having to cram into the car? It's chef's kiss chaos."

If I didn't know Renard Laveaux, I'd have no idea that gargoyles are such troublemakers.

"Deal. If we tell my angel first, they won't have a choice." I grin evilly. "Now, let's start planning the route and which places we're going. I want to enjoy this as much as possible before we all get thrown into the deep end with school starting."

"Agreed."

"She's a fucking sadist!"

The annex fills with noise, rousing me from the work I was doing. After we finished our planning, Renard took off to his perch to 'decompress' for a while, and I tracked down Jinx to give her some attention. The playlist on the speakers was soothing, so I hunkered down to get my planning completed. The fine arts professors I'm working under all sent lengthy emails full of things I need to put together in the next two days and though the tone of their missives was irritating, I want to make a good impression.

Just because Apex didn't have a well-supported arts program doesn't mean I'm a fucking bumpkin.

Fitz laughs as he, Felix, and a *very* sweaty, dirty bunny come barreling into my calm workspace. "Baby Girl, if she didn't make everyone show her their fitness levels, she wouldn't be able to develop individual plans for you. Plus, she has to assess the strength of the Cappie team. These wimps won't have what it takes to compete with the other schools, much less the public schools."

"Ugh, stop making sense, Fitz. You're supposed to agree with me and curse Zhenga's entire heritage."

I grin as Felix rolls his eyes at the two dueling pouts being aimed at one another. "By the look on the Raj's face, angel, it doesn't seem like you're being fair to the lioness."

Felix snorts hard. "She isn't. Yes, it was grueling and hot, but nothing Z did differed from what Fitz and I did with the male team. In fact, she practiced right alongside our team."

"And fuck, are these kids *pampered*. I mean, shit. I thought our whiny Council heirs and adjacent business morons were spoiled rotten." Fitz kicks off his shoes, then comes over to flop on one of the large cushions with a disgruntled expression. "Noooo. They might be spoiled, but these fools are being told they're in peak professional competition level condition, but they are *not*."

Tilting my head, I reach over and brush the hair that's escaped from his topknot out of his face. "Really? The children of athletes and all that shit are soft? By Bloodstone standards or… normal pred standards?"

"Uh, by any fucking standards, bro," Felix says in disgust. "Z was about to lose the plot when one girl asked if she could schedule practices so they didn't fall around her moontime because it makes her slower."

I frown. "But…"

"Exactly. No pro-league is going to even consider that shit. Hell, no serious competitor would even ask that," Fitz growls under his breath. "We have our work cut out for us and we will not make friends with the parents. We can't have the Khan name on this bullshit or dear old Dad will be displeased."

Dolly walks over with an ice cold bottle of water from the fridge, her skin flushed and smelling delicious from her workout. "At least I wasn't as insipid as the others. I think it earned me a few points with Zhenga."

"More than you know, Princess. You might have groaned, but you did every gut wrenching step of the run and continued working until she called time. Trust me, that earned you some credit." Felix rakes a hand through his hair and frowns as he looks at the surrounding mess.

"What the hell is all this?"

I chuckle. "While you guys are out sweating to the whining, my bosses sent me a shit ton of work. After Ren and I finished getting the list for our shipping excursion done, I dug in. I want to get it done so we can spend time together tomorrow, too."

His eyes narrow. "*Our* shopping excursion?"

"We're *all* going? Everyone?" Dolly beams and claps her hands, suddenly finding her second wind. "I'm so excited! I definitely have to go grab a shower so we can get moving. Fitz, come on. If you hurry, I'll let you massage my troubles away before we go."

'Let you?' Felix mouths at me with a smirk.

"Fuck off, big bro. She can let me do anything damn thing she wants while you chuckleheads nurse your blue balls in here." Fitz bobs his brows, flipping Felix off before trailing along behind our girl like a happy puppy.

"He's absolutely off his rocker for her," I murmur with a fond smile. "It's amazing."

My ambush mate sighs and nods, his own expression soft. "She's amazing."

"Agreed."

FORGIVENESS

Delores

By the time Fitz and I emerge from his soapy adventure, the rest of my guys were waiting in the living room. I threw on a crop top and joggers with flip-flops, so I'm comfortable trying on clothes and Fitz mirrored me. It gets eye rolls from everyone but Chessie, but he clearly does not give a fuck. His confidence is one of my favorite things about him and I wish I could wake up with even a fraction of my excitable tiger's self-esteem.

"Are we ready?" I ask as I adjust the strap of my small crossover bag.

"*Absolument.* The Captain had one of his crew bring the Land Rover around." Renard rises, dropping his keys in Aubrey's hand before he comes over to kiss my cheek. "*Alons*[1], gentleman."

Aubrey heaves an annoyed sigh as he joins us, shaking his head. "As you can tell by the French, he's excited. He and Chess mapped out some grand plan."

Chess grabs my hand, squeezing the one Fitz isn't hogging to thread our fingers together. "We found the best stores and route to take while minimizing the exposure along the way. I'd think you and Felix would be pleased, Aubrey."

"Less talking, more walking," Felix grumbles from the back. "We'll never get home if you all don't shake a leg."

"Sir, yes, sir!" I call over my shoulder. "Over and out."

"Dionysus on a unicycle, this is going to be a pain in my ass."

Fitz snorts as we all walk down the hall to the back entrance. "I'm sure we could arrange that, bro. I see they have an interesting dungeon on the list. Our girl might enjoy topping your grumpy ass."

My face turns bright red, but I clear my throat loudly. "I just might, Fitzy, but you go first."

"If I get to watch that? Hell yeah. Peg me 'till next Tuesday, baby girl. I'll even ask nicely."

"For the love of Zeus' singed balls, Fitz!"

I'm going to enjoy the hell out of this, even if I'm a tomato the whole way.

LETTING AUBREY DRIVE WAS A MISTAKE. THE DRAGON maneuvered the huge SUV like he would his giant winged form, and I thought Felix's head was going to explode. Chessie looked a little green, too, but since we've been on solid ground for a bit, it's gotten better. The tiny bookstore is in the Adams Morgan district of the city and the brick row houses filled with boutiques, bars, food and music are adorable. It seems like a hip, young profession type section of the city—perfect for our first stop.

Once we finally find parking, I hop out to look around. I haven't been to the Capital since I was a small child, but the excitement in the air here is palpable. I'm sure this vibe differs greatly from the ones we'll find in our other stops, but as someone who has traveled little, I'm eager to explore.

Lucille took me more places in the womb than out of it.

"*Riddles & Relics?*" I look over at Aubrey, who rolls his eyes. "I guess they carry more than books?"

"Assuredly, lunchable. It's obviously run by someone connected with the Kavarits. It will have to suffice." He sniffs and grabs my hand before Fitz can, flashing him a toothy grin.

"Hope you're wearing flame retardant undies, Baby Girl. This will be *very* interesting."

I frown, wondering why on earth I would need that in a bookstore. Rennie's lips quirk up as he holds the door open and we enter to the tune of tinkling bells. My jaw drops as I look at the interior, feeling a bit like I stepped into the damn TARDIS. The store stretches back much further than I would have expected and instead of being three stories like it appears, it's one huge open space with bookshelves spanning from floor to ceiling on every wall. Electric torches light the room, but only dimly, because the decor is right out of the fucking Mummy. I half expect to see Brendan Fraser come sauntering out of the back with his adorable grin and earnest eyes.

What? That cast is so hot I'd do them all and I'm fairly sure I'm straight.

Making sure I don't have a little daydream drool on my chin, I lean in to whisper to my dragon. "What *is* this place?"

"Hello! Welcome, welcome!" The booming voice cuts him off before he can answer and when I look over, I have to pick my jaw up again.

Holy. Mother. Of. Zeus.

Apparently, I'm not doing a good enough job of hiding my reaction to the three hot men who just entered the store from the back room of the shop in a line. Fitz lets out a snarl and Aubrey grips my hand so tightly I have to bump his shoulder with mine to get him to let up. I open my mouth to say something, but Felix pushes his way to the front, standing in front of our group like he's the king of the lions on the big rock. The testosterone chokes me a bit as the others shift into a weird pack position around me, their shoulders stiff.

The triplet who spoke smirks and I can tell he's the troublemaker of the group. He has high cheekbones and spiky, coal black hair razored at the sides with big brown eyes and sensuous lips. His brothers share his features, but one is much more muscular with very short cropped hair and the other is lithe with long waves. They are clearly comfortable letting the extrovert handle communication because neither responds to my guys' aggressive stances.

"Oh, for fuck's sake," I mutter, letting go of my dragon and pushing out of the alpha male clump. Once I'm standing at the front again, I smile at the sexy bookshop guys neutrally. "Hello, I'm Dolly and these are my…"

Damnit, I was doing so well taking charge.

Chess chuckles from the back, and I know they're all waiting for me to get myself together. I take a deep breath and look at the hotties with a proud grin. "These are my boyfriends. Sorry, I'm still getting used to that."

Once the words leave my mouth, I'm surprised to feel Felix step behind, pressing his front to my back to murmur so low even *I* almost don't hear him. "That's my girl, Princess."

My eyes flutter as I lean into him, soaking in the sensation of my dominant tiger touching me like a sponge. A throat clears and I know it's the jokey guy, so I force myself to croak, "I need books for the start of the semester at Capital Prep. We're transfers from Apex."

That gets their attention and the other two men fan out along the counter with narrowed gazes. Muscle guy cuts in before the other two can respond. "Your men are too old to be students. Are they staff?"

"Yep," I reply with a shrug. "What can I say? I'm a lucky bunny."

Bunny seems to confuse them, but the long-haired one studies us carefully. Something about his expression tweaks my instincts, but it doesn't seem dangerous as much as… angry. Finally, he points at Aubrey accusingly. "*You* are the coal sucking *Draconis* inhabiting our library. Don't bother denying it."

I don't see him change as much as I *feel* the rage in my gut. It might be from Rennie, who I know has to be holding my straight laced boyfriend back; I don't think anyone else could manage it. But he's going to lose it and if I'm going to get what I need for the semester, these guys can't kick us out for some weird dude thing. Turning on my brightest smile, I look at the joker, hoping he's reasonable.

"Family rivalries aside, I need the books for my second year classes. If you all want to whip them out and measure, you can do it once I have what I came for. I'll happily window shop elsewhere while you do so."

That gets a bark of laughter from both groups of alpha men, and I smirk in satisfaction. The best way to distract *any* male is to mention their dicks, and I'm getting fairly accomplished at knowing when to pull that card.

"I enjoy your spunk, young one. The puzzle of your heritage is intriguing as well, so we will do as you suggested and put aside our grievances. Perhaps old Khufu deserved a rest after so many years of service. You may have granted him a boon in disguise." The triplet with the wavy hair is soft-spoken and his tone radiates intelligence and kindness. He's likely the leader and his short-haired brother is their enforcer. That would fit some of the pack dynamics we learned about in Shifter Basics last year.

"I appreciate it… oh, you didn't give me your name. I'm sorry," I reply sweetly. "What are your names, gentlemen?"

The feeling of satisfaction flows through me again and I think this time it might be Felix I'm sensing. He's appreciating my strategic information gathering.

"I'm Chisisi, and these are my brothers, Ramses and Asim," the playful Sphinx says after their leader nods. It's not surprising the long-haired one is named after a pharaoh—royalty love to assign their children important names.

Poor Felix and Fitz can attest to that for sure. I'm not sure about Aubrey and Ren, but they don't like to discuss their pasts, so I have no idea. I shake my head, dispelling that concern as I gesture at each of my men, using their titles purposefully. "This is Felix and Fitzgerald Khan, heirs to the Khan empire, and their adopted brother, Chess. You picked out Lord Draconis, but this is Monsieur Laveaux."

Renard snorts behind his hand, his tail flicking up to stroke down my spine. "Our Queen forgot to mention she's Delores Diamond Drew, heir to the Drew Council seat. So humble, *ma petit lapin*."

I turn bright red, putting my hands over my face when the triplets look at us in amazement. Unlike Lucille, I'm not a fan of waving my ass around in public; in fact, I only throw that bullshit in the ring when I'm trying to make someone think twice about killing me. I don't enjoy strutting around making people bow to me because I won a 'fame' lottery. "Yes, yes. My mother is a horrid monster and I'm the black sheep… er, bunny, of the house."

Ramses tilts his head at me, his eyes dark and glittering with something I can't pinpoint. "Any enemy of the Council is a friend to the Kavarits. They do not serve exotic shifters as much as seek to leverage us for profit. Please give Chisisi your list, Dolly. We will gladly assist you."

"Make sure you double the order," Fitz says as he pushes forward. "We need two of everything to use as bait."

The stoic Asim cracks a small smile. "Your enforcer is thinking ahead, rabbit. Listen to his counsel, as I would do the same if it came to the safety of my mate."

Oh, god, not the mate thing again.

Even though I know it's true based on the shit I learned from Zhenga last year, I still haven't wrapped my head around the whole 'forever' thing. I know it's because I have rejection trauma and I came to the school expecting to die last year, so I haven't really made long-term life plans. All the online research I did this summer helped me realize that's why I'm having such a hard time not panicking when it gets mentioned. It's not at all that I can't imagine holding onto the guys for as long as we all live; it's that I'm still sure they'll find something better and zip off into the sunset.

"Why are you so tense, Princess?" Felix murmurs into my ear as I watch the sphinxes gather my books and papers. "I can sense your prey side spiking."

Turning my head, I look at the worry on his features and lean forward, giving him an impulsive kiss. The surprised rumble of pleasure soothes me, and I sigh against his lips. "I was thinking about our date. You have so much to compete with, Raj. However will you top it all?"

His laugh is dark and sexy, making my thighs clench. "I think I can manage, Princess. Don't worry about me; worry about how you'll make it through without losing your voice."

Fuck yes.

"I can't wait, *Sir*." He groans and I giggle. This is going to be a long ass day if they're all going to play with me like this in public, but I'm not complaining.

In fact, I'm looking forward to it.

---

1. Come

For You

Felix

The Princess might have cooled the temperature, but I can sense the unease in the rest of my ambush. Aubrey is still bristling over the pointed emphasis on his name, and Renard swooped in to save the day by taking him and Dolly to the romance section. Small giggles and dark laughs are coming from that area while the arrogant sphinxes gather her textbooks and materials.

I'm a bit surprised by how physical 'book heavy' the courses at Cappie are—Apex moved mostly virtual a long time ago. I suppose it would be even harder for the pampered children of the famous to get their work completed by tutors and au pairs if they had, though. My classes aren't prone to plagiarism and chicanery because they're mainly physical activity, but I know the others have had the issue even with Apex's tech.

"What's on your mind, Felix?" Chess murmurs as he pretends to look at a large table of art books.

My lips curve and I shrug. "Fitz is yammering with those douches and our girl is distracting the dragon. However, it hasn't settled either of our unease, has it?"

The cheetah turns the color of a tomato, dipping his chin. "Well, no. This is unfamiliar to me, so I'm not sure how to make myself feel less… chest thumpy."

"It's good that she brings it out in you, brother. I watched Fitz flounce around like a jackass for years and wondered how you stayed so calm. Now I know confidence was the issue—you had to *believe* you were worthy of demanding what you wanted."

His eyes widen and he whispers, "How did you know that?"

"Because Fitz never made you feel less, but you never asked for more until you wanted her. Something about our girl makes us *all* realize our exile doesn't define us—even me." I give him a rueful expression, letting Chess know I'm in a similar boat. "Watching those clowns eye our loved ones isn't easy, but she made it clear she wanted to be drama-free."

At that moment, my twin bounces over, his eyes dancing with mischief. "What are you fuckers glaring at? The Kavarits are cool as fuck. I invited them to the first Games match. They played on the Zong Zi… Zow Zeeng… oh, fuck it. That U&M team."

Chess and I exchange an irritable glance as our brother bounces around, but the cheetah speaks first. "*Zhuǎnxíng*, Fitz. But you were close this time."

"Yeah, that. High school only, but they seem pretty cool. You said we need more friends, right? Why are the two of you still acting like you have lemons shoved in your asses?"

Sighing, I cross my arms over my chest. "I don't like how they look at the Princess. And… Aubrey hates sphinxes."

Fitz pauses for a half a second, then bursts into laughter. Chess is as puzzled as I am, but my twin is cracking up so hard, tears start running down his face. He can't even breathe long enough to do more than hold a finger up—luckily for him, *not* the middle one— so I fume as I wait for him to stop.

"Fitz, for the love of Neptune's crabs, give us a break here," Chess grumbles as he rubs the back of his neck. "What's so goddamn funny?"

"You… the two of you…" He mimics an angry face that cannot possibly be how we look. "Fuck, you're worse than the Capsaicin Crusader over there. This is the *best day ever*."

My arm shoots out and I grab him by the collar, tugging him eye to eye. "Fitzgerald…"

"Oooh, he's gonna 'Raj' me 'cause he's jelly." My brother hoots again and wipes his eyes, not remotely concerned with my death grip on his shirt. "You need to get out more. I invited them to the game because they're funny as hell *and* I had a little 'meet cute' in mind for Baby Girl's gangster friend."

I drop him as his words hit me like a bricked bat. "Well, shit."

"I *knew* I sensed something," Chess mutters under his breath.

Fitz reaches over and ruffles the cheetah's topknot, making him look adorably messy. "Baby, you know better. No more nakey time outside the fam; it's a rule."

He crosses his heart as he pouts at Chess, and I roll my eyes. "Yes, thank you for *that* image. But you could have told us you were playing Cupid, dummy."

"I just *did*…duh."

Sometimes, I'm not sure how I managed not to murder my twin long before we got to Apex.

"Let's go see what the others are doing over in the non-textbook section, shall we?" I roll my eyes at Fitz, but he grins like a loon in return. I think he enjoyed seeing Chess and I get possessive— perhaps even set it up. He's always on us about showing emotion more. *Troublemaking little shit.*

"C'mon, Chessie. Maybe the poetic prat and his savory scholar found more of those racy books that get Baby Girl all blushy. I *love* when she reads them to me." My brother drags the cheetah along, babbling about dirty books with gusto, and I shake my head.

Fitz excited about reading is a new one; I'll give her that.

Putting aside my irritation at the proprietors of this place, I follow them downstairs. The levels set below ground are cool and dimly lit, like a movie temple just as the main floor is, and it's hiding how massive their inventory really is. The flying duo is each leaning against a shelf, watching Dolly as she slides around on a ladder with her bum in the air as she reaches for things. They could help her, but hell if I can blame them for ogling instead. It's a sight to behold and even I can admit that.

"Baby Girl, I see London!" Fitz yells as he barrels down the aisle. Our friends give him a dirty look, but he doesn't notice as he tugs Chess along to stand underneath her. "And now I see France."

"I've told you to *stop* calling my pussy that. You are *not* Napoleon, you lunatic," she replies as she stretches up to grab a thick tome that must be several books in one. "Rennie, look I found the one with the girl who pretends to be a boy."

"Excellent choice, *ma petite*. Did you find a paranormal one, too? One with dragons should be amusing," the gargoyle says as he bobs his brows.

"No *dragons!*" Aubrey growls. "They don't do it right and I can't abide poor research."

My brows furrow as I look at them all in surprise. "Does she have you *all* reading smutty books with her?"

A ripple of sheepish looks runs across my entire ambush and I snort. "Holy hell, Princess. You even converted the literary purist. Good on you."

She turns on the ladder and crosses her arms over her chest, arching a brow at me. "Perhaps you'll be lucky enough to find out *why* they all like reading with me now that you're not being such a tool, Raj?"

Ouch. I deserved that one, I suppose.

"Fine. Just nothing with wolves. I fucking hate those flea-bitten assholes."

Dolly rolls her eyes and holds her hand out, ticking her fingers one by one. "Good goddess. No dragons, no wolves, no TSTL chicks, no law enforcement, no this, no that… it's getting harder to find things based on all of your rules, boys."

Fitz pouts. "Hey! No one likes the po-po, D. That's fair."

I shrug. "He's right."

Huffing, she holds her free hand out and Renard takes it so she can leap off the ladder to the floor. "Thanks for the assist, Rennie." Dolly pushes up on her toes and kisses him lightly, then hands Aubrey the books she wants to add to the pile he's holding. "Did you guys come down because they're ready for us?"

Chess chokes, putting his hand over his mouth, and I slap him on the back. "No, we followed Fitz. He seemed very interested in your… reading habits."

"Of course he is. We like to re-enact things," she says as she winks at me playfully and sashays past us towards the stairs. "I make a fabulous pirate queen."

"She really fucking does," my twin says with a sigh. "She can run her sword through me anytime."

"Less jaw flapping and more stair climbing," Dolly calls behind her. "I want to get the clothes next!"

If this happened in a bookstore, I can't imagine what that is going to be like. Zeus help us.

"I found the uniforms in your size, Baby Girl!" He bounces in, dropping them over the closed door of the dressing room.

If someone told me that my twin, Fitzgerald Ulysses Castor Khan, would be caught dead running around a women's boutique picking out clothes for his *mate* with our resident brooder, I would have laughed in their face. It's only been a little over a year since Delores Drew sashayed into our world and the changes still amaze me constantly.

Renard and Fitz are zipping around, picking out all manner of shit for her, and once she wiggles into them, she comes out into the weird atrium to do her runway walk. Occasionally, someone shouts a suggestion to the two hyper shifters and they come back with a different style dress or pants. I feel like I've stepped into the Twilight Zone.

Even the snarky lizard is tossing in his two cents.

"Fitz, they have to be altered; I'm sure of it. Apex's were cut for girls with less… meat than me, so I had to go up a size and have them tailored. Capital Prep isn't likely to have any better selections."

I frown as our girl calls that out from behind the door of the room she's changing in. She's built exactly how she needs to be, and I don't like the insinuation that she's defective because she doesn't fit into the minuscule garments in her own size. "Princess, this is one of the premier stores for our kind tucked in this area; are you sure about that?"

Her head pokes out of the room, fingers curled around the door as she shrugs. "Pretty sure. They cut clothes from smaller sizes every year, it feels like. Even my prom dress was tailored, but Luc didn't make me feel like a shit about it."

"Come here, Princess." I crook my finger at her, expression serious as I lean back in my chair. Her cheeks flush and I can tell she wants to, but isn't certain what to do. Looking over at Chess, I jerk my head at the curtains serving as a door to our waiting room. "No one comes in. Now, come out, Princess."

Dolly sees Chess smiling at her reassuringly and nods, pulling the door to the dressing room open to reveal her half dressed body. She's wearing a loose uniform skirt that hangs low on her hips, thigh highs, and a rosy pink bra. Her long blond hair is cascading over her shoulders and holy fuck buckets if she isn't a naughty dream come true. She walks over to me, eyes full of doubt as she murmurs, "Yes, Sir?"

Grabbing her full, round hips, I bring her closer and inhale her scent. Her stomach is soft, though I can feel the muscles she's been working on with César over the summer. The gentle curves of her body feel like home and all I want is for our girl to understand that we adore every single one of them. So I spin her around, pulling her onto my lap so she can see the hungry gazes of our family. "Do you see that, Princess? Look at what you do to *all* of us."

"Fuck fashion," Fitz growls softly as he adjusts himself without shame. "You know I love every inch of you."

My hands settle on her thighs, massaging the thick muscles that give her rabbit leaping abilities. "These help you jump and run— though I imagine they feel fucking fantastic wrapped around your ears."

"They do," Chess says with a mischievous smile. "I'd rather die smothered in you than at the hands of those hooded freaks, Angel."

Dolly's skin heats under my palms, and I know she's struggling with being turned on and embarrassed at the same time. Her newfound sexuality is a fragile thing—she's learning to accept her wants and needs as normal, no matter what. That's why she often ping-pongs between seductress and shyness. It's endearing as hell and I love it, even if I don't admit it out loud.

"Shhh! Chessie. Someone might hear," she hisses, as she squirms around in a *very* distracting manner.

"Princess," I groan as I grab her to still her ass. "Do you trust us?"

"Of course I do." She twists, making me clench my jaw as she looks at me earnestly. "But…"

Placing a finger against her lips, I give her a dark grin. "Shhh. You have to be very quiet, like a good girl. Can you do that?"

Her eyes widen and she nods a little, though I can feel the tremble that runs over her frame. I jerk my chin at Fitz and the smirking duo across from us. "I think our girl needs us to show her rather than tell, gentleman. As long as she behaves, she gets rewarded. Capiche?"

A chorus of growls precludes movement, and I look at Dolly seriously. "Tell me the word, Princess. I know Fitz well enough to know you have one."

"Beetlejuice," she whispers. That gets a few chuckles, and she flushes bright red. "I won't say it by mistake; that's why!"

I lean in and kiss her pouty lips gently before gripping her chin. "That's good, baby. Now, I'm going to put you on display for our family and we're going to show you how beautiful we think you are. But if you make noise, we have to stop. Understand?"

She nods and I arch a brow, waiting. Her eyes dance when the realization hits and she looks at me defiantly as she says, "Yes, sir."

So deliciously contradictory—I can hardly wait to get her alone. Alas, this will have to suffice for now.

"That's our girl," I rumble.

My hands splay over her thighs, pulling them apart to hook over my own. She draws in a quiet breath and I lift the hem of the skirt slowly, revealing the matching dusty pink scrap of lace she's wearing underneath. It has Fitz written all over it and I'm proved right when he dives across the tile on his knees to kneel in front of the shivering bunny. His eyes skate to mine and I nod, watching Aubrey and Renard move to either side of us and sink to the ground.

"Baby Girl, you smell like blooming honeysuckle and it's *killing* me," my twin mumbles as he darts forward to bite her inner thigh. His teeth leave red marks and I'm pleased to feel the sharp intake of breath against my chest. "I owe you another pair. Put it on the account."

That said, he tears the flimsy material away and tosses it over his shoulder. Her scent fills the air and every single one of us groans. The legends say the smell of your true mate is like being enveloped in a silk glove and stroked—I never believed it until now. My entire body is screaming to touch her, mark her, make her mine before anyone else can. I know it's the tiger and when I look down at my twin again, I can see the strain in his features as well.

"Do it, Fitz, or you lose your spot," I growl as my hands tighten on her legs. I'll leave bruises, but my tiger likes that possibility, so I continue gripping her.

With that, Fitz buries his face in her pussy, and Dolly melts into my embrace like a complacent little sub.

Excellent.

Risky Business

Delores

The second Felix's voice changed to that commanding tone, I was a goner. It's hard to explain—I've spent most of my life forbidden from making my own decisions, but the way he demands things has this undercurrent of care I've not experienced before. I want to fight him a little, but I also want to give in and let him tell me what to do. I haven't unpacked all of that yet and with Fitz lapping at me like I'm his last meal, I sure as fuck can't now.

Being quiet as his tongue twirls around my clit in complex patterns is damn near impossible. My eyes are closed and my limbs are quaking in Felix's grasp; I have no idea how I'm going to last. Two fingers slide inside of me and I'm not even sure whose they are, but my body squeezes them eagerly. I dig my teeth into my lower lip when another pair of hands unsnap my bra and fingertips brush over my hard nipples. There's so much stimulation that I feel like I'm on fire. Suddenly, one of my dominant tiger's hands leaves my thigh to encircle my throat, pressing lightly on it.

Oh, my.

I feel him waiting to see if I'll blurt out my safe word, but the light squeeze is enhancing the sparkling sensations all over my body. Pressing my head into his shoulder, I give permission to teach me this new kink as I wriggle against the mouth, giving me so much pleasure. Felix puts a bit more pressure on the arteries on the outside of my neck and my hips buck into the hand fucking me.

"Such a good girl, Princess," he whispers in my ear. "You're doing so well. Give Fitz the first one, baby."

Holy mother of…

Fitz's teeth clamp down right as Felix stops talking and I have to bite hard on my lip to keep from screaming. The orgasm hits me so hard I feel every muscle tighten up, then release into jello when the crest fades. His hand lets up at my throat as I pant hard, unable to move while my blood thrums in my veins. Someone tweaks a nipple and it makes another shock wave ripple over me.

"Baby Girl, you fucking squirted!" I open my eyes to see my crazy tiger with my juices all over his face and a glazed look in his eyes. "I came in my goddamned pants like a dumbass teenager. Holy shit."

The hard presence at my back confirms Felix has control of himself, and I look over at the gargoyle staring at me hungrily. "That was so—"

I don't get to finish because Rennie swoops in to kiss me hard and fast before I can. His tongue sweeps over my lips and through my mouth possessively, growls rumbling into me from his mouth. A low chuckle from my other side tells me Aubrey is amused—and closer to me when I'm naked than he's ever been before. He places a light kiss on the outer curve of my breast, then nips my skin.

"I believe that makes it my turn for an appetizer, bite size."

My breath catches. "I don't think I can do it again…"

"Of course you can, Princess. Let the dragon heat you up again and perhaps you'll get a cock after that."

Motherfucking shit, Felix Khan is good at this—not that I have a comparison, but I'd do damn near anything when he uses that voice.

"Yes, Sir," I mumble as someone arranges my legs, draped over the taller dragon's shoulder while Felix brushes his thumb over my pulse point. I've lost all concern that we're in public or anything else going on in the world; I'm just letting them guide me towards feeling good with no worries.

Chess' voice feels far away as he says, "Use the dragon parts, big guy. I love watching her face when she's surprised and aroused."

"Bad cheetah," I mumble as Aubrey inhales then traces the shape of my throbbing pussy. "Dirty mouth."

A sharp rap on my thigh gets my attention and Felix growls into ear, "No noise, Princess. That's one."

My eyes slide shut again when a fluttering tongue moves from my clit to slip inside of me. Suddenly, it's alternating between fucking me and flickering over my g-spot like a mini-vibrator. I have to bite my lip again to keep from screaming and my hips rock into the motion eagerly. I didn't think I could do this again after that huge O, but they flooded my body with heat from the attention of my grumpy book dragon. Whatever the hell is happening with his dragon tongue is *fucking amazing,* and I'm probably ruined for life.

"She wants to scream, *mon ami.* I can practically taste her pleasure," Rennie says before he leans in to lick the blood droplets off my mouth again. "I'm quite enjoying the razor edge you have everyone on."

"Son of a bitch."

That's Chess groaning and I pry my eyes open to see Fitz lifting the cheetah's dick out to stroke it while they kiss. My core clenches at the sight of them together and I struggle to stay quiet as I ride my dragon's tongue with the two snarling preds in my ears. The wave builds in me as Fitz gets more aggressive with our lover and I let out a ragged breath.

"Please…"

Felix gives me another slap, this time closer to my pussy, and I feel another flood of fluid leak out of me. "Don't be a brat, Princess. You want your reward, don't you?"

I nod, leaning my head back into his shoulder and writhing. A sharp sting on my inner thigh almost makes me shriek, but I lock it down as the climax rushes towards me at the small amount of pain. Grinning to myself as my body shudders, I catch a piece of skin on the tiger's neck and gnaw lightly in retaliation.

He didn't say I couldn't bite, only to be quiet.

The sound he makes is exquisite and I'm not ready for him to lift my dragon away, smirking at the glazed donut state of his face before placing me face down on the small sofa. "You, Princess, have been a bad girl. I'm saving your punishment for later, though, because we didn't negotiate boundaries properly. Agreed?"

My face rubs against the fabric on the couch as I nod, my eyes fixed on Fitz as he takes care of Chess. I don't want to speak because I'm already neck deep, but the urge to reply 'yes, sir' is real. Felix smooths his hand over my ass slowly and I try to remember how to breathe when I think he's going to take me right here for the first time. But he steps away, and the next thing I know, a tail is crawling up my leg.

"My turn, *ma petite*. You can give us one more, *oui?*" His hands grip my hips and before I can respond, his cock is plowing into me from behind.

The size of it stretches me, and I bite down again to keep the noise to zero. My men are claiming me and destroying me and I'll be damned if I'm not loving every second. Pushing up on shaky arms, I rock back into his thrusts eagerly. His tail slips between my battered thighs and I feel the tip toying with my clit. I shudder again and my eyes roll back in my head; my brain is officially mush.

I am an ex-bunny.

"Just a little more, Princess. Squeeze him tighter and Fitz will let Chessie come."

That Felix is still in control is hot as fuck and I do as instructed, gripping my gargoyle tight inside and he lets out a string of curses in French that would shock the habit off a nun. Chess makes a growling whimpering sound not long after and the clever tail coaxes the last enormous wave of pleasure out of me after that. When the ripples dissipate, I collapse on the couch, letting Rennie hold me up. I'm not even sure I *have* bones anymore.

"Holy Aphrodite, bro, I think we broke her."

I smile drunkenly at Fitz's comment, but I don't move. I'm definitely going to need a few before I can pretend to be functional.

"Indeed, Fitzgerald. You and Chess clean up—find whatever the hell else you want and have it delivered to the library. Get everything she needs while we help her come down," Aubrey says authoritatively. "Don't get all fancy shit; she needs to relax, too."

Mmmm, I sure do… especially if this kind of play is going to be the norm. I feel sleepy.

Gentle arms tug me away from Rennie, and Felix's voice rumbles in my ear as he carries me to a chair. "Don't worry, Princess. We're going to clean you up and get everything taken care of. Just rest and when we leave here, we'll feed you."

Oh, I could get used to this.

By the time I could wobble out of the boutique, Fitz and Chess had everything taken care of. I'm not sure where I'll put the massive stacks of clothing, shoes, and Hera knows what else they had piled on the counter, but the owner looked less perturbed than I would have expected. My cheeks were pink as we filed out —something Rennie took great pleasure in needling me about as we walked down the street.

Our detour took longer than expected and I note the sun is slowly sinking into the horizon. Tomorrow is the last day before the other students and staff will arrive. I'm less nervous than I was earlier in the day, but the firm support of my guys is part of that. After their demonstration, I feel much more confident about walking into the snake pit I assume is waiting for me.

"What do you feel like eating, lunchable?"

My lips curve as I tilt my head at the dragon. "*Lots* of food. Like I could devour a fucking buffet."

They all laugh and Fitz tugs on my hand, dragging me to his side before ruffling my hair. "You need a feast fit for a champ, Baby Girl. You earned it."

His praise makes me flush again, and I dig my elbow into his ribs, making him yelp. Chess snickers from his other side, and I shrug a little. "I'm just glad I didn't make all of you wonder what the hell you were thinking by taking on a newb like me."

Felix stops short, causing us to crash into him. Turning around, he arches a brow at me. "Did anyone seem worried, Princess?"

"No... but..."

Rennie shakes his head. "No buts, *ma petite*. Chess was extremely accurate when he pointed out how lovely you are when you're discovering something new. You are still learning who you are as a shifter, as a person, and as a sexual being. There's no way to do it wrong."

"Unless you're her douchecanoe ex," Fitz mutters.

That makes me laugh and I give him a grateful expression. The hyper tiger always knows how to bring me back from the insecurities my past baked into me and his insult was the perfect thing to say in the moment. "Okay, okay. I'm uncooked dough; I get it."

"You sure as hell make *me* rise, baby girl."

Felix smacks his twin on the back of the head, but he chuckles. "I think that sentiment is shared, bro. But he's right, Princess. If you're feeling unsure or worried, you just need to talk to us. As the others have pointed out, you're going to be our mate and we want to make sure you feel happy and safe."

Shit. I'm going to leak; how embarrassing.

Pulling a pair of sunglasses out of my purse, I put them on and clear my throat. "I appreciate that, Felix. You guys and Cori and Rufus are the first people in my life who haven't wanted to use me for their own gains, so I'm still getting used to that. But it doesn't mean I don't believe you or that you don't hold special places in my heart. You know?"

Chess walks over and kisses my cheek. "I absolutely do, angel."

"Chinese?" Everyone looks at Fitz as he studies his phone and he rolls his eyes. "Don't be assholes. Baby Girl knows I'd crawl through glass for her, but someone had to find food before her bunny blasts us with blue shit until it's fed."

The Raj pinches the bridge of his nose as if the conversation is physically painful, but he sighs. "As usual, my brother is right even when he's being a dickwaffle. Where are we going, Fitz?"

"Are you all deaf? A Chinese buffet is the *obvious* choice for a starving bunch of preds. Follow me, assmunches!" He grabs my hand, pulling me along as he strides through the thickening crowds in the artsy district. "We're hitting up the *Happy Kitsune*. It's got a five claw rating and I can't wait to inhale some crab Rangoon."

Leave it to Fitz to dispel all the heavy emotions and make us all laugh at the same time.

DIRTY MIND

FITZ

I DON'T CARE WHAT ANYONE SAYS—WATCHING MY BABY GIRL PUT away enough food to feed a small army is hot. Last year, I felt like she was still monitoring every bite that went into her mouth because of that bitch mother of hers and the Petty Plastics. Now she's dabbing her mouth with a napkin daintily after seven plate-fuls of various foods each of us suggested she try. I fucking love how happy she looks, and I'd skin someone alive if they upset her.

Of course, I'd skin someone alive for fun most days, but upsetting our girl is the cardinal sin in my world.

"Are you ready to finish our outing, angel?" Chess is looking at Dolly like she hung the moon and my heart swells in my chest. He's come out of his shell so much since she stumbled onto our public show in the library, and that's another reason the lovely bunny rabbit has my eternal devotion. The others may not have noticed, but I see him growing more confident day by day and it's brilliant.

"I think so." A small belch escapes her lips, and she looks scandal-ized, covering her lush lips quickly as her face turns red. "Excuse me! Oh my goddess, how embarrassing."

Snorting, I roll my eyes. "Baby Girl, that wasn't even a *real* burp. Don't apologize for a normal bodily function. Have you *heard* the dragon after he goes hunting? I'm surprised he didn't break the fucking windows over the years."

Aubrey glares at me as if he'd like to set me on fire in the middle of the damn restaurant, and I laugh even harder. "Fitzgerald Khan…"

Luckily for me, Felix steps in before I set the scaly Shakespeare off again. "Stop it, both of you. Princess, Fitz is right. You don't have to be embarrassed about enjoying your meal. I didn't want to make you self conscious, but I'm glad to see you consuming enough fuel to feed your bunny. You need more energy after you emerge and you weren't getting enough last year."

Dolly blinks and sticks her lower lip out. "Why didn't you guys say anything? I knew there had to be a reason I was tired all the time, despite getting as much sleep as I could."

I grin wickedly. "When I let you…"

"Fitz!" Renard sighs and reaches over to take our girl's hand. "*Ma petite*, you must know none of us are stupid enough to criticize what a woman eats. Even if it's clinical, it's just not a smart plan."

Good one, soaring sonneteer!

Her brows furrow, and she thinks about it for a moment, nodding when she decides. "Okay. I'll give you that. I would have told you all to bite me if you tried to comment on my food intake. It was one of Lucille's favorite topics and I would have been triggered."

"Now that we've cleared that up… shall we hit the last store on the list?" Chess grins a little and I cover my mouth to keep from laughing. "I'm sure we can handle the ones in the middle with online orders and we don't want you too tired for Zhenga's practice tomorrow."

"Mmmm. Skipping the big box stores isn't about making sure we have time to visit *Dungeons, Dragons, and Daddies?*" The gargoyle has a sparkle in his eyes as he leans in on his elbows, looking at my cheetah knowingly. "Because I call bullshit if you say 'no,' Chester."

The table erupts in guffaws when Chess turns a lovely shade of pink and the spicy lizard spits his drink out. Clearly, he didn't think about how Aubrey would react and I fucking cannot *wait* to see what happens when we get all these stodgy assholes in that kind of place. Renard and I are the most adventurous of the group, so neither of us will be perturbed, but even my commanding bro doesn't use a lot of equipment.

"Chess!" Baby Girl hisses. "You picked this place? I thought you were the *good* one!"

His lips curve and he shrugs. "Maybe I've been converted."

Dolly buries her face in her hands, shaking it from side to side as she groans. When she finally looks up, all five sets of eyes are on her, waiting for her assent. "Fine! Fine. We'll go to this incredibly embarrassing den of iniquity, but you have to *promise* not to make fun of me when I don't know shit. That means you, *Monsieur Kinky Tail.*"

My grin is so big it hurts as I jump out of my seat. "He agrees. We all agree. No shenanigans in the sex shop. Come on, baby girl. Let's have one last hurrah before this shit show starts at the snooty school."

The flustered bunny rises, taking my hand as she looks at the rest of our family. "Get moving, you pervs. This is your big chance to see me turn into a literal fruit as you explain what all of this dirty stuff does."

I couldn't have put it better myself.

DUNGEONS, DRAGONS, & DADDIES IS IN THE 'RED LIGHT' DISTRICT, so we have to take a brief drive to get there. When we arrive, I'm surprised to find it in a small plaza with a bookshop called the *Feathered Quill* and a dive bar called *Inky Depths*. I guess krakens run the latter or some shit—which makes sense, since this place is on the river. I'm not sure which avians run the bookstore, but I hope like hell we're not going to run into another dragon in this kink palace.

Having the Lusty Lizard run afoul of sphinxes was bad enough; Odin forbid he finds some rogue dragon to fight with.

"We should check out the other places, too," Dolly says, looking around the hidden shopping area with wide eyes. "I've never been to a seedy bar."

"And you're not going tonight, either," Felix rumbles as he takes her elbow. "With the weird magic fucks and random kidnapping threats, I'm not eager to step foot in places we haven't checked out." He pauses and looks at Chess. "We *did* vet this place, right?"

Chessie grins as I tuck him under my arm. "I double, triple-checked this with Fitz's tools. It's clean—no Council *or* ties to any of our families. But you're right, I have no idea about the other two places."

"Why do bad guys ruin *all my fun*?" our girl mutters as she kicks a rock. "It's a pain in my ass. Don't say it, Fitz."

Chuckling, I give her an innocent look. "Who me?"

"If you believe *that* shit, I've got a castle in Bavaria to sell you," Aubrey says with a snort. "But I believe you're being inaccurate… we can obviously have *plenty* of fun without the pall of our enemies. Tonight is a perfect example."

Dolly smiles softly, pulling away from Felix to walk over and kiss the dragon's jaw. "You're right, big guy. They can't mess up our private time, even if they're putting me in a rapidly shrinking cage."

"If we're done being sappy…" Rennie winks at her and she huffs again, turning on her heel to stride towards the big steel dungeon doors on the front of the store.

I snicker, tugging Chess along behind her without waiting for the sourpusses. The excitement of exploring this world with our girl is flooding my veins now that we're here and I can put up with all their sniping as long as I get to waggle some tentacle dildos until she turns the pink I adore. "Probably shouldn't say sap inside here. Who knows what freaks we'll run into?"

"Duh. You're here, right, Fitzy?"

Ugh. Low blow right in the balls, but I fucking love it. Baby Girl is sexiest when she's confident.

"Behave in here, you miscreants. We don't want to be invited to leave before we get to explore."

My brother puts in his best 'in charge' face and I roll my eyes. "You can take charge in the bedroom all you want, *Raj*, but I'm second in command until you give real orders. I'll have as much fun as I want."

That gets a laugh out of my baby girl and I see the nervousness in her posture fade a little. She's adventurous in private, but I know her lack of experience eats at her. It's cute that she worries about disappointing us simply because we've got decades or centuries on her; however, if she realized just how fucking dopey we all are for her, she wouldn't fret. Even my twin is besotted as hell—I know because he's letting her see the real Felix.

It's a gift very few get to experience since our exile.

As if to prove my point, Dolly whirls back towards the big, castle-like wooden doors and pushes them open with her shoulders squared. The blond hair makes her look like a Viking queen, and I add that role to my internal 'play' list for later. Blond braids and a sword sound like a rocking good time. Maybe I can get Chessie to play along, too. I bet if I—

My internal monologue comes to a screeching halt when we walk into the dimly lit store. We knew this place was shifter owned because of the background, but they did not prepare me for the nirvana in a strip mall we discovered. Much like the bookstore, it's massive inside, but it has levels going up instead of down. The main floor is lit with purple lights, but the upper levels have color coded lighting starting with blue and ending on the top floor with a UV glow. I bounce on my toes, adrenaline pumping through my veins as my tiger prowls inside.

"Holy fucking Hela," I whisper to my twin. "We found the *real* Valhalla run by people who actually know what the fuck they're doing. I may never leave."

Aubrey rolls his eyes and rubs his hand over his face. "As impressed as I am, I fear Fitz's mounting enthusiasm is going to get us banned for life. Considering the combined current lifespan of our family, I fear that will be a very long time."

"Don't worry, big guy. We can keep him mostly calm," my beautiful bunny says before smiling at me in a way that makes my dick twitch. "Fitz, if you can keep it under wraps, you can pick out all the weird stuff you want and we'll negotiate later."

Letting out a quiet war whoop, I salute her and take off into the purple hazy level to find out what delights lurk here. I know the rest of them are probably losing their minds, but that's because they don't get me like she does. Chess comes the closest and my twin after that, but my baby girl knows without having to ask that I'll return anything that makes her uncomfortable. I'd never push her on sex shit because she lost her virginity to an assface who manipulated her emotionally.

I know V-cards aren't actually as important as the older dipshits make it out to be, but it was hers to share, and he stole that decision from her with his lies. I won't ever do that to her.

A display of glowing, oddly shaped dildos gets my attention and I pause, coming out of my head to study them. "Hmm. Alien, unicorn horn… ouch… wolf knot… gross. Oooh…this one is interesting, and it works with that sexy strappy thing…"

That's when the group finds me and I get to watch our girl turn the lovely rosy color of her nipples from head to toe. "Fitz! I was joking about that."

"I wasn't," I sing-song. "And look at Chessie! He likes the train idea, too. Take a sniff, baby girl."

"For fuck's sake, Fitzgerald!" the dragon growls as I beam at them. "That's not even… accurate. It doesn't look… like that!"

"It doesn't?" Chess says with a puzzled expression. "Do you have a cloaca, then? I thought that was wyverns? But they're even more rare so I don't have *actual* evidence…"

Felix blinks, his head turning slowly as he looks at me. "Are you picking a dildo you think looks like his when he's a dragon? Thor's hammer, Fitz!"

I shrug. "I'm fucking curious. You assholes can *not* tell me you're not curious about what Dragon Daddy and Gargoyle Grampy are packing when they're shifted. They could google what tiger and cheetah cocks look like. Everything about them is *speculation*."

That makes Dolly turn even redder and I know it's because she's felt the emo professor's big boy for herself. She socks me in the shoulder and grumbles, "This is a little weird. Admit it."

"It is not! And now I know his giant pole is *definitely* special, 'cause you're trying to distract me. I'm buying this inaccurate guy, his cumtube, *and* the harness, baby girl. If the heaving hot pants wants to prove me wrong, he's going to have to *show* me." I hear Chess groan, but they're all full of crap. I can smell everyone getting excited and I'll have my big orgy if it kills me.

"He doesn't have a cloaca," Renard says helpfully. "This is not *that far* off, though the spines aren't big—"

"Enough!" Aubrey roars, then softens when Dolly giggles. "If you insist on pursuing this line of thought, I bet the black or blue rooms can match our French poet."

Everyone laughs and I shrug. "I plan on investigating this entire place, my winged weenies. I'm sure we'll have boxes full of fun to teach my baby girl how depraved we are."

Now, to lure him to the ropes and restraints on the red level so I can get him all worked up.

My grin spreads as they stare at me, and I shrug. "I think we need to hit up the red level next. Baby Girl's bondage box is dangerously amateur. Any of you want to help me fix that?"

As predicted, no one protests.

Hell yeah.

TROUBLE

DELORES

T HE COOL WATER OF THE SHOWER COURSES OVER ME AS I FINISH getting the conditioner out of my rainbow locks. Learning to take cold showers was hell at first, but since they help me calm down the increasing urge to grab one of my men and go to town as well as maintain my color, I've accepted it. I took a fuckton of them over the summer when we were separated and I know from Zhenga's classes last year it's because my shifter hormones are in high gear.

Being a teenage bunny and finding… mates… I haven't claimed causes that, apparently.

I have one last day of semi-freedom while people arrive and I intend to kick ass at practice, then make the most of it with my guys. Fitz's shopping spree included *five boxes* of goodies that had them all so giddy we could barely get to sleep when we got back last night. It was late and this damn Pred Games thing was early, so nothing got taken for a test run, but I can feel all the fun times gear as if it's haunting me.

Smiling to myself at how easily our family is coming together after the disaster at Apex, I finish up and head into my room, wrapped in my towel. As predicted, there's a sparkling hot pink workout kit waiting for me, and I shake my head. Rennie gets a kick out of leaning into Felix's original 'Barbie' nickname and his stuff reflects that. Even the damn tennis shoes match, so I know I'll at least *look* the part of the spoiled princess the other team members will expect me to be.

Getting them to believe it so they leave me alone is another thing entirely.

Once I'm dressed, I scoop my hair into a tight ponytail and grab my bag. I'm the last one here this morning because Felix and Fitz went to meet Zhenga for a strategy session before practice, and Aubrey drafted Rennie for library duty. The latter grumbled, but since Betsy hasn't arrived yet, he could convince him with stern glares. He would have taken Chessie, too, but my sweet knight got an email requesting he meet with the guidance counselor to go over some of his additional duties as their assistant.

I'm a little nervous about making the trek down the lane and through the tunnels to the underwater field access alone—I have no idea what terrors await me at Capital Prep when more of the students arrive.

Luckily, the moment I step out the front entrance to the library, the Captain comes scampering up with a crooked grin. "Aye, lassie! I'll be escorting you to practice as Raina's busy in the Aquatic dorm. She wishes ye well, though."

I smile and shake my head. "They knew I wouldn't feel safe until we get the lay of the land, right?"

"Aye. Our most generous gargoyle made certain the loyal prey from Apex were given jobs here, and we all mean to repay him by keeping his future queen from anyone who might harm her. You'll have eyes on ye everywhere ye go that are friendly, too. Don't worry your whiskers, Miss Dolly."

"Oh, for heaven's sake, Captain! Just Dolly is fine. Didn't Raina tell you that?" I chuckle as we walk down the path past House Reptilian, frowning as a dark vibe makes me shiver. I'm glad we made that my 'fake' warren, but something about it gives me a wiggins, even from here.

He arches the eyebrow without a patch at me. "She did, but my crew is well trained. None of our men will do Admiral Renard the disrespect of calling his mate such a familiar name."

Admiral? Did they promote him? His band of merry prey is so incredibly odd.

"Okay. But remember, he's not my only… uh… boyfriend. I don't want the others to get jealous," I tease gently. "Be nice to them, too."

"Of course, lassie! Now that we are no longer at Apex, all the friends of the Admiral are part of our crew. That includes Betsy, first mate of the books, and the ship's medical staff and…"

He goes on for a few minutes and I realize that somehow, my brooding boyfriend must have saved the jobs of almost all the prey who survived the attack at Apex. Not only his closest friends, like those who worked in the Tower or the nurses who saved me, but the herbivore who maintained the grounds, the pigs and mole rats on the cleaning staff, and even the capuchins and macaques who worked in the kitchens. My soft-hearted gargoyle probably couldn't stand them losing their livelihoods because some dick-weasels decided to bomb us.

Rennie is the biggest mother hen of any gigantic, exotic predator and it makes me squishy thinking about it.

"I really appreciate it, Captain. I'm learning to defend myself and I'm getting good, but I can't watch my back *and* my front. The guys have to do more work here than at Apex, so they aren't able to follow me all the time, either." I wrinkle my nose as we enter the tunnel from the stairs and the walls surrounded by water make my heart rate jump.

"Their tube impresses me. It's like the underwater cafeteria, but it keeps the Games area separate." The raccoon shifter squints at me as he tilts his head. "Are ye sure yer ready for this, Miss? Even prey watch the college and pro Prey Games—they are not for the faint of heart, lassie."

As he swipes his card with tiny hands, we enter the secure tunnel to the island where the practice arena and the actual Games stadium are. They don't give clearance to people who aren't in or working with the teams. They ferry fans over for the actual matches and that boat doesn't sail when it's not a game day. Felix pointed out that if I don't make enemies on the team, I might even be moderately safe here.

"I know, but I have fantastic coaches and being part of something this big might convince weaker preds to leave me alone. At least, that's the guys' theory."

The Captain doesn't look convinced, but he nods as he opens to the doors that lead to the practice arena. It's another Khan sponsored building, but Felix assured me they own arenas in all the major academies. Besides the Leonidas', the Khans have more influence in sports than all the other families combined. Fitz confirmed it has to do with sports book betting and the program at Bloodstone, but I feel like that's not the only thing they're doing by donating expensive facilities. That asshole who fathered them is as crooked as my parents and grandfather, and eventually, I'll use it against him.

I just have to survive this murdering motherfucker and the cloaked cockwaffles first.

"PICK IT UP, LADIES! YOU WOULDN'T CATCH A SICKLY GAZELLE, much less a competitor at that speed!"

Gritting my teeth, I dig deep and push harder to pass the front of the pack so I'll cross the line before the rest of them. The larger assortment of female competitors today gave me pause at the start of practice, but as time went on, I felt the daggers aimed at me when I could outshine most of them. I tried *not* to do it; I really did. But just like now, Zhenga wouldn't let me stay in the middle of the group by putting less effort in. She refused to let me be less, so I wouldn't threaten the new girls—which is sweet, but it's going to cause a lot of fucking bullshit.

"Careful, DD, or those things will black out your eyes!"

My eyes widen as the shrill voice of Gold surprises me so much I almost stop short and cause a pileup on the track. Instead, I sprint past the starting line and straight over to the bench to flop down and guzzle water. I don't look in my ex-friend's direction—that's what she wants more than anything. Attention is all the Heathers live for and if I stop allowing their immature behavior to affect me, I win. This is a new school with new rules and it's the perfect place to establish them as insignificant bullies rather than rulers of the roost.

"Aw, did that upset the whittle bunny?" This time it's Pink and I have to fight not tense up. "I guess knowing you'll still be a freaky loser at this school would be upsetting. Now that we're here, the people have something to aspire to."

Does she even hear *the bullshit coming out of her mouth? Gross.*

Before I end up laughing and ruining my untouchable act, another voice cuts in. "Coach Z! Who let the cheer morons on our field? I knew that high-pitched doggy whine had to be coming from somewhere. There are *mutts* in our midst."

"Holy fuck," I whisper to myself as I look up to see the group of girls I was avoiding fan out in an alpha female formation in front of the Heathers.

Their leader is the one who spoke—a tall, muscular jaguar shifter named Selene, whose mother is a famous pop star and father is an ex-Pred Games World Champion. But her gang comprises four other preds, just like Gold's, though they couldn't be more differ-ent. Unlike my old frenemies, these chicks aren't dressed the same or even the same species.

Selene has a rainbow cadre of infamous friends, including Charlotte Bruce, a great white shifter; Jaiyana Faez, a crocodile; Roswitha Faust, a grizzly bear; and Kyaw Aung, a fangy python. Chess looked them all up when we saw the team roster earlier this week—their parents are diplomats, royals, rappers, sports stars, authors, and a fashion designer. The Faez family is an actual goddamn brand name, so she's definitely not going to be intimidated by Gold's stature.

I watch the Heathers mirror the new group—who I'm secretly going to call the Queen Bees—and I wonder if there's going to be a non-sanctioned rumble in the middle of the grass.

"Ladies!" Zhenga comes storming over to the two groups squaring off, her expression annoyed. "Coach Rockland requested time on the field for her squad to practice with their new members from Apex. Let's not have blood spilled from our cheering section—at least, not today."

My lips curve as I watch the Bees stand their ground, but the Heathers know how dangerous Zhenga can be when she gets mad. They've seen her in the Games at Apex and these new chicks haven't. It makes for an interesting stand off until a skinny woman with a long neck and ratty beehive comes rushing out of the stands squawking loudly. The sound is actually worse than Gold or the others shrieking and my sensitive bunny ears ring with the noise.

Who the fuck is this disaster and how do I avoid her as much *as possible while we're at Cappie?*

"Coach Zhenga is right, my lovelies. These are our mighty heroes, battling for our alma mater in the gladiator's circle and along with their muscled male counterparts, they deserve our undying admiration! Our squad are their muses, and they will show their appreciation for us when they are victorious."

My eyes move between the two groups of glamazons and then to Zhenga, hoping someone will tell me what the fucking hell is going on. I pull my phone out of my duffel, shooting a text to Fitz as the two coaches have a confab in front of their groups.

> BabyGirl: Someone needs to look into this Coach Rockland woman who runs the cheer squad.

CSpot: She's my new boss.

TigerWoody: What?!

TigerKing: Why?

EmoBatMan: This sounds as if it will be problematic.

LustyLibrarian: Could everyone stop making enemies for a day or two until we deal with the ones we already have?

> BabyGirl: I'm not making enemies! The Queen Bees on my team just had a standoff with the Heathers. There's a mean girl brawl about to pop off, so she and Zhenga are trying to settle them down. Something about the way she speaks... makes my gut clench.

CSpot: She's also an author... She asked some really uncomfortable questions.

TigerWoody: That's it. I'm taking her tongue for a jar.

> BabyGirl: Fitzy, I love my collection, but we can't do that until we know why she's creeping me out. Maybe she's just icky, but not evil.

EmoBatMan: What kind of author, Chester?

CSpot: Self-published, but I didn't ask because I was trying to get out of there.

TigerKing: Princess is right. We have to
tread lightly until we have a foundation
here. Fitz will hit the dark web and Aubrey
will use the library. Chess, go charm the
admin office. Renard, talk to your network.
We'll discuss tonight.

BabyGirl: What do I do?

TigerKing: Behave, Princess, and let us
help you. When we're all home, we'll
reconvene while we do that damn chip
search we forgot about.

BabyGirl: Yes, Sir!

TigerWoody: Keep edging him, baby girl.
It's funny as fuck.

I smile at the screen and lock it before I put it back in my bag. We're not taking any chances on security this year, which is why Felix is focused on making sure we don't forget things like the trackers. I hate thinking about some damn things buried inside of me that help my mother stalk me, but we have to cut off her access. That she hasn't reached out yet after I was called to school early doesn't bode well.

Looking up at the crowd of women yelling at one another, I ponder for a second.

Maybe the enemy of my enemy is my friend?

BEST FRIENDS

DELORES

"UGH, I CAN BARELY *WALK*," I GROAN AS I TRUDGE OFF THE FIELD for the day. It took Zhenga and the gangly cheer coach almost a half hour to work out where the cheer squad could practice that wouldn't put them in the line of fire and kept the warring girl gangs far enough away from each other. She made us do these ass aching sprints called 'suicides' while they plotted their detente, and I feel like I'm going to die.

I thought César was bad; Zhenga makes him look soft.

Fitz chuckles, pausing for a moment to give me his back. "Hop on, Baby Girl. Z isn't known for being the only chick to compete in the male games for nothing."

I blink. "She *what?*"

"Yep. She petitioned the fucking league and won the right to jump from the women's team. It's why my bro let her fight him all the time. He knew she wouldn't *let* him win."

Felix snorts. "Until she started using it for—" He coughs. "Well, until she was unscrupulous for a while."

My eyes narrow and I'm surprised to hear a low growl echoing out of my chest. Both the tigers smirk when I have to shake my head to stave off the bunny's instinct. "Stop making that face, both of you. I can't control it!"

"*That* is why we're looking so pleased, Princess. Your Battle Bunny doesn't like the idea of Z using matches to cop a feel and neither of us hates it one bit." Felix bobs his brows as I hold on to his twin, letting him carry me down the tunnel to land.

"Fine. But it's just biology," I grumble. "Don't get all weird about it."

"How is it the two of you have managed to fucking switch places? Now you're all soft and she's bristly. I can't keep up," Fitz complains. "You need to bang it out and get this shit under wraps."

"Shut up, Fitz."

Giggling into my piggyback partner's hair, I squeeze him. "I don't think anyone expected you to be such a matchmaker. You're practically throwing me at people."

Fitz stops, turning his head to put his nose against mine. "Not people, Baby Girl—our family. I don't mind sharing you with our family, but anyone else will die painfully. Understand?"

I roll my eyes, booping my nose against his as I return the crazy look he's giving me. "Ditto, baby."

"Are you two done? I'd prefer we exit this fucking sci-fi monstrosity with our wits about us, if you don't mind," Felix retorts drily. "We have no idea what the fresh hell is on the other side of the airlock."

"Understood, General Dick-tator!" Fitz says with a mock salute that makes me snicker.

"We're all going to die. I can see it now."

Fitz ignores his brother, climbing the steps to the top without hesitation, and opens the door to the waning sunlight. We all scan the area quietly before walking onto the path that leads to our part of campus. There aren't many people in this half, so we head for the library quickly, skirting around to the back where the private entrance is.

Just before Felix waves his arm at the door, a flash goes off, damn near blinding me. Fitz stumbles backward and for a second, I'm certain I'm getting dropped on my aching butt. He recovers in time for me to see something flying away into the sun, but I can't make out what the hell it is.

"What the fuck was that?" Felix snarls as he rushes to help me off Fitz's back.

"I don't know, but I doubt it was good," I reply grimly. "Apparently, we're not even safe by air."

"Just fucking great."

"Fuck, Angel. There's another one."

My head thunks against the back of the couch as I watch Chess run his detector wand thingy over me with a shocked expression. This is the fifth RFID they've found on me and I'm feeling like an endangered species on a nature show. I don't know what the actual fuck Lucille needed all these chips in me for, but I'm guessing they were injected with vaccinations throughout my childhood.

Lucille Drew, giving credence to conspiracy theorists everywhere with her bullshit.

"Even our father didn't tag us with that many," Fitz mutters. "I'm going to enjoy skinning that woman for a parlor rug."

The image makes me chuckle. There's a rug from a similar threat in Lucille's office. It's been there since I was little and she brought me in to watch them deal with an accountant who was skimming off the top. The spectacled puma always gave me the creeps even though she insisted I called him 'Uncle Dutch', so I was less upset that he died than about losing my favorite nightgown to blood splatters.

"I know how to skin," I say with a shrug. "I could help." They all look at me like I've grown a second head and I sigh. "Life lessons from Lucille were rarely fairy tale material."

"Yeah, but——"

Aubrey cuts Rennie off before he can ask, and I give him a grateful look. It's not a memory I feel like reliving, especially since we're currently removing my psycho mom's access to my whereabouts one by one. I have a feeling this will finally prompt a phone call and when it comes, it won't be pleasant.

"Dolly can skin. Good info. Did we get them all, Chessie?" Fitz rubs his hands together with a devilish gleam in his eyes. "Because I think we should feed them to a couple of randos in the cafeteria so she doesn't know she lost the feed."

Bless his crazy, non-judgmental mental heart.

"Good plan, Fitzgerald," Aubrey says as he scoops up the pile. "I'm sure the kitchen simians will be glad to help."

"I'll speak to the Captain in the morning. His crew can redistribute as they see fit." The gargoyle's eyes are filled with mischief and I feel tension finally deep out of my frame. "You should heal those quickly, *ma petite*, so no one will be the wiser."

"Let's move on to our assignments for the day. What did you find out about this new player on the board, Fitz?" Felix gives his brother a look and Chess immediately gets up to wheel the Cappie board over so he can make notes.

We already have the old rivals listed with small summaries and a map of campus in black and white so we can highlight territories and paths. Hopefully, it won't look as ridiculously unbalanced as the one on the Apex board does, but who knows? This place hasn't given us much chance to get a feel for its atmosphere because it's been a ghost town until today.

"I was slightly limited in what searches I could start on my *phone*, bro. But it's weird so far. What I know so far is more geared towards her 'author persona' than her real identity." My hyper tiger rubs the back of his neck, giving Chess a rueful expression. "Looks like Carina Raquel Rockland graduated from that defunct private academy the Hopewells ran until a decade ago. She's held a lot of random jobs related to counseling since, but only one of note: Capital Prep."

Aubrey grunts, shaking his head as he looks at Chess. "None of you were here when Rainbow Ridge Academy had to shutter, but they lost accreditation. It was a big pyramid scheme designed to make those hypocritical fuckwads a fortune off preds who wanted their kids to attend a school that 'accepted everyone.' Unfortunately, all they fostered was a slew of uneducated morons because it was all a facade."

I frown, remembering Purple having a bunch of issues in late elementary school that Pink held over her head for a while before getting her father to 'fix' it. Lucille was on the warpath about making sure I had all these lessons in ferocity around that time and I didn't pay attention to whatever Purple had going on. It was hard to focus when I barely slept because of the nightmares.

"That explains why a fucking scavenger is allowed to be part of an elite five staff," Fitz mutters. "Job placements were likely part of a settlement with the families who paid for their kids to attend."

"It's what the Raj would have done," Chess agrees. "He wouldn't return money, but he'd throw his weight around."

"What else did you learn, Fitz? I'm interested in the author portion especially." Renard's wings pop free and I can tell he's feeling agitated. I frown, peeling myself off the cushions to sit in his lap, and his wings surround us protectively.

Lacing my lips against his ear, I murmur, "What's wrong, my lyrical lover?"

He shakes his head, and the wings tighten. "I don't know. Something about this is disturbing my gargoyle. It feels… unsettling."

"It should, you big softie." Fitz grins as he holds up a finger. "Rockland isn't a well-known high tier family name and since she's a scavenger, I can't find a damn thing about her provenance."

"Zeus help us, he's watching the Princess' mysteries again," Felix mutters. "The gargoyle is right, Fitz. If you can't locate her family, we need to know what the public persona says."

"Okay, okay. I was saving the best for last, you tight asses. The suspicious guidance counselor is a romance author called C.R. Rockhard."

"Oh, gross!" Everyone looks at Chess as he brushes himself off like he's been infected. I pat Rennie's knee and he lets me out of my cozy wing haven to go to him. The cheetah is still muttering as he shakes himself, his face full of disgust.

"Chessie," I say softly as Fitz joins me in flanking him until he stills. "Tell us what's got you acting like you need a radiation shower."

His eyes are dark and I can see the animal flickering in them. That's unusual for our placid mate, so I tug his bun free and stroke his hair gently. He purrs a little and Fitz sits his chin on the opposite shoulder. Once we're enveloping him, I feel his heart rate slow.

"I thought she was being friendly. She showed me around the office, lamenting that I'm only there part time, and asking 'get to know you' questions. But every once in a while, she'd ask something too personal, then laugh it off when I hesitated. It was uncomfortable, but I tried to keep her happy since we need allies."

Dual growls escape Fitz and me, making Chess flush and Fitz hold his fist up for a bump. Once I oblige, I ask softly, "Are you comfortable relaying what she asked that made you so upset?"

Chess nods and sighs. "It was about Fitz and I. A little about Felix and the other Apex employees, but she came back to Fitz and I more than just in passing. It felt like… she was testing the waters to see how much I'd tell her. I felt weirdly profiled as a gossipy gay man."

That makes Aubrey shoot out of his seat and walk over with a dangerous fire in his eyes. "I will crisp her, Chester."

"Hey, knotty knight. I want to defend his honor. You can have the leftovers," Fitz complains.

"How many times do I have to tell you that thing is not cor—"

I arch a brow at them both, pulling back from the embarrassed cat to interrupt their squabble. "No one is crisping, removing tongues, or doing *anything* to this creepy bitch until we know what the hell her game is. Maybe she's a spy for Lucille or someone sent by the hooded dicks? We can't waste opportunities just because she's gross as hell."

Felix gives me a pleased smile as he motions for us to be seated. "Princess is right. With so many unknowns, we have to be strategic. There's a ton of research to be done on shit from Apex, much less this new garbage. No deaths until we can maximize the effect."

"He didn't say 'no *maiming*' so I'm good," Fitz crows. "I hope you have space in that trophy case, Baby Girl."

"You know I do," I reply with a wicked grin. "Surprise me."

"By Hades toga, you two are so fucking creepy," Aubrey grumbles. "Just kill people and be done with it."

"Some people deserve to suffer first, Buffalo Bibliophile. It's justice." Fitz winks at me and I giggle.

Even his insults are getting more high-brow. I love it.

"Can we stop focusing on me now that I've shared my experience? The admin staff here are worse than the owls at Apex; they're all raptors of different types, so they despise felines."

"Great. That means they'll hate me, too," I groan. "We all know what raptor birds do with rabbits. Mattie is an exception."

"Fine. We'll move on to Aubrey, since the Brooding Bard is probably waiting for his info."

Felix's very 'Fitz-like' nickname is so jarring that we all laugh and the cloud hanging over the room disappears.

Until my phone beeps with a summons for tomorrow afternoon after my first day of classes—with the mysterious Ms. Rockland herself.

Dog Days Are Over

Delores

Dragging myself out of bed this morning was no small feat. After Chess' admission last night, the boys decided they were *all* staying in my room again. We piled in and got comfy with a movie, leaving it on until everyone dozed off. I think everyone was feeling protective of our cheetah, and though the guys didn't specifically say it, that meant they needed to be close.

I'm not complaining—the family blob in my bed is the most safe and accepted I've ever felt in my brief life.

But they're all gone now—off to prepare for early classes, appointments, or visitors in their respective positions here. Since my first class of the day is Acting, followed by Voice, I'm not starting at the crack of dawn. I have Shifter History after my break and it worries me more than the first two. It might be a day full of new professors, but the last Shifter History professor made my life miserable until I ended his. The odds of me getting a decent person teaching a class based on the Council's curated narrative aren't good.

My cheeks flush as I pull on the skimpy uniform Cappie requires —one even more revealing than the one Apex forced on us. The rules here say I have to be wearing it between the hours of seven a.m. and five p.m. when classes are in session, regardless of what class I'm heading to. The duffel bag of clothes to change into when I get to Acting is sitting next to my messenger bag. I hope they have a locker room in the arts complex because I don't want to get stuck carrying all my gear every day.

After I pull my hair into a ponytail and add a little makeup, I check my bag to make sure I have the tech, chargers, and materials I'll need for today. I have a copy of my schedule on my phone, but I also have a printed copy with the map on the back. Since people messed with my access to tech last year for the first part of the semester, I don't want to be left blind if the Heathers found a sponsor after the dust-up at practice.

Taking a deep breath, I close my eyes and focus on centering myself. Today is important—I'll see Rufus and Cori for the first time in months and meet my new professors. I can't let all the insecurities and doubts I shed by the end of the year come back just because my old enemies followed me here. Capital Prep is a whole new world and a student body full of people who don't know the Delores Drew I am now.

This is my chance to start fresh and I'm going to take it.

I squat down and pet Jinx's head. "Everyone deserves a second chance, right, baby?"

Her mew makes me smile and I watch her scamper back to her treehouse before I head out.

Hopefully, I'm not being naïve again.

"*BUENOS DÍAS!* MY NAME IS ADRIATICA LOS FELIZ AND IF YOU ARE new to *Capital*, I will be your theater and speech instructor. I am also the head of the Theater department, so questions you have about the program should be funneled through me."

They gave us access to lockers, so I just returned from changing and storing my stuff to find a colorfully dressed woman clapping her hands for attention in the middle of the room. My eyes dart to Rufus and Cori, both of whom are leaning against the wall behind her with matching grimaces. That doesn't bode well, but I turn back to the professor quickly so it's not obvious I picked up on their displeasure.

"This is an upper level course, so I expect all of you—especially our transfers from Apex—to keep up with our pace. We have many talented young performers in this program and now that it is being funded appropriately, our schedule will be rigorous. We will begin with warm-ups. Take your places and prepare to stretch."

She doesn't give further instructions, but I notice the girls from the Pred Games team striding to the front to stand in a starting position for yoga. Taking their cue, I find my space near the back so I can observe their routine without being a spectacle. This isn't how classes ran at Apex, and Professor los Feliz obviously has a more structured approach.

That's why my besties look irritable, I'd bet. We had lots of leeway and now we don't.

By the way she takes us through the moves, I know she's some sort of feline. The grace our new professor moves with is unmistakable —I know because I spend a good amount of time watching my three big cats. Her eyes flick to her new assistants occasionally, and I feel my bunny's annoyance when she rolls her eyes at Cori. My friend is a talented dancer, but she struggles with balance in this type of situation because of how she's built. If this woman picks on her, there's going to be a problem.

"Now that we're warm in body, we must get our chords ready for speaking!"

Everyone shuffles around until we're in a circle and she leads us in a bunch of weird exercises where we make loud sounds and trills.

I'm used to some of them from vocal lessons, but they have not asked me to mimic other animal sounds. It feels ridiculous, but the Cappie students don't seem a bit fazed. When we finish, Rufus walks around with packets, winking at me as I take mine. I'm going to have to wait for the skinny on their experience with our odd drama teacher, but I bet it's good.

"This is our first production for the year?"

I recognize the voice belonging to the brash jaguar from my PG team immediately. She's the one who squared up with Gold and her followers are right behind her again. I never caught her name during the practice they deigned to show for, but her attitude tells me she expects to be on top of the heap here.

"Yes, Selene. The first quarter production will be a small play. We will audition for it during our next class and start rehearsals immediately after casting. The performances will be right after midterms."

Her beautiful features mar as she looks at her friends. "I don't know this play. Do any of you?"

They shake their heads, and I look down at the synopsis for a moment, studying it. A growing sense of horror fills me as I read and my eyes dart to my friends. They both look uncomfortable, and I realize they likely complained about it, but their protest fell on deaf ears.

"#Viral is a recent work by a new playwright and I'm very excited to explore its themes! It's perfect for a high school or college setting. Though the speaking parts will be all female, we will have plenty of ensemble and backstage positions for the guys."

Dear Hera, please let someone who has powerful parents complain before we embark on this theatrical Titanic.

"It's an amazing idea," the crocodile in the group coos. Her insincerity practically oozes from her words and, paired with her species, I make a note to give her a wide berth. So much about this girl suddenly reminds me of Bruno and I have no interest in finding out if her bad side is as terrible as his.

I pull out my phone quickly, making a few notes about the people in this class, so I'll remember later.

> *Selene (?): Pred Games, jaguar, head Cappie girl; unafraid of Heathers*
> *(?): crocodile, one of Selene's girls, Pred Games team*
> *(?): grizzly; one of Selene's girls; Pred Games team*
> *(?): python; one of Selene's girls; Pred Games team*
> *Adriatica los Feliz: feline?; drama and speech; very structured; doesn't seem to like Apex transfers; gives Cori dirty looks so must want to die*

Unfortunately, I'll have to rely on my detective skills here because if every professor cares so little about making sure they acclimate the new students, I'm going to have a rough go for the first few weeks. Chess and Fitz can pull rosters and do some digging, but until then, I'm flying blind. I'll need to be *very* cautious about who I interact with and how until I know what side they fall on, Council-wise.

As for the hoods, who the fuck knows?

"Thank you, Jaiyana! I am looking forward to seeing all of you audition on Wednesday." Professor los Feliz smiles broadly, but I sense something behind it I can't put my finger on. It might be paranoia because of Abel last year, but she's not saying exactly what she means. "One of my new assistants will pass out the syllabus, schedules for the rehearsals for this production, and your homework for the weekend. After that, please break off on your own or in groups to read through your sides for the audition until the end of class."

I wait patiently until Cori comes to me, Rufus following as they lead me to a corner at the back of the theater. The rest of my classmates are moving to their own spaces as well, so it doesn't stick out when they follow me. Once we're all together, I rush forward and hug them tightly. A feeling of safety comes over me, and I sigh. "Thank hell. I missed you guys so much."

Rufus chuckles and pulls back a little. "Well, isn't this adorbs, Coco? Our scaredy bunny is showing emotions and touching people! What *have* those boys done to you, boo?"

Smacking his arm lightly, I wrinkle my nose. "Make fun of my trauma all you want. You know you love me."

He sniffs and Cori bursts out laughing. "You two are the *worst*. Stop sniping 'cause we have a *ton* to catch up on. Talking on Fang-time was not enough and I can't wait to hear all the tea about your summer, D."

"What summer? I worked for Luc, which is always great, and I trained with César, but otherwise I was locked up like freaking Rapunzel," I mutter. "Lucille had her goons watching my every move when she wasn't in residence."

"So sad, Dollypop. Coco worked for my Aunt Brandine in the salon and I did my usual underhanded shit for my family. It was a blast, but not having you there was a total drag," Rufus says as he settles on the floor. "However, we *will* claim you tomorrow night in our dorm so we can fix that mess you're calling hair."

I throw a pen at him, narrowing my eyes. "How was I supposed to upkeep this without you guys? It's not like I could go to Lucille's people and I sure as fuck wasn't going to attempt it myself. Is it really that bad?"

Cori giggles and nods, her curls bouncing. "You have like four inch roots, babe. Didn't those boys say anything to you?"

"They have informed me they firmly believe I look perfect no matter what. And no, I'm not telling you about my lesson regarding that tidbit." My face heats, and they both snort in unison. "So, no. They will not tell me if my dye job needs work—like ever."

"That's what we're for; don't worry. I have *zero* problem telling you when you're a hot mess, girl." Rufus winks and Cori elbows him, making him choke on his gum. "Damn it, Coco."

"Now that we've established my shitty self-care routine, can you guys tell me about this chick?" I hold up the play pages with a frown. "Tell me about this disaster waiting to happen. Does she have some sort of agenda or is she really this clueless?"

"Clueless!" they chorus, and I groan.

I will not enjoy this class one bit.

New in Town

Delores

Madame de Bouvier ran my voice lessons exactly how I'd expect. In fact, so far, she's my favorite new professor. She was pleasant, if not a little mousy for her species.

As I exit the Cappie version of the Shird from my second day of classes, I ponder for a moment. I'm uncertain I want to venture through the tunnel to the cafeteria on my own, and I also don't want to call for an escort. I saw one of Raina's men watching this morning as I walked to the building next door; he seemed shy. He's probably lurking around here somewhere, but the quokka doesn't know me yet and I hate to force him to interact.

Maybe I'll grab food at our quarters for now and leave the main campus for my afternoon classes.

Heading down the path, I look up at House Reptilian and frown. I have to go there soon to rumple something of my stuff and make it look like I've been around. It feels even more foreboding now that students are here and I can't figure out why. It just has an icky vibe, so I don't want to be anywhere near it. I thought it was my bunny at first, but the more I think about it, that doesn't feel accurate.

I shake my head as I scan my arm at the back door of our new home, muttering, "I'll make Fitz come with me. That will fix it."

"You'll make Fitz go where, Baby Girl? Do I need to crack someone's head already? Show me who and it's done."

Blinking as the tiger in question bounces over like a Disney character, I laugh softly. "No, you don't have to beat anyone up. My dorm building is still creeping me out and I decided you should come with me tonight."

He picks me up, throwing me over his shoulder and patting me on the ass despite my squeals. "No problem. I'm always happy to guard your body. Plus, I can *discourage* anyone who thinks they can gawp at my girl. Win-win."

"Put me down, you ape!" My voice sounds exasperated, but we both know I don't mean it. I'd let Fitz Khan manhandle me anyway he chooses anytime and my protests are weak.

"I can only assume you meant to say 'pretty please with a cherry on top, oh masterful and sexy boyfriend of mine,' so I'll let you go once we get to the kitchen."

"Hmmm. No, I don't think I forgot to say that. Felix isn't here." My lips curve as he makes a sound of betrayal and stops mid-stride. Before I know it, Fitz is nose-to-nose with me, grinning like a crazy man.

"I'd literally *pay* for you two to get your shit together and bump uglies, Baby Girl. My brother desperately needs to let himself go for once, and you need someone to rein you in a little." He dips his head to kiss me lightly and cocks his head. "Now, come eat before you waste all my touchy time with verbal sparring."

This. Freaking. Guy.

I let him lead me over to the counter, plopping on one of the stools and letting my bag hit the floor. He whistles as he pulls a bunch of stuff out, assembling a huge sandwich that looks fucking delicious. Fitz winks as he pushes one towards me and the other at the chair next to me. When he joins me, I pick it up and groan as the flavor rolls over my tongue.

"Damn, Fitzy. You make a mean sandwich when I send you to the kitchen," I say as I wipe my mouth. My eyes dance as I give him a playful smile. "You're on post sexy time food duty from now on."

He rolls his eyes, licking his chops clean. "Don't give me too much credit, Baby Girl. Chessie made the aioli; I'm sure of it. By the taste, I think your bunny likes the garlic…what's up with that? Speaking of which, I don't ever think I've seen you eat a carrot, and that's just freaky."

And there goes his ADHD again.

Instead of asking why the hell he's wondering about carrots, I just shrug. "Not much for them unless they're cooked—never have been. I guess it is a bunny sin, huh?"

His face lights up and he nods, then sips his soda. "Yup. Though, you eat meat and I guess that's odd, too. I'm just glad you don't pick at salads and shit because you're dieting all the time. It would make the brooding brothers and Chess lose their minds. They're such henny penny motherfuckers."

I arch a brow. "Says the guy who carried me from the door and made me lunch?"

"I don't know what you mean by that," he shrugs and finishes his food. "Now eat up so you have energy for my afternoon delight, woman."

Well, if you put it that way.

It's a pity I can't have Fitz for lunch every day. Or Chess. Or… Okay, I'd accept a rotating lunch schedule; I'm not picky. I mean, who'd complain about big sandwiches and big O's for their mid-day break? Not this bunny, that's for sure.

I sigh as I leave the library. It sucks that I didn't get to see anyone else, but Aubrey was swamped with the dreaded password reset shit he dreads every semester and Rennie was in class. Felix and Chess were both in their offices meeting with students, though I'm not sure why my royal tiger would need to. Maybe he and Zhenga are plotting shit for the Pred Games schedule? It wouldn't surprise me. They seem determined to turn the Cappie team into a juggernaut. I like Felix has something that makes him excited. He hates the shifting classes with a passion and this seems to make him happy.

I'm not even worried about him spending so much time with Coach Z.

"Fitz isn't the only one having growth," I mutter as I head into the tunnel. Apprehension fills my veins as the airlock closes, but I know there's a new quokka behind me. He waved when I walked out, and I knew he was the afternoon companion. Truthfully, I feel better with someone following along, even if they don't talk to me.

Raina's triplets don't *look* threatening, but neither did she until she pulled out a compound bow and went Legolas on those hooded freaks. I learned a lesson about underestimating an opponent just because they aren't a pred that day. Triplet Two is probably packing heat, but he will not show it unless we face an issue. Interestingly, the quokkas dress like bikers, not pirates.

By the time I emerge from my musings about my raccoon friend's little harem, I'm at the end of the underwater tunnel and I swipe my card to exit to the main campus. Looking around, I note the various dorms, then the pathways leading to the student buildings. The center is *very* exposed and I'm not a fan of all the places someone could dart out to attack. I remember the weird flash bang from the other night and look up to see what must be an avian shifter class above.

Nope, don't like that, either.

"Don't worry, girly. They aren't allowed to fly around unsupervised at night or on weekends."

I blink in surprise, looking at my quiet companion. "That's good to know. It's a bit jarring to have them circling like this."

"Agreed, ma'am. I'm no fan of winged preds, either."

He doesn't elaborate, but he falls in step with me as I head for the Scholastic Complex. I decide to bridge the gap myself. "You can call me Dolly. Raina and The Captain do and any mate of theirs is a friend of mine."

"Bowser," he replies with the bright smile his kind are known for. "My brothers are Banjo and Kirby. Don't say it… our mum was an old school gamer."

Stifling a giggle, I press my lips together to get a hold of myself before I speak. When I finally have control, I ask, "Felix calls me Princess—please tell me you call Raina that."

His cheeks flush bright pink as he mutter, "Peaches. I call her Peaches."

That does it—my control snaps, and I burst into laughter. Apparently, all men are assholes and even my raccoon friend has to deal with it. "Oh, my."

"She gets very cranky," Bowser admits. "But I love it and her response."

We stop at the front of the building, and I wipe my face. "Thank you for this. I was very nervous about this class because of my experience with a bad professor and you've calmed me down a lot. I really appreciate it."

The quokka winks at me despite his embarrassed color. "I had a feeling you needed a pick me up, girly. My Princess adores you and I'd do anything for her. Be safe in there. Kirby will be here to walk home with you if none of your men shows up."

Giving him a little wave, I head up the stairs of the oddly shaped building. There are lots of students filtering out, but I don't make eye contact. For the moment, I just want to learn about the landscape of this place. I recognize a lot of faces from social media—children of movie stars, musicians, politicians and more—but none of them seem to know me. That's a good thing in my book; I'd rather get recognition on the Games field than from the shenanigans in my past or my family name. My classroom is on the second floor and once I hoof it up the steps, I stand outside it to peek inside.

No one problematic yet—score.

A rough jolt sends me sprawling into the room and I have to employ every skill I learned this summer to stay upright. When I whirl around with my fists raised in position, I see Gold smirking at me with her acolytes behind. They all looked pleased with themselves for nearly flattening me and my bunny sees red inside. A swell of fury threatens to consume me, but I school my expression as I look at the girls who seem incapable of simply fucking off to live their lives like adults.

"What is your problem?" I ask coolly. My hands drop to my waist and I mimic the cocked hip pose they're all in.

"That Capital Prep also allows trash in its student body," Gold snarks. "Now you've sullied *two* respected institutions, loser."

These fucking chicks are psycho. I haven't seen or spoken to them in months, yet here they are still doing this childish nonsense.

"Grow up, Heather—that's directed at *all* of you, by the way. This obsession with abusing me in public is pathetic and immature. You didn't scare me off last year and you won't succeed this year. I don't *care* if you think you're better than me; your opinion doesn't define my self-worth." I sniff and flip my ponytail at them, spinning on my heel to walk to the back row to take my seat.

"You'll be sorry, DD. Mark my words; we have *plans* for you." Pink calls out as I go.

Snorting as I drop into my chair, I give them a wide, toothy grin. "Knock yourself out, ladies. The more you show everyone exactly who you are, the less your narrative makes sense. With time and distance, your focus on drawing this bullshit out is going to look like what it is—a desperate attempt to stay relevant by punching down. Chew on that for a while."

I reach into my bag and pull my tablet out, purposefully ignoring them as I peruse my notes from earlier in the day. Adding their names to my list of people's details, I don't respond to any further comments or growls. The other students are certainly watching, especially those close to Cappie's current power structure.

I'd bet texts and DMs are whizzing to the celebrity mean girls' group from my acting class as we speak. Those two cliques fighting one another for control of this school can only help me, and I'm happy to let them duke it out while I solve the mystery that brought them here.

After all, as long as they don't go after me or my friends, I don't need to deal with them, right?

My nose wrinkles as my brain protests because that was the old Dolly. I did that when I ran with the Heathers and look where it got me. *Fuck.* Sighing as I look around the room, I realize I'll have to stand up for anyone either bitchy group picks on and it's going to put an even bigger target on my back.

Just fucking peachy.

RISE

DELORES

I'M PRETTY SURE BEING A DICK IS A REQUIREMENT TO BE A SHIFTER History professor. They probably ask about it on the application to teach at the academies. That's the only explanation that makes any sense.

Herr Helmut Blitzen is an enormous aquatic shifter—my nose said shark, but I'm not as familiar with those—and he stomped into class like he was storming a beach in battle. His dark, glittering eyes looked over all of us hungrily and landed on me so quickly I know he was told who I am. He didn't call me out like Abel; no, he simply called on me so many times I looked like the class dunce within minutes. The questions he asked about Council 'victories' weren't things covered in last year's curriculum, and I'm not sure if that was because Abel sucked or because he skipped ahead.

The result was the same, regardless. Everyone laughed at my expense for the entire class.

My eyes drifted to the clock constantly, watching the hand move wistfully as he bellowed and flashed his teeth. Instead of mouthing off like I did to Abel, I answered calmly and apologized for my lack of knowledge. He didn't seem pacified by it, so that strategy won't work for the rest of the semester. The only thing that *might* save me is having Aubrey give me private tutoring and reading far beyond our place in the texts. I'll have to dedicate time daily to preventing him from humiliating me in every class which really chaps my thumpers.

"As if I have time to fuck around with this shit. Between Pred Games, people out to kill me, and fucking four productions a year, I'm already booked into oblivion. Now I have to make time for some cockwaffle's neurosis, too." I mutter as I leave the Scholastic building.

My brain is aching as potential schedules whiz through it. I can survive on less sleep and work on some of this shit on the weekend, but I also have five fucking boyfriends I actually *want* to spend time with. That's not counting my besties, who I missed like a piece of my heart all summer. I thought Cappie would be *less* demanding than Apex—everyone has always ranked my school at the top of the heap for standards. Maybe that's just PR, too?

Hell if I know. All I know is I'm screwed and now I have this meeting with Coach Cuntmuffin.

Sighing, I walk down the steps and head to the Dupree Student Center. The guidance offices are located there; Chess told me where to go last night while we were watching the movie. Cappie allowed him to teach some of the minor theater classes—apparently, the professors here hate all the technical courses, so he got those. However, his secondary role was guidance liaison for Apex transfers, so he spends half his time working for this woman.

Based on his experience the other day, I'm extremely uncomfortable with that. I thought she was odd at practice, but I figured it was the nature of being a cheerleading coach. The girls who gravitate towards those teams are pretty specific, if my memory of Shifter Secondary is correct, and you'd have to be a little weird to deal with them and their parents. But the story about her fishing for greater detail about Chessie's private life and our discovery of her pen name made me wonder if there's more to it than lack of social skills.

According to our Google searches on her 'work,' I believe I know exactly who this chick is and what she was doing.

"You need evidence, though, Dolly, or you can't accuse her."

With that last pep talk, I step off the elevator onto the third floor and take the right turn, Chess told me. Coach Rockland's guidance office is at the end of the hallway, sitting on the edge of the building. My nervous cheetah told me it's huge, full of expensive snooty furnishings, and has a spectacular view of the campus. None of those things contradicted our suspicion that her position here was a bribe to keep her family from demanding money back from the defunct Rainbow Academy, so another strike goes against her name.

I knock on the door lightly, waiting until I hear a sing-song command to 'enter' ring out. Opening the door cautiously, I walk into an office that reminds me of the one for the dictator from the magic movie except it's not decorated in pink, but *rainbow*. Everything in the room is a different color and the walls are a coordinating gradient. Posters declaring popular slogans like 'Born This Way,' 'Yas Qween,', 'Slay All Day,' 'Love is Love,' and 'Proud ally' are framed on the walls facing her desk. Under them are bookshelves filled with textbooks, reference books, and stacks of novels, but I notice most of them have the pseudonym Fitz found on the spine.

Likewise, single books are nestled in cubbies with small decorations to create displays for each title on the top shelves of each low case.

Holy mother of Cerberus, this place is a shrine to her own ego. I'm in serious trouble.

The woman in question beams at me from behind her standing desk, walking on a treadmill as she gestures for me to sit in one of the garish armchairs facing her. "Welcome, Delores! I'm so happy to have you join us at our elite institution. Forgive me for not letting you in, but I have to get in my steps and dictation. I may not be as prolific as some, but their derision can't stop me!"

I nod, confused by her response. It sounds like she expects me to know details about her I'm not privy to and I'm unsure if it's because she believes she's *that* well known or if she's just clueless. I don't want to set her off, though, so I give her a tight smile. "No problem, Coach Rockland. I have to admit I was a bit surprised by this appointment; I was unaware I needed to see you once we settled my schedule."

She laughs—a throaty, condescending sound that makes my skin itch. "Oh, no. This isn't about your schedule. I called you here to discuss your mental health."

What?

"I'm aware of your… interesting emergence and the subsequent issues that plagued you at Apex last year. Several students expressed their concern about your delusions and victim complex, so under our protocols, I contacted your mother."

My face goes from friendly to blank within seconds. I know what's expected of me as a Drew or Rostoff—whichever Lucille wants to equate me with this week—and I cannot allow this woman to glean any knowledge of my emotions. I don't know if this is a trap set by my psycho mother or my ex-BFFs, but since they're both involved, I have to be strong. "What did my mother say about these spurious accusations?"

"She admitted you had a rough transition to your animal, and that she was constantly disappointed in your inability to handle challenges thrown at you during your first year as a college student. By the time we finished speaking, she agreed with my assessment that you should have two counseling sessions a week with me until I feel you've worked through your issues." Her smug smile makes my stomach turn, but I don't even blink.

I nod and tilt my head. "When will these sessions be scheduled? My schedule is quite full and my mother expects me to excel in every aspect of my school work. I cannot allow something as trivial as 'therapy' to derail my achievements here."

Keep it frosty, Dolly. Don't let her know how angry you are.

"I'm adding them to your schedule for the first semester now, but I see space Monday morning and Thursday afternoon. You will be here on time, ready to work on your self-centered delusions, and we will resolve your needless hatred for the people who are simply trying to make you a better person despite your... handicap." Her smile is bright and friendly, but I can see the malevolent glee under it. It's tinged with some sort of eagerness as well and I don't understand it. "We will also discuss your narcissism and how it's led to the nymphomania you're engaged in. Talking about this aberrance in great detail will help me understand how to fix your broken mind."

Suddenly, I get what's happening. My eyes dart to the decor and then back to the vulture smiling at me as if she cares deeply for my well being. *This is all a trap, and it wasn't set by the Heathers or Lucille.* No, the scavenger sitting in front of me forged this steel cage, and it benefits her more than anyone who lent their hands to building it. Coach Rockland knew the moment the Heathers visited her to spew their bullshit that she could force me to come spill my guts to her if she embarrassed the great Lucille Drew enough. Lucille played into her hand expertly and now she's got an unwilling captive to mine ideas for her fucking books.

As soon as she's done scraping everything she can out of me, she'll declare I'm miraculously cured, no doubt.

I don't let her know I've figured out her play, nor do I show one ounce of emotion. "I appreciate you working with my schedule and calling me into your office to explain the situation. Is that all you need from me today, Coach?"

"Oh, my. You should call me 'doctor' while we're in session, Delores. I *am* the one tasked with making you a presentable member of our society, after all. Your repaired image will all be because of my hard work and talent. I cannot *wait* to write up the specifics for a book."

My eyes narrow for a second, but I get it under wraps. *Like hell she's going to use my misfortune and hard work to profit.* "As far as I've been told, ma'am, you're not a doctor of any kind. I wouldn't feel comfortable giving credence to a false narrative simply to enhance your self-worth. I'll stick to Coach, thank you."

Despite my even tone and unreadable expression, Rockland doesn't take my declaration well. Her cheery facade snaps, revealing the darkness lurking under it as she glares at me. "We will see about that, Miss Drew. I am the one in charge; I have more sway than you. If it takes more strident methods to get you under control, I won't hesitate to use them."

"Last year, I learned to accept that I cannot control the actions of others, only my response to them. If you choose to employ less savory efforts to curb my free will, I cannot guarantee what damage that might do to you in the long run. But threatening me won't do much—my mother is far superior in that arena and I know she will follow through." Rising to my feet, I pick up my bag with one hand and push the emergency button on my phone screen with the other. "If that's all, I have homework to attend to."

She slams her palm on the handle of the treadmill, stopping it to jump off and advance towards me. Vultures are carrion eaters and looked down upon by almost all preds, so I know I have a tactical advantage if she attacks. I may be prey, but they trained me to be a pred, so I won't pull my punches if it's defending myself. But she doesn't come close enough to get physical—instead, she pauses at the edge of her desk with a cunning grin.

"Miss Drew, you'll find I don't threaten anyone. I make promises and I offer my sincere help to those who need it… like you. You needn't fear my sessions; no, use them to become a better version of the lowly prey animal you turned out to be. With my help, you'll rise to a modicum of respect in line with what you deserve."

Don't react, Dolly. She wants you to attack her so she can call you crazy. Reel it in, bunny rabbit.

Before I can respond, the door pops open and I see Fitz's glowing eyes and a toothy grin. He looks as if he's barely controlling the crazy as he clears his throat. "Ah, there you are, Miss Drew! They have sent me to fetch you by Coach Zhenga for a Games strategy session. Forgive me, Coach, as I must steal her away."

I look at him, then the nasty counselor, my eyes suspicious. *Why is he talking like a fucking butler in an Agatha Christie movie?* The whole thing is weird, but he definitely got my distress call and he's trying to save me, so I nod. "Absolutely, Professor Khan. We were finished here, anyway."

"Oh, please. As if it's not well known this girl is sleeping around with half the staff, including you," Rockland says, waving her hand. "You have no right to end my meeting before I say it's done."

Fitz's grin widens, and the psycho fills his eyes as he steps further into the room. "Thank fuck. I was already tired of pretending to be nice." He cracks his neck and steps closer to the vulture, his expression more menacing than before. "Since you know, I can make it crystal clear that Dolly is *our* girl, just like Chess is *our* cheetah. If you so much as wear a perfume that bothers them, I'll take great delight in plucking every one of your feathers individually before roasting you on a spit to feed to the reptiles. And since that sort of thing was my *job* for the ambush, I am skilled at making it last for weeks."

Rockland arches a brow, but I can almost taste the fear in the air. I take Fitz's hand, giving her a big fake smile, and follow him out the door without another word.

I've won this round, even if I don't know what the next holds.

Heathens

Fitz

IF MY BABY GIRL HADN'T PUT THE KIBOSH ON KILLING PEOPLE before we know what their game is, I would have strangled that corpse nibbling bitch with my bare hands. I can tell whatever she said has Dolly shaken because the icy exterior she erected hasn't melted and we're halfway through the tunnel. Her posture is ramrod straight and the grip she has on my hand would make a lesser pred cry.

But I'm not a lesser pred and if she needs to crush my hand bones for a couple hours, I'll live. It won't be the first time it's happened.

"Baby Girl…" I start, but she shakes her head emphatically.

"Not here."

My brow arches, but I catch her looking around furtively. She believes it's possible there's surveillance in this stupid tube and honestly, she's probably right. I would have thought of that myself —hello, hacker—but I'm so fucking angry about her being upset that it's clouding my brain box.

"I just wanted to ask about your first day. I can see it went very well, though." That almost gets a laugh out of her and I beam.

"Yes, it was quite pleasant," she lies. "Capital Prep is an excellent school."

If anyone believes that horseshit, I've got a swamp in Florida to sell them.

I muffle my chuckle with a cough and squeeze her hand lightly. She was okay at lunch, despite the weird Theater professor, so all of this tension is about her stupid fucking History class and the guidance cunt. My mind races with ideas on how to fuck up her ridiculous cheer squad and make her pay in tiny ways that will cause the avian to molt with anxiety. Even if I can't come at her directly, I guarantee the winged wankers will help me figure out less obvious ways to torture the bitch. It's Ren's specialty and I know he'll play along.

"You're coming over for dinner, right?" It occurs to me I need to keep up the pretense she's not coming home to the library every night, especially since we haven't checked out her dorm recently. "Felix and Chess are coming, too."

Her eyes light up as she gets why I'm saying it so loudly. The rules say only the Flaming Hot Cheeto and Grumpy Goliath can live in that space—there has to be an explanation as to why we're all there at night. Felix, Chess, and I are *supposed* to be living at our off-campus townhouse. Since our girl arrived, we've barely set foot in the damn place, and I doubt it will get any better as the semester goes on. I should probably get that crew of prey minions to move most of our stuff in over a couple of nights, so we don't have to make trips back and forth.

"Of course I'm coming to dinner. I want to talk about everyone's first day and how your classes went, too."

The tiny wink she gives me makes me roll my eyes and I chuckle softly. Dolly is smart as a whip, but stealthily, she is not. We'll have to work on creeping and crawling so she doesn't stick out like a sore thumb. Even if she spent the past year cultivating a look that definitely begs for attention, she needs to know how to blend into the background if we're going to solve the mystery of the dead kids and the hooded freaks. I'm sure we'll have to sneak around a bit to find clues.

When we reach the other end of the quiet passage, I wave my badge at the scanner and the lock opens to let us out. Breathing in a deep lungful of fresh air, I let it out slowly. I don't know why these assholes at Cappie didn't just build a goddamn bridge instead of that underwater birth canal, but I really fucking hate it. It's too contained, and the access is out of my control—I don't fucking trust it a bit.

"We need to figure out a way to bypass that nightmare," I grumble as I take her hand. "It feels like we're asking to be ambushed or gassed or some bullshit by being in the damn thing."

"Are you claustrophobic, Fitzy?" Dolly grins mischievously. "I would never have known."

"Hell no. That thing feels like a giant trap a Bond villain would devise. The airlocks? The glass? I mean, I'm just waiting for someone to declare 'the sharks got smarter' and a fucking megalodon to bust through it."

Her eyes widen, and she clamps her hand over her mouth for a moment. I know she's trying not to laugh, but I'm serious with this shit. I have a bad fucking feeling about that tube and my tiger refuses to let it go. I'm about to growl at her when something drops out of the trees, making us both scream like bitches. When my vision clears, I see Renard double over, laughing so hard he can barely stand.

That mother fucker, I'll…

I bum rush the chortling gargoyle, knocking him to the ground and rolling around as we take swipes at one another. He's still cracking up as we tumble around, but I'll show his ass. Scaring the absolute *fuck* out of our girl is *not* funny. My ears prick up at a tinkling sound and suddenly, I realize I'm punching him, but Dolly is actually giggling. In fact, she's flat on her ass, clutching her sides as we wrestle, and she might even be crying.

"Baby Girl, I'm defending your honor. The least you could do is… ow, damn it!" I snarl at Ren when his tail yanks mine. "You're a fucking cheater, Laveaux."

She sobers a little, wiping her eyes and trying to catch her breath before she replies. "I'm sorry, Fitzy. It's just… he got us. We're so big and bad, but he literally scared our pants off dropping from a tree. I mean… he's not invisible. How bad do we suck?"

Put that way, it is pretty humorous.

I stop wailing on Renard as I chuckle softly. I'm more embarrassed than mad, anyway, so she's right. "Okay, okay. Pouty Prankster wins this round."

"*Merci*, Fitzgerald. Your concession is much appreciated." The shifter in question leaps to his feet and holds his hand out to me, then to our girl. "I was watching for your arrival, but you needed to lighten up."

Snorting, I grumble, "I don't know if making me jump out of my fucking skin is the right way to tone down the mood."

Dolly brushes off her butt, picking up her bag and grinning widely. "It worked pretty well, honestly. I needed that laugh, and so did you."

Renard winks, then bows. "At your service, as always, *ma petite lapin*. Felix wanted someone to watch for another aerial attack as we entered. That flash looked like a flash grenade on the feeds and it makes all of us nervous to think someone is using human weapons to distract or disarm us."

A flash bang? Since when the fuck do any shifters need human shit? Have we made yet another enemy?

"That seems like overkill," our girl says thoughtfully. "We weren't prepared for air, so they could have dropped a damn coconut from above to knock us out and it would have worked. Could it be about testing our defenses?"

I blink, then burst out laughing again. "A coconut? Would it have been migrating?"

They snort and roll their eyes, but Renard is the first to reply. "Fitz, you've been watching entirely too many human movies with them."

"I strongly disagree," Dolly says as she links one arm in each of ours. "Now take me home and feed me, boys. I could eat a water buffalo."

Yes, ma'am.

"Chess, this is *delicious*." Dolly slurps up another noodle, making my cock kick in my pants as she groans happily.

I could kiss my darling cheetah for making this Italian dish, and the smirk on his face says he knows it. He wipes his mouth, smiling broadly before he says, "I knew you'd like it. I made sure it was spicy enough for the big guy, but not so much it would burn everyone else's tongues."

She grabs another piece of the cheesy bread and takes a bite, chewing it with more indecent noises. Every eye at the table is watching her and when she realizes it, she turns bright pink. "Stop it, you guys. I had to live on fucking *salads* most of the summer because of Lucille's watchdog and his pack of dickheads. Having actual food for the past few days has been glorious."

"But... you're... a bunny?" Felix says with an amused look. "Are you complaining about lettuce and shit?"

"Don't be an ass, bro," I mutter as I scoop some more pasta on her plate. "Our girl likes a big helping of meat on her plate, and I'm not complaining."

My twin blinks, then actually laughs, making everyone else follow suit. Man, I really love how he's opening up. Felix has been punishing himself for so long that I can barely remember how much fun he was before the weight of unrealized expectations crushed him. His eyes dance as he watches Dolly dig in with gusto and he twirls a wineglass in his fingers. He's enjoying himself without the aid of a hefty tipple of scotch and it's fucking beautiful.

"I suppose you're right, Fitz." Felix turns to Chess and claps him on the back. "Good job, bro."

I'm about to add my tidbit of wisdom when I get distracted by the swipe of a pink tongue over pouty lips. *Fuck.* My eyes narrow as I watch her closer, scenting the change in the room greedily. If we can clean this shit up quickly, we can probably work in some naked time before—

"Calm down, Fitz," Aubrey says, bringing me out of my trance. "We still haven't discussed what happened after snack size's morning classes."

Dolly growls under her breath and wrinkles her nose. "Ugh. I was trying to avoid that garbage. Fine, I'll spill. But everyone needs to put down their pointy objects. *Capiche?*"

The others share a concerned look, then they glare at me when I shrug. "She's right. You don't want to have a weapon in hand."

"I *am* a weapon," the dragon snarls as he leans back in his chair. "But I'll try to keep it cool."

How do you argue with that shit? The motherfucker burnt down the Library of Alexandria as a child. He's not wrong.

"Go ahead, Princess," Felix says as he puts down his fork. "Tell us what the hell has you on edge and Fitz scrambling to cover."

"Shifter History was… as expected. Blitzen is a dickwaffle, and he embarrassed me at every turn. He didn't take any sides or let either group of mean girls pick on me as much as force me to look stupid. I'll have to study my cottontail off to get ahead, so he can't do it every day all year." Her brows knit as she looks down at her napkin, clearly frustrated with herself.

"You aren't to blame for that, *ma petite*. Even your friends agree that your mother purposefully kept you ignorant to control you," Renard says softly. "Flames and I will work with you to get you up to speed."

"Ugh, I know, but I *hate* feeling dumb. It's just another thing they can point at and say I'm unworthy. As much as I know it's not true, I can't help but get upset. I don't know how this asshat knew what button to push, but it fucking sucked." Dolly flops back in her chair, looking up at the ceiling with a long sigh.

"I get that," I interject. "People have always treated me like an idiot because they didn't know how to handle me. But you did, Baby Girl, and now my head's clearer than it's ever been. Sometimes smarts aren't just in books, you know."

She smiles softly, getting up from her spot to walk over and plop down on my lap. One hand brushes over my hair, pushing it out of my face before she leans in nose to nose. "Fitzgerald Khan, you are not, nor have you ever been, stupid. Anyone who thinks so will die before they finish saying the words. Cross my heart."

"Awwwww," Aubrey says, his voice laced with playful sarcasm. "Look how cute our family psychos are. It's adorable."

My brow arches as I point a finger in his direction. "You, Flaming Fartknocker, better be nice or I'll spill the tea about your antics. We lost a *lot* of shit before the beautiful bunny bounced into our lair."

He snorts, blowing a smoke ring in annoyance, and I know I got him. "Fine. Be body part collecting weirdos all you want. It's perfectly normal and not at all worrisome. Carry on."

"Tell them the rest, Baby Girl," I say as I turn back to her. "They need to know why you hit the distress button."

She makes a huffing sound, but leans back into my arms as she complies. "That cunt cheer coach called me into her office to tell me she'd had reports of my 'delusions' from last year from other students. Then, in her infinite wisdom, she called Lucille, who sold me up the river, and they decided I have to get 'counseling' from her twice a week until she feels I'm cured."

"What?!" Chess blurts out, toppling his chair as he stands. "No way. You can't."

"I have *to*," Dolly replies glumly. "She's made it part of my schedule and run it up the flagpole. I could get banned from shit like the Pred Games and performances if I don't do what she's ordering. Lucille signed off on it, too, so I can't even work that angle."

"Guys, there's something really wrong with this woman," I cut in. "Her office looks like a unicorn barfed in it and she has all these posters…"

Dolly groans. "Her office is this giant shrine to her books—and based on the color scheme plus her poking at Chess, we can guess what that is. The posters are full of generic ally slogans and she's got a bunch of authors I recognize on the bottom shelf where there are books that aren't hers."

I didn't get *that* part and now I'm ready to boil over. *How fucking dare she try to—*

"Fitz, calm down," Felix booms as he stares at me. "Princess, tell us why you hit the button. This is all bullshit, but it's not why you panicked."

She nods, dropping her gaze to look at her hands. "She called me a narcissistic nymphomaniac and implied I'd have to discuss my decline into that life in great detail to work through it. The look in her eye was so predatory that I knew something wasn't right. When I tried to leave, she started talking about control and her sway, but I could feel the *hunger* radiating from her. Not to attack me, but… to force me to talk."

The gargoyle's wings pop out, and he flexes them with an agitated look. "*Ma petite*, we will work on getting this woman's edict reversed, but I cannot stress enough how little you can reveal to her. No matter how emotional she gets you, no matter what she uses to prod your wounds… do *not* tell your story."

I frown, wrapping my arms around her tightly as I stare at the broody shifter. "Why is that, Rock Man? What's got your tail in a knot now?"

"I was worried when Chester mentioned all the questions, but I thought perhaps I was overreacting. Now that Dolly has had a similar experience, I can express my fears." He throws his napkin down and paces across the room. "Many years ago, I took up residence in Italy. This was after my exile and before I came to Apex, of course. I met a writer, and we became friends… Suffice to say, they stole my story as inspiration and I've had to watch it echo through time, reopening my wounds every time I see the blasted tale."

"I don't recall any gargoyle tales that are that well known," Aubrey says as he frowns. "Are you sure…"

Renard smirks as he turns to us. "He was human, so I did not tell it as a gargoyle and his true love. The thief wrote it with different characters and that's all I will say about it for now since it is not the point. I am only trying to caution our bunny rabbit that every word she says may end up in a new romance novel that goes viral."

I groan, thunking my head back against the chair. "Could we hit *pause* on collecting new enemies for a bit? I'm at fucking capacity for planning people's deaths for a while. Look at our fucking board; it's full of assholes trying to screw us over."

"Er, sorry." I look over to find Chess diligently making notes about the shitty vulture woman on the board in his precise script. "I thought I should…"

"No, no." Felix waves his hand. "You were right to add her. And Renard is right about giving the bitch details. Unfortunately, it means someone is going to have to read her drivel to see if we should be worried."

"Not it!"

Everyone shouts at once and my twin sighs. "Fine. *Fist, Fang, Claw, Bite.*"

Dolly beams as she sits up. "Oh, I'm very good at this. Rufus taught me."

"Best two out of three?" Renard asks as he clears the plates. "We'll go after we finish cleaning up."

"Agreed," we chorus.

I'll kill that little gangster shit if I end up having to read this nonsense.

Bad Feeling

Delores

The next morning comes way too early. Rennie ended up being the loser in our little tournament and I think it *almost* made up for him scaring the hell out of Fitz and I. Once I grabbed the power shake Chess had ready and my stuff for Shifter Basics, I booked out of there before the sniping got too intense. I feel bad for my poor gargoyle, but I think out of anyone, he'll be the least upset by whatever the fuck he finds, so it was a good outcome.

Besides, all I can focus on right now is heading for Felix's class.

He was long gone by the time I got up, which means he was up before dawn. That doesn't surprise me a bit, but it worries me a little about what the hell he has in store for us. The email to our class this morning said we'd be in the practice arena for the Games, so he's not planning a repeat of the dreaded whiteboard shit from last year. I have no idea what he's doing instead, but knowing my grumpy Raj, it will be grueling.

"Good morning, Miss Dolly."

The sound of a cheerful voice gets my attention and I realize this must be quokka triplet number three, Kirby. His smile is even brighter and I can tell he's the joker of the group by his playful tone. I smile and let him catch up as we make our way to the airlock. "You're Kirby, right? I've met Bowser and Banjo, but I haven't met your armadillo or skunk friends. Is the skunk related to Argyle in the infirmary?"

Kirby nods enthusiastically. "Indeed! They are cousins, and yes, Percy is as prickly as his relative. As you mentioned, our last member is Holliday, and he's in charge of weaponry at Apex, so that's where he is here as well. You may see them for trips in the evening, as they start even earlier than this for their positions."

By Poseidon's seashell jockstrap, that's early as fuck.

I swipe my card at the entrance, looking at Kirby curiously. "I can see the laundry being open that early, but why the armory?"

He shrugs and gives me the broad quokka grin again. "No idea. It's always been that way, though, Miss. I suppose those who work there expect it. Sometimes, you find them entirely staffed by nocturnal creatures, which makes it easier. Holliday is an oddball that way; he prefers night to day."

We stroll over to the secondary lock, swiping again and entering the tunnel that heads to what I heard people refer to as 'Arena Island.' Looking around as I walk down the underwater pathway, I take the suggestion Fitz made about looking for security in my surroundings. Besides teasing Rennie mercilessly with Aubrey, he also declared himself in charge of teaching me stealth.

According to my crazy tiger, he thinks we'll have to sneak onto Apex's campus at some point and there could be other less than scrupulous activities involved in getting answers about our enemies. Fitz swore Felix agreed and so here I am, checking for hidden cameras in the tunnel as I walk to class.

If you told me this would be my life last year, I would have laughed in your face.

The airlock to the field stairs beeps as I wave my card again and I arch a brow as Kirby follows me. His brothers seemed uncomfortable entering pred spaces, but he trots along like it's no big deal as we cross the grass separating the main stadium and the practice field.

"Why are you walking me through the pred area when your brothers didn't want to enter them?" I ask curiously.

Kirby shrugs. "Raina and The Captain said our gracious gargoyle's orders were to accompany you until we knew you were safe with allies. You are not safe until you have been deposited at your class and I see it with my own eyes."

My nose wrinkles. "You guys take Rennie pretty seriously."

"He is the protector of the prey staff, Miss Dolly. Before his arrival, it was terrible to be one of us. Our families have worked at Apex for many, many generations and the stories prior to him are bleak. We are very grateful for his protection."

Wow. Is Rennie like the prey staff Hercules or something?

"I didn't know that. He doesn't talk much about himself—I only knew about The Captain because when I first toured Apex, I saw him threaten some aquatic shifters giving the crew trouble during feeding time." I grin a little, remembering how scared I was of the hulking form of his gargoyle then.

Stopping at the pitch, Kirby chuckles. "I imagine he was on a tear. Our benefactor is soft with those he cares for, but he is mighty in defending them."

"Well said," I agree as I see Felix glaring. "Time for me to get to class. Thank you, Kirby."

"Anytime, Miss Dolly."

With that, I turn and head over to where my grumpy boyfriend is tapping his smartwatch with a look of irritation.

Doesn't he know good things come to those who wait?

"GET A MOVE ON! I KNOW FOR A FACT AT LEAST A HALF DOZEN OF you are on the Pred Games teams. You have to be faster than this, even in non-shifted form," Felix growls from where's standing at the edge of the circle. He's pacing as he watches every single person in our class run the dreaded suicides. My tiger is in rare form this morning—he's had us run two miles worth of laps and after that, he started on stretches and then these damn things.

I suspect he's using this as extra practice for the Games.

To be fair, he's right about the amount of Games athletes in this class session. The Cappie Plastics and the Heathers are all sweating away, though the latter group is whining as if it pays by the word. There are a few male Games competitors as well and they're from Cappie, so they aren't handling Felix's first day punishment well. It seems like they're the male counterpart to the Plastics, but they haven't harassed me like my ex's group would, so I mostly ignore them.

Huffing as I continue to push my muscles to the point of exhaustion, I watch the interaction between Selene and Gold. Their respective cliques keep knocking into one another or causing 'accidental' trips. I can tell Felix has noticed, but he's ignoring the plaintive cries from both sides as he focuses on the rest of the class. He didn't have patience for one set of spoiled brat bitches, much less two competing for Queen of Petty Bullshit. Besides, he's got members of *his* team panting like they're going to die from exercise that isn't as rough as what Coach Z demands of the girls in practice.

That's making his tiger prowl, and I'm a little excited that I can sense that.

A whistle blows and we all jog over to the edge of the circle to drop onto the benches. They passed water around and I consider dumping it on my damn head. That's how hot I am. But I don't, because my next class is Speech and I'm barely going to make it through the stupid tunnel and the Arts Center in time. My saving grace is that the Plastics *might* share that time slot with me and if so, Professor los Feliz won't want to yell at them. Crossing my fingers for that bit of luck, I toss back a gulp of water with a sigh of relief.

"You're all a bunch of spoiled, ill-trained weaklings. None of you would survive Bloodstone and you may not survive this semester if you don't shape up. I suggest anyone who had to sit early or barely made it through this round consider a private regimen to get up to speed." His eyes light on me and I know he's pleased, even though his expression doesn't change. I can read the praise in his gaze and it makes my flushed cheeks even hotter.

Fuck, I'm a sucker for his 'good girl' eyes. It's embarrassing.

"Now that I have a decent baseline on your physical capabilities, I want everyone to drop and give me a hundred push-ups followed by a hundred crunches. When you're finished, you can hit the locker rooms to clean up and head to your next class early. Don't even *think* about cheating; I'll know."

I wing a prayer of thanks to the universe. Thanks to César and his torture sessions, I'm good with that amount of calisthenics. I won't collapse and humiliate myself as long as I can keep my aching thighs from betraying me. Walking over to the grass, I flop down to do the crunches first. I've barely started when a shadow falls over me and I see Felix giving me the tiniest of grins as he looks down.

"Make sure you do this correctly, Miss Drew. I'd hate to give you detention."

If I didn't ache from head to toe, I might take him up on that.

"I promise to do them correctly, Sir," I say sweetly. His chest rumbles and I laugh, starting my crunches as if I don't have a care in the world.

"Brat," he mutters as he walks away.

I keep doing my exercises as I'm told, knowing the longer he holds out on this date thing, the hotter it's going to be.

And I'm going to keep pushing his buttons the entire time.

As I predicted, even with the extra time, we barely made it to Speech. Rufus and Cori weren't in this class, so I checked my phone to see if they'd messaged yet. The group chat was full of complaints about their morning classes and it helped me get through the massively boring introduction to this class. At Apex, we had so much freedom to learn our craft on our own, but it appears here, we're going to be spoon fed every aspect of theater slice by slice. Thinking about it makes my brain hurt, but I make it through Speech and Music Theory without falling asleep.

I walk out of the Shird, squinting at the midday sun and cursing Felix's morning exercise. My break today is small and I pull a power bar out of my bag. I have just enough time to chow down while I sneak into my stupid dorm to ruffle shit. Fitz will be upset that I'm going by myself when I asked him to come, but we haven't worked it in yet. I'm worried some asshole hall monitor or my roommate will report that I'm not where I'm supposed to be. It's not like Apex where I abandoned a single room on a floor by myself; someone's going to figure it out if I don't get this shit done.

House Reptilian looms in front of me like a giant bug. It's shiny and slick, like a reptile's skin, and rounded like it's coiled up. It's giving off a vibe that makes the hair stand up on my arms, but I suck in a breath and head up the steps, anyway. The front door has a badge scanner like everything else, so I scan in and look around. Dark woods and wrought iron are part of the gothic decor, making the common room look like they have designed it for Halloween. There's two people curled in big chairs reading, but everything else is quiet—eerily so.

This was a bad fucking plan.

It's too late now, though, so I stride over to the elevator and push the button for the fourth floor. The damn thing is old, rickety and has an open cage as the doors. I can't help but wonder if that's for aesthetic because Cappie sure as fuck has the money to upgrade this bullshit. It stops with a jerk and I get out, walking toward my assigned room. Another card swipe has me inside and I close the door behind me.

"Thank hell no one's here," I mutter as I look around.

They placed the various clothes and personal items we bought all over my side of the room. I assume Raina helped the crew do this because they shelved books with little knickknacks in vignettes, clothes are in the open closet and draped over the desk chair, and they made the bed with fluffy pillows and stuffed animals. If you didn't know me, this could easily fool someone into thinking I'm here occasionally.

I turn to look at the opposite side of the room, snorting when I see it's filled with science books, lab coats, hefty texts and plain furnishings. The pred who lives here is obviously majoring in one of the many science or tech programs the Ericksons sponsor. Nothing personal is lying around, only materials for classes like beakers and pipettes, plus vials of various liquids strewn across the desk. There's a weird chemical equation on the desk and a bunch of scribbled notes with molecules.

My brows furrow as a zing of energy races through my veins. It's like my instincts are telling me this is important, so I pull my phone out to snap pictures of everything I can. I've never felt a buzz like that before, but I know in my gut I've found something the guys should see. *Who the hell is my roommate, anyway?* Listening for a moment to make certain no one's going to surprise me, I rifle through the papers until I find a name on one.

Kinsley P. Crandall

Frowning as I rack my brain for why I recognize that name, I put everything back in its place. I don't have much time before Piano, so I have to get moving. I take the time to rumple my spread like I've been here to nap, leave the wrapper from my bar on the desk, and move around some shoes. I squint for a moment, then put a book by the pillow, hoping it looks like I was reading.

With a final distrustful gaze at the space, I turn on my heel, exiting to the hallway. The elevator is creakier on the way down and the students in front of the fireplace haven't moved. This is the fucking dorm where time stands still, I swear.

"At least you got in and out without having to deal with anyone," I tell myself reassuringly. "You can run this weird shit by the guys tonight."

As long as nothing else happens before then, of course.

Spellbound

Aubrey

Having control of the staff accounts at Capital Prep was a boon I did not expect. At Apex, I was able to reset things and if needed, start new accounts, but this school has a much more intrusive system. To prevent leaks about student mishaps to paparazzi, the network admin can get into any account and check activity—from DMs to email to browser history. Fitz figured it out within minutes of inspecting my system when we arrived and I've done my best to avoid intruding on people's privacy ever since.

However, the conversation about this creepy counselor made me wonder if this is her typical MO or if she's chosen our girl as her first experiment. Rennie is reading through her skimpy backlist to find specific keywords I should look for in her digital footprint, but once I had a break today, I couldn't help taking a look at her most recent behavior.

Despite how invasive it felt, I feel justified now.

'Coach' Rockland's internet searches reflect a desperate need to gather information not only on Dolly, but all of us as well. She's done multiple searches on the tigers, Bloodstone, Chess, and his parents' disappearance. There are articles about my family and Renard's, plus a wealth of shit on the Drews. She's messaging with a contact that I'd bet my scaly ass is one of those bimbette girls who keep coming for the lunchable and another who seems like they might be on the Council. Both are feeding her tons of info via cloud storage on all of us and the happenings at Apex. That points a finger at displaced staff making a quick buck off of the things they witnessed.

I'd be troubled by this by itself, but emails to Dolly's mom, the head of Cappie, an agent, and yet another mysterious source give me pause. This woman clearly has no moral code and she'll do anything to get ahead, including damaging someone who is supposed to be under her 'care.' My evidence agrees with the snack size; her mother is being snowed by another master manipulator. But her ex-friends are in this ass-deep, as are others I will need Fitz to help me locate.

Pulling my glasses off, I rub my hand over my face. There's so much going on all at once that I believe it's being orchestrated to keep up constantly reacting. Attacking Dolly on her way to school was reminiscent of the disappearing students, but it was too coordinated. The team prevailed—but should they have? I'm not certain because eyewitness accounts are mostly inaccurate and colored by bias. Perhaps the real goal was to put us on high alert so we're distracted from seeing others things.

"But what?" I whisper to myself as I stare at the trash in the counselor's recent history. "Was it to keep us from focusing on staff and student deep dives before school began?"

If so, it worked. The attack and our decision to create a second home base for our girl took time. The extra jobs we were forced to take on here at Cappie take extra work. Even Dolly's heavy course load and piles of work are eating up more free time than they did at Apex. Maybe *all* of this is to prevent us from doing more sleuthing into the hooded freaks and the Council. One or both of those factions could influence enough people to make this shit happen.

This is something we have to examine as a group—I'll bring it up at dinner.

I flick the mouse, scanning through a few more emails before I call it a day and head back to our new nest. Suddenly, a few words catch my eyes and the fire in my belly starts to burn. Squeezing my sparkly bunny in my left hand, I try to breathe slowly as she's been teaching me. It's hard, though, because this load of bullshit just became the number one topic I'm going to address when everyone is back. We can't let this happen; it'll draw attention from much farther away than these silly elite schools.

Pondering for a moment, I pick up my phone and call my companion. He's been grumpy since he drew the short claw, but I don't call for no reason. He won't ignore me.

"*Bonjour, mon amour.* You're interrupting a perfectly enjoyable funk."

"Apologies, but I believe we need to bring the bear and badger into the fold. I've discovered some troubling correspondence on the carrion eater's system." I wait for him to think about, squeezing the bunny reflexively as I grit my teeth.

He lets out a slow breath. "If you are suggesting it, I don't doubt it. I will contact them. They can join us for dinner and, perhaps, offer a fresh perspective on some of the enormous amount of shit we're juggling. It's only been two days, *mon ami*. None of us will be able to keep up with the deluge if it continues to accumulate like this."

"Exactly. From the minute Fitz went to get her, it multiplied exponentially. This isn't normal."

"I'll take care of my part. You have all your ducks in a row for the presentation. Oh, and make sure to let Chester know we will have guests? He hates to be unprepared."

I snort. "I know. He's turning into a clone of you."

"If only, *mon amour.* If only."

Right.

WHEN I FINALLY FINISH PRINTING ALL MY DOCUMENTS FOR THE meeting, I head through the corridor to our quarters. The smell wafting from the kitchen is delicious and I inhale deeply. Though Rennie and I get sustenance from other sources, I've always enjoyed eating. When I discovered he'd trained as a chef, he spent months making all sorts of delights, but since we were always alone, it eventually waned. I thought he might start again when the Khans stormed our fortress of solitude, but he seemed content to let them go home most nights.

Dolly's changed everything, especially since Thanksgiving last year.

Chess has taken over the cooking, but my mischievous mate frequently joins him in the kitchen. I'm waiting for him to admit he's Cordon Bleu trained, but getting personal details out of Renard is a slow process. I've had the benefit of centuries; the rest of them are just beginning to peel away the rock hard exterior that isn't solely his shifted form.

Admitting to our relationship is a big step.

Bypassing the main room for a moment, I go into our room to change into more comfortable clothes. This is my big change, I suppose, and proof that even an ancient dragon can learn new tricks. Moving into this place we set up to be comfortable for all of us cemented the formation of a family—a clash— for me.

I don't lounge around in my pressed work clothes; no, I wear sweats and tees like the rest of them. It was hard switching over because it made me feel more vulnerable and less distant from them. But it also felt like the right thing to do. I can't expect our girl to be honest with us or the others to share their tales if I don't start letting them in.

Shaking my head, I sit the papers and my tablet on the dresser so I can strip. I toss the dirty shirt and pants in the laundry bags and pull on my new home garb. Looking in the mirror, I pause for a moment to see the expression on my face. Amazingly, I look happy and not like I want to roast the entire campus on a spit. Of course, I *do* want to toast most of the fucking people here, especially those we know are gunning for our girl. But I don't look like a thundercloud coming over the hill ready to burst and cause havoc.

A tiny mew startles me and I grin bigger, stooping to pick Jinx up and set her on my shoulder. Her small claws dig into my shirt for purchase and I walk over to get my stuff with the shoulder mounted kitten in place. Hopefully, the rest of them are arriving and we can distribute all of this shit so Dolly isn't burning herself out trying to balance it all. She feels responsible and she's going to be even more stubborn once she hears my news.

Fuck. I hate being the bearer of supremely bad news.

"Dollypop, I'm super jelly you have digs like this. They have me on the third year floor of the fucking *dog* house and let me tell you… floral scented bathrooms it is *not*," Rufus says as he waves at the hallway. "Not to mention you have your own chef, you brat."

Fitz glares at him, rumbling softly as he shoves my bestie into our sunken nest area. "You're not moving into our MojoDojoCasa."

"I told you letting him and Princess watch that Barbie movie on the tablets this summer was a bad idea."

I pinch the bridge of my nose, sighing as I look at Felix. He's conveniently forgetting we set that up so he wouldn't drive down and do the exact thing he did the minute we weren't watching—sneak into her house. "It's done now, isn't it, Raj?"

"Don't be a hater, Prof," Rufus says to the room at large. "You asked us here for a reason, right, Coco?"

The colorful polar bear nods, her curls bouncing as she hops into the big couch and sighs happily. "Yep. Ru-Ru's correct—you wouldn't have curtailed your sexcapades to have us over if it wasn't important."

"Guysssssss," Dolly groans. "Stop. No sniping. That means you, Rufus, and all the rest of you testosterone-fueled a-holes. Cori, however, is perfect."

"That's what you get for liking dick, D. If you just swung the pendulum, I bet—"

Snack Size looks over at her, glaring as she puts her hands on her hips. "No longer my favorite. Behave. I have to go get this Predhub uniform off so I can join you."

I arch a brow at her, eyeing the wilted hair and sheen on her skin. "You changed back into after Zhenga's practice?"

An aggravated screech is my only answer and I chuckle as she stomps away. "What did I say?"

"They make us put it on between seven and five pm. Her practice ended before five so she had to re-dress for the walk home or risk demerits if someone tattletale saw her." Cori sighs and looks down at herself. "That's why I still have the damn thing on."

"Amen, sis," Rufus replies. "These tight asses really enforce that shit, too. I already got ten for venturing out for breakfast in PJs. The heads in the doggy kennel are real cocksuckers and *not* in a good way."

"At least they stuck you with something remotely similar. They put bears in with *cats*, if you believe it. It's ridiculous and they hate every single ursine in the building. Our head glares at me like she wants to use my ass to sharpen her claws."

Dolly comes back wearing an oversized tee that belongs to Fitz—the Bloodstone security logo on it tells me that—and a pair of yoga pants. Her hair is tied back in braids and she's got bare feet with sparkly toes. I smile at her cozy appearance, moving over so she can drop on the couch with her friends. "I'm sorry you guys got shafted coming here. If it wouldn't get you in trouble, I'd find a better place for you."

Felix looks thoughtful for a moment, but he shakes his head and walks over to the kitchen. "Chess, is this ready? I want to get whatever the big guy has to say before we eat." I give him a surprised look and he shrugs. "You have that pensive look and you're dancing. It means you found something and you don't like it."

He's absolutely right and I'm a little stunned. Am I that predictable?

"I found a lot of bullshit, but one thing in particular concerns me the most. And I had Rennie call your friends, lunchable, because our boards are too full—which is also part of the problem." I find a seat on the end, waiting for the gargoyle to curl in his usual fashion nearby. "Chester, you'll want to come in here."

The cheetah pauses, looking at me curiously before he fiddles with dials on the stove. Once he's done, he comes in and very carefully sits next to Fitz.

Smart move.

"As everyone but your friends knows, my position at Capital Prep allows me more access to digital information than my position at Apex did. Between my access and Fitz's skills, we've been compiling data, clues, background, and more on the players in our mysteries. Today, I did some peeping in staff accounts. I can actually see everything they do, including access to WiFi with their own devices." I frown, still uncomfortable with that level of spyware in their system.

"Famous people and politicians," Rufus says with a nod. "Not a shocker, honestly. Imagine what the paps would pay."

"Indeed," I agree. "But I was really looking at the worst offender so far…our Ms. Rockland. There's an absolute fuckton of shit she's up to that isn't kosher but… The most pressing one is a contract with her agent for a new book. Her proposal is full of holes—whether it's ignorance or purposeful, I don't know—but it appears to be about… you, Nibblet."

Dolly's jaw drops and she pops out of her seat, striding over to me with a furious expression. "Are you fucking kidding me? She's trying to profit off a story about *my* pain?"

Felix tilts his head back and I know he's trying to rein in his temper. The tail that flicks over my ankle tells me Rennie is doing the same. Chess has his fists balled on his lap and his face is red, but the real surprise is Fitz. His expression has gone completely neutral and everything about him is almost…blank.

That's not good.

"I'm sorry, cupcake, but it seems like she is. The email had a whole script prepared for public promotion and a schedule for all the places online and in person she plans to send releases to. I assume she put it in motion the minute someone confirmed you'd be attending school here."

"No worries. It won't be an issue if they can't find any pieces."

At the tight words from Fitz, our bunny moves from me to him, sitting in his lap and stroking his hair off his face. "I love your crazy, baby, but we can't do that right now. Anyone who knows her plans could bring the Council or Sibbies here. If she's a plant for one of our other enemies, it will tip them off."

"Excuse me, psycho family?" Rufus grins as he arches a brow. "While I *love* me some chaos and blood, I think Coco and I are a bit lost. We're not privy to all of the enemies and whatnot."

"Why are you here then?" Fitz grinds out as our girl tries to soothe him.

"Because we can help," the bear says as she bounces in her seat. "I don't know everything, but I think Rufus has a possible solution to *this* one thing. Tell 'em about Farley."

Who in the fuck is Farley?

Can't Break Me

Delores

Leaning back against Fitz, I tilt my head as I wait for Rufus to speak. It occurs to me that with the overarching drama at Apex and my personal shit, I don't know much about either of my best friends. It makes me feel bad and I rub my arms as the feeling of unease spreads through me. Have I been a bad friend? I'm not sure, but I know that's because the only friends I've ever had were the Heathers. The dynamic there is nothing like what I have with Rufus and Cori which means I don't have any comparison to examine.

"I'll try to be brief since all these alpha males seem set to pop," Rufus says with a smirk "Dollybear, you don't know a lot about my family, but I'm sure your knuckle draggers checked me out. They run a specific illegal trade throughout the Northeast because they moved from the South about a hundred or so years ago. We were well known bootleggers even then and had a huge feud with another family in the area. It was a long one and a lot of people died, so near the end, a splinter faction moved up North to start a new empire."

My eyes narrow because this sounds pretty familiar, but I know Rufus' family is a predstasy cartel or something. Surely no one was selling that in the 1800s? "Okay. But what does that have to do with this?"

"Patience, D." Cori winks and socks Rufus' arm. "Get on with it, drama queen."

The badger chuckles and shrugs. "I can't help myself. Anyhoo, my great-whatever grandpappy and granny and some of their bazillion kids moved up North to similar country to what they left. They started a new empire that over the years, morphed into what it is now. But they took the structure their daddy used to be successful and expanded it with some very stringent rules. Each generation would have enough children to supply a few heir possibilities plus children who will go into legal, business, and political pursuits. That way, everything we need stays in house."

Felix gives him a sharp look. "So the McCoys basically breed a never ending supply of badgers to keep their community isolated and non-infiltrated? Sounds like something my father would do."

My friend shrugs and gives him a toothy smile. "As I'm the top of the heap for heir apparent despite my 'handicap'—as Granny calls it—I have access to damn near everything in the family. That's where Farley comes in."

I bristle at his sexuality being called a handicap, but it appears Rufus has made peace with it. He's fought his way to the head of the clan status regardless and I assume that came with a lot of blood and teeth. "Who's Farley?"

"And what the hell good will a drug dealer do us?" Aubrey grunts. "Except for possibly making Fitz jizz in his pants."

"Oi, Snarky Salamander! My love juice is reserved for Baby Girl and Chessie. None of it's getting wasted in my fucking sweats."

"For the love of Hades' sweaty nuts, *Fitz*," Felix growls, "let the gangster speak."

"Why, thank you, Professor Khan. I've always depended on the kindness of strangers," Rufus drawls in a sugary accent. When his joke doesn't land except for Cori and I, he rolls his eyes. "Tough crowd. Okay, so like you surmised, we have an entire firm of lawyers who handle various specialties and it's just your luck that the meanest, most vicious honey badger in that place is also the most skilled intellectual property lawyer in the country. Farley guards all of our proprietary blends of legal shit humans consume like pot and vapes with a wink and a blade to the kidneys."

"We can't *kill* her," I blurt nervously. "I mean, not yet? Who knows what she's shared? My reputation is in tatters as it is; I can't have some ridiculous bullshit floating out there suggesting all sorts of crazy shit I didn't do."

"Relax, Dolly," Rennie says with a slow grin. "I think I see your tattooed friend's point. He's saying his relative is a skilled litigator in both the shifter and human realms. He'll be able to dig into putting the kibosh on this lying bitch legally. If he's as vicious as Rufus claims, this should tie her hands for long enough that we can knock some other players off the board."

"*Exactement!*[1]" Rufus snarks. "Farley will do anything I ask because he owes me for saving his bacon when we were kids. You don't have to worry about some insane bill—not that one of these assholes wouldn't foot it—because this is a quid pro quo situation. Should I let him loose on the corpse gobbler?"

Looking around at my guys, I read their responses on their faces. They think it's a good idea, but they'll go with whatever I decide. Cori squeezes my hand and I sigh, knowing she's in, too. "Okay. Send your honey badger to fuck her up. Anything that gets some of the pressure off that nonsense is good. I haven't even considered how Lucille will react if it gets out because I'm savoring her lack of contact."

"You know that's bound to change soon, Baby Girl," Fitz says as he buries his face in my hair. "Just like Felix knows we'll hear from our asshole father soon."

Another growl rumbles through me and everyone laughs. I know they all think it's cute that I consider the current Raj one of my targets, but I'm serious as a fucking heart attack. I'm coming for that man for what he did to the cats and he'd better sleep with one eye open once I get the resources. My new *'Fuck 'Em Up Sis'* list is extensive and much more ambitious, but I'll get through it if it kills me.

Which going after my mother and the Raj of Bloodstone just might.

"Regardless, that takes Rockland off the board for the moment. Thank you, Rufus," Chess says as he puts an asterisk next to her name to note her as 'in progress' before continuing. "Who's next?"

We all stare at the list on the board quietly.

Current Enemies & People To Watch

Hooded Freaks???
Student Murderer???
Apex Poisoners???
Lucille & Bruno Drew
All Heathers– Gold, Pink, Purple, Silver, Yellow
Todd and douchebags squad?? (Maybe?)
Khan Raj
Weird Smelling Person Ren Won't Talk About
Sphinxes (Aubrey insisted.)
Plastic Cappie Mean Girls & Guys (Maybe?)
Helmut Blitzen
*Carina Rockland **
Random unknown spies for either side?
Whoever is throwing shit from the sky?

"I don't suppose ignoring the ones without a specific name or description is possible?" Cori asks. "I mean, Ru-Ru and I can help watch the Heathers, the Todd-bros, and their new rivals in classes when we see them. But some of this is too vague to follow up on."

"No shit," Aubrey growls. "Every time we found new clues at Apex, a body dropped or one of the minor players caused enough trouble that it distracted all of us. And the working theory I wanted to discuss is that it's all connected in some way. Everything is happening at once now—from more demanding jobs and to classes to constant bullshit from random people who should have no skin in this game. It's orchestrated chaos."

Rennie beams and claps his hands. "Oh! This is my area of expertise. Chester, please flip a board to a clean side. I want to write everything in a bubble and do some shit while you all discuss."

Chessie does as he asks, looking confused, but Aubrey waves him on. "Let him go to town. Renard is excellent at *wei qi*[2] and this is more like that than chess."

"You think one or both sides of this shit we're caught in the middle of are purposefully pulling enough strings to make life chaotic so we don't have time to look into them?" Fitz says. His brow furrows and I run my fingers through his hair as he thinks. "In a totally Psy ops wielding perspective, it makes sense. Look here so you don't see what we're doing there."

"How do we combat it?" I ask impatiently. "Because, not going to lie, but I'm really tired of feeling like every minute of every day here will be scheduled to prevent some fucker from humiliating, attacking, or flunking me."

"Isn't that normal college?" Rufus smirks and shrugs. "The key is to chip away at it and not let the bastards grind you down. Let's divide up the duties and we'll make this shit our bitch."

"Exactly. I need Fitz's help doing some higher level tech things with my access," my dragon says in a begrudging tone. "I think Snack Size needs help being grilled on Shifter History—more advanced than her level so that drill sergeant can't embarrass her."

"Oh! She has people walking her, right?" Cori claps her hands and beams. "I'll make like twenty sets of flashcards and bring them. Anyone escorting her with have them on a ring and can quiz her as they go!"

"Noooooooo," I moan. "Not everywhere."

"It frees up time, Princess. Your friend has an excellent idea because if she makes that many we can give them to the Captain's crew." Felix arches a brow at me, his expression reproving. "Unless you want to spend *more* time studying than with us?"

"Fine." I cross my arms over my chest and Fitz peeps over my shoulder, his arms tightening on my waist. "Stop it, you big perv." He ignores me and everyone laughs again. *Assholes.*

"That means we can star the Blitzen fool, Chess," Aubrey muses. "Do we think we can leave the dingbats to fight each other but keep an eye on them? Outside of talking to the creeper, they haven't done anything you can't ignore, right, Nibblet?"

I think about it for a moment and nod. "For the moment. But I think we have to add someone. I didn't get to tell you guys about it yet, but the more it stews, the more I believe this is important."

Everyone looks at me in concern and I clear my throat. Going to the dorms alone wasn't smart, but I can't always call people every time I move. If my enemies force me to have a twenty-four hour bodyguard, they've won. I'll be in a cage of my own making and I can't allow that. It gives weight to the claim that I'm weak and maybe I was last year, but I'm not now.

"I went to the Reptile Pit today after class to futz with my stuff." Fitz starts to protest and I hold up my hand. "Don't get mad; I know I asked you to come but I wanted to get it over with, so I did it."

"What did you find? I don't know anyone from that place so far." Cori frowns as she looks at Rufus. He shakes his head in agreement. "What the hell classes do they take?"

Felix strokes his chin, thinking for a moment. "I've had a few in Shifter Studies. They're quiet and shifty. I met a few snakes and a gator. Apparently, the crocs prefer Aquatic and the gators always go to Reptilian. No one mentioned why, though."

"I haven't seen any in the library."

Rennie shrugs. "Some lizards and snakes in the lower English courses—one Gila Monster, which I found fascinating. Crandall or something."

"That's my roommate!" I whip my head around, eyes wide as I think about the possibilities. "Her desk was full of chemical molecules and equations and shit that looked suspicious. I got this weird vibe from the dorm and it got worse in my room. I took a bunch of pictures so you and Aubrey could check this shit out."

"Your bunny?" Felix asks curiously and I shake my head.

"No. It wasn't her. I had this overwhelming feel of foreboding in the dorm, but when I glanced at her side of the room, I was *drawn* to the desk. I haven't ever felt anything like it, but I knew I had to check it out. Once I did, I couldn't stop myself from documenting everything. It felt so important." Chess walks over and I hand him my phone so he can send the pictures to everyone. "I really think Kinsley Crandall has something to do with… part of this… but I don't know what or why."

"Baby Girl, you know that's the only poisonous lizard, right?" Fitz sits his chin on my shoulder. "I mean, we still haven't figured out the poison shit. A Chemistry major would be a perfect puppet for creating a poison no one has in their databases."

"Fitz, you're a genius!" I grin and turn my head to give him a smacking kiss. He flushes and shrugs while the rest of the room breaks out into loud chatter. I clear my throat and they all look at me again. "Okay, so Aubrey and Rennie will look into this poison stuff then?"

"We will, *ma petite*. That's another star we can add."

My stomach growls abruptly and Fitz pats it lightly. "I say we eat, then we'll do the rest. Our girl is starving and since we have guests, I can't feed her my cock. I suppose pot roast will have to do."

"Fitz," Felix sighs in exasperation. "For the love of everything holy…"

"It's okay, Sir." I wink when his eyes flash. "I'll keep him in line until we get our work done."

"I'm holding you to that, Princess."

Rufus frowns and kicks the table. "So fucking unfair they're all taken. I'm registering a complaint."

My crazy tiger looks over with a smug smile. "About that…"

---

1. Exactly
2. Also known as 'Go'

PROBLEM CHILD

FITZ

Not only did I help solve shit for my baby girl, but I even did her punky friend a huge dick-flavored favor. She was *extremely* grateful this morning in the shower and Chessie was similarly happy with me last night. I need to get the two of them in my bed together when we're not all sacked out, but I was waiting until I thought my girl was ready. Given her recent behavior in the boutique, I think it's time. I grin to myself as I walk across campus at a leisurely pace, dreaming up scenarios that make my cock twitch eagerly. A random student gives me an idd look as I whistle a jaunty tune, so I snarl in his direction. It makes him scamper off like prey.

What a fucking waste. At least the rich kids at Apex had a little backbone—Cappie kids are soft as butter.

My two classes this morning were a drag. Not only do Cappie kids have no balls, but their computer science department must have been run by a total moron. None of my advanced kids have a fucking *clue* how to do anything not based in the Erickson Tech OS. Their hacking skills are nil, so they won't be worth spit when they get out of here. No wonder *U&M* is the choice of the geek squad preds. All these fuckwhistles are good for is mid-level management, not actual programming.

That sounds like I care, but I honestly don't. I can revamp my curriculum to allow for their *many* deficiencies and assigning them a bunch of crap they'll struggle with means I can cancel in person classes while they work in the lab. It's exactly what I did this morning so I could take this stroll over the green to study the patterns of the avians overhead while I made my way to the admin building.

Chessie isn't here today, so nothing I do can be linked back to him if I'm caught. Baby Girl had class early with my brother and right about now, she should be in a three hour block with our cheetah. I didn't tell anyone about my plan, but I definitely checked out the schedules on the fridge to make sure no one would get blamed but me. This little stealth mission is all Fitz Khan.

"Here goes nothing," I mutter as I jog up the steps to the entrance.

If Capital Prep is anything like Apex was pre-magic bomb, there's always staff in the main office. However, once you walk past it to the elevator bank, no one's ever watching the other floors. Maintenance and security might take up residence on the back half of the first floor, but those morons are probably just like the dipshits at Apex. They sit in their break rooms and watch TV until someone forces them to get off their ass to do work. That's why it's staffed with lowest tier preds—it's a shit job no one wants.

I give the birds in the office a jaunty wave as I pass the window. They look down their noses at me, but only because I'm still whistling. I don't give a single fuck about their judgmental bullshit, so I push the button for the lift, lifting my arm to pretend to look at my watch. If I'm pressed, I'll say I'm meeting Chessie and it's doubtful anyone will know whether he's supposed to be here or not.

I am *a super genius, even if my girl's the only one who recognizes it.*

Hopping in, I run my finger over the screen that lists the floors and what offices are on them. I don't need to break into the ass-sucking counselor's abode—Ghost Pepper and Frenchie McPout-face have her covered for the moment. Besides, I'm more inter-ested in her digital slime trail than the eyesore she works in. No, I want to worm my way into a bigger preds safe space today: Head-master Bathalzar Slechtsrijven.

None of us have met the pompous ass, but we've all snorted at his pretentious emails. I'm not sure why someone who is supposed to be running this place is never around and doesn't address students or staff in person, but I guarantee his office has something we can use locked away. The bell dings, interrupting my thoughts, and I step off on the fifth floor confidently. My attitude says I belong here and that alone should keep anyone from questioning me.

But there's no one here—not a damn soul.

I pause, taking my phone out of my pocket to turn on the flash-light. Holding it up like I'm trying to get a signal, I watch the screen to see if there are cameras in the waiting room that weren't listed on the school security grid. I looked it up after that night with Dolly in the tunnel, but there was a suspiciously small amount of them. There has to be a secondary grid buried in some subdirectory of the system and until I find it, I'm checking every space I enter.

When I'm satisfied there's nothing to worry about, I cruise past the empty desk of his assistant and down the hall to the double doors that must be his office. My eyes widen as I look at them, unsure how I've gotten so lucky. "What a douche canoe. He has a regular old lock on this place."

The knife Felix always preaches about is clipped to my belt, so I grab it and bend down. Mine isn't so plain, which is why I'm able to pop lock picking tools out of the handle. I make short work of the basic thing and put my tools away. The doors swing open slowly and I stare at the room it reveals. Everything is giant sized, though I suppose that makes sense for a fucking hippo shifter. I flash my phone around before I get too far inside and once I've confirmed this place is clean, I tuck it away.

Wouldn't do to leave evidence lying around by mistake.

"If I were a lazy fuckwad, where would I keep damning evidence?" I tap my fingers against my lips as I study the big hutch against the far wall. I'd lay money that has a TV in it, so not there. The bookshelves are crammed with serious looking tomes of every variety, but they seemed unused. I doubt this jackass has read anything in here; it's probably all decoration. That leaves the cabinets behind his desk and the desk itself, so I stride over to examine them.

My eye twitches as I look at the gorgeous, hand carved piece. The damn thing is made entirely of African blackwood and I'd bet my last dollar it was either a gift from or procured by my dickhole father. Not only is this shit expensive as fuck, it's also a protected species. Some stuffed shirt motherfucker having a desk the size of a goddamn grand piano made out of it is obscene, especially since it looks as if it almost never gets used. Even I know this kind of thing should be in a museum. My idiot sperm donor probably let it go for a favor of some kind years ago—maybe even one that made certain my brothers and I ended up at Apex instead of any other school.

I hate dickweasels like this and I'm not sorry I broke in here now.

"Cabinets first since they aren't making my tiger angry," I say as I whirl around to look at the imposing wooden structures. These have a keypad, so I'll have to do more than a little fiddling with tumblers. I reach into my other pocket and pull out a plastic badge with a specialty chip in it. Waving it in front of the pad, I check to see if its RF signal is corruptible. The small beep tells me it is and I grin. "Child's play."

Taking my phone out again, I remote into my main system and scroll until I find the security grid. Once I have it, I wave the card again and this time, the lock's information pops up on my screen, digits flying by as it calculates the code for me. When it comes up on my screen, I smack my hand on my face in absolute disgust. "One two three four five? Is this moron serious?"

I punch it in with vicious stabs, muttering about the combination on my luggage in a tribute to the fantastic movie Dolly had us watch about space pirates. This entire day has been like a Fitz birthday blowjob full of fun and I get the feeling I'm going to find something amazing to show everyone. The drawers open one by one, showing me files of various types as they slide forward. I kick the ones that look financial closed—I assume he's crooked so I don't care about money laundering—to search for personnel and student files.

"You should have digitized this a long time ago, Hungry Hungry Headmaster. Now I'm going to take pictures of all the dirty secrets and no one can stop me."

Flicking through sections until I find this year, I pump my fist. *Fuck yeah.* The student files are alphabetical by first name—something that is fucking strange *and* works in my favor. It's like I'm being guided by Lady Luck today and I'm going to leave some shit for whatever deity is helping me for sure. Fitz Khan isn't stupid enough to ignore this much goodwill in one damn day. Sorting through until I hit 'T', I sing-song to myself, "Where are you, *Todd?*"

I owe that shitstain a comeuppance for making my baby girl hurt. She might have taken her revenge and I took his fingers, but I'm not *done* with him yet. Call me petty, but causing her ex pain makes me a little giddy. When I find the file, I plop it on the desk and start rifling through it. It looks like a dead end until I hit a contract in the very back of the folder.

"Well, well. Isn't this interesting? The two-fingered twat has been sold off to the new member of the bitch squad. Maybe that's why

Dolly hasn't seen either of them yet?" I snap a photo of the marriage contract between the Maclachlans and douchebag Todd's family, then put everything back in the drawer.

Moving quickly, I go through each Heather's file, then switch the staff files. I take pictures of anything I'm not sure about and slip them all back into place. Sighing, I turn to the huge desk behind me and frown. It's not going to have a keypad and knowing the kind of craftsman who probably made the damn thing, the triggers for the locks won't be obvious. I knew this would be the hardest part, which is why I saved it for last.

I drop to my hands and knees, crawling underneath and start feeling for odd protrusions or switches. It's slow and painstaking—something I'm not made for. Grumbling as I feel my natural hyperactivity start to peak, I close my eyes. Chess and Dolly tell me if I just breathe and try to focus on this one thing, I can keep it together long enough to finish what I'm doing. I don't believe them, but I try anyway as I feel along the wooden furniture.

As if by miracle, I hit a spot near the back corner and all five drawers spring open. *Fitz for the win!*

"Now let's see what kind of treats you have for me, my beauty," I whisper as I scoot out from under the damn thing.

The top drawer is boring—pens and office bullshit. All I find in the next two down are full of extra shirts and snacks. I hit pay dirt in the very last one in the form of a laptop that does not look like the official ones given to us by Capital Prep. In fact, this one looks like a personal system that probably doesn't have much protection. Grinning, I boot it up and flex my fingers.

Here's hoping it's not full of hippo porn.

Whatever It Takes

Delores

Felix drilled us until I almost dropped again, so by the time I changed back into my uniform and found my escort, I was moving like an elderly rabbit. The smiling Captain just adjusted his stride, chatting with me about his new duties with the Aquatic House and in the river that splits the campus. Apparently, the swimming bunch here aren't nearly as shirty as the ones at Apex, though there are a few transfers who still need a poke. He dropped me at the new Shird with a salute and toddled off, grumbling about inspecting House Reptilian's indoor pools before he sailed back across. The words 'sailed back' hit me and I made a mental note to bring up the possibility of an emergency watercraft to the guys later.

Once I got to Costuming, Chess had assignments already handed out, but he'd kept one for me. Our costuming and set design courses are running parallel to the productions for my other classes, so we've got basic ideas of what we'll need to start despite the casting not being finalized. I flipped through my assignments based on the #Viral play, noting which characters I would have to schedule fittings with, then worked on my designs quietly. In

Chess' classes, no one bothered me or any other students—everyone worked and only looked up to get help.

Talk about knowing how to wrangle a group of students—he didn't raise his voice once.

My gentle knight pulled me aside before I left the stage after set design, kissing me breathless. Together, we chuckled about rewarding Fitz for helping Rufus, then I reluctantly walked outside to find a new escort waiting. Surprisingly, this time it's Raina and she's all smiles.

"Miss Dolly!" She hugs me tight before we start towards the dreaded tunnel. "I've missed seeing you, but the Captain says your fluffle takes most meals in your nest."

I blink at her in confusion as I hold my badge up to the scanner and we head inside. "My what?"

The raccoon tilts her head at me. "Your fluffle, Miss Dolly. That is what a family group of bunnies is called. Did you not know that?"

Of course not. I'm as ignorant of prey shit as I am pred shit. Fucking Lucille.

"No, I didn't. The guys have been arguing over whether it's an ambush or a clutch or a clash. Mostly, I ignore their chest beating," I admit with a rueful grin. "Terms don't matter much to me; having people with care about me is the most important thing."

"Aye, that's true. But, if I may say so, *you're* the Queen of that group, Miss Dolly. It should be called *your* term, not theirs." She waits for me to scan us out of the tunnel and I realize she managed to distract me from my nervousness about this stupid tube with ease. "The Captain may refer to us as his crew in public, but I assure, it's *my* gaze in private."

Now I've learned two things within a span of minutes from my masked friend.

"Raina?" I ask as we start across the green.

"Yes, Miss Dolly?"

I look at her seriously. "One, *please* just call me Dolly. You're my friend, not my servant. Two, can I ask you about prey things sometimes? I mean, I know I'm only sort of prey and we don't know why but... I feel like I know nothing about either side of me. It's dangerous."

Her face lights up and she nods enthusiastically. "You absolutely can! I'd be honored, Mi--Dolly. In fact, I can make up cards like the ones Miss Cori gave my men for your history classes."

"I appreciate it, Raina. I'm so glad we became friends in the cafeteria last year—truly. You've been amazing and I haven't taken the time to thank you properly."

We stop in front of the academic building and the raccoon puffs up happily. "You don't owe me anything. You and Monsieur Renard are the kindest preds we know. My gaze will always be loyal to your fluffle." She stops and snaps her small fingers, then digs in her apron until she finds a card. "Oh! I'm supposed to ask a question. Let's see... 'what was the cause of the Great Divide?' That's an easy one, Dolly."

I frown, wondering if the prey are taught different answers than us. "The Great Divide was when shifters and magic users stopped interacting. Magic users were abusing their powers to gain control over many powerful shifters and their families, so we fought until they were forced to go into hiding."

Raina raises a brow, her expression curious, then she flips the card to verify my answer. "Is that what they teach you?"

"Yes?" I reply as I watch her. Her head shakes slowly and she shrugs. "Is it wrong?"

"Maybe not wrong, Dolly, but certainly not accurate. We're taught a much more global picture in our schools, I'm afraid." Her gaze turns fearful as she looks around. "But perhaps we should discuss that at another time."

"Got it." I force a smile and give her a little wave, climbing the steps to head up to Shifter History. The information that the Council is serving us history written by the 'winners' isn't news, but I wonder how much the ignorance preds have about their real history is coming to roost with weird ass magic people blowing up one of our schools.

The main question is: why the fuck now? What kicked this shit off after hundreds of years of nothing?

I don't have that answer, so I just head into class with a frown.

"That's another mark, Miss Drew. How you survived your first year in that hellhole you transferred from is beyond me," Herr Blitzen sneers. His huge body is straining the seams of his dark suit, but unlike my kind dragon, he looks like a stocky goon.

In fact, he looks like someone Bruno would employ. Gross.

Pursing my lips, I force myself to grind out an apology—*again*—as the rest of the class snickers. Most of these 'children of famous people' don't know the answers, either, but they're happy for him to pick on me. The Heathers use it to call out nasty barbs and because the Cappie kids are self-absorbed assholes, they laugh at that, too. Ignoring all of them at once has become the gauntlet I use to meditate away stress.

"She was banging half the staff; that's why," Pink says loudly enough for it to float over the entire classroom. It gets her another cheap laugh and phones all over the room buzz. I'm sure she's uploaded the clip of her voice already with some cheeky hashtag.

"That won't be the case here," Herr Blitzen harrumphs.

Okay, that's it. I'm not letting a middle aged dickwad professor riff off me, too.

I push to my feet, knowing there will be recordings of this before I can finish speaking. Looking out over the room, I let the red bleed into my eyes as my bunny fills my body with strength. My voice is calm, but menacing as I pin everyone—including the shark professor—with my infuriated gaze.

"Despite Heather's inability to do basic math, I was not nor will I ever be, sleeping with half the staff of Apex. My fluffle consists of five men who are my fated mates, so sorry if you were hoping to fill out an application, Prof; I'm full up and you wouldn't make the cut."

His eyes widen and he starts to stomp over to my desk, but I hold up my hand with a crazy smile straight out of Fitz's playbook. "I wouldn't, if I were you. The last Shifter History professor who crossed me hasn't been heard from in a while."

"I knew it," Gold growls under her breath. "Daddy couldn't find him anywhere when we moved to Cappie."

Turning my distinctly unhinged look on her, I just stare until she looks away. "Make no mistake: I am *not* the Delores Drew these girls knew in high school and I'm *not* the one who started Apex with no one by my side. If you're coming for me, I suggest you attend the first Pred Games match Saturday night and see who I am now. That's your one chance to make a better choice."

I watch all the phones lower, making sure I don't back down an inch as I gather my things. Flipping my hair in a Heather-esque move, I stalk over to the door, turning to blow the room a kiss and flip them off before I slam out the door.

Motherfucker that felt good.

The elevator is too slow as I ride down and a small shred of regret creeps in. The guys are going to *kill* me for mentioning Abel, especially after we worked so hard to cover up his death with the explosion. My outburst is one of the things César was working on with me—taming my bunny's fury—and I'm going to get a lecture from him, too. It might have felt great to fuck up all those people, but I'm definitely going to pay on so many levels. I might even—

The phone in my pocket buzzes and I'm so distracted, I pull it out without checking the Caller I.D. before I answer. "Go for Dolly."

"Delores Diamond Drew, that is not how you answer the phone!"

My eyes widen and I almost drop it when I hear her voice. Lucille has been noticeably absent since the guys finagled my early trip here and I was almost convinced she stepped on the wrong toes and someone killed her. *Or was that hoped? Fuck if I know.* I take a deep breath, ratcheting back the temper that I allowed out for my classroom outburst. That won't work with Lucille and I'm not in the mood to add Bruiser to board today.

"Lucille," I purr. "*Please* accept my apologies for the rudeness. Today has been a stressful day and I answered without checking to see who was calling. It won't happen again."

The venom in her voice is palpable. "It had better not because I've seen your little performance today at that low-rent academy."

Holy shit does she have a fucking 'Delores' alert on the Preynet or something? I bet she does.

"Lucille, I—" Before I can respond, she growls into the phone and I fall silent.

"Delores, I *never* thought I'd be in a position to say these words and I'm furious to lose a perfectly good yacht over it. However… today you were the perfect image of what a Rostoff should be." She sighs heavily and I hear her sipping a drink, so that must have physically pained her to say. "Your grandfather texted me to pass on his approval. You'll find a large bonus in your account from the family coffers."

I blink, unsure what the hell I'm going to say. Dmitri's dirty money is *not* something I want and I sure as hell don't need his approval. I don't even want Lucille's fucking praise and I've figured out just how much I like that shit lately. Her words just make my skin crawl and I shiver as I stare at the phone.

"Delores, are you there? You'd better not have hung up on me, you little—"

"No, Lucille. I'm sorry. I lost service in the elevator for a moment," I lie smoothly. "But I appreciate your call. I hadn't heard from you in so long I was concerned. I almost checked in with Mattie to confirm your safety."

Her scoff is incredulous. "Never be worried about me, my chunky lagomorph. Lucille Rostoff Drew is a force to be reckoned with, not a tragic headline. I had Council business to attend to and the renovation of Apex is more complicated than we assumed. Those things are far more important than verifying my disappointing progeny is alive."

And there's the real Lucille.

"I understand. In the future, I'll remember that." I look around, hoping to see my next escort here early, but there's no one here. I don't want to stand around until the stupid appointment with Coach Cuntface, so I'm going to head over to the Admin building alone. "Is there anything else I can do for you, Lucille?"

This time, her voice carries a threat and its unmistakable. "You chose to enter the Games with our name, Delores. Your father, grandfather, and I will not tolerate a loser wearing our name in public. Whatever it takes, you will win that match or they won't know where *you* went afterward. Do you understand?"

I swallow hard, biting my lip until it bleeds. Coach Z has been working with me and I'm doing well, but I don't know shit about my opponents. The rosters for each team aren't released until *after* the first match of the season to prevent 'unsportsmanlike conduct' in the pre-season. It's code for murder and maiming, but no one seems to bat a lash. However, my mother just made it very clear that if I don't win, she'll have me dispensed with.

"Yes, Lucille," I murmur, working hard to keep the wobble out of my voice. "I understand."

"Good. I look forward to seeing your victory."

She hangs up abruptly and I dig my shades out of my purse so no one can see the uncertainty in my eyes as I walk across the green to the offices. If her goal was to throw me off my game, she's succeeded for now. The great manipulator knows exactly how to push my buttons so I lose my confidence and my strength.

That's because I wasn't lying to Rockland last time we spoke: Lucille does not make idle threats.

FIREWORK

DELORES

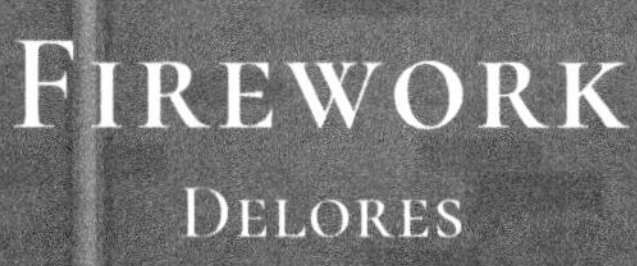

AFTER MY FIRST 'APPOINTMENT' WITH THE DAMN NOSY COACH, I know for certain we have to put a stop to her shit. She started out fairly normal, asking questions about my childhood and my parents. Despite wanting to out Lucille and Bruno, I kept my answer vague so she couldn't play back any hidden recordings to use for notes. I'm already dancing on a wire with my mother, especially considering my pimp grandfather has taken notice of me. Rockland is stupid enough to give hints about her work in progress to press or online sycophants—any of which could find their way back to my sociopathic family.

I did my best to shut down like Fitz docs and give her nothing but a blank wall, even when she probed into my emergence and near-death experience at the Vom Prom. Truthfully, I'm neither hurt nor angry at my old life anymore. The way it happened damaged me, but finding out where I stood was more valuable than any other lesson before it. If I'd come out a weak pred, I might have stayed with my sexually incompetent ex and treacherous friends for a long, miserable life.

But Rockland doesn't need to know any of that. I'm not on board with my likeness being used for her personal profit, no matter how she justifies it.

My reticence aggravated her eventually, though, and she made tea, sitting a mug of what she called 'healing herbs' next to me with a fake smile. Unfortunately for the conniving vulture, the Heathers taught me not to accept drinks from people I don't know unless they're sealed or prepared where I can see every step. Using my phone, I texted the guys to get her out of the office. *It says a lot that no one even asked why.*

Once she excused herself to check on the fire alarm that suddenly started buzzing, I poured the tea into my empty water bottle and gathered my things. I figured Aubrey would know who to send this to in D.C. He took a position working at the National Library one day a week while we're at Cappie to get us access to its archives and files. I knew he'd probably met someone who could analyze this to see what the hell this woman tried to drug me with.

It'd be fucking great if people would quit trying to poison, maim, assault, or kill me for a day.

Her absence made it easy to scurry out without her knowing and I headed home with Bowser on heels. He left me groaning about my homework load, off to see Raina and their gaze. I, however, went inside and barely had time to eat and finish my work before I fell asleep at the table. When I woke up again, it was to my alarm this morning and a flurry of texts in the group chat letting me know where everyone would be today.

Which brings me to the class I'm currently tuning out while I think about all the damn shit I have to deal with between now and Sunday night. Professor Kamara Rakoto is lithe and vicious looking in her pinstriped suit and Edna Mode glasses. I've only had one another class with her, but I can tell she's a big cat and that she takes her subject matter *very* seriously. She expects the students to as well, but her teaching methods don't make it easy. International Diplomacy should be pretty interesting, but so far she's had us outlining chapters and memorizing by-laws. It's as dry as can be and as tired as I am, I'm struggling to focus.

I almost cry with joy when a message pops up on my tablet.

Ru-Ru: How's your day so far, Dollybear? Coco and I are ready to rock your first Game!

Coco: Rufus had the best idea. You're gonna love it.

Dolly: Ugh, if I make it to Saturday. This class is gonna kill me.

Ru-Ru: Diplomacy? But it's a blast. You debate and argue; I love that shit.

Dolly: Not in my class. We've done nothing but take notes and outline for two days.

Coco: What the hell? Professor Rakoto is pretty popular as far as we've heard. No one would like her if that's how it always goes.

Dolly: Great. Lucky me. Somehow, I got the pod person version of the cool teacher.

Ru-Ru: We'll look into it, Queen D. If there's a story, I'll sniff it out.

Coco: Are you free to do your hair tonight? We can come over for bitch, bleach, and bad movies.

Dolly: Definitely. I have to get it done before the match. Felix is supposed to go out with me afterwards.

Ru-Ru: Uh... are you sure that's a good plan? I mean, the Games are... feral. It gets preds all sexy and sweaty and ready to fuck.

Coco: That's why it's a good idea, Ru-Ru!

Dolly: I probably should have remembered
what Fitz did, huh? Way to be naive, Dolly.

Ru-Ru: At least now you'll be motivated to
win by something other than your bitch
mother.

I'm about to snark back when a loud roar echoes in the room. My head flies up and I see the boring professor with angry golden eyes I recognize even from this distance. *Holy shit, Rakoto is a tiger. Does that mean…?* Swallowing hard, I watch her prowl from the front of the room to my desk where she glares a hole in my head. I click the screen of my tablet off, then turn to look up at her with a sheepish expression. Even if I'm not a fan of her method of getting my attention, I have to try not to piss off every teacher I have.

"Miss Drew. I know you have a different expectation of classroom behavior since you attended that *other school* last year, so I'll give you this *one* chance to redeem yourself." Her red lips curve over pointed incisors as she looks at me. "You'll write five pages on the original treaty of Bloodstone Isle and have it in my email by Sunday at 11:59 p.m. Otherwise, I'll write you up."

Is this woman kidding me? How the hell am I supposed to get that done along with all my other homework and *the first pred Games match?*

Gritting my teeth, I nod and mutter a 'thank you' loud enough for her to hear before ducking my head again. We didn't find anything suspicious on this woman in our background checks, but no one mentioned her being a goddamn *tiger,* either. I mean, I'm pretty sure there are some tiger ambushes across the world who don't belong to the Raj, but it's not many and I doubt someone from one would be working at this university.

No, Kamara Rakoto was placed here for a reason long ago and now she'll be the perfect asset for the twins' father.

Frustration floods me and I almost bang my head on the desk. This whole 'chaos in a bottle' attack shit is fucking up my entire life and I'm getting sick of it. I stare at my tablet for a minute, then I open the outline for the boring ass shit she's teaching. My lack of focus is gone—it's been replaced by anger and determination. The minute this stupid class is over, I'm heading to Rennie's Shakespeare class where I know he'll let me work on whatever the hell I please. I'll get her stupid punishment done today and then rip someone's freaking head off at PG practice.

That idea makes me grin and I pick up my e-Pencil, scribbling notes about the Canine-Feline Declaration of 1909.

This bunny always feels better when she has a plan.

As predicted, my soothing gargoyle allowed me to work on the ridiculous paper as long as I promised to read our assignment with him this weekend. I enjoy hearing his deep, accented voice read lyrical prose and I plan to make my grumpy dragon sit with us while he does. The solution makes me smile, especially since I have that essay ticked off and now I can vent my fury out at practice.

I guess Fitz and Felix were right about my participation having unexpected benefits.

Striding into the airlock with the quietest quokka, Banjo, I gather all the fury and rage that has been building up over the past week. Apex was a nightmare before the mystery and murder started, but since the night of the explosion, things were mostly calm. I missed my friends and my guys, Lucille was a shadowy threat, but I had time to breathe. Since the moment I left for Capital Prep, the universe has been piling obstacles and assholes in my path like I'm cursed. I'm fucking tired of it and tired of being nice.

I slam my badge against the second scanner and stalk down the tube at a rapid clip. Banjo is probably having trouble keeping up, but I don't care right now. All I want to do is get changed and climb in the ring with whomever Zhenga pairs me up with today. It's the first time we'll be doing full contact battles and my adrenaline is pumping like a freight train in my veins.

No matter who it is, I'm ready to rumble.

Banjo waves when we hit the grass and I give him a small smile before heading into the locker room. Luckily for me, Coach Z banned the cheer squad from using our facilities outside of the field. I assume Felix helped her with that blatant middle finger to the corpse licker; this arena is here due to Khan machinations. Her dimwits are relegated to changing over in the Leonidas stadium and walking to the practice field. It protects me while I'm naked, at least, even if it won't help me anywhere else.

"Your uniforms are being delivered to your dorms today," Zhenga calls from the front of the room. "They are made to fit only you, per our measurement session. You will receive a new one after every match as long as you remain eligible to compete. That means you must be academically, physically, and competitively eligible to participate that week. Athletes must have a three-point-five or higher, be uninjured, and stay in the rankings. You are also prohibited from competing if you are on any kind of behavioral probation. Keep your noses clean, ladies."

I feel her eyes on me and I sigh into my locker. She's probably trying to warn me about the Heathers. They'll be subject to the same rules on the squad, so they know they can fuck with me if they make me retaliate to their shit. *One fucking day. Just one day without bullshit would be fantastic.* Pulling on my new team practice gear that has appeared in my locker, I wing a thanks to the sky that each piece is vacuum sealed in plastic. After the tea fiasco, I'm not willing to take anything, even clothing, someone could have messed with.

This level of paranoia is unfair. I should be partying and having fun in college, not fending off psychos and magic wielding freaks.

Stowing my shit in the locker, I pause to text Fitz to make sure the electronic lock can't be breached while I'm away. He doesn't have classes today, so I know he'll be on the sidelines with Felix and the guys team in the main stadium, but he'll have his phone. I almost wish he would come to our practice today, but I know he'll be at the game Saturday. He can witness the fruits of his friend's training again that night. Tonight is supposed to be Felix's and I don't want him to barge into our plans—whatever they are.

"Let's hit the field!" Coach Z shouts and I rise from the bench, letting the bunny inside fill me with her pent-up emotions.

It's time to burn off the fury that is consuming me in a sanctioned fight. I just hope Zhenga hasn't put me against someone who can't handle what I've got roiling inside of me.

I don't know if I can leash her now that I let her out.

Legend

Delores

"Miss Drew, you'll be fighting Jaiyana. Selene, you'll face Braylynn. Roswitha and Allizia. Kyaw and Philippa. Helena and Beatrice. Absinthe and Norma Rae. Francesca and Ashlée. Elizabetta and Denita."

I watch as Zhenga hands out the assignments, feeling panic roil in my gut next to the anger. Jaiyana is the *last* person I'd want to have a practice match with because of her species. The crocodile in her already triggers my memories of Bruno and though Selene's jaguar would be a keen second, I have less fear of Lucille than my father.

At least, physically.

Bruno has never pretended to like or need me for anything. In fact, his cruelty was almost worse than Lucille's because it was obvious he didn't give a single fuck if I lived or died—not once. Lucille doesn't love me, but she had a use for me, so I felt something from her besides hatred. My father hasn't looked at me any different than he would dog shit on his shoes my whole life. When he meted out his punishment, I could *feel* the pleasure he took in making me bruise and wail. I'm nothing to him and that bone-deep fear of not knowing how far he'd go is edging through me now.

"As you know, at college level, the Games are *not* the same as what you watch in the pro leagues. You may not kill or permanently maim another participant. If the refs believe you cannot control your beast, they *will* call the match and give the victory to your opponent. Cheating is closely monitored, so don't think you can get away with claiming you didn't 'mean' to blind someone." The lioness pauses and gives each one of us a serious look. "If I think you'll be a liability in the match, I'll bench you and hold new tryouts for your spot. Do you understand?"

"Yes, Coach!" the team choruses.

I catch her eyes, nodding as she looks at me curiously. She has to know I don't have any known rivals in this group and I'll do the best I can. Much like her competing in the male Games as the only female ever, I'll be the only prey animal to ever grace the college field. It's going to draw a big crowd—especially if Lucille's reaction to my status can be trusted—so Zhenga's coaching career could also be on the line. I've got a lot riding on this damn thing and if that's not enough pressure, I know it will set the tone for what people can and cannot do to me at Cappie.

You can do this, Dolly.

I hear a couple hoots from the stands as I take my place in the circle to face Jaiyana. My eyes flick over and I see Rufus and Cori clapping in the stands. Their support helps ground me and I turn to look at my opponent as she gets ready. Jaiyana is tall, broad shouldered, and has glittering dark eyes common to her species. Her long black hair is pulled back in a tightly bound French braid and pinned up so it can't be used against her. We aren't much different in height, but her muscles are toned and tight like she's been training for this most of her life. Given her father's career in the Games, I'd bet she has.

"Ready?" Zhenga says as she holds up a hand. Our eyes meet hers and she grins. "Fight!"

Jaiyana advances, clearly favoring the aggressive opening. I grapevine along the edge of the circle as I watch her, learning the walk her body moves and looking for weaknesses. A low rumble comes out of her throat when she realizes I'm not meeting her in the middle and I see a flash of the slitted gaze of her reptile in her eyes. We're not in the water, so she doesn't have the advantage of depriving me of oxygen that way, but I see her fists clench. She'll throttle me the second she gets her hands on me.

I'm faster and I know if I use that to keep her moving, she can't get me in the barrel grip.

"Are you scared, little bunny?" she sneers.

I hear Selene and the other girls snorting from their places in the line up. They're not really my enemies yet, but if I beat this girl, they will be. No Queen Bees like seeing their brethren knocked off their pedestals. My lips curve as I shrug at her, noting the way she holds one shoulder lower. *An old injury, perhaps? Noted.* The croc steps forward, pushing into the circle further so she can get within reach. She's hoping to intimidate me, throw me off by being as big and aggressive as possible.

Unfortunately for Jaiyana, I'm very used to more vicious preds than her taking this tack. Lucille has always loved playing with her food and Bruno delights in pain. "No. I'm wondering why you haven't jumped in if you're feeling so damn froggy. Worried you'll lose to a lowly prey animal?"

My words have the intended effect because she leaps into motion, lunging for me in a smooth move. But I dance away, letting claws slip from my fingers as I whirl behind her. As soon as she hits the ground, I take a swipe at her leg and she snarls as blood drips down her tanned leg. She's rolled over to sweep the uninjured leg out within seconds, catching one of my ankles. I stumble, barely keeping my balance as I try to get out of her reach.

Jaiyana has an advantage on the ground, like in water, but I have the edge on my thumpers.

When she doesn't knock me down, I hear both clapping and booing from the peanut gallery. I don't let it bother me as I crack my neck and start circling again. I'm not sure how I'm going to tap her out; she's much stronger than me and I can't slit her damn throat. Pushing that thought out of my head, I take a breath and let my bunny fill me more, knowing my eyes are red and I'm probably sprouting fur. I know I can't open the cage entirely because I'm prohibited from the ending she wants, but I need her strength to defeat this chick. By the time I've got my brain settled, I feel the hairs on my neck stand up and I know she's coming.

My legs flex as I leap out of the way of the charging crocodile. As soon as I land, I turn and send a spinning kick at her face. It connects, knocking her almost out of the ring with the force. My face gets redder as I remember how much more psi I have in my legs when the rabbit is loose. I need to be careful. Sucking in a breath as Jaiyana comes at me again, I duck to the left to avoid her right hook. An uppercut from my left rings her bell again and she screams in frustration.

Anger makes you sloppy.

Fitz's voice in my head helps me stay present as the stocky shifter grabs my arms. Suddenly, her clothes tear and she's half-shifted, just like Bruno. Fear makes my heart race and my eyes widen as ears, tail, and more fur pop out. I'm losing control quickly and I have to take her down before I get myself in serious fucking trouble. I grip her arms back, digging claws into her scaly skin. Mine are much longer and sharper, so she lets out a loud growl of pain.

"You bitch! That will scar," Jaiyana hisses.

My eyes narrow at her and I keep my expression calm as I grit out, "You'll live. You're a fucking alpha and the heir to your family. Why weren't you at Apex?"

She gives me a toothy grin and I'm reminded that crocs have the strongest bite of any animal on the planet. "Small pond, big name isn't how the Faezs roll, appetizer. Plus, Cappie has the best Games team. Now, where do you want it?"

I snarl back at her, letting go with my left hand to whip it out in a backhand to her jaw. She didn't expect that, so she reels back and I'm able to scamper back enough to break her grip. "I think you should be asking me that question."

"My father—"

Fuck that. I spent my life hearing that from my ex-friends.

Ignoring her sentence, I plant my back foot, readying for her to spring forward as she drones on about her stupid parent. When she gets within range, I lift my leg and kick as hard as I can. She goes flying across the ring and lands in a crumpled heap before she can even finish her list of shit her dad did. Wiping my forehead with the back of my hand, I mutter, "... is *not* in this fucking ring."

Zhenga looks at me in shock, blowing her whistle and jogging over to the prone reptile to check on her. Whooping from the stands tells me my friends are going nuts, but I'm too numb to check. I let out a long shuddering breath, putting my hands on my knees and bending over. I barely got my fear of Bruno under control to handle this, but if I've really hurt Jaiyana my Games career is over.

I doubt that would have been so at Apex, but Cappie is so much softer than my old school.

Warm hands land on my shoulders and I whirl around, using my elbow to hit the person who touched me without permission. A groan and a soft growl get my attention, so I open my eyes, startled to find Felix and his yellow eyed tiger doubled over behind me.

"Shit. Shit. I'm sorry, Sir," I pant as I stand up. I think my arms might be bleeding a little and I'm definitely bruised, but I'm not as hurt as Jaiyana for sure.

Felix gives me a heated look when he finally catches his breath. "That was a foul, Princess. No striking the ref."

Giving him a sheepish look, I walk over to look up at him shyly. "Instinct. I was trying to come down from… this and someone touched me."

"Fair enough," he says as he grimaces. "We want you aware and fighting back, so I'll let that one slide. You did well, Princess. Fitz will *love* the video I took."

I wrinkle my nose and snort. "He'll be putting it in the spank bank the second you hit send, you know. I'm surprised he's not here."

"He said 'It's your turn tonight, bro. Chess and I are reaping the spoils tomorrow when she kicks someone's ass' and then sent me packing from practice." Felix looks amused, but we both know Fitz isn't kidding. "So I came to see how you're doing."

"I did okay," I say with a sigh. "But Jaiyana was sort of a bad first try. Her shifter form makes my bunny angry and scared because of…"

His expression darkens. "Your father. You know we're going to kill that bastard, right?"

My eyes dance. "Only if you get to him first. Now help me hobble to the showers, Professor. As long as I didn't cripple that bitch, I have to get these injuries healed for tomorrow night."

"I suggest soaking in the big tub when you get home. You need to be mobile for tonight, Princess. I won't take it easy on you just because you had a scrap today."

Tilting my head, I arch a brow at him. "You still haven't told me where we're going, Sir. How will I know how to dress?"

He shrugs, his eyes dark as he wraps an arm around me. "Casual is fine. No jewelry, nothing flashy."

"Mmmhmm. Shoes?"

"Walkable, not tottering nightmares."

I stop, narrowing my eyes at the smirking tiger. "If you're taking me rock climbing or some physical bullshit, I'm going to yank your tail as hard as I can."

His laughter rolls over my skin and he squeezes me lightly as we walk into the empty locker room. "No, nothing like that. Don't worry; I'll feed you and then we'll have a fucking amazing time, I promise."

Letting go of him, I hop over to my locker and grab my shit, winking at him over my shoulder. "I'm going to hold you to that."

Play With Fire

Felix

It took immense control to leave her in the locker room to change. My tiger has been pacing for months because he knows my twin and Chess have been with our girl while we have not. It's not that we can't share as much as the alpha instinct; I'm the Raj and I should have gone first. But that's my own fault for pushing Dolly away for so long. All my brothers have experienced more with her than I and the only obstacle was my own stubborn need to punish myself.

It was hard to admit Fitz has been right about letting go of the past for years.

Shaking my head, I make my way to the library to mentally prepare for tonight. One of the Captain's crew will be there to escort her back and I know she'll head straight for her room to get ready. Dolly's consistent ability to distribute her affection to all of us equally is one of the things that finally pushed through my shields. She really cares for each of us in a unique way and makes sure no one feels left out no matter what. It never comes off as forced or fake—despite being so young, our bunny sees us as individuals and treats us accordingly.

Of course, the way she's helped my twin open up and show the real man underneath is part of why I like her, too.

My smile is genuine as I wave my hand at the scanner on the back door. I hadn't realized how little this happened before she showed up and blew a hole in our carefully regimented group brooding. But now, it's coming more easily and more often. Dolly's effect on even the stubborn ass dragon echoes through our new 'nest.' Renard has it decorated to the nines, Chess fills the air with delicious food smells, and Aubrey doesn't snarl when Fitz bounces around like a hopped up rave kid. Her presence eases us all and I take great pleasure in watching it.

"Felix, is that you?"

I grin as Aubrey calls out from the living room. He's taken to spending more time in our gathering space on off days than in the library—another change I approve of. As much as the ancient lizard and I butt heads, even I realized he worked far too hard as a result of outliving his past mistakes. "Working from home, Lord Draconis?"

He rolls his eyes at me from where he's sprawled on the sunken couch with his laptop and a scotch. Jinx is sitting above his head, purring like an outboard as the dragon stabs at his keyboard. "Fuck off, Raj. How did the practice match go?"

My eyes darken as I remember and he laughs in a matching tone. "Our girl conquered her fear and took down a crocodile. It will probably cause her problems later, but I could see how much it boosted her confidence when she won. She should do well tomorrow if she can keep that focus."

"Shit," he mutters. "I bet it was hot as hell, but if it was Hercules' kid…"

I grimace and nod. "There'll be videos of it. He'll come down on his kid like a hammer and practices will start being dangerous for the Princess."

Aubrey sits up and pulls off his glasses, cleaning them on his shirt as he sighs. "We knew this could happen when we encouraged her to join the team. If she did well, she'd shake up the status quo like Zhenga did and it would make her a target for the bigger assholes."

"But it should ward off the lesser preds. They won't want to mess with her for fear of getting beat by prey or taking the chance away from one of the head bitches," I finish for him. "Either way, we knew there was a down side, but we had to take a gamble."

"Who could have predicted the counselor bitch coming out of nowhere to add another enemy to the board?" Renard walks in with a smile and drops onto the couch in a boneless pose. "Hopefully, Chess will have news that the gangster's uncle is working his magic. The other professors are child's play next to that."

I frown. "We know the History dick is messing with her. Who else?"

He shrugs and leans his head back. "She's certain she won't get any good roles from her theater classes because the jaguar who teaches it must be linked to Hecate and her kid. The tiger from her diplomacy class had a good reputation when Fitzgerald checked her out, but *ma petite* came to my class with a punishment after only two sessions. I'm uncertain what reasons the latter two have, but Dolly will struggle this semester."

Son of a bitch. When I find out who's pulling these strings, I'm going to rip them to pieces.

"Perhaps the show tonight will discourage some of these syco-phants from continuing their bullshit," I muse. Stroking my chin, I let a hungry smirk take over my face as I look at my friends. "I'll have Chess tip the media off beforehand."

The dragon narrows his gaze at me, looking suspicious. "Where in the hell do you plan on taking the lunchable for a date that the paparazzi will follow?"

I snort. "My dear spicy gecko…it doesn't matter where I'm going. If I'm there, the cameras will show up. This is one situation where it is absolutely good to be the King." They both roll their eyes at me and I shrug. "Plus, I might even please my asshole father enough to send another bonus. I'm sure he'd be pleased if it bought our girl another crown."

That makes them grin broadly and I wink as I leave them, heading for the room Renard cleaned out for my ambush. It was an office before, but when we decided that everyone staying in one place was better, his crew of prey animals took care of it within a day. I shut the door and pull out the clothes I plan on wearing, making a note to myself that I can offer Dolly's friends a private place in our townhouse just over the academy border. They seemed unhappy with their dorms and if they're good at sneaking, they can get in and out without anyone knowing.

A rainbow haired bear isn't exactly stealthy, but we did make our secret entrance in a camera blindspot. That should help.

Now I have an unorthodox date to get ready for and a bunny to surprise.

Time to get clean before I get dirty.

WHEN I EMERGE FROM THE ROOM, THE REST OF THE GUYS ARE sitting in their usual spots trying to pretend they aren't waiting for Dolly and I to leave. She's not out of her room yet, so I stride over and give them all a derisive look. "Full house, tonight, hmm?"

Fitz laughs and slaps his leg dramatically. "Very funny, bro. Now tell us where you're taking my baby girl. Cross my heart, I won't shadow you."

Uh-huh.

"No way, jackass. You're practically stuck to the Princess with a magnet. I was amazed you didn't intrude on her date with Chess as it is."

Aubrey grins and shrugs. "He's easily distracted with shiny things."

"Ha! That's fancy talk for 'Broody McFrenchKiss got him drunk and we challenged him to a Smash Preds tourney.' They *tricked* me," Fitz whines and pouts a little as he looks at me. "You won't do that, will you, bro?"

I arch a brow. "No. I'm ordering you to give us some fucking space this time."

His face falls and though I didn't put the whole 'Raj' thing behind the command, he knows I'm serious. My brother isn't actually *trying* to invade Dolly's dates because he's jealous; he's simply so excited about our family that he can't help himself. He's always been the most social of the three of us and our exile was hard on him. "Fine. No stalking for Fitzy. Buzz kill."

Chess scoots over, always ready to soothe his tantrums. "Baby, I'll keep you busy while our girl and our king have a little alone time. Remember… he's been alone the longest now that we know those two are bonking."

Renard snorts and opens his mouth to retort, but he's cut off when Dolly comes out of her room.

She took my sparse information and ran with it, donning tight black satin jeans and a vivid purple halter. The short lace shrug she has on doesn't cover her tatts and her belly ring sparkles in the lights overhead. I grin, letting my eyes skate down her legs to her feet, noting the spike-heeled boots that lace up to her knees. Her hair is in wild rainbow waves around her face, accenting the dark smoky look of her makeup. Her friends come bounding in behind her, winking at me before they wave and head for the back door.

Of course the Terror Twins were involved in this badass look our bunny is sporting.

"Who let them in?" I ask, waiting for Dolly to approach.

She rolls her eyes and walks over to me, then does a little twirl. "Don't be a grouch, Sir. Did we do a good job with the outfit?"

Reaching out, I haul her close and place a light kiss on her forehead. Her honeysuckle and candy scent makes me smile. I murmur low, "You look positively edible, Princess. Are you ready to go?"

Dolly nods, pulling back to note my simply black dress pants and black oxford. "Curious as hell, but definitely ready."

Giving my twin the middle finger before he can ask, I take her arm and wave to the others. "Don't wait up."

"Hey! She has a match tomorrow, dickhead. Don't you dare—"

Fitz's voice is cut off when we walk out the back door and head for the parking lot past the Shird. Dolly snickers as she looks up at me, her lightly tanned skin almost glowing in the moonlight. "He's going to worry about that all night, you know."

"He let you fight a bunch of magical hooded freaks with him. Fitz is the *last* person who gets to comment on your safety." I pause for a moment when she frowns, then add, "Besides, he knows he can track the car and phones. Plus he has a fucking satellite, Princess. He'll be fine."

"Oh, I forgot about that. You're right." Dolly beams up at me, her concerns gone.

Aubrey owes me a hundred bucks; I knew *she realized how closely he tracks her.*

PULLING INTO THE DARK PLAZA IN MY PHANTOM, I LOOK OVER AT Dolly with a satisfied smirk. Her expression is confused. Last time we were here, we absolutely refused to go into *Inky Depths* until we did research on its ties to the underworld. This time, I'm bringing her here on purpose.

"I thought you said this place is controlled by Lucille's family and we couldn't go in?" Dolly frowns and tilts her head at me. "Now we're here for a date?"

Chuckling, I take her hand and kiss her knuckles lightly. "Princess, I know the others took you to fancy places, dancing, or quaint picnics. But unlike them, I've had a hard time fighting the urge to let you spread your wings and I want that to change. I may be able to issue demands in the dark…" She grins and I can see her flushing. "…but I need to show you that I trust you to be a part of the team."

"You just said Fitz let—"

"Did a good job of riling you up, didn't I?" My eyes dance as I nip her fingertip and she squirms in her seat. "I said that to make you huffy and it worked. But we researched this place after we left and what Fitz found was that it's not what it seems."

"It's not a dive bar?" Her expression is disbelieving as she unbuckles her seatbelt. "Cause it really looks like a skeezy dive bar."

"Not *just* a dive bar," I reply as I open my door and hop out. Walking over to her side, I open her door and wait for her to emerge, all shapely curves and legs as she rises to stand in front of me. My cock notices, but I shake my head to clear it. "The bar is a front for the illegal Pred fighting rings downstairs."

Her eyes widen and she throws her arms around my neck in excitement. "We're going to an illegal fight? That's so fucking *cool*! What kind of fight? Is it bare knuckle or are there weapons or…"

I cut her off before we start for the door, holding one finger up. "Princess, I need you to breathe. I'm not sure what they'll be running tonight, but I do need you to promise me a few things. Otherwise, I'll never survive this shit. Got it?"

"Negotiate with me, my King. I'm ready to plead my case." Her eyes twinkle as she puts her hand on her hip, arching her back a little in a move that probably works on my brother.

Hell, if it wasn't so dangerous in this joint, it'd probably work on me; who am I kidding?

"One, do you have your knife?" She nods and I frown, wondering where the hell it's stowed. "Two, I need you to stay where I can see you, no matter what. Even if I'm not close by, I have to be able to see where you are."

"Got it. Stabby weapon, stay in sight. Anything else?"

Rolling my eyes, I sigh heavily. I have to be crazy doing this shit, but I'm still going to have Fitz tip the media off once we're inside. "We see the soft Dolly at home, but here? You need to be Delores Drew, heir to Lucille Drew's throne. No mercy, no favors, and no quarter—otherwise, there could be trouble."

Her bright red lips spread into a knowing grin and I watch as her posture changes immediately. The warmth in her expression and tilt of her head turn regal as she gazes back at me with an arched brow. "Like so?"

She looks like she'd stab a bitch with her heel, so yeah, that's what I asked for.

"Excellent. Come inside with me and we'll see what trouble we can get into." Taking her arm, I transition to my own 'Khan heir' deportment as we stalk to the entrance of the bar quickly. I open the door for her, letting her make the entrance I knew she would before I step in behind her.

"Your Majesty," the bartender dips his head and I sneer.

"Where are the rings?" I bark without acknowledging his misstep. My father would have him killed for calling me that and most non-Khans know it. It's his favorite trap and most cruel test of loyalty—which King do they acknowledge.

"Down the hall, through the curtain, and take the elevator to the ground floor," someone offers from the crowd.

Dolly doesn't speak, just surveys the room as I give them a sharp nod. Once we move, the noise resumes in the bar and I lead her down the cramped hallway. "See what I mean?" I whisper.

"Yep. Act like royalty and be feared like royalty," she responds. "I know what to do."

Good thing she does because I'm not sure I know what the fuck I'm doing at all.

Animals

Delores

Felix couldn't have surprised me with his date choice if he'd donned a grass skirt and done the hula. I mean, he's *always* the one bitching about letting me put myself in danger. This is decidedly *not safe* and our lack of backup makes it even more dodgy. But he looked sincere when he said he wants to trust me, so I'm following his rules for the moment. I don't mind his bossy, royal 'Sir' stuff if he's not being a dick and the dominant thing is fucking *hot* in the bedroom.

Control is Felix's weakness, and for now, he can have it.

We step into the elevator and my tiger cuts his eyes up briefly to let me know there's a camera in here. I clocked it when I walked in because Fitz has been teaching me about stealth and being aware of my surroundings is lesson one. We haven't gotten to lesson two yet because he's waiting until I've honed my skills to his satisfaction and, much like his brother's bossiness, I like Fitz the spicy teacher. Nodding imperceptibly, I move closer, facing my date and straightening his collar. It doesn't need it, but he takes that moment to lean in and brush his lips against my ear.

"You need to behave down here, Princess. Remember, I don't need saving, even if it looks like I do. Everything has a purpose."

My facial expression doesn't give away what he said, instead I tip my head back and close my eyes as if he's being naughty. That's a much more interesting picture for anyone watching security, even if it goes public somehow. I don't know what Felix thinks we're going to find out in this place, but there has to be more to our trip than letting me put on a show for a bunch of criminals. I turn my head to nuzzle his cheek briskly so I can reply.

"I'll do everything exactly how Lucille would; cross my heart."

That covers a broad spectrum of crimes and punishment, but he doesn't need to know that yet.

"Good girl," he says before his teeth sink into my earlobe firmly.

I shudder, cursing the effect of his tone on my barely there under-garments. My pants are tight enough that any friction will drive me crazy, but he's not even touching the money spots. *Evil, evil king.* Pulling back, I pretend to air kiss his nose and stand tall as we reach the bottom floor where the doors open. Before I move, I scan the scene while Felix holds the doors open, noting everything I can until I stride out. His lips curl for a moment, then he offers his arm as we walk into a cavernous underground with gambling tables, a bar, TVs hanging from the ceiling, and an enormous sunken area halfway to the other end that must be the fighting ring.

This place runs under the bar and most of the parking lot outside, I realize suddenly. They've put a strip mall full of seedy shit on top of their highly illegal operations underground. No one would assume this place is down here unless they knew and the amount of money lying on tables, being counted by roving cashiers or bet on the fights has to be astronomical. There are easily three hundred slimy assholes—both rich and poor—assuaging their addictions in this weird cave of vice.

I feel eyes on me as we walk past the roulette table, so I look over at Felix with a haughty smirk. "Where shall we start tonight, darling?"

The yellow of his tiger flashes at me, and he cocks his head to the ring. "I'm feeling bloodthirsty tonight, Princess."

Something about the way he responds trips my wires, but I nod, allowing him to lead me over to a booth by the entrance. Felix arches a brow at the cougar running the gate and the cat swallows hard, scrambling out of his chair to find someone else. I'm not sure what's going on yet, but apparently, lowly mountain cats don't serve the king.

"Excuse me."

I whirl around, my eyes narrowed as I hear a leopard purr behind us. It takes a lot to keep my face from showing relief when it's not Lucille, but the woman looks like a distant relative. Knowing I can't show any fear, I glare at her as if I'm going to attack. "You dare sneak up behind us like a coward? Do you know who we are?"

Felix pats my hand on his arm, giving the slinky cat a magnanimous smile. "Forgive my Princess. Her temper is genetic, I'm afraid."

The leopard nods, looking suspicious before she replies. "I am aware of your reputation, Prince Felix. We have not had the pleasure of your presence before, nor your girlfriend, Miss…"

"Drew," I reply in a tone that would make my mother proud. "My name is Delores Rostoff Drew—something you'd do well to remember."

That gets her attention. Her eyes widen and she bows her head briefly. "Of course you are. My apologies, Miss. I did not intend any offense to you or the Prince. Please pass on my sincere gratitude to your families for my position here."

Our families?

If my tiger is feeling uneasy, he doesn't show it all. Instead, he gives her a piercing stare as he replies. "I would like to join the card—next. I'm feeling spry tonight and I haven't had a good workout since Bloodstone. I believe you can make that happen?"

My entire body tenses, but I cover it by leaning into him with what I hope is a vicious smirk. He didn't tell me he was going to jump in the fucking *ring* with a bunch of psycho criminals! How am I supposed to keep my reaction to that bottled up? I feel the leopard looking at me, and I know she's watching to see if this is a set-up. Name dropping freaked her out a little, but not enough to risk her tail for a bored royal.

"Baby," I say as I lick up his cheek. "You know I love when you're covered in blood. It's sexy."

His jaw ticks, but Felix turns to give me a searing kiss. We battle for control for a moment and when he pulls away, the cat can see I bit his lip until it bled. That should do it—the children of Lucille Drew and The Raj of Bloodstone being violent nut jobs makes perfect sense. "Then blood you shall have, Princess."

"Yes, Miss Drew, Your Majesty. I understand. Allow me to organize your request," the leopard says, as she watches us. She speeds away, and I watch, tilting my head.

"She's going to start the book first, isn't she?" I give my date a wry look and he nods, eyes dancing in amusement.

"Most definitely. But you're doing very well, Princess. I almost believed you for a second." His arms wrap around me and he leans in to whisper, "Don't worry about me, remember?"

I snort. "I saw the Staff Games, Felix. Fitz took over, but he didn't *need* to. I'm not worried you'll lose; I'm concerned about our presence being noticed by people we don't want attention from. And I wasn't lying…I do like you covered in blood."

His grin is feral. "Perhaps the attention is the point, little bunny. Sometimes, hiding in plain sight works as well as fading into the background."

"Whatever you say, Sir." I wink and follow him as the leopard gestures for him to come closer by an enormous door marked 'Staff Only.'

Here we go.

***

My stomach is full of butterflies as I stand in the roped off box our 'host' brought me to while Felix gets ready. I know why he wanted me to give off the 'fuck with me and die' air when we came in; he knew I'd be left alone while he did this. I'm keeping up appearances, looking around with a steely gaze and haughty tilt to my chin as I eye the people surrounding the VIP section. It's not protected by anything other than a grumpy-looking bouncer and a few velvet ropes that will stop absolutely nothing from getting in.

If something goes wrong, the crowd has to believe coming after me will cause their immediate deaths.

As the current competitors tear into one another, I walk along the partition, sliding the tips of my claws on it idly. I keep a bored expression on my face, only barely glancing at them occasionally as I walk back and forth slowly. The movement is draining a little of the energy coursing in my veins, but it's also cementing the impression that I could give a fuck less about everything around me. In truth, I'm studying the exits, the cameras, the people, and everything else Fitz told me to watch for. It's both practice and practical because I have no idea how this risky ass gambit of my tiger's will play out.

The Khans are universally feared, and he is the rightful Raj; everyone knows that even if they don't accept it. If that evil old fucker dies, they'll never choose a weaker royal to spite Felix. At least, I don't think so. Fitz told me the new 'heir apparent' is a slimy little shit who abuses the females and can't fight his own battles. Their ambush is too ruthless to put an idiot like that in the top seat, unless someone is pulling his strings. Felix putting on this show might ruffle some feathers—his enemies could see he's not the beaten down wreck he was when he first arrived.

But then, my enemies might see how fucking fierce he is and reconsider; it's a delicate balance.

A loud alarm sounds and I realize it's serving as the bell. Looking down, I note the bloody mess in the ring that used to be a wolf. They don't hold back in the underground scene, and the lioness who was in the ring is pawing at the air in victory. Before I can blink, it shifts and my eyes widen as I stare at a naked Coach Z pumping her fist in the air. She's covered in blood, especially at the mouth from ripping the throat out of her opponent. It takes everything in me to continue meeting her eyes as she winks from the spotlight, but I give her a sharp nod of approval.

Zhenga makes a few more loops around the circle, letting the announcer go on about her stats and her family line. When she's in front of me, she cuts her eyes to another section of the crowd. Following her gaze, I have to lock it down again when I see my new nemesis, Kamara Rakoto, standing in the shadows of the back row. *What the hell is she doing here? Is this why Felix wanted to come?* Coach Z moves on when she knows I understand, smirking and waving at the crowd despite being clothed only in wolf's blood and gore.

That's one part of shifter behavior I haven't gotten used to yet—zero fucks given about public nudity.

I pretend to yawn, dropping into one of the lush seats and crossing my legs as I pull my phone out. The excitement is dying down and I know it's only a matter of minutes before they announce my boyfriend. That's going to set them off like a firecracker and the kitsunes running bets around the crowd will start whizzing like the Flash. I can't look as if I give a shit until Felix comes out; it has to look like his victory is a foregone conclusion in my mind. It is, but rich people always have this air of untouchable *ennui*. Lucille is always draped in it unless she's angry, so I know exactly how to play this.

"As always, the Leonidas Liquidator has decimated her prey! Up next, a real treat for our fight fans: a surprise addition to the card. In a shocking turn of events, we have *royalty* among us tonight!"

That gets the crowd's attention, but I don't move. I know who's coming and they need to see me continuing to ignore the world around me.

"Get ready to place your bets, because we're going to see blood and gore. Our top fighter, Brutus Leonidas, the exiled heir, will fight yet another cast off from a family of vicious cats. Make your choice between Brutus and the exiled heir to Bloodstone Isle: Prince. Felix. Khaaaaaan!"

Gasps, hoots, boos, and screams of delight fill the arena as Felix strides out in a pair of fighting silks, wrapped hands, and nothing else. He doesn't need those wraps, nor did he need the oil adorning his gorgeous tanned skin from head to toe, but I know why he did it. He looks more like the exile he was when he came to Apex than ever—I've seen pictures—because his hair is growing out, his stubble is roguish and he's wearing a flippant smirk only perfected by the insanely wealthy.

This is being recorded on so many devices that it will go viral within seconds of the fight's conclusion.

I finally stand when his eyes move to me and he strides across the ring, ignoring the ref and his hulking opponent. Leaping up to the top of the barrier, he holds on, waiting for me to approach. When I get close, he uses one hand to hold himself up and the other to grip my chin while he kisses me hard. I have to grit my teeth not to fucking *swoon* at how strong he is, but when I pull away, I mirror his cocky expression as I look at the crowd. He hops down, strolling over to the ref as if nothing happened, and I let out a slow, calming breath.

From that moment, it's like everything moves in fast forward. The bets end and the match begins with a slow study of one another. The lion is gigantic for this species and much like the wolf Fitz fought at Apex, I assume he has to be juicing. It's likely the reason he got the boot from the Leonidas' family—they're known for harsh penalties in the League if they catch players enhancing themselves. From the Pred Games to the Prey Bowl, they don't allow cheating in their sports. But this guy? He's three times as big as even a shifted male lion should be. That doesn't stop Felix, though, because, like me, he's using that size to his advantage. His half-shifted tiger is sleek and fast, so the lumbering dickface can't get a good grasp on him.

Until the steroid freak gets his tail and a loud, tiger roar fills the air. Felix completes his shift within *seconds*, something I haven't seen before. This is what a *real* alpha of the species looks like: absolutely in control of every inch of his forms with no hesitation. His body rolls and his fluid motion allows him to escape the big dude, but not without a bleeding gash on the appendage he wrenched free.

First blood makes the audience lose its mind, especially since it's Khan blood. I know it doesn't mean shit, but they all think their champion is going to beat a future king. It's making the tension notch up and I raise my hand indolently, not even looking around as I wait. A server appears as if by magic and I grunt over my shoulder, "Scotch. Now."

Sounds good, right? Hopefully, I can choke this shit down without making a face.

My glass appears so quickly you'd think they teleported and I rise to walk up to the barrier as I sip it slowly. It's expensive; I know because it's not burning as much as I assume straight liquor should. TigerFelix sees me and a minor flash of recognition runs through his eyes as he darts forward to swipe his claws over the lion's flank. He must approve of my act because he's continuing his fight without pause, attacking the big cat over and over until the air is thick with bloodlust.

I let my gaze flick to where Rakoto is and I note she's staring at my guy as he finishes his opponent with expert precision. She has to know he was holding back at first, and her expression is irritated as hell when the ref jumps in to pull TigerFelix off of their prone champ. The fight runners don't want him killing their golden goose, despite not caring if Coach Z destroyed her opponent.

Sighing loudly, I toss back the rest of the scotch and slam my glass down in a show of anger. I want them to think I'm pouting that Felix didn't get to murder the other cat; it's one hundred percent how Lucille would react. Though, I'm not convinced she wouldn't shift, jump in the ring, and do it herself if she was mad enough. It's not out of her wheelhouse at all. Killing people is her second favorite hobby after torturing me.

"And the winner is the future king of the ambush, the Bloodstone Brawler, Felix Khan!"

When the announcer holds up his hand and he starts his victory laps, I nudge my way past the bouncer, heading for the locker room as we planned. My gaze is dark as I look at anyone who meets my eyes and they give me a wide berth when I stalk to the staff area. No one even speaks; they simply move the hell out of my way as I pass.

If this wasn't part of Felix's plan, it's a hell of a side effect.

Ignoring yet another bouncer, I push open the door and stride into the room like I own the place, leaving gaping idiots in my wake. Felix isn't here yet, so I plant myself on a bench, legs stretched out on it as I lean back. The alcohol is buzzing in my veins now, hitting the adrenaline from the fight and having a little chemical party in my brain. I'm not drunk, but I'm definitely a wee bit buzzed, so it's good this place is empty. Watching Felix literally tear that moron apart without breaking a sweat has me worked up, especially since I know we're doing this to piss people off.

I think my chaos loving gargoyle is rubbing off on me because I find that idea delicious.

Power Over Me

Felix

I COULD HAVE ENDED THE FIGHT SOONER, BUT I LET IT DRAG OUT for the assholes who will no doubt have this online before I towel off. The scratch on my tail is irritating, but it will heal quick enough. I shifted as soon as I was out of the view of the fans and now that I've shaken off the money grubbing promoters from this place, I'm headed for my true prey: Dolly.

Flinging open the door to the locker room, I stalk in, chuckling when I find her reclining on the wide bench between the lockers. Her eyes are dark and she gives me a lazy smirk that makes my cock twitch. My Princess is a blend of whip smart sarcasm and adorable naiveté—both of which make her fascinating. She's prey raised in a pred world with no understanding of how anything works, but she's picking it up like a prodigy. She's fire and ice and cotton candy with zero apology for it.

I can't get enough of it.

"That was brilliant—not to mention hot. But that was your plan, right, *Sir?*" she says as she sits up, placing her spiky boots on the ground. "You wanted everyone to see me being rich and unaffected so they'd think twice, especially after you tore that juicing dickhead apart?"

My lips quirk as I toss the towel aside and drop onto the bench, straddling it as I scoot closer. She leans back as I get in her space, ever the playful minx, and by the time I answer, she's almost bent over backwards. "I did. Brilliant of you to work it out, Princess."

Dolly snorts, her hand coming up to brush the hair out of my face. "It didn't take a genius to figure out your plan had more than one level, Felix. The King is *always* looking at the whole chessboard and you are most definitely the King."

Swooping in, I kiss her roughly and her hands wind around my neck. Her fingers bury in my hair while our tongues battle for dominance. Her aggressiveness surprises me, but I like it; it'll make her submission that much sweeter. Teeth tug at my lower lip, just sharp enough to almost pierce it, and I growl loudly. The others weren't wrong about the bunny having a little bloodlust under her skin; the trick is keeping it from clouding her mind before she's ready.

"Careful, Princess," I rumble against her lips when we separate for air. "You're being quite naughty."

Her lips curve before she pulls away, arching her brow at me knowingly. I watch as she leans down and unzips each boot, letting the leather fall to the side. Her fingers slide under the hem of her ripped jeans and a small tab flips out. Tugging on it, she slides it upward and suddenly, the inner seams of her pants are parting like her boots.

My eyes widen. "What the hell?"

"Courtesy of Fitz, I imagine. I didn't realize how they worked until I put them on tonight," she chuckles, continuing to reveal skin until she reaches the apex of her thighs. She's wearing a barely there scrap of black lace with thin straps and I groan.

Merciful Bast, this fucking girl is going to kill me.

"Turn around. Get on all fours and be still," I growl in a low voice. "Otherwise, I'll stop."

Her eyes flash red briefly, but she lifts her right leg up and over us both in a move only a dancer could accomplish. I grit my teeth as I watch her slowly adjust until she's kneeling on the wide bench with her thighs spread and her hands holding her up. Her round ass is sticking up, so I squeeze it hard enough to make her bite back a strangled sound.

"Quiet." The order is followed by a sharp smack to her right cheek and I feel the shudder run through her. Her scent is intoxicating as she fights the instinct to be vocal, and though I love the sounds she makes, I also know she *loves* being told what to do almost as much as she enjoys fighting me. "Hold still."

I turn over, putting my back on the wood as I scoot underneath her. Once I'm settled under her bare thighs, I inhale with a hungry grin. I'm not worried about someone intruding; they wouldn't dare disturb me after the show in the ring. But we don't have all the time in the world, either, so I grab her legs to spread them further. Diving into her wetness, I lick a line up her slit before moving to her clit. Nipping it lightly, I flick my tongue over it and suckle, alternating until she's flooding my face with more heat. I grip her tightly, using the jerks and harsh breaths of my girl to measure how close she is. Every time I sense she's getting too close, too fast, I pull back and make marks on her inner thighs as she shivers. I want her panting with need before I'll take her over.

The thought makes my cock twitch in my shorts and I double my efforts, lashing her with my tongue until she lets out a strangled squeak. Growling in reproval, I bite down and I know she's damn near ready to explode. Our girl loves public fucking; I've seen how hot it gets her. Dolly isn't perturbed someone will see her; in fact, the possibility makes her wetter. I thrust my tongue inside her quickly, bringing her closer and closer until she's trembling again, then pull my mouth away.

"Do you want to come?" I ask as I blow cool air over her hot pussy. "Are you waiting for me to give permission?"

"Yes, Sir." Her voice is a throaty whisper and I almost fucking jizz in my goddamn fighting shorts.

Fitz would never let me live that shit down.

Leaning forward, I nip her again and wetness floods my face again. "That's my good girl. When you're ready, you may."

I bury my face in her pussy again, letting go of one thigh to shove three fingers inside of her roughly. She squeezes them like a vice, riding on my digits and my tongue until her hips jerk hard. I feel her orgasm as it hits her and continue working her until her panting breaths get slower. When the shaking stops, I slide out from under her and roll to my feet.

Dolly is vision as she leans over the bench, head pressed to the wood and her ass in the air, thighs slick with juices. She's not even naked, but I can barely control myself as I straddle the bench and yank her hips towards me. Leaning over her back, I rumble in her ear. "Hold on tight."

That's all the warning she gets before I drive my cock into her and my fucking eyes roll back in my head. My fingers dig into her hips hard, likely bruising them as I fuck her hard, brutal, and fast. I've been waiting so damn long to do this and I haven't done it with anyone I gave a shit about in even longer. But the tiger inside of me is starving for her and I can only do so much to hold back.

As if he heard me, my skin ripples and claws escape. My eyes widen but my Princess arches her back and slams back into my thrusts when they slice into her. The primal part of me lifts his head to roar, and it rumbles out of me, rattling the surrounding lockers. Nose twitching with the scent of fucking and blood, my tiger is straining my ability to stay completely human and I've never felt this way before. I don't know if I can keep this up much longer.

Dolly lifts her head, looking over her shoulder at me with a feral expression as she squeezes my cock inside. Her brow arches over deep crimson orbs as she rasps, "Here, kitty, kitty."

Mother. Fucker.

My hand slips to her clit, rubbing it as my hips snap and I feel the inevitable taking over. Fangs burst from my mouth and my cock swells as our bodies slap together loudly. I blanket myself over her back, grinding into her and waiting until her walls flutter around me. I lift my head, scenting the air again as her climax crests and my dick buries in her as deeply as possible. The swelling continues as the barbs we learned about last year latch on and she thumps her head on the wood when another orgasm rolls through her. That's when the urge grabs me by the throat and won't let go.

Bite. Mate. Mine.

I grind my back teeth, pushing at my tiger hard to keep him from taking over. It's not time yet, and she's not ready. Plus, she hasn't fucked the dragon yet and it wouldn't be fair. My claw tips dig into her hip deeper as I fight the beast inside of me, roaring for what he considers his right. The struggle helps my dick calm and with a relieved breath, I feel the hooks release to allow me to pull out of her. I swallow hard as cum leaks down her leg and it riles my inner pred up again.

"Felix?" Dolly rises, ignoring the mingled juices as she walks over to the bin and gets two towels. When she returns, I grab her and pull her close, inhaling the honeysuckle smell mixed with sex. She lets me steal the towel so I can clean her up while she threads her fingers in my hair. "What's wrong?"

I lift my head after I get her sorted. My lips curve in a rueful smile. "The tiger enjoyed your insubordination a little too much."

She frowns, then suddenly she gets it and her cheeks flame. "Oh. Well, I wouldn't have minded. I like teeth."

That makes his ire flare at me, and I groan while I wipe myself down. "Fuck, Princess. You'll get him started again."

"Not really a problem for me," she replies as she bends to zip up her weirdo pants and then her boots. "But it would keep us from blowing this joint to get some food and I'm literally ready to eat a water buffalo."

Hell yeah, that's my girl.

"Give me a minute to dress and we'll do just that. Do you want to eat out or bring it home?" I don't tell her about the tiger's demand to mate her. I need to talk to the guys and we have to get all our animals to agree on it before we bring it up with her. No fucking way am I letting a five-way asshole pred fight hurt her feelings or fuck up our family.

"I thought you already did that…eat out, I mean." Her playful wink makes my cock stir again, and I blink before I laugh.

"And I'll do it again, after we get some food in you, Princess. Have to keep your energy up so you're ready for tomorrow." I wink back, tugging on my clothes from earlier.

Once I'm dressed, I look at her freshly fucked hair and face, brushing a few errant strands aside but not fixing it entirely. This, too, is a look I'm hoping the cameras capture.

After all, the Queen to Felix Khan's kingdom should look like she's been satisfied.

The Greatest Show

Delores

Waking up this morning was a trial. I was sore and covered in random marks that stung under the spray of the hot shower. Felix was gone, but a lone rose was in his place—*le fucking swoon*. I threw on one of the big shirts in my basket, grinning when the smell was Aubrey. I haven't taken the laundry out to the hall for pick up yet and most nights, some combo of my guys sack out with me.

Chess was waiting for me with a huge breakfast and he sat with me until I finished every bite, smirking at the way I moved as we chatted. I asked him if he knew about Zhenga being in the underground fights and he nodded, throwing out a blasé answer about keeping tabs on people. When I sat back and groaned, patting my full belly, he just laughed.

Apparently, I need a lot of energy today, and he plans to provide the fuel.

The next boyfriend to show up was Fitz, and he was the one to put the video on the huge flatscreen on the wall. As predicted, the whole fight and my walk of fame after our locker room hijinks were remixed and went apeshit viral. His eyes sparkled with mischief as he pointed out my 'just fucked' hair—*thanks Felix*—before tugging me into his lap.

His laughter drew out Rennie and Aubrey, both of whom watched the damn thing on loop for a few as they gave me teasing looks and tossed out little barbs about my haughty persona. The worst part was reading the comments; they ranged from drooling people saying dirty shit about *both* of us to angry morons bitching about the announcer calling Felix the future king. If I could have reached through the screen to choke them, I would have.

Fitz's response was, "Fame brings out the assholes, Baby Girl."

He's right—my experience with social media after the Vom Prom proved that.

By the time everyone calmed down, Chessie had the table cleaned up and was making notes on the board with this week's accomplishments. I told him about the mysterious Rakoto woman in the stands and how Zhenga made sure I saw her. That moved her from question mark status to a solid 'bad guy' in my mind, so we need to get someone on her. Fitz let me know defeating Jaiyana has me on the Plastics' radar; they've started their own little hate campaign online. Unfortunately for them, the viral video has quashed it, so we let it go for now.

Aubrey and Rennie booked us time this coming week in the National Library for research so we can compare our maps from Apex to some of their texts. The library here is ill-equipped compared to my old school, so they want to sneak out Monday night after dinner to use the more comprehensive archives. It's a good plan, but with my workload, it will take a chunk out of my homework time.

Not that it matters if the people trying to kidnap or kill me succeed.

We continued working until lunch, then Fitz declared it was time to get ready for the Games. The others grumbled, but he sent me packing to change into workout clothes and when I returned, we went outside to the back lawn.

Now he's looking at me in my yoga pants and sports bra like he wished he'd made another choice. "Fitz, what are we doing?"

"Shit. Distracted." He shakes his head and grins. "We're doing yoga and stretches and meditation shit. Get in a mental place where all that other stuff is gone before it's time to head to the arena. The Games are dangerous and you need to focus and get your body unkinked."

I arch a brow.

"Bad joke, I know," he chuckles and shrugs. "I can't help it. You're covered in tiger bites and scratches. It's making me itchy and horny."

"I doubt me bending in funny positions and groaning is going to help."

"Won't know until we try, Baby Girl."

Famous last words.

***

Adrenaline is pumping through my system as I stand in front of my locker. Dusk fell, and the guys had Kirby walk me over to the Games arena. Since the female Games are first, Felix and Fitz will be in the stands with the rest of my boyfriends until they have to join their team. I know Cori and Rufus will be there; they've been texting all day with updates on my viral infamy with the Khan heir. Rufus swears it's going to pack the crowd like the girls' Games had never seen and that makes me even more nervous.

If I don't do well, there will be so many consequences I can't even parse them —no pressure.

When I arrived, they were setting up the ferry on the other side of the river and it didn't look bad, but that was probably just students. It's been a couple hours since then and I've kept to myself, staying in the mental zone Fitz and I created at our Mojo-

Dojo home. He hasn't stopped calling it that since Aubrey grumbled and it cracks me up. Of course, my feminist AF tiger would choose to make our place 'me' centric; he's never once balked at any of my quirks or damage. He just supports me like my personal cheerleader, no matter what, and has no compunction about letting me find my way.

I shake my head as the different ways the guys and my besties help me, my heart swelling at the comparison to everything before them. My life is truly different now and I'm able to be the person I always wanted to be. For that reason alone, I have to show all the people who doubted me when I turned out to be a bunny that I am a force to be reckoned with. The thing they consider my detriment is my strength, and I won't hide in the shadows to avoid conflict anymore.

They yelled 'run, rabbit, run' once, but now they're the ones who need to run because I'm coming for all *of them.*

My lips curve up as I pull on the snug Capital Prep jersey and matching booty shorts. Competitors need to move and shift without worrying about restrictive materials. However, like all pred events, they also want us branded with their logos, so the uniform gets destroyed at every single match. I took off Rennie's choker at the house because the crowd doesn't need to see the magic, but also I was afraid they could use it against me. Someone could steal it from my locker or get a grip on it in the ring— neither of which is optimal. Even my hair is braided in tightly tucked dual French braids to prevent hair pulling; I'm not giving whoever I fight any quarter.

"Time to line up, ladies!" Zhenga yells from the doorway.

Shutting my locker, I walk over to the line-up. She's got us in order of appearance and I'm near the end. I don't know if that's better or worse, but I can feel the Plastics stare as I take my place. Luckily for me, they can't arrange an 'accident' because none of the matches are paired until right before we go onto the field. I suppose there's wiggle room if they have friends on other teams or minions, but I've never seen them drag along anyone like the Heathers do. No, those girls handle their own shit and have the power to do it without needing sycophants. They're a different breed of bully, though just as dangerous.

My eyes close for a moment as I remember what Fitz told me this afternoon. *"Baby Girl, there isn't a motherfucker on the planet—much less that arena—worth wondering if you're good enough. You're Delores Drew: a survivor, a warrior, and we love you. Remember that we believe in you."* It made me watery and almost does now, but I steel my spine and jut my chin out.

I'm ready to rock, no matter what happens when we jog out.

The line moves, so I follow along, staying in my confident zone rather than paying attention to the shit going on around me. I don't whisper with the others or listen to the extremely *loud* crowd echoing in the tunnel as we wait. When the announcer calls our names, my gaze is hard and I've got my game face on as I run behind Denita. She's in front of me and I can feel her nerves as we hit the lights and sound of the jam-fucking-*packed* stadium. Someone murmurs about never seeing this many people here before, but I let it wash over me while I watch her run across the field to the benches.

A roar of applause and boos in equal measure is a cacophony when they called my name. I expected as much, so I make my path across slower, letting them all know I won't be cowed. My eyes catch on the front row behind our bench, and the smile that splits my face is impossible to control.

Sitting there in one long line are my guys in a ridiculous pink, sparkly version of the Capital Prep jerseys that say 'Drew Fluffle' in curly letters. My number is on them, and I'd be willing to bet Rufus put my name on the back, too. There's something on the sleeves I can't read, but even Felix is standing in his Barbie-style jersey clapping. Rufus and Cori are on the other side of them in their own jerseys and I'll be damned if the Captain, Raina, and their entire crew aren't there talking with Luc.

They all came, and they're here to support me.

I give them a brisk nod, schooling my face again as I approach the bench when it hits me—a gaze that makes the hairs on the back of my neck rise. When I glare up into the crowd, I notice the boxes for VIPS. That's where it's coming from: Lucille is here. My mask drops for a moment as I look up, raising my hand slightly to flip the box off at my side. Not everyone will see it, but *she* will. Her eyes miss nothing and that will whip her into a froth like no other worrying someone else saw me.

Take that, Mother.

***

With every match, my anxiety grows. I'm managing it thanks to my guys' tutelage, but the Heathers are flipping and spinning around like concrete-footed orangutans. They give me death glares when they pass and I've seen their gross Coach watching me as well while she talks into her phone. Lucille and Bruno are sending their own icky vibes and my fear of failure is edging at my consciousness. I can't let myself down and I *definitely* can't let all these jackals witness me failing on the first try. I know I can't win every time, but *this* time, I have to.

"Next up, Annalise Bérgamon of *Academie* versus Delores Drew of Apex Academy. Delores is representing both Apex *and* Capital Prep tonight in her Pred Games debut!"

Just fucking great. Thanks, announcer dude.

I jump to my feet, looking out into the audience with a stone face, then stride over to the ring. The ref steps in the middle and I wait for the showboating *Academie* student to make her way here. Every one of them has strolled up like a fashion model and spent five minutes posing for the flashes. She finally stands in place for that part and I have to control the gut deep urge to roll my eyes. This isn't the runway; it's a damn fighting competition. But I let her do it as canine scents fill my nose.

She's not a wolf, but definitely has the smell of a dog in her aura. *Possibly a hyena or dingo?* My lips curl up a little when I consider getting revenge on a dingo, even if it isn't the ones who chased me last year. Honestly, I've got a lot of mutts to mete out justice to, so it doesn't matter what kind. Just being one of their species helps me amp up my bloodlust. The bunny inside pushes forward, imbuing me with strength and fury as I wait for her to stop hamming it up.

Before I can stop myself, I grunt, "Yo, ref. Are we modeling uniforms or fighting? For fuck's sake."

My opponent's eyes cut to me, an icy glare washing over me as the ref coughs and walks forward to call the start. Madame Chien didn't like me pushing her out of the spotlight and it's got her off-guard. I can use that. Dropping into a loose stance, I wait for the whistle and when he blows it, I shoot to the left before she can charge me. Annalise is quick on her feet, though; she's able to catch herself before she tumbles, unlike Jaiyana.

That's it, little doggy. Attack in anger with no plan.

Smirking as I dodge her next feints, I curl my fingers into fists, waiting for my moment. When she gets close enough to bark some nonsense about my mother, my left shoots upward to knock her back with an uppercut. Before she can clear the ducks from her vision, I follow it with a jab and a leg sweep, taking her to the ground. Unfortunately, her ankles find mine and she locks them, tripping me as I move away.

Now we're both on the ground scrabbling and I kick with all the power of my rabbit. My legs are the strongest part of me and it shakes her loose, but my victory is short-lived. A low snarl alerts me she's shifted—an oddity this early in the match. Annalise must realize I won't be the pushover she assumed. Jumping to my feet, I square off with the canine, noting her spots.

She's a hyena like Todd and his idiot friends… excellent.

The feral response from my bunny surprises me, and I blink as the red fills my eyes. Fabric rips as the half-shift takes over and grin around my pointed teeth. *This bitch has* no idea *what she just unleashed.* As soon as I'm shifted, I run at her with the increased speed of my animal. She leaps into the air to meet me, so I aim for her throat with my fist. The punch knocks her back with a yelp and I dive to the dirt, pinning her as my claws dig into fur.

I can barely see my opponent through the haze of anger flowing through me. Loud growls and barks fill the quiet arena as I pummel her over and over, muttering, "Stay down, you fucking mutt."

But Annalise must be as dumb as the Heathers because she keeps squirming and fighting. Her teeth catch my arm, making me roar as blood drips on the ground. That wasn't illegal, but it was dirty as fuck. Snapping my teeth back at her in a taunt, I wait until she ducks away from them to bury one hand of sharp claws into her leg.

The smell of blood is getting heavy in the air and deep inside, my rabbit wants me to finish it.

Shaking my head, I work to clear the mist when those thoughts come to me. I smack the ground three times to show the ref she's out and rise to my feet, dusting my fur off. Except that's when the goddamn fool comes barreling into me from behind before the whistle blows and I end up on the ground eating dirt. My back cracked when she hit me and I groan as I spit out the grass, then tilt my head until my neck and spine crack again.

I was going to let her live to compete again, but now I have to teach her—and everyone watching—a lesson.

Flipping my body over, I grunt as the bruises and scratches ache. The enraged dog has drool dripping from her maw as she snaps at me and I make a disgusted face. "By Mars' sweaty bits, woman, get a hold of yourself."

Her answer is another bark, and I realize she's *not* an alpha. She can't talk, nor can she think like anything but the animal. And she doesn't have the push. Satisfaction courses through my veins as I fake a slash at her face, forcing her to look at me. My arms go limp, knowing she'll head for my throat.

When she does, I move like lightning. My hands shoot up to grip her throat and I squeeze as I pray this works. Looking her right in the eyes, I boom, "Concede!"

A gasp rolls over the crowd at my shout, and it slowly turns into a roar when the hyena yips and goes totally limp.

The feeling of power that slams into me is immense. I toss her off me, getting to my feet and glaring down at the whimpering canine with a smug look on my face. *You could end her now*, the bunny whispers. But I don't want to do that—not for a game. So I step on her back leg until I hear a crack as loud as her hit made on me, then hold one arm in the air for the ref. He comes running over in a flash, blowing his whistle over and over as if that would stop me from continuing if I chose.

My eyes finally clear as applause and shouts echo through the stadium. I see Fitz jumping the fucking rail from his seat in tiger form, followed by CheetahChessic. They dart around the guards, hoping to stop them as if it's child's play to land next to my feet in a protective stance. A loud roar follows them and before I know it, I'm flanked by the three kings, all half-shifted into massive goddamn creatures and a tiger as they stare into the audience intently.

If anyone was thinking about vengeance, this display put a libido on it before it even began.

"In a stunningly ruthless display of *alpha dominance,* the winner is Deloooooores Dreeeeeeeeeeeee!" the announcer shouts in a surprised tone. "We are witnessing *history* today at Capital Prep!"

My breath heaves as I feel all the eyes on me and the guys while the medical team carries Annalise off the field. I know this will make people angry, but I can't keep being the bigger bunny. At some point, I had to draw a line in the sand and today was that day.

I only hope I chose wisely. Time will tell.

Crazy In Love

Chess

It took a bit for the fervor in the stadium to calm down. Fitz lifted Dolly in a fireman's carry once he shifted back, and to all our surprise, she let him caveman her off the field. Ren had clothes because of his damn amulet, so he went to fetch her things while Aubrey snorted smoke and took to the air. Felix headed for the boys' locker room to get dressed for those matches, and they left me to follow my two mates as they stomped over the grass to the tunnel entrance. I'm pretty sure everyone else was as hyped as us, but Fitz growled them off.

He called dibs on tonight, after all.

My angel has been quiet as we walk, and I think she's sorting through her brain. The last time she went super saiyan, she wasn't really conscious. This time, however, she made rational choices and that messes with your head the first time. I know how that is; they forced me to do much worse in the ambush trials. I could almost *feel* her wrath from the field, though. Deep inside, there's a kernel of darkness that recognizes the darkness in all her mates—which means she came damn close to killing that hyena.

Fitz would have, rules be damned, and shrugged it off if they penalized him for a match or two. He's always been more reckless than Felix and me by leaps and bounds. But that's the nature of being the second to the king: you always have to be ready to defend the crown. And Fitz Khan would tear the world apart for the people he loves, no question. That's why he's lugging her on his shoulder—if someone tries us, he'll be the one dismantling their spine, not her.

"Chessie?"

I smile when I see our girl looking up at me from his back. "Yes, Angel?"

"Do you think I did the right thing?"

She's adorable when she looks both fierce and unsure.

"I do. The *Academie* girl came at you dirty and if you'd let it stand, it would have set a precedent for the entire season. Right, Fitz?"

He snorts. "You did better than I would have. She'd be carrion food if it was me. Fuck their rules."

See?

She lets out a long breath and nods, her eyes on me as she finally smiles. "I did the focus thing, you know. Like you taught me, Fitzy."

I arch a brow, curious how *Fitzgerald Ulysses Castor Khan* could teach anyone how to focus. "What focus thing? And why don't you use that?"

My lover stops at the entrance, giving me a glare as he swipes his card. "First off, I was helping her center *her* mind. Second, mine doesn't *work* like that."

"It's true," Dolly pipes up. "He was squirrely as hell while I did the whole yoga-Jedi-balance-mind-and-body thing. I had to stay focused and balanced, but he danced all over the place like he was on something."

Chuckling, I tuck a strand of hair behind her ear before we head into the underground. "That makes *much* more sense. Those who can't teach?"

"Exactly," she giggles, as Fitz smacks her ass playfully. "Hey!"

"You're full of sass now that you beat someone up. That's more like me than you want to admit, Baby Girl."

He's right, too. Now that she's out of the headspace she was in for competing, Dolly is back to being herself, but bubblier. Getting some of the frustration she's buried inside out is good for her. "I think he's got you nailed, Angel."

Her eyes dance and then she winks. "Not yet, but soon enough, baby."

Gulp.

***

Fitz doesn't waste any time. The second the door to our quarters opens, he strides down the hall to Dolly's bedroom and dumps her on the bed. His eyes are golden as he growls, "Out, Jinx."

The sand cat looks up from its perch and sniffs before leaping to the floor and sashaying out the door. I chuckle softly as he kicks the door shut. Looks like our lovable psycho is ready to rock. Dolly props herself up on her elbows, smirking at him knowingly as he paces back and forth.

"Fitzy, stop that and get over here." Her voice is husky, and it makes my cock twitch in anticipation when he does exactly as she commands.

When he moves, I walk over as well, crawling onto the bed with them as a flush creeps up my neck. From the second I saw Delores Drew through the library window, I wanted this moment—and now it's here. Fitz looks over at me, his features delighted as he rakes his eyes over us both. His head tilts and his voice is raspy when he speaks. "Did you know, Baby Girl, that the day your beautiful feet hit this campus for the tour, Chessie wanted this? When you saw us through that window, we could see *you* and, for the first time, he asked if we could share you. He'd never once shown an interest in a girl I had the hots for, but the minute he saw you, his dick went insane."

She blinks, taking that information in for a moment. Her eyes are blown as she looks up through her lashes at him, then at me. "All you had to do is ask, my knight. I can't think of a better place to be than speared by a kitty sword fight."

"Fuck," I mutter as I press my swollen cock against her thigh. "You're getting a dirty mouth, Angel."

"Better fill it with something to wash it out, Chessie. I've got business with her golden pussy."

I laugh softly as our girl grins and nods, allowing him to climb over her until he's between her thighs. A soft noise escapes when he buries his face in her heat and I scoot up on the bed to line up with her mouth. "Are you okay with this?"

"Get over here," she growls softly, her hands wrapping around my hips to tug me close. My body shudders as she rubs her nose along my leg, making little breathy sounds as Fitz devours her. When she gets to my shaft, her tongue runs from my balls up the bottom to the tip. She toys with balls on my piercing, flicking her tongue over all four before taking the head into her mouth.

My balls tighten, and I have to consciously struggle not to rush her. She's suckling gently when Fitz does something that makes her moan and jerk, swallowing me down faster than I expected. The vibration makes me sink my hands in her hair, holding on tight as she adjusts. Her body is shivering now, so I thrust faster as the orgasm takes her under. When it fades, I look down at her, then at Fitz. He's giving me a fangy grin and I know what he's going to do.

While my angel continues to torture me with her mouth, he leaps off the bed and heads for the chest of toys we bought at the store. He comes back with a bottle of lube, squirting it in his hands as he prowls over her. I see her eyes widen, so I run my hand over her hair soothingly. Fitz won't hurt her and I know he's been subtly working her up to this before today. The delicate way he handled courting her and teaching her all the things she didn't know tells me he wouldn't spring a new thing on her tonight.

I know exactly when his fingers slip inside of her to stretch her ass, because my cock pops out of her mouth as her head falls back. She reaches up to stroke me firmly while she writhes against his hand, making deep guttural sounds that draw pre cum out of my tip. Her tomb rubs it in and I hear her curse—that's another finger. "Fitzy, make sure she's ready."

"Oh, *mon amour*, I will," he rumbles back. "I want us to fill her so full she sees stars."

Son of a fucking bitch. I love when he's being filthy.

"Do you want that, Angel? Would you like Fitz to bury his dick in your ass while I ram into your pussy? Are you ready to take us both?"

"Hell yeah, I do," she mutters, then looks up at me with a crooked grin. "I don't know if I'm ready, but I trust both of you to help me get there."

That makes Fitz growl again, and she squeaks when he works another finger in. I know his cock is like iron because we've dreamed about this since we met her, but it's *so* much better live. Dolly is gripping my shaft like she's trying to wring the cum out of me before it's time and her breasts are bouncing as she rides my love's hand. The scent of blood from the match covers her, pairing with her honeysuckle and Fitz's musk in a way that makes my inner muse spiral out of control.

"You're a vision," I murmur as I look down at her. "We're going to make you feel so good, love."

Her hips buck and she pants as she lifts her head to glare at Fitz. "Enough playing. I need one of you inside me *now*."

"Yes, ma'am," Fitz says as he pulls his fingers free and salutes with the other hand. He grabs the lube and lathers his dick up with a shudder of pleasure. "Chessie, lie down so she can climb up on your dick and ride you. I want to see it."

My lips curve as I do as he instructs, watching both his hand stroke his erection and our girl roll over onto me with lithe grace. She pushes up on her hands, looking down at me with blown pupils and a hungry expression. "Ride me, angel, then Fitz is going to fuck your ass."

Levering up, she catches my gaze, then sinks down onto my cock with a rumble of pleasure. Her wet heat squeezes me and I have to grit my teeth. This is about sharing her, and I have to make sure she comes again before Fitz will give me permission. I rock into her as she moves, loving the feel of her gripping me and making soft moans. When Fitz gets behind her, his eyes lock on mine and I can tell he's having trouble holding back. The second his head breaches the tight hole, she throws her head back, and a strangled sound escapes her lips.

"Do it, Fitzy. Just do it," she says in a dark voice and, to my surprise, he complies. His cock buries in her roughly, bumping along with mine, with only a thin layer of tissue between us. Dolly's fingers dig into my sides as she adjusts to being split, but it's not long before she rocks on me again.

"That's our girl," Fitz says, as he wraps one hand around her hip and another around her throat.

My eyes widen as I watch him put a little pressure there, knowing she's a child of violence and fuck knows what her father or mother did to her. But my angel moans and leans into his grip, arching and swirling her hips that grinds her clit on my pelvis. My shock fades when she whispers, "Harder, Fitzy. I can take it. Fuck me— both of you."

Golden eyes meet amber over her shoulder and the primal in the room notches up. My cheetah *loves* that demand and I can *feel* Fitz's tiger. His fangs are out as he slams into her in opposite thrusts from mine and I know he's going to leave marks in the places he's holding onto her. I reach up to tweak her nipple, tugging and twisting as her moans turn to shrieks.

Delores Drew belongs to us and she's completely at our mercy—willingly. It's so fucking hot I can't stand it.

"Make her come," Fitz orders as he pants. The tiger is rippling over his skin now and our bunny's claws are digging into me.

We're all right on the edge of something enormous, but I know we can't do it yet. Instead, I let go of one breast and slip my hand to her clit, rubbing until she begins to shake and shout with pleasure. Wetness floods my dick as she gets closer and when I sense she's on the edge, I pinch and she screams loud enough to rattle windows.

As soon as her walls wave around me, I know I'm going to lose it, so I look at Fitz pleadingly and he nods. My fangs lower and I move from her chest to her wrist, bringing it to my lips. Teeth digging enough to make my animal happy but not break skin. I bite when the climax slams into me like a fucking brick wall. Wild roars fill the room and I watch Fitz with cat eyes as he, too, clamps down on a shoulder. We all hold on desperately until the waves of orgasm finally fade, but I don't stop toying with her bud.

"Chessie, I can't," she whines as I flick my thumb over her fast and hard.

Fitz is hoarse when he gives her ass a slap and snarls, "One more, Baby Girl. You can give us one more."

His cock slides out of her, but mine stirs, so I move and suddenly she's quivering again. By the time it's over, Dolly is slumped on my chest like a rag doll and my lover is returning from her bathroom with two warm cloths. He lifts her off me, despite her protest, and settles us side by side.

"Now, my loves, we clean you up and get us tucked in. Tomorrow will be a calm day, as you'll be sore."

His hands drift over both of us gently and though I don't want to, I feel my eyes flutter and sleep takes me before he's even finished.

Scars to Your Beautiful

Delores

Fitz was right—I was sore enough on Sunday that I lazed around the house, eating and working on homework. Rufus and Cori came over for a bit, jazzing up the place with their excitement over my subtle 'fuck you' to my mother. Everyone was chill as hell; even Felix and Aubrey joined us in the big work nest. The day was so perfect I hated to go to bed and have it end.

But it did, and for the next few days, I had to grit my teeth through the snide remarks from my detractors and evil professors until Thursday, when I finally escaped the clutches of my shitty Rockland appointment. Tonight I'm going to the National Library with Rennie and Aubrey to work on finding information about the maps we saw at Apex. I got completely caught up on my work for classes by yesterday so I could focus solely on this. The hooded twatwaffles have been quiet and we haven't heard a peep about the dead body since it happened, but I *know* that will not continue.

It's never as easy as they finally fucked off to bother someone else.

When I get back to the library, I wave at Banjo and head to the back, moving my arm next to the sensor. I giggle when I think of Raina tossing all our removed chips into various things that some of my enemies might have consumed. Maybe it's a bit asshole-ish, but I also adore thinking about Lucille or the Raj wondering why the fuck we're off doing whatever the Heathers or Plastics do when they're not bullying me. It's extremely satisfying, so I forgave myself for doing something a little over my lines.

"I'm back. She behaved—mostly—today. A lot of the questions were about the Games and the viral vid." I frown as I think about it for a minute. "I wonder if Farley has started his campaign yet."

Aubrey appears in the doorway of the main room, walking out with a fond smile. "In due time, I'm sure. The tattooed badger swore it would be swift when it happened, so I doubt we'll have to wonder."

Grinning, I reach up to grab Jinx off his shoulder and cuddle her. "Are we still going to the big library tonight? If so, should I dress sneaky or what? Lucille never took me places where *humans* might be about. The first time was with you at the little bunny fair."

"I think normal clothes will do, though I advise against a skirt."

I arch my brow at him. "Why? Too tempting?"

"Too revealing for flight, lunchable," he scolds. "We're going incognito to a spot where the Captain left a vehicle then driving. We don't want people knowing you've left campus."

Since the last I was off campus without a full fluffle, we got attacked. I see his point.

"You don't think you and Rennie can protect me?" I pout teasingly and he rolls his eyes.

"Bite size, you can also protect yourself, as evidenced by the battle scars from this weekend. But we are far more likely to draw attention fighting those freaks than Fitz and the crew. My size alone…"

I bite my lip and bat my lashes at him. "How would I know about your size? You've been holding out, dragon."

His eyes darken and he takes Jinx back, growling under his breath before he says, "Go change. We leave in a half hour."

"Sir, yes, Sir!"

Aubrey snorts. "That *does not* work on me, nibblet, only the Raj. You'll have to try harder."

Phooey.

***

There's no way to describe flying on a dragon's back over the city while your gargoyle lover goads him into a chase. I held on so tightly I was afraid it might hurt him, but Rennie just laughed as they dipped and spiraled through the air. Fully shifted, they're equally enormous and the playful race wasn't the stealthiest way to get to our hidden car, but by the time we landed, my heart was racing.

I may be an adrenaline junkie.

Yet another fancy old car awaited us, and Rennie's smug look as he tore down the highway made Aubrey squeeze me to his chest. I had to tap his arm so I could breathe a couple times, but otherwise, I had no complaints about being wrapped up in his enormous arms. I don't think he minded as much as he let on, either, because I *definitely* felt something poking me as we sped towards our destination.

When we pull up to the imposing building, I swallow hard. Like many famous places in the capital, the National Library is a 'shared space.' Both humans and shifters roam free in the Library, the Smithsonian, the Capital, and lots of other well-known buildings. The treaty the Council made after they broke with magic users allowed our government to meld into the shadows, creating a second powerful cabal underground. At least, that's what my jackass History teacher said. I doubt it was that clean, nor was it as easy as Herr Frozen Cock says, but it's what I have to go on for now.

"Are you okay, lunchable?" Aubrey tilts his head when the car stops, observing me.

"I… I'm nervous," I admit as I dip my head. "What I know about interacting with humans is limited to TV and movies, so I'm afraid I'll break some super secret law or something."

Rennie snorts and shakes his head. "*Ma petite*, you're making a mountain out of a molehill. Humans are so conditioned to see what they expect to see that they write off everything as solar flares or gas leaks. Even our fiery mate's snafu has been written off as an accident in human lore."

"Of *course* you bring that up," the dragon grumps. "I was *eight*, for fuck's sake. My clash overreacted because the humans overreacted and…"

Aubrey throws his hands up, and I can almost feel his misery over the past wafting from him. Reaching up, I take his wrists and lower his arms, then place my palms on his. My eyes are soft as I look at him earnestly. "You're right. A child who didn't know how to control himself should have *never* been put in that position. Your clash, your parents, your family… they all failed you by sending you away to Apex. There were other ways to resolve the problem, but their own shame and guilt caused them to place blame where it didn't belong. But *we* don't care if you destroyed a bunch of old paper and books, Aubrey. Our family cares about *you* and who you've become since then."

"Awwww. *Ma cherie*, that was lovely," Rennie says, pretending to sniffle. "It made my stony heart grow three sizes!"

Both of us smack him and we all laugh. Aubrey gives me the most gentle smile I've seen yet as he flips my hand and kisses my knuckles. "Thank you for saying that. I'm still a long way from forgiving myself, but that's the dragon in me." He pauses and gives me a curious look. "But who said I came directly to Apex, snack size? You realize how old I am, right? It didn't *exist* when they sent me to these lands."

I frown, looking at my hands and wishing I could count on them, but I know Rennie will give me hell. "Well, in *theory*, I understand how old you are but… If you didn't get exiled straight to Apex without passing 'Go,' where the hell did an eight-year-old dragon end up?"

His lips curl up and he shrugs. "Here and there. Keep in mind that when I arrived, this land was only populated by native cultures of humans and shifters that fled the old countries after the many wars. It was a millennium before the human explorers came to these shores and another three centuries before they created the Capital. By then, the shifter wars and the split with the magic community had divided the supernatural community. I came to this area before them and stayed until Apex was founded."

"And until I arrived, he was a miserable, solitary wretch who lived in his giant horde-filled lair and commuted to school," Rennie says with a grin. "It took *forever* to lure him into moving into my lair."

My head spins as the two of them share more in five minutes than they've given me in over a year. "Holy shit. You guys are old. Like forget robbing the cradle, your crusty old pervs." My eyes dance as they both look horrified, and I pop the door open to hop out. "Catch me if you can, grumpy old men!"

Taking off, I run towards the King Neptune fountain, taking in the architecture and the portico busts on the outside of the build-ing. Humans don't know the serpents and nymphs are real things, but I enjoy imagining the Captain and his crew wrestling krakens or gigantic serpents, regardless. My men are calling for me as I walk around the rim, so I turn to wait for them to join me. Aubrey huffs as he comes close, yanking me into his arms.

"You, bite size, are far too sassy for your own good. Spending so much time with those whipped tigers is rubbing off on you." He grins as Rennie comes up behind me, caging me in between them.

I snort, leaning back into my gargoyle as I wink at him. "Oh, I'm rubbing something. Be nice to me or it won't be you." His eyes widen and Rennie sniggers when I reach around to smack the dragon on the ass. "Now, mush, old man! We have maps and books and hours of research to do."

"I already regret telling you any of that," he mutters as he lets go. "You're as much a brat as him."

"But you love me exactly as I am, big guy," Renard says as he holds his arm out for me. "Let's go."

The question is… does he love me, too?

***

Two hours later, I'm slumped over the table, my eyes already bleary from studying tiny, spidery handwriting in books so old they damn near fall apart if people *look* at them. Aubrey was the only one allowed to fetch anything from the super secret 'shifter antiquity vault,' so Rennie and I began by pulling out tons of maps to compare with the ones we have pictures of.

Nothing matched up, but we checked all the Capital's secret infrastructure and anything we could find on Apex. The only point of intersection was the map we'd already sussed out as being the tunnels under my old school. Everything else didn't fit a damn thing we tried, including the Library itself, the Smithsonian, and a bunch of other famous landmarks in town. I'm miffed we don't get to go steal the Declaration of Independence like in the movies, but alas, breaking into any of the human monuments was also ruled out.

"What the fuck *is* this shit?" I mutter. "This book is like a bazillion years old and it doesn't mention the 'Society.' The maps Aubrey has probably predated the fucking caveshifters and they don't show the stuff we're looking for. Are the ancestors fucking with us? That has to be it, right?"

Rennie gives me a rueful chuckle as he pushes his hair out of his eyes. "I fear we're searching through archives that may have been sanitized after the Treaty. The Council and the heads of state probably shuffled all the good shit to hidden lairs."

I blink. "That's it!"

They both look at me with tired eyes. "Apex is sought after for donations as tax shelters and by estates, right?"

Aubrey nods. "Yes. And everything has to be authenticated and verified to reside in its most guarded archives."

"That's why we found mentions of the Society in the new books! Everything the Council wanted to keep secret about the Treaty and magic was in books that most likely got distributed among wealthy, loyal families. No one is ever in danger of finding it *unless some heir donates it.*" I grin as both of their eyes light up when they get what I mean.

"Sparkly pixie nuts, lunchable. You did it!" I smirk as Aubrey takes his glasses off and cleans them furiously. "The books you and Fitz read were part of a large submission from multiple overseas families. Someone with a *lot* of clout in their family tree wanted to get rid of dusty old books, but didn't know what they had."

"Uh-huh. And to be honest, you don't read them all, ScalySpice." He grins at my attempt at a 'Fitzname,' and I shrug. "So who knows how many *more* books like that you have down there?"

Rennie and Aubrey look at one another, their expressions dark before they turn back to me. Finally, Rennie speaks. "You realize that means we have to go back to Apex? It's guarded and blocked off while they deal with the mess the hooded dicks left, so we'd have to break in."

Beaming brightly, I shrug. "Fitz has been teaching me to be sneaky. Besides, we don't have to go in the hard way. Won't Raina and the others know how to enter from the prey tunnels that lead to the outside where their housing was?"

Aubrey smacks his forehead and groans. "I can hear him humming *Mission Impossible* now. Bast, save me."

My brows furrow, and I tilt my head at Rennie, who still looks troubled. Usually, he loves mischief and giving the finger to the Council by breaking into Apex undetected is up his alley. "Why so serious, Frenchie?"

He boops me on the nose and sighs. "No more superhero movies. To answer your question, I'm worried about this plan. The Captain's crew and their friends told us prey animals weren't having much trouble with the aftermath there, but the way it affects preds has stopped construction many times. When we retrieved the things Aubrey and I needed, we were run down for days afterward. The magic there is dangerous and still wrecking havoc."

I close my book, coughing as some dust flies, then scoot my chair over to him. "You know more about magic than the rest of us; I can tell. Why won't you talk about it with us? We need to know more than internet rumors about different users and powers."

Shaking his head, Renard pulls away, looking at his hands. "I can't, *ma petite*. I've never been able to discuss the things that happened when I was younger, not even with Flames. There's still too much pain and regret. We will have to work with what we have until we can't."

"By the wings of valkyries, Rennie, calm down," Aubrey hisses. "I can see him flashing over your skin and if any of the humans see it, we're fucking toast."

Renard looks startled, and I turn bright pink when he looks at me questioningly. "I-I'm used to him. I don't notice when you rock out anymore."

His grin is gentle, and he takes my hand to squeeze it. "I won't complain about that, *cherie*."

"Yes, yes, we're all adorable and that's great, but lock it down." Aubrey rolls his eyes and picks up his stack of archive materials. "I'm taking this back, so we're welcome to visit again rather than getting us blacklisted. If you two can keep it together for the few minutes until I return, it'd be super."

Giggling, I wiggle my fingers at him. "Off you go. I'll try to keep him mostly presentable."

"As if I believe *that*," the dragon grumbles as he stomps away.

Turning to Rennie, I twine our fingers together. "Someday, you'll be able to tell us about the orchid and the amulets and all of it. I promise. But I won't push you if you're not ready because none of you have ever pushed me. You just have to know that no one in our family will be mad at current Renard for past Renard's dumb mistakes. Okay?"

His smile is genuine as he strokes his long fingers over mine. "Sometimes, I forget you're the young one and we're the elderly folk when you act like that. It's quite irresistible."

"I hope so because you geriatric cradle robbers are stuck with me," I shoot back. "No take backs."

"Annnnd then you say things like that and I hear Fitz coming out of your mouth, so that illusion shatters."

I shrug. "What can I say? Bunny see, bunny do, baby."

What? That was a super mature comeback.

Can't Hold Us

Delores

We don't have a match this weekend, so by the end of practice Friday, I'm ready to check out from the stress of week two at Cappie. Rufus and Cori are coming over for a 'Team Badass' meeting to pull together all the intel we've gotten this week and plan our secret outing to Apex on Sunday. I can't convince anyone to stay behind despite the dangers we've heard whispers about from our prey friends, so we have to coordinate. Eight people running around an off-limits site with weird contaminants and enemies isn't something Felix takes lightly, so I expect him to be in full-on general mode.

He's hot like that, so I don't mind.

The Games practice was exhausting—Zhenga worked us hard and the daggers from the Plastics made my skin itch as I waited for a cheap shot to come out of nowhere. It never did and I'm thinking they won't hit me from behind like the Heathers. No, I think Selene and her crew are more of a 'head-on,' public view group of meanies. That means I need to be careful of everything I do in front of them, because they'll likely capitalize on my mistakes rather than sabotage me. Just the pressure I need to make me even more paranoid.

"Miss Dolly, you seem tired," Kirby says. His bright smile draws a matching one out of me. I can see how Raina loves her triplets so much. It's impossible to frown when faced with big quokka smiles all the time.

"Not physically, no. I mean, yes, practice was hard. But really, the constant vigilance is making me droopy, you know? I've got so many enemies to watch that it's like I'm traipsing through a field of landmines all day." I swipe my card at the first gate and we walk through, heading towards our destination.

The quokka nods, looking pensive for a moment before he replies, "I understand more than you think. That feeling is what most prey feel most of their lives. You weren't raised like us, so it's very draining to know you have to be on guard. We consider it part of life, so it's not nearly as taxing."

I blink. *I'll be damned.* Kirby hit the nail on the head without meaning to. My animal hadn't emerged for most of my life and after the prom, she ran on fury and vengeance. Once we got used to Apex, we knew what to watch for, so it was easier, especially with the prey tunnels. Now that I'm stronger and embracing the way I was raised rather than my animal nature, being so passive is causing an exhausting conflict inside of me.

"Hades' fiery toga, Kirby. I think you figured it out." He looks at me curiously, and I sigh. "My bunny was very prey-like when I first emerged, but I've spent the past year allowing her to follow the pred instincts my parents taught me. All this worrying and darting around to avoid attacks is taking away the power I gave her. So I'm tired because everything inside me is in conflict."

Nodding, he beams again. "I don't pretend to understand how you can get your bunny to be vicious, but the Captain has told us about your fierce fighting. If you've trained your animal to be a predator, Miss Dolly, she will not be satisfied with behaving like prey anymore. She will want blood, just as they all do. You can't fight that or it will fracture your peace with your animal."

That's why the Games practice and matches give me such a high—I'm setting her free again.

As we swipe again and head up the stairs into the waning sunlight, I look over at my escort. "I won't get you guys in trouble by refusing to let you do what Rennie asked. But I am going to fight back more and hold my ground when I'm not in the ring. I think giving my bunny what she needs will help me take back my control."

"Excellent idea, Miss Dolly. Though, perhaps don't tell anyone I helped you with it. Just in case." He gives me a sheepish smile and I know he's worried I'll go off the rails only to blame him.

I shake my head and wink as he walks me to the back door of the library. "It's our secret, Kirby. Give Raina a hug for me and say 'hi' to the others. Okay?"

Kirby salutes me and waves as I move my arm over the scanner to go inside.

Time to show these overprotective alphaholes that I'm not fucking around.

***

"Pass the cheesy bread," Cori yells from her spot with Rufus. He's ignoring her as he texts furiously and my friend elbows him in the ribs. "Earth to Ru-Ru."

Chess takes pity on her, rising slightly from his spot at Fitz's side to hand her one of the bread platters. "I think he might be besotted."

Fitz puffs up on my right side, grinning like a loon. "You're *welcome.*"

A glass appears in front of me, and I look up to see Aubrey carrying two other glasses in his hand. He brought me a Dr.

Pepper without being asked when he got scotches for him and Rennie. "Thanks, big guy."

Rennie laughs as the dragon grunts and climbs back into the nest with their bounty. "Fitz's gambit was rather ingenious, I have to admit. The triplets at the bookstore seem to make your sketchy friend happy, and it means they'll be less grouchy if we have to go shopping again."

"Yeah, but now he's so attached to his phone that he's gone *deaf*," Cori grumbles as she takes a bite of the food, then moans in happiness. "Thank hell Chess remembered my non-meat loving preferences by substituting cheese."

Wrinkling my nose, I pluck a pepperoni and cheese stick up as I wink at her. "Chessie is good at making sure everyone has exactly what they need."

That gets Rufus' attention finally, and he looks up from his phone with an eager expression. "Do tell, Dollypop. We'd *love* to hear about it rather than everyone talking around me."

"Perhaps they wouldn't if you put down that wretched thing for five seconds?" Aubrey says as he downs two pieces of the 'Heat Lover' pizza Chess made for him and Felix. "I believe Fitz would call it… hashtag rude?"

Felix and I laugh, barely avoiding getting crushed by Fitz's rush to get to Aubrey to fist bump. He flops back down next to me as he sighs happily. "Nice one, Tangy Tightass. Very topical for an old fart."

His taunt earns me a sharp glare from my winged warriors. Fitz overheard me teasing them when we got back from the Library and he hasn't stopped poking at them since. It's probably going to get his ass fried or dumped in the river, but my playful tiger isn't one to back down simply because there are unpleasant consequences. I lean back into Felix, trying not to giggle as they both grumble under their breath.

"I hate to quash the fun," Felix begins, but Fitz's snort stops him. He reaches over me, his fingers giving the closest nipple a hard twist.

My jaw drops as Fitz yelps and I turn to look at the Raj. "Did… did you just give your brother a purple nurple?"

The entire table bursts out laughing, and I lean in to nuzzle his jaw with a soft chuckle. His expression is smug as he shrugs. "Perhaps even I can be taught new tricks, Princess."

"I'm *definitely* quacking about this," Rufus mutters as his fingers fly over the screen of his phone. "And yes, it's the stupidest fucking name possible. That's what happens when morons like the Ericksons let their bimbo daughter re-name their products. *Quacker* sounds like a little kid wants a saltine."

Cori rolls her eyes and steals the phone, tucking it under her butt. "No more quacking, asshole. We're here to spend time with Dolly and make a plan for Sunday."

"She's right," I reply before he can shoot back with a zinger. "And our Tiger King has a royal decree, so zip it."

Felix pinches my ass this time, giving me a stern look. "*Don't* call me that. But yes, I was about to open the floor to plan our raid on Apex. If we get it over with, we can be merry and shit afterward."

"Be merry and shit," Fitz says, as he rubs his nipple. It must have been a hard one, because he's still pouting. "You're such a buzz kill, bro."

"The Captain says there's a tunnel on the northwest end that will take us through the sections under the woods." Rennie looks at each of us, making sure we're paying attention before he goes on. "But that won't get us everywhere we want to go in a straight line. There's another at each corner and he recommended we split into groups to meet in the middle so we can explore all of it in one go."

I frown. "Splitting up is *never* a good idea. It's what gets people killed."

"Only if they're virgins and that ship has sailed in this room," Rufus snarks.

The guys guffaw at his quip and Cori elbows him again. "Don't be a dick. Professor Renard is right and so are his prey friends. Well… but so is Dolly."

My dragon looks amused as he looks around. "So all us non-virgins should be safe to split up or…?"

"I don't know," Felix says as he scratches his chin. "The tunnels are long and winding. Some sort of weird magic is making preds sick according to the rumors. We have no idea how many hidden places could hide hooded freaks or booby traps. It feels dicey."

This is getting us nowhere—it's dangerous no matter how we do this and we have to do it.

"Okay. Maybe the answer is we need four groups with enough strength for us to feel relatively safe." I sit up, grabbing a notebook and pen off the table. "If we also ask the Captain's crew to come, we have fifteen people. It'll be uneven, but if we have Aubrey, Fitz, Rennie, and Felix lead the teams, we can organize by strengths." I draw a little combo on my paper, sticking my tongue out as I decide who goes where.

When I finish, I hold the list up.

Aubrey Rennie Felix Fitz

Cori Chessie Dolly Rufus

Banjo Captain Kirby Raina

Percy Holliday Bowser

"That's… brilliant," Chessie says as he looks at the list. "It's fairly even in terms of attack power—I think—and each group should be able to defend themselves. Do we have something to communicate underground, Fitzy?"

"You paired me with the crazy gangster, Baby Girl," he pouts and crosses his arms over his chest. "Maybe I don't want to share my toys now."

"Fitz, I cannot think of a single moment since I've met you where you *didn't* want to share your toys with me," I drawl sarcastically. "Answer Chessie, please?"

Felix holds his hand up and mimics pinching with his fingers. "Stop pouting and share, brother."

"Fine, fine." Fitz tugs me away from his twin and wraps around me tightly. "Yes, I have some earwigs and radios that will work. Might be one per team, though. I'll order more in case we're going snipe hunting again later, but I wasn't prepared for such a sizeable group."

Rufus looks up from the phone that he somehow got back from Cori without her knowledge. "I'm awfully hurt, baby Khan. I'll have you know I'm fucking dangerous in a scrap and I have a sixth sense for nasty shit before it goes down. My Memaw had the gift, you know."

"No shifters have 'the gift,' you fool," Rennie mutters as he rolls his eyes. "Not even gorgons, as few as there are."

"Believe what you want, Pierre le Pessimist, but my Memaw is never wrong." Rufus runs his hand through his hair and shrugs. "I'm not so talented, but I've got killer instincts."

"Are we done flashing dicks around?" Cori smirks, then winks at me. "Because I think we all have stuff to contribute and there are enough people who underestimate us without us helping them out. So knock off the measuring contest."

I almost stand up and clap. Cori hasn't been nearly as sassy this year and I don't know if it's the new locale or her lack of hook-ups, but I was a little worried about her until now. "You tell 'em, sis."

Felix rubs his hand down his face, looking at us all like he wants to bang his head on the wall. "Groups set, then. Renard, contact the crew while we use the board and maps to plot our course. Chess, if you will?"

"We need lists of what to look for and what to grab," I add as my cheetah goes to pull the boards over. "Everyone should have copies on paper and on their phones. Oh! And knives."

Cori arches her brow as she looks at me curiously. "Knives? We're preds, Dolly."

I shake my head and my tiger grins. "Felix says we never go anywhere without a knife and it's saved our bacon more times than I can count. Rufus, you've got enough to give her one, right?"

"Dollybear, I've got enough knives to carve up the entire Games team and serve them for dinner before even one goes dull. I'll arm our girl." Rufus' fangs flash as he winks at me and I sigh.

"You know, I'm thinking I simply *attract* crazy."

"Duh."

Gee, thanks, Fitz.

Killer Queen

Lucille

Pacing across my ex-accountant's pelt on the floor, I glare around the room as if it holds the answers to my unrest. Since Bruno and I came home from Cairo, the chessboard has changed dramatically and the moves were not my doing. First, my errant progeny finagles her way to that substandard academy early and then she dares to choose to represent our family in an age-old competition I didn't approve of. I could strangle that bulky himbo in charge of the Leonidas pride for allowing his own wayward daughter to register Delores, but he's far too useful to the Council. His teams travel the world ceaselessly and it makes various branches of my father's and Bruno's businesses *much* easier.

That doesn't mean I won't show him who's really in charge; I simply have to be smart about it.

I'm almost pleased when I hold my hand out and it's immediately filled with a martini glass. Matilda was on her best behavior this summer because I made it known Delores was under the watch of Bruiser's security team in the house with no witnesses. Accidents happen and who's saying she might not get caught in the crossfire of a poorly planned home invasion? *Not me.* My threat kept her on her toes so well I thought she might have a nervous breakdown, but luckily for her, she held it together.

Being surrounded by weaklings is nothing new, of course. Dmitri drilled the importance of cannon fodder into me at a young age, and I took it to heart. Spineless lackeys are expendable, but useful for so many things. You don't want to choose someone too intelligent to follow you everywhere or you set yourself up for an internal coup. So I keep the addlepated Mattie and Bruiser close because they're just smart enough to carry out commands, but not quite enough to revolt.

Bruno would lose his scales if he knew his treasured brute was actually loyal to me. It's delicious.

"Matilda, what reports do we have on the progress towards repairing my school?" I tap my claws on the mantel impatiently as I stop to watch her flutter about the room, looking for the right files. Couriers bring me the most classified documents in writing and I burn them once I've digested the information. I don't trust that fool Erickson not to betray me, and there are simply too many loopholes to be exploited in digital communication.

The pale-faced bird finally stops flapping around the room like a toddler in a towel cape and walks over with a sheaf of papers in her hand. She's trembling as usual, and I roll my eyes as I snatch them from her. The top page is some ridiculous scientific nonsense about worker safety—as if I care about that. Snorting, I toss it aside and move to the next report. It shows a fifty percent slow down in worker output and rising costs for injuries. "Who approved paying for this?"

She blinks, gulping as she walks over to look at the expense report. "It's part of the negotiated contract, Madame Lucille. Titus McLachlan was in charge of it."

Of course he was. That sneaky feline owns most shares in the worldwide hospital network as part of the legitimate wing of the Khan empire.

"I'm going to string that tiger up by his toes," I snarl as I look at the mounting charges. "Who cares if the workers are getting sick? They have a job; it should be enough. This was a gambit to line the Raj's pocket."

Mattie swallows again, his eyes blinking behind the stupid glasses before she says tentatively, "Madame, I agree, but perhaps if they are too ill to work, it will continue to impede your progress? Also, the rumors among the lower tier predators and the prey may prevent us from replacing anyone unable to continue."

My jaw tightens when I see the wisdom in her words, but instead of thanking her, I thrust my empty glass at her. Taking it, she scurries off to the pitcher like her feet are on fire as I seethe. The partnership with the Khans is a necessary evil on many fronts, but I dislike allowing anyone to siphon money within my organization —regardless of the reason or legitimate purpose for it. One cannot maintain an iron grip on underlings who are also immoral if you do not make examples of those who act out. I will have to punish Titus for his largesse in a public, yet very definitive manner.

Too bad his wimpy heir discarded my dish rag daughter. I could have taken that away with a manufactured scandal, though perhaps…

"Matilda!" I snap. She runs over with my fresh drink, looking pathetically terrified. "Find out everything you can on that idiot child of Titus and do it now. I believe I know how I'll reward his… *ingenuity* in our contracts."

Blinking, she takes out a notepad and scribbles on it quickly. "Yes, Madame."

"Also, pull every record we saved from prior to the blast at my school. I want to see all the files on incidents there last year. Get birdbrain on the phone if you have to." Sipping the ice cold martini, I smile to myself. My plot might hit two targets with one mortar and the thought pleases me.

"Is there a particular incident or student you want information on, Madame?"

Ha! Nice try, featherhead. No, I won/t be giving you detail to pass to Delores.

"No, I simply want to look at everything. I need to match it up with the escalation in violence for the insurance paperwork in this file." I wave the papers I haven't even looked at towards her and she nods. Turning away to gaze at the portrait of my father on the wall, I stir my drink as I consider how I will arrange things to suit my machinations. It has to appear believable and not be traceable to me, so I'll use Bruiser. He has plenty of disgusting contacts in the underground world that won't ask questions.

With my revenge on the thieving tiger settled in my mind, I examine the next set of papers. They aren't helpful, so I head to my desk to file them. I sit my drink down and shift my right hand, pressing a paw pad to the scanner on the drawer. I take no risks with security, even in my home. Dmitri often spoke of trusting those closest to you the way you'd trust a starved animal and I concur. Anyone can betray you and being prepared minimizes the impact.

"Where's the intel file on Delores? I want to review her progress outside of that performance in the ring last week. She didn't know I was there, but given her profile has risen astronomically since she started at Capital Prep, I have to keep a much closer eye on her." Leaning back in the plush chair, I wait for my assistant to flit about again and when she brings me the next files, I growl, "This had better be complete. I lost my contact at Apex and had to purchase a new one mid-year. I do *not* want to suffer the same setback this year."

"B-But, Madame… we could not have predicted a murderer would randomly select our mole for execution. How shall I instruct your team on your wishes?"

I roll my eyes and sit up, pushing the button on my intercom. *"Bruiser! Idi syuda."*

The lumbering bodyguard appears within less than a minute, dipping his head as he enters. "Madame Lucille. What may I destroy for you?"

My smile is fangy as I tilt my head at Matilda. "No destruction— at the moment. Your skills are required to investigate my current contacts at Capital Prep. I do not wish to have a repeat of the lost connection from last year. Drive up there tonight and tomorrow. Do what you do best."

The look on his face is gruesome and I know anyone he gets his hands on will suffer if they don't comply with his orders. "As you wish, Madame. I will vet them completely, even if it requires pressure. Do you have further instructions while I am on campus?"

He means do I want him to visit my chubby leech; I'm not stupid.

"Perhaps. I will think about it and, before you leave, visit me again for clarification." I cut my gaze to my shivering hawk assistant. I don't want her warning my daughter that Bruiser is coming and I'll make certain to activate the communications blockers after I dismiss her.

"Understood."

Bruiser exits the room and I shuffle my papers again, pausing as I inspect the details of the trackers I've had in Delores since she was in diapers. Squinting, I eye the data, then click the mouse on my computer to look at the posting of the foolish eldest son of the Raj. Something doesn't add and I can't quite—

Ah-ha. Very clever, Delores. Very clever, indeed.

"Matilda!" I startle her again and she scampers over to appease me. "I need to speak with the cybersecurity head and Doctor Rankin *immediately*."

"Yes, Madame. Right away. May I inquire what I should tell them about your call?"

I snort, giving her a sharp look. "No, you may *not*. You will call Doctor Rankin first and patch him through to my office. I will have you reach out to Brutus after I get what I need from Rankin. Is that clear enough or should I try it in smaller syllables?"

"N-No, ma'am. I mean, yes, Madame. I understand." She pushes her glasses up and writes on her pad again. "Is there anyone else I should contact?"

Leaning back in my chair again, I ponder her question. I'm going to find out why Delores' trackers *all* show her scattered across the campus when I know she's in a video placing her at *Inky Depths* at the time in question. Once I do, I'll dispatch Bruiser to deal with the techs, who should parse my intel and missed her brief excursion. Then I'll call that sleazy old feline on Bloodstone and discuss our strategy for his wayward sons and their adoptive orphan.

"No. However, I require a mid-afternoon snack. Tell the cook I demand *fresh* food and it had better arrive quickly lest I head down to check on it myself."

That gets her moving. My ridiculously mousy bird secretary is fond of the head chef and she'd swallow her whole tongue before allowing him to be served on his own platters. Smiling to myself, I push the button on the intercom and call for Bruiser again before she returns. He stomps in, arching a brow inquisitively.

"She can't be trusted not to spill her guts to Delores." He nods, straightening his jacket as he waits. "Not only do I want you to shake up our contacts and verify their covers, but I want you to find out everything that's happened on campus these past few weeks. Sniff out what my daughter is hiding and how we can monitor her better, then find weak points we can exploit later on. I need to know what she might stick her nose in before she does it."

"And if I find out who was responsible for our contact's death? What is your wish, then?"

"Don't take them out until we know what their game is. The Society or the Council did not coordinate the murders at Apex.

They are likely linked to the little show that destroyed my school, Bruiser, and I want vengeance for the affront. No one survives interfering with my plans, but we cannot strike back until we know what they want."

"Consider it done, Madame."

"Now go threaten the kitchen staff. It will shake up our avian friend until I get the communication system locked down."

"With pleasure."

ZOETROPE

RENARD

THOUGH I AGREED WE NEED TO COME HERE, I STILL HAVE GRAVE misgivings about being back at Apex. The campus had an unsettling feeling to it during the aftermath of the blasts, and I couldn't figure out why. Being back here in the dead of the night, even with our reinforcements, feels similarly wrong. We aren't even *in* the tunnels to cross the border onto the land yet and my gargoyle senses trouble.

"We must be careful, everyone. The rumors are very specific about how long preds can stay on the grounds before they become ill. I know Fitz has given the leaders earpieces and radios that will penetrate the tunnels, but check-ins are not optional." I look at my family, then *ma petite*'s friends, and last, my prey crew. "When Fitz hacked the hospital records, the symptoms were severe and there is nothing here that is worth anyone being injured."

Aubrey looks doubtful as he gazes at our ragtag crew. "Tell me the codes again."

"Code Lannister for a coward who might stab us in the back," Dolly says with a salute that makes her look ridiculously adorable.

Fitz grins as he rubs his hands together. "Code Shonda means someone's going to die and I'm not sorry."

I look over at Aubrey, and he rolls his eyes. "We really need to get control of their TV consumption."

"Don't diss Grey's, poetry boy," Fitz shoots back as Dolly giggles. "We're learning a shit ton about what *not* to do in emergencies, right, Baby Girl?"

Aubrey groans, putting his hands over his face as I sigh. "Fine. Everyone knows the codes and has the maps. Felix and Fitz, your teams should head to the right at the fork and ours head left. The priority is getting into any locked rooms, especially those marked with Council names, and looking for anything relating to the four maps we haven't figured out yet. Check-ins are every thirty minutes."

With a grimace, I watch as everyone starts into the tunnel that goes beneath the forest surrounding Apex. I'm concerned, but I don't see any other option to help us unravel all the mysteries we're facing.

Hopefully, the team leaders can keep their charges in line and safe.

***

My group is headed for the areas around the forest atrium we discovered last year where we found the damn paintings. There were quite a few locked doors in the areas around that little temple, and I want to break into all of them. Aubrey's group is headed for the library/Tower underground to look at his precious archives. Felix has the quadrant under the lake and Admissions, while Fitz branches off towards the Shird and the Ring. Despite all the prep work, something about the campus is making my skin itch and my amulet buzz.

"Perhaps the leftover magic?" I murmur to myself. "But the scent is here, and it's not fresh, but not old, either."

"Is something wrong?" Chess looks at me curiously and I shake my head, then nod. His reaction is comical, then he asks, "Are you sensing something the rest of don't? Not to be nosy, but I feel you're holding something back. I mean, it might be personal or you're just not sure…"

The Captain speeds up a little without being asked and I try to figure out how to explain to my friend that I'm sensing things that simply cannot be real. I was *there* when it happened and I know the result like I know the back of my hand. *Yet…* Since the night Delores joined me at the club, the traces of a person long gone and a past I choose not to confront have come roaring back. I don't know how to admit I'm afraid I'm having some wild delusion.

Or worse, that you're somehow right.

Huffing at the voice in my mind, I let out a slow breath. "I keep having this *feeling* that someone or something that cannot be real is present. It's made me question myself and my sanity, *mon amie*, because I know it cannot be possible. So either I'm losing my mind or someone knows about things no one should ever know about from my past. Those options are not optimal."

"Well, I doubt you're losing your marbles, Ren. Your brain is trying to tell you something and if you're the only one who knows the story, only your interpretation is being considered. I know you're pretty close-lipped about the past, but you might need another perspective." Chess shrugs and shines his light on the wall, holding his hand up. "Look at this."

My frustrations melt away as I join him. When he pulls the light away from the rock, there's a design I recognize from the pillar we had to shine a light on. Something about it tugs at my subconscious, but I can't make the thought actualize. "They applied this with some sort of paint or magic that only illuminates when the torches aren't lit."

"Aye," The Captain says as he walks over. "There are many spots in the tunnels with these markers. We paid them no mind, as preds are an odd lot. Shouldn't have been anyone down here other than prey, but none of the scallywags made the glowing sigils."

I rub my hand over my face, realizing whatever this plot is trying to accomplish, it's been in the works for a long time. It's unclear why Dolly's arrival triggered the beginning of their machinations, but she said the hooded attackers mentioned looking for her. She's young, so it couldn't have been *that* long, but why would they seek her, anyway? Turning to Chess, I motion for him to snap a picture. "I suppose they could be here to guide their acolytes."

"X marks the spot, eh, Your Grace?" The Captain nods and points to the tunnel ahead. "We need to be following only the same mark, then. Others might lead to different outcomes—good or bad."

"Yes. I assume the marks, if there are more, will correspond to the ones from the pillar as this one does. Whether they'll give us any new information, that I cannot say." I turn to Chess and grin. "Perhaps you can use your night vision? Mine is better in a form that does not fit well in these tunnels."

"Can do, Your Grace," he snarks and I glare.

It's not my fault the prey think I hung the moon because I don't eat them, the little shit.

"Knock it off, Chester," I growl as we head down the tunnel. I can feel the temperature changing, so I know we're going deeper underground without a noticeable descent. These tunnels were crafted expertly and I can't help but wonder if they were originally for prey passage or if this 'Society' we can't find info on has always used them for their various needs.

As if he can read my mind, Chess murmurs, "If these really were constructed for a secret society, I feel like we haven't hit the 'main area' yet. It's not like I have experience, but everything you read or watch shows big gathering zones or temples where they do—whatever the hell it is they do. Have you ever seen something like that, Captain?"

"Nay, lad. I've been all over the place, though not in places locked or sealed. There are quite a few little nooks and crannies we can try to bust into that might lead us to the treasure. If I'm not mistaken, we're almost past the edges of the lake near your Tower, Your Grace. Further forward will take us under those cursed woods."

We've been walking for a while, so I glance at the screen on my phone. *Time for a check-in.* Pushing the tiny button on my earpiece, I open the mic. "Check-in, teams."

"Team Badass, all good!" Fitz crows loudly. "By the way, there's weird fucking glow-in-the-dark shit on the walls as we're headed to our zone. "The hillbilly mafioso is taking snaps, but they're spaced out pretty well. You can't see them with the lights on."

"Bioluminescent," Aubrey mutters. "And yes, Team Delta is finding them on the way to the archives as well. I have Cori documenting, so I can study them when we're back home."

"Team Alphahole found ours and I took pictures, too," Dolly cuts in.

It's hard not to laugh, as I can almost hear Felix sighing at the moniker. "Good. Then we've found something that may be useful to reverse search, even if nothing else turns up. We're almost to the woods. How close are the rest of you? And how is everyone feeling?"

They all answer in unison, and I groan. "One at a time. Status, Badass?" Fitz relays their position and condition without too much nonsense. Then I continue until we're all accounted for. The prey and Dolly seem perfectly fine, but each of the preds admits to a small amount of fatigue. My group is similar, but I also feel fine. "I don't know why *ma petite* and I are exempt from the effects, but that's another clue. It's not *just* prey; somehow, there's more to it."

"Okay, we've checked in, Ren. Let's focus on the task, not chatter on the headsets. Everyone, again in a half hour. Good luck," Aubrey says curtly.

That means he's close to his Apex hoard. Dragons get very touchy when their hoards are close by.

Chess gives me a knowing grin and I shrug as I click the headset off. "Aubrey is still learning to share his treasures, I'm afraid. He's done exceptionally well with our girl, but I worry once they consummate, he'll need to calm his dragon considerably. He was a bit… spicy after she and I…"

"I was amazed when Fitz agreed to share her last year," Chess admits. "He's always been open to me joining his random hook-ups, but it didn't interest me. I was worried he'd flip his lid when I admitted I wanted her, too."

I blink, thinking about that for a moment. "When was this? He seemed 'all-in' from the beginning. It surprised me how eager he was to encourage everyone, in fact."

The cheetah gives me a sly grin. "The first day we saw her on the tour at Apex. There was a shared voyeurism moment at the library and I told him. He jumped on it immediately and it made everything so much easier. I hadn't met a female I was attracted to before, much less a prey animal."

Chuckling, I nod. "I knew the moment Flames stormed in a-flutter about this new library aide that he allowed in his archives. It took many years for him to allow me access to each of his hoards one by one. Although he hasn't told her about the primary one yet, so that will be an adventure."

"Ahoy, Your Grace! There's a sealed door here," the Captain calls over his shoulder. "Perhaps you'll be able to decipher the writing?"

I walk over to the door, studying it for a moment as I nod. "This is Dutch. We've located the Erickson family's room."

Chess squints at it, tilting his head. "For a tech family, this actually doesn't seem difficult. There's just a sliding puzzle and I assume it opens the door."

The Captain takes the watch while the two of us kneel by the carvings in the door, sliding pieces around as we try to figure out how to get inside. Hopefully, the others are having similar luck, because the later it gets, the more on edge I feel. Whether it's the leftover magic or something else causing my paranoia, I'd like everyone to get off the Apex campus and back home sooner rather than later.

"I think I've got it," Chess says, and with that, the door clicks open and we head inside to rummage through the Erickson's hidden treasures.

OVERWHELMED

DELORES

"TELL ME ABOUT THE STUFF YOU GUYS FOUND," I WHISPER TO Cori and Rufus as we paint a backdrop. "By the time we all met up, I was exhausted, and the guys were grumpy as hell. Aubrey looked like he was going to smite someone because we had so much stuff to haul back."

Rufus smirks and shrugs. "Your crazy boyfriend had us digging through the Leonidas room like a drill sergeant. We found a lot of records that show they're being paid for a lot of placements on teams by elite and Council members. They're also fixing matches in a lot of leagues big to small because of that idiot younger brother of Coach Z's."

My nose wrinkles and I frown. "That's disappointing, but not surprising. I think Z is being railroaded, but she's also not super happy with anything about her family."

"Well, our trip to the library with the grumpy gecko was pretty successful," Cori says as she paints a bathroom wall. "He grabbed a ton of books he hadn't gotten around to cataloging last year that look really old. Banjo and Percy loaded everything in the carts after he packaged them up. He was pissed he hadn't thought of this when he gathered his stuff this summer, but after we checked every inch of his secret cave, he was satisfied."

I sigh, knowing he got behind because of all the bullshit I brought to his door via my idiot exes and dead people. "That explains why he was so pissy by the time we left. He probably feels guilty. I know Rennie was also toting a shit ton of *non-techie* stuff like maps and scrolls and stuff. He and Chess were really shocked by the lack of computer-y things in their room. We'll have to go back in a couple of weeks and see if we can find more rooms."

"What did he say they mean?" Cori asks as she hunts for a fresh cup of water to rinse her brush.

"Aubrey and Rennie are comparing them all. Some of them have weird languages and need restoration," I reply. "Chess is going to help and we're meeting tonight to discuss what they've found. Are you coming?"

"We would be if anyone *invited* us. You could have texted before today, you know. What if I had *plans?*" Rufus complains. Cori ducks her head and shrugs, walking away quickly. I give Rufus a questioning look and he sighs. "Since I started sort of seeing the triplets, she's a little sensitive. She hasn't found anyone at Cappie yet, and I think it's frustrating her."

"Aw, shit," I whisper as I look in the direction my other bestie went. "We're both so busy and she's feeling left out. Damn, Ru-Ru, we suck."

He shakes his head, giving me a rueful smile. "No, we don't. I know you don't have that much experience with real friends, but we can only do so much if she doesn't talk to us. I deciphered why she gets mopey, but she didn't *tell* me. I love Coco, but she knows we're not psychic. No amount of dropped hints and shit makes up for direct communication."

I know he's right, but I still feel bad. Cori has been amazing, and I don't want her to feel sad.

"That's true, but I still want to help. Maybe I should see if Fitz can keep his eyes peeled? He did a good job with your guys." I wink at him and I'm surprised to see Rufus actually blush. "A very good one, by that look."

"Don't be crass; it doesn't suit you," he sniffs, and I burst into giggles.

Cori appears from backstage, smiling as she holds up new brush cleaning cups. "What's so funny?"

"Dolly's boyfriends," Rufus cuts in. "They're all aflutter because they're worried someone will pay the Leonidas' to fix one of the college level matches. But I said she'd just whoop whomever's ass with her weird blue wizard shit…"

"Shhhhh!" I scold him as I look around. He might not want Cori to know he was talking about the triplets, but he also can't distract her by spilling my shit in public. "We have no idea who's listening around here. I don't want audio to get leaked online by Pink or Selene's people to get leverage."

"Not to mention the creepy old vulture you have to see again today," Cori adds as she glares at our friend. "How long do you have to keep feeding her vague bullshit?"

Scooting down the set, I work on another section of the backdrop. "Until she releases me. I have to prepare myself every time I go so I have a believable, yet completely fictional, account of my life, so she thinks I'm 'sharing my pain.' It's annoying as hell."

"Farley texted me this morning, by the way." Rufus snaps his fingers and pulls his phone out of his pocket. "He says—and I quote—the 'bitch is off her rocker and I've sent the paperwork, so don't worry.' In our family, that means he's sent one of the Postman."

I watch as Cori's eyes widen, and I pause. "Who the fuck are the 'Postman,' Rufus?"

His grin is almost feral as he shrugs. "The McCoys don't trust anyone not from the family. We don't use the mail—Memaw assigned a branch of the tree to be and raise what we call the 'Postman.' They handle all correspondence personally. I look forward to seeing what happens when one of them shows up on campus."

"They're fucking huge, D. Like the biggest goddamn science experiment badgers I've ever seen," Cori interjects. "And they barely speak. Brandine had some stuff that had to be delivered and the one they call Goliath came to the salon while I was working this summer with his brother Jethro. Ru-Ru said they're all that big, too."

Satisfaction courses through me, and I grin broadly. "By Hecate's hemline, I hope I'm there when they show up. Seeing her shake with fear would be the cherry on my sundae. It'd be even better if I got to see it more than once."

"Girl, the Postmen *never* ring twice. If that doesn't stop her, the next move will be the Messengers."

Arching a brow, I look at Cori and she shrugs. "Okay, tell us about the Messengers."

"Stupid, nosy, snide bitch," I mutter under my breath as I stalk across the green to the tunnel. "Who the hell gave her permission to ask about my *goddamn. sex. life?!*"

Bowser looks at me in shock and slows down, letting me pass him. I'd laugh, but I'm so angry at Rockland right now that it's probably a good idea for everyone to stay out of my way. The Postman hasn't arrived yet, so she was digging into my boyfriends like a pirate on a treasure hunt. She had the nerve to ask me what things my 'older men' have convinced me to experiment with and whether there are group activities.

As if I'm giving that bitch a single detail of my sexy men's moves for her poorly written trash.

"You know it's garbage when Rennie is threatening to gouge out his eyes if he has to read 'one more Predhub-rip off' scene in these disgraces to novel writing. He's way too nice to say something like that if it's not awful." I grumble as I kick a rock before I swipe my card at the entrance and stomp inside.

My phone rings and I pull it out. Fitz's face fills my screen and I can't help smiling. The picture is crazy—he took one of himself hanging upside down from the outside of the library after he scared me one night. Clicking the button, I answer, "Hey, crazypants. I'm halfway home. I think I scared Bowser with my ranting."

"Ranting? Who am I killing? Gimme a name, Baby Girl."

"Ugh. No one we can actually kill, Fitzy. You know Rockland time makes me angry." I wave at the scanner and exit the tunnel with the quokka hot on my heels. "I think I'm going to stop and futz with the stupid dorm room, since I'm already in a bad mood."

"Fuck that! I'm coming; don't you take one more step into that snake pit until I get there," Fitz yells.

I don't even have time to argue because he hangs up. Cursing under my breath, I give Bowser an apologetic look. "Uh, you get off early, man. Fitz is—" Before I can finish, the hyper tiger is running across the lawn of the library towards us with a war whoop. "...here."

My furry escort smiles broadly. "I'm glad, Miss Dolly. You look brighter already. I was worried about you until Mr. Fitz called."

Mr. Fitz? Good Goddess, Raina's men are all so damn polite and adorable.

"Baby Girl!" Fitz says as he swoops me up and spins me around. I can't help but smile and some of the anger fades as he twirls us. "I missed you. The winged weenies are squabbling and Chess is teaching. My brother is off with your friends, helping them haul their stuff to our townhouse. I was bored to tears."

I smack my palm against my forehead. *How did I forget to even ask them about the move this morning?* Neither Rufus nor Cori brought up my stern tiger's offer to let them hunker down in the townhouse they'd rented. It's right outside Cappie's borders, and the secret access point they created for themselves will work fine for my friends to slink in and out. "Are they excited? I hate they had to do this when I couldn't help."

His grin widens. "Well, the fluffy gangster was giving him a *lot* of shit last I heard, but I think he'll live. Now, let's go fuck up your room and see if this sneaky roommate is actually there."

Waving at Bowser as he heads off, I take Fitz's hand and tug him towards the creepy building. "I actually hope she's not. We'll have better luck rummaging through her shit if she's not."

"I love a good room toss. Lead the way," Fitz says as we head inside. His eyes cut around the outer room as we walk in and I feel his disdain.

Like last time, there were students curled in chairs by the fireplace despite the heat outside. Today, there are even more people curled in random spots with books. I haven't been in the other dorms, but the people in the Reptile house seem pretty studious. No one looks up as I tug Fitz to the elevator and we get in. I'd say it surprises me, but honestly, this school is so damn weird that very little shocks me now.

"This thing is older than all three of us Khans put together," Fitz grumbles. "Yet another reason I'm glad you're not actually living here. It feels like it's going to shake apart."

"Of all the things trying to kill me here, I don't think the elevator is our biggest enemy." I lean into his arms, letting him surround me with his warmth. "Promise me you'll behave if this chick is in here? We don't know enough about her to knock her off the board yet."

"If she was part of the poisoning at Apex, I won't get the chance, Baby Girl. The Habeñero Hothead is gonna smash her into bits. He was so pissed about ruining his suit and having to slog through all the vomit." Fitz smirks as his fingers trail over my arms. "But he'll probably let you watch if it makes you feel better."

I think about that for a moment, then shrug. "That would be an acceptable outcome."

Fitz growls and squeezes me, grinding against my ass. "I love the vicious streak in you, Baby Girl. Don't let anyone make you feel bad for it because it's hot as fuck."

"It doesn't make me… like her?" I ask quietly. I don't think I've ever voiced that before, but it's been on my mind. There's so much about our world that's shitty and unfair—most of it based on the ability to kill weaker beings.

"Absolutely not." He snorts and kisses my ear. "You aren't cruel or manipulative like your mother. You don't abuse people like your ex-friends. The empathy you show others, even the prey animals and shit, is what makes you better than them. But that doesn't mean you can't be formidable and fearsome."

The door opens and I sigh. "Thanks, baby. I needed to hear that."

"Anytime, Baby Girl. Now let's toss this place so I can get you home for dinner."

Horns

Fitz

This creepy place makes me extremely glad we convinced our girl to stay in the MojoDojo. All those weird kids making vacant doll eyes at us as we walked to the elevator and then the death trap? Not a ringing endorsement for her safety. Plus, it's on the fourth floor and the middle is *never* a good strategic position. Following her down the hall to her actual room, I roll my eyes at the dim lighting and décor; this place is some sort of weird homage to haunted houses or something. She swipes the Cappie card to get in and we walk into the pitch black dorm.

"I'd say she's not here, Baby Girl," I drawl as I let my eyes adjust. "Unless she's sleeping at four p.m."

Dolly flicks the lights on and I'm about to make another snide remark when she puts a hand on my chest. "Oh, shit. I think she's got a friend sleeping—*oh my fucking Goddess, Fitz!*"

A growl rumbles out of my chest at the tone in her voice and I step in front of her, my body poised to strike at whatever has her scared. "What? What?"

She trembles as she shrugs me off, walking around my defensive post to get closer to the bed. "That's—that's… it's not… That person isn't *sleeping*, Fitz."

What? Is she saying they're dead?

I sniff the air, confused when I don't smell blood or decay. The eyes are closed and the girl's skin isn't turning gray. *How does she know?* I stalk over to where she's pointing, intent on keeping her from panicking more. She might be fine with death, dismemberment, and bodies, but it's completely different when you find them lying in a bed that should be yours. They have traumatized our girl enough as it is; she doesn't need this.

The nerdy looking girl is lying peacefully in the floral sheets as if she's sleeping. Once I pull back the sheets, I can tell they did not kill here her. The slice on her neck is deep, and she likely bled out recently, but there's not a drop of gore anywhere in this place. It's like she was killed, cleaned, and moved here purposefully to send a message— which is likely right on the nose. The body hasn't been long, so whoever did this doesn't know my baby girl isn't living in this room.

"Stay back. I know you can handle shit, but you don't need to see this," I say as I whip out my phone and start texting. I'm not saying anything out loud; we haven't swept this room for bugs and who the fuck knows if this is a setup. I put my finger to my lips, and she nods, her face pale as she complies without a word.

TigerWoody: At Baby Girl's dorm. Code Black. *Again.* Need a crew and Henny *now.*

EmoBatMan: On it.

TigerKing: Again?

CSpot: Is my angel okay? Are you okay?

TigerWoody: Everyone calm down. And someone stop the Lizard Lothario before he comes stomping over. We don't want to draw more attention to this.

EmoBatMan: Good call. Felix?

TigerKing: On it.

LustyLibrarian: I'm fine, Fitzgerald. I know it's not prudent to cause a fuss, given the circumstances.

CSpot: But are you both okay?

TigerWoody: Yes, love. Baby Girl and I are fine. But this… problem… is lying in her dorm, in her bed, and it's been cleaned and staged. No accident.

EmoBatMan: The Captain and his crew are on their way and I messaged Henrietta. Luckily, that oaf in charge is never here, so she's in charge in an emergency.

TigerKing: *snort* At least we know she won't want to make a big deal. This will stay under wraps because she's a puppet.

TigerWoody: I'm going to do a little forensic shit in here. See if there're clues before anyone gets here. I'll send a picture of the face for Chessie to run through my programs.

CSpot: I'll try to I.D. her, babe.

TigerWoody: Over and out, dickheads.

I close my eyes, working to suppress the hyperactivity coursing through my veins because of the adrenaline. Baby Girl needs me to focus because she looks ready to keel over. Taking her hands in mine, I tug her over to the desk on her roommate's side of the room and plant her in the chair. "I'm going to look the body over to see if there's anything Aubrey can submit to his friends at the museum. We know they won't call the Sibbies, but if I can narrow this down, we'll know who to aim for."

She nods quietly and I go back to the corpse, intensely glad it's fresh and we didn't walk into decomp stench. I snap a picture of the face first, sending it to Chessie, then I let the tiger's eyes bleed in. The change sharpens my vision and I hover over the uniformed body to examine it. It'd be easier if I had gloves, but if I find something, I'll use claws to avoid prints.

"Should I… see if there's anything we can use to preserve… things?"

"Good idea, Baby Girl. But cover your hands before you touch anything not out in plain sight. It makes sense you might leave prints on a chair, but not on drawers or inside of stuff. Remember what they do on the mystery shows, right?"

That gets a small chuckle and I smile to myself as I continue my way down the torso. Dolly rummages quietly, and I hear a sound of satisfaction when she must find something useful. I'm about to turn around, but then I see them: two long blond hairs caught in the buttons on the sleeve of the girl's jacket. The body has short black hair, so it's not hers.

This is the clue we need to find out who the fuck is killing students, and I found it.

"Baby Girl, what did you find over there? I need something to carry this."

She walks over, holding up what look like tubes from a lab. "Will these work? This Kinsley chick had lots of lab stuff last time, so I knew looking around might lead to shit we could use."

I nod, giving her a proud smile as I take the capped vial. "Perfect. Keep a watch for the calvary while I do this, okay?"

Her face is a little less pasty than before, but her spark is still gone. She just nods and walks back to the desk, sitting quietly. *I don't blame her, but I also don't like it one bit.* Shaking my head, I go back to the body, sliding two claws out to pluck the hair off the cuff. It takes a little doing to get it in the tube and sealed, but once I do, I stuff it in my pocket. Having our own evidence is crucial and I trust the Council's flunkies about as far as I could throw the dragon.

"Fitz?"

"Mmm?" I reply as I go back to searching for more clues.

"Who is she? Do we know yet?"

I sigh, looking over my shoulder at the guilty expression on her face. She thinks they killed this student because of her, but I doubt that. It's far more likely they were killed for no reason at all except to inspire fear. Just like her bullying friends, psychopaths and sociopaths like to play with their food. If they didn't kill this girl to mess with her, they'd be killing someone else for another reason. My father taught us that from the time we were cubs, with his capricious whims and frequent tirades that lead to bloodbaths.

At least I have a fucking reason when I tear someone to bits.

"No, we don't. I sent Chessie a picture and—" My phone dings and our eyes meet. I stand, backing away from the corpse as I check the screen. "Oh, fuck. This isn't good."

"What? Who is it?" Dolly shoots to her feet, hurrying over to see what I'm looking at. Her skin goes white again and I have to hold her arm when she sways a little.

The fucking dead girl is her absent roommate that Aubrey's been researching as the poisoner—and now she's dead in Dolly's bed.

This is so *not good.*

"Fitz Khan, we're only two weeks into our guest stay at this institution!"

Henny is fluttering around like a chicken who sees the sky falling. I have no idea how the Irritable Iguana handles her; it's annoying just to witness. Huffing, I look over at the Captain and Holliday as they carefully wrap the body in plastic. They seem to know what they're doing—something I should ask the Flying French Fry about. Everything the two of them have done looks familiar from Dolly's mystery shows, and I'm a little impressed.

But then, who the fuck knows what that poetic prat had them do this summer?

I wouldn't put it past him to get his minions trained in crime scene shit after we got everything out of Apex. Renard always seems one step ahead of everyone else, watching the pieces move while he perches on shit and smirks. He's got that Moriarty vibe—*focus, Fitz.* I rub my temples, letting out a frustrated sound when I have to stop my brain from running off again. It's gotten easier since my baby girl came along; she's worked with me on reining in the chaos in my head. But when I get emotional, it's a fucking challenge.

"Henny, you know damn well Dolly didn't kill this girl. Whoever she is, we stumbled on her while picking up some books from her dorm. I was escorting her to the library to study." I try to look nonchalant, not wanting to give away exactly what she planned to study. We don't need the administration questioning why she's spending so much time there.

The frazzled avian throws her hands up, squawking something in a high pitch I don't catch. Dolly does, though, because she stands up to face the assistant to our absent Headmaster. "Ma'am, I don't know what happened here, but I-I don't think I can stay in this dorm. It's too gruesome after this."

Oh, clever girl.

"Where do you recommend you stay then, Miss Drew? You cannot live in the other dorms as it's too much of a temptation. Despite your skills on the Games field, a mob would be too dangerous. Your mother will be furious if we put you in jeopardy."

"Ahem," I say with a bright smile. "I believe there's room in the library staff quarters, Henny. I've visited my friends there, and it seems to have open rooms. Perhaps having staff members to watch over her would make Dolly feel safer. Obviously, the dorms have proven themselves too exposed to allow her to continue living there."

Dolly blinks her big blue eyes and fat tears roll down her face. I have to look away as she works the Shirdal woman with those badass skills that *should* have gained her a part in the stupid play here. She's upset; don't get me wrong. But this little show is about using this bullshit to our advantage. Our girl may be worried, but she's not stupid and she's always using that gorgeous brain in her head. It reminds me of Felix sometimes; he's always watching the angles, too.

That's why he's the King and Delores Drew is our motherfucking Queen.

"I suppose I could clear it with Professor Draconis. He's rather protective of his space, but he would never let a student remain in a dangerous situation." The bird hems and haws for a moment, then nods, looking at the Captain. "Can you have some of your crew assist Miss Drew in packing up after we examine this entire scene?"

"Aye, Madame. Consider it done." When she turns away, he looks at Dolly and winks. The little shit knows everything in here is throwaway and that's likely what he'll do. We purposefully made sure our girl didn't need a damn thing. She left here so no one could use it against her.

Henrietta turns back to us, looking tired and strung out. "Fitz, please take Miss Drew to the library with her things. I'll contact you when I have an answer. Captain, I'll expect you to handle all of this quickly, quietly, and then meet with campus security to file reports. I have to contact the Headmaster and after we identify her, the student's parents."

That said, our fearful leader gives us one last reproachful look and leaves.

"Guess we're not calling law enforcement," Dolly mutters. "*Quelle surprise.*"

"Baby Girl, I love it when you talk all *voulez-vous*, but for now, let's go home." I take her hand, squeezing it as we walk to the door. Before we leave, I pause. "You know what to do, right, gents?"

"Anything we find, make sure the Admiral is informed," Holliday says grimly. "Aye, aye."

I slip my other hand in my pocket, feeling the tube there. "We're going to catch this son of a bitch and make him pay; I guarantee you that."

And the price is going to be very, very *high for making my Queen upset.*

RIVER

AUBREY

WHILE I'M INCREDIBLY GLAD OUR BUNNY CONVINCED HENNY TO allow her to move in, I can tell the incident earlier in the week is weighing on her. Fitz brought her home, and she waved everyone off to take a shower before heading to bed. She spent her free time this week working on homework and doing yoga in the backyard. Everyone but Fitz tried to give her space so she could process, but it's been several days now and she's still hiding out. I could deal with that if it was the only bullshit going on, but Rennie has been moping since we did our trip to Apex and Felix is damn near ready to burst because we haven't gotten answers about the hair Fitz found.

My dragon is very displeased that our family is not happy, which makes me cranky.

That's why I got up in the middle of the night to pace around the living area, staring at the boards in irritation. There are connections we aren't seeing and machinations we're not prepared for. I hoped being forced to come here might calm down some of this chaos, but it's ramped up. We've got more people and more clues, but none of it seems to lead to anything but more questions. The situation is infuriating because we're going in enormous circles only to end up back where we started with dead bodies.

Except this time, they left it in Snack Size's bed.

A soft noise from the other side of the library doors makes me pause. There shouldn't be anyone in my library at this time of night. All the assistants are long gone and the cleaning crew comes in the morning. Scales ripple over my skin as I stalk towards the doors, growling low as my dragon rears his head. I'm going to *murder* whoever dares to break into my space, then I'm going to kick both Fitz and Rennie's asses because their security failed.

My wings break free as I wave my arm at the stupid scanner and stride onto the large, ornate main floor. It's dark and there's not even the scent of another shifter in the room. My eyes bleed to my dragon's as I look for heat trails. When I see a faint trace, I grimace and head for the bookshelf that conceals the way down to the underground archives. The intruder is headed for the most valuable pieces in the Cappie collection, and that ignites the fire in my gut, making my blood burn with fury.

I can't wait to crisp this motherfucker after they give up who sent them.

The shelf swings out when I pull the correct combination of books and I push it closed quietly. Making my way down the roughly hewn rock stairs, I work to contain my fury. They have hunted me in the past—all dragons have, at some point—but the factions after our bunny aren't torch wielding idiots. They have money, power, and influence, so there's no need to fear a college girl, even if she is an heir with an anomaly. She might have never even discovered the blue lightning if they hadn't tried to level Apex last year. Nothing they're doing is stopping whatever is coming; it's making it more certain, so they're getting more desperate.

"Too bad for you, sacrificial lamb," I mutter under my breath. "They sent you to get roasted."

Creeping around the corner, I make my way into the cool, dark archives as I look for the thief. A small light catches my gaze and I make my way towards it silently. This criminal is bold; I'll give them that. They're sitting at the table, looking through the volumes I stacked on the tables yesterday. My eyes narrow as I get close enough and snatch the hood off their head with a snarl of triumph.

Except all I see is our bento bunny's rainbow locks in a messy bun and her pale face with purple circles under her eyes. She gasps and frowns at me, crossing her arms over her chest. "Aubrey! What the hell are you doing?"

"Nibblet, I should ask *you* that question. It's three a.m. on Friday. You have Diplomacy in four hours. Why are you down here flipping through these old books?"

She looks uncomfortable, shrugging in response. "I can't sleep. It's been hard to do since we found Kinsley's body."

Arching a brow, I sit on the edge of the table, folding my wings back as I study her. "I thought you were okay with dead things."

"Don't be ridiculous. I *am* okay with dead *things*, but this was a dead *person* in *my* bed. I can't miss the symbolism," she says with a sigh. "Kinsley might have been on our suspect list; hell, she might even have been the poisoner. I'm not worried that she met her fate so much as that someone may have mistaken her for me."

I hold my hand out and she lets me pull her to feet, settling her between my legs. "I don't believe anyone could mistake that girl for you. You look like one of my adorable sparkly unicorns and she looked…normal. Bookish, sure, but pretty normal."

Her lips curve up, and her expression makes my chest tight. "You know what I love about you guys?"

"Our sharp wit and asshole tendencies?" I quip.

Dolly giggles and reaches out to tweak my nose playfully. "Well, yes. But more than that, I really love that when any of you try to make me feel better, you don't feel the need to tear other girls down. Like, you make me feel special and pretty, and I love it, but not at the expense of being a dick to some other woman—even if they deserve a good asskicking."

I give her a surprised look; it's not what I expected her to say at all. "You're not perfect, snack size, even though it feels like you're perfect *for us*. However, it's unnecessary to compare you to anyone else because they can't compare—they're not *you*."

Her eyes widen for a second, then she darts forward, pressing her lips to mine as her arms wrap around my neck. My dragon lets out a mighty roar inside as our tongues twirl around in a hungry kiss. My hands land on her hips, holding onto her as she burrows into me eagerly. When our lips break, I run my finger over her lower lip.

"It's three a.m. and you haven't slept in days, snacklet."

"Mmmm. That's true, big guy. Maybe you should wear me out so I can finally get some rest."

And there goes every good intention I had because she said that while the dragon is far too close to the surface.

Picking her up, I feel her wrap her legs around me as I walk towards one of the empty tables. She leans in and bites my lip, eyes dancing with merriment as she tugs on it. As soon as her butt hits the heavy wood table, I pull back and growl softly at her. "You're a brat, cupcake, and don't think for a second it will work with me."

Dolly leans back on one hand, smirking as she unzips the hoodie to reveal her tiny sleepwear. "Seems to work for Rennie. Why not me?"

"Because he's learned when to be a brat and when to do what I say. I can't say the same for you," I reply as I pull the tee shirt over my head. "However, if you figure it out, perhaps I'll consider it."

Her eyes darken as she sees the scales that erupt over my chest and spread down my arms. Swallowing, she darts her tongue out to lick her lips before she looks up through her lashes. "You're half-shifted."

I nod, giving her a fangy grin as I lean forward until her back is on the table. My wings flex and spread wide, helping me balance as I lick a fiery trail over her collarbone. "Mmmhmm. I have plans for later, bite size, and you need to get used to me first."

A shiver runs through her frame and I don't know if it's fear or desire, but my dragon is happy with either option. Moving to her shoulder, I bite down, making her gasp and dig her nails into my biceps hard. "That's it, little bunny. You can't break me; go wild."

My answer is a soft growl and, to my surprise, she darts forward to sink her teeth into my opposite shoulder. It's not quite vicious enough to break skin, especially in dragon form, but I feel it and groan. She laps her tongue over the mark and adjusts until I arch her body into mine, close enough to make the fire inside spark again. *This is what I want; I want her to let go of her primal side without fear.* As a reward, I nip and bite my way down her chest, ripping the flimsy bralette in half so I can sink my teeth into a nipple.

"Fuck, Aubrey," she breathes. One hand comes up to bury in my short locks and for a second, I get why they're all growing their hair out.

I bet my squishy collection she's a hair puller.

Blowing hot air on the tense bud, I hold on to my inner beast carefully. Her nails dig in again and I suck her nipple, sliding one hand down her side to her hip. Hitching it on mine, my hips grind into her in time with my mouth. I lift my head, moving to the other breast as her chest heaves, noting the honeysuckle scent permeating the air. I want her dripping before we fuck because I don't intend to hold back, even in a half-shift.

"I can smell you," I mumble against her skin, then nip her firmly. "My dragon likes it; in fact, he's desperate to get out."

"Let him out. Just… please, Aubrey. I need more."

Chuckling softly, I squeeze her hip and sink my teeth into the curve of her breast until it leaves a mark. "Impatient little thing now, aren't you? You get more demanding every time, I hear."

"I know what I want," she shoots back. "I'm not afraid to ask for it."

"That's good, bite size. The occasional shyness is cute, but I like the sass, too." I follow the line of her ribs with my tongue, heading for her quivering stomach. It's still soft to nuzzle, but she's getting a little muscle under there from her training. They clench as I kiss my way to her belly button and when my tongue rims the edge, she bucks her hips up. "Now, now. Don't rush me."

"But…"

A firm smack on her thigh makes her stop wriggling, and I grin. Those tigers have trained her well; I'm impressed. Though, thinking about her taking control is just as hot if I'm honest—just not with me. An idea occurs to me as I nip her hipbones, so I pause for a moment. "You're behaving so well, but I wonder what you'd do if your reward was to be in charge?"

"Of you?" Her tone is incredulous, and I shake my head as I squeeze her again.

"Absolutely not, lunchable. The dragon would never allow it. But perhaps if we had Rennie with us?" I trace a line up the groove of her leg, then move to do the same to the other side. "He's *very* flexible that way."

I lift my head, interested in her reaction and I'm pleased when I see the blown out pupils and glazed expression. She nods at me, obviously trying not to move as my chin hovers over her pajama covered mound. Tucking that plan away for later, I dip my face to inhale her scent again and this time, the growl I let out is pure animal. I give into the dragon, letting go of her to spread her thighs wide on the table. She's soaked; I can see the wet spot on the tiny silk shorts. Tearing those off, I toss the pieces aside, then gather her juices on my fingers. Her eyes meet mine as I lick the fluid off of my fingers before her head thunks down on the table.

"If you knock yourself out, this will end quickly," I warn her. My response is a strangled sound when I expose her swollen clit and repeat the trick with the hot air. "I'm sorry; did you say something?"

"Fucking hell, you tease, touch me!" she snarls. Her ass lifts off the table, pushing her pussy into my face eagerly.

That's what I'm looking for—the fire in her that calls to mine.

"Tell me what you want, little one. I want to hear it." She huffs and I sense her hesitation, so I flick the tip of my tongue over her and stop. "You're a big girl. Use your words."

"I want you to devour me until I come," she pants.

"Mmm. Nope. Be specific." I grin wickedly, knowing this is pushing her boundaries a little, but she knows the words to stop. "Direct me, cupcake."

Her body squirms for a moment, but I hold myself out of reach until she whimpers. "Fine, you stubborn asshat. I want you to lick and suck my clit while you finger me until I come on your face."

Perfect.

"As the Queen demands," I retort. Burying my face in her heat, I nibble and nip the tender bud while two fingers slide into her. Her core clenches around them immediately, rocking into my face at the same time. I need her to do this on top one day, but for now, I'm going to get her ready for what's coming. My cock could cut diamonds; that's how hard it is. This won't be a gentle ride. "Keep talking."

Dolly gasps as I work another finger into her cunt, continuing to lick and suckle as she writhes under me. "Th-There. Do that... again. P-Please."

"This?" I mutter, muffled by her pussy. Her thighs have settled around my ears tightly, but I don't care. To make my point, I thrust all three fingers in roughly, then pull back. She doesn't answer, so I bite her clit again and she mewls loudly. "Or that?"

"That. That. More teeth. More, more," she pants as her hips rock on my digits faster. "More of everything, Aubrey."

Grinning ferally, I follow her pleas and slip a fourth finger in to continue stretching her as she slams into my hand. I turn my head and bite the inside of her thigh roughly, sucking the skin against my teeth until she whines. I repeat that on the other side, feeling her body tightening. She's very close and I know exactly how to send her over the edge.

"Are you ready, little one?" I ask as I look up at her. My fingers are still sawing in and out quickly and she's flushed from head to toe.

"For what? To come? Fuck, yes."

Diving back in, I use her dripping juices to work one finger into her ass. She squeals and I lick my lips as I watch her ride my hand wildly. Right when I think she's going over, I let the dragon out more, curling the long forked tongue around her clit to flick it rapidly. Her back comes off the table when the orgasm crashes into her, but I keep working the dragon tongue over her sensitive spot as she gasps and shudders and jerks. It's a secret weapon and if she thinks this is the end of the night, she's dead wrong.

Her body goes limp and I rise to my full height, wings spread as I whip the sweat pants off. Ranging over her, I lean in to lick a droplet of sweat off her jaw. "Ready to fly, little one?"

She gives me a mischievous grin and her eyes turn dark crimson as she half-shifts seamlessly. Twitching ears, soft fur and sharp claws greet me before she flashes the oddly pointed fangs. "Now I am."

No blood. I growl at the dragon internally when he pushes through my hold to release my tail and the larger incisors. He doesn't like it, but we all promised no one would mate with our girl until we knew she was ready for it. She's getting there, but not yet. "Good girl."

My cock slams into her and she lets out a sound I've never heard in my life. It's a cross between a scream and howl that shakes the surrounding shelves. The dragon loves it, so I pull my hips back and repeat the motion. Her claws dig into my arms, definitely not following the blood decree I gave my animal as she holds on. The table creaks when I thrust again, but I ignore it when her muscles clench around my dick. There's no stopping the knobs and knot from swelling; it's too fucking amazing, and she's too damn wet. My body knows it's finally fucking its mate and while I can't mark the marks, physiology doesn't listen to reason. A squeak gets my attention and I shift, pushing deeper into her to hear it again.

Fuck, this girl makes the best noises I've ever heard.

"What-what the *hell* is *that*, Aubrey Draconis?" Her question ends in a high-pitched moan and I damn near preen.

"Later," I mutter as I grab her hips and hold on, slamming into her over and over as the pleasure makes me sink into the primal. I can't focus enough to answer her and I want her to come at least once more before we're locked in position for however long it takes for my fucking dragon to calm. "Squeeze harder."

Her eyes flash and I almost choke when I feel an odd electrical tendril move over my frame. Panting as it dances over me, I throw my head back and roar. My wings extend above us and I gnash my fangs together o kccp from biting the shit out of her. The hunger is bone deep, so I let go of one leg, rubbing her clit until she finally shrieks and the shivering starts up again.

"You... fucking... cheater..."

Looking down at her with the eyes of the beast, I smirk and pull back, thrusting once more as hard as I can. That sends us both tumbling over the edge with roars and screams that make the entire room echo. I'm about to flick her bud again, trying to coax her to one more climax when there's a loud creak. I don't even have time to react before the table cracks in half, dumping us in a sweaty, sticky heap of limbs.

Our eyes meet, and the laughter that tumbles out makes my heart swell with happiness. Tears leak from her eyes as she works up to a cascade of giggles that would make a cartoon character proud. I can't even be mad; it's my fault. Dolly wipes her face, then places her hands on my cheeks before she kisses me. When she pulls back, the look on her face is full of adoration and amusement.

"Fitz will *never* let us live this down, you know. We didn't just defile your library; we fucking *broke* it!"

That starts the laughter again, and I have to admit she's right. None of them will ever let this go and there's no fucking way that noise didn't wake someone. The archives aren't sound proofed and we just fucked like demons.

"Ahem."

I look up from our tangled spot on the ground to see the tiger in question, looking so excited he may not sleep for a week. Chess and Felix are smirking as well, and my gargoyle is lazing on top of a tall bookshelf as he looks at us upside down.

"I believe I've been told *over and over* that there's *no humping in my goddamn library.*"

Dolly giggles and I scrub my hand down my face. "That's correct."

"Looks like someone's buying a new table," Fitz sing-songs. "And now I can fuck anyone I want anywhere I want, you scaly hypocrite."

"Fitz!" Chess says, as he looks at us sheepishly. "No, you can't."

"Yes, I can!"

I look down at our girl, feeling the flush creep up my neck. "Are you *certain* I can't crisp him?"

"Nope. No crisping."

Damn. This is going to suck.

Wake Me Up

Delores

It took two weeks for Aubrey to get the table in the archives replaced, and the guys definitely didn't let him forget his own egregious breach of his rules. They riddled our nightly work sessions with ribbing that made me both bright red and turned on to varying degrees. I'm doing well with expressing myself when we're alone, but I still get squirmy when we have Rufus and Cori there to join in. They're supportive and gentle—well, Cori is—but I'm working to shed the trauma I had after Todd tossed me out like garbage.

It helps that the guys are fucking determined to make me feel like a supermodel even when I have fucked up hair and morning breath.

"Miss Drew, are you paying attention?"

Blinking back into reality, I give the eagle-eyed tiger a bright smile. "Yes, Professor Rakoto."

"Perhaps you can tell us what the primary reason for the assassination of the Archduke was and how it impacted both shifter and human history?" Her gaze narrows on me as she stalks closer, but I don't let it bother me.

Finding out she's a Khan puppet makes it infinitely easier to cate-gorize her as an academic threat, but not a physical one. She can treat me like shit and try to embarrass me, but unless the twins' father puts a hit out on me, I'm fairly safe. I lick my lips as my brain works to find the answer she wants, even if it's not what actually happened. Once I remember this is the guy I coined the 'Archduck,' I'm able to breathe easier.

"The Archduke was the younger brother of the Emperor of Austria-Hungary. European shifters could worm their way into many of the royal families in the previous centuries. Unlike in this country, so many of the heads of state between the latest part of the Renaissance and the Industrial Revolution were not actually humans. The European and Asian Councils had great power at the turn of the century, but many of the families were still at war with one another over business interests."

She sniffs, folding her arms over her chest. "Why does that matter?"

Because he didn't fucking duck and that's what lead to World War I, you twat.

But I don't say that; I simply smile again. "It's important because the Emperor's son died and the Archduke became the heir appar-ent. He made choices in his personal life that angered the crown, but they couldn't cast him aside because of interspecies marriage because of the Crown Prince's death. Neither preds nor prey were happy when he married his swan lady-in-waiting because the two sides had been battling for lands with one another and the humans for many years. Thirteen years after their wedding, a member of the prey resistance faction assassinated them in a public appearance in Sarajevo and it lead to a declaration of war between the species."

"Very good, Miss Drew. How did the humans get involved? Why do they think this war belonged to them?"

The classroom is silent as I pause again. I'm sure the Plastics and the Heathers think I'm going to whiff this, but Rennie has made sure I'm ready for anything. "As it is now, very few humans are aware of our existence and have no idea we walk among them. So the humans believed a rebel from a nationalist faction shot a human leader and the two countries went to war because a human assassin killed a human royal. The other causes of the Great War involve all three species, as they cannot make rational decisions in large-scale disputes."

Of course, if the Councils hadn't declared revealing ourselves treason after the Magic Treaties, the Archduke could have ducked or even healed his wounds before he got to the hospital.

"Excellent, Miss Drew. I'm glad to see you are catching up with the rest of your peers. I was worried you were lagging so far behind that you'd flunk the first semester and have to repeat it next year."

My lip hitches and I open my mouth to retort when the door flies open. The frame is filled by two beefy looking bear shifters and our nervous Headmistress from Apex. She hurries over to the professor, who nods and looks directly at me. *This is not good.* I calmly pick up my phone, texting the group chat to let the guys know it seems like I'm being pulled out of class for something and to track where I am. When Rakoto calls for me to join the cadre at the door, I hit send and shove my stuff into my bag.

I don't know what the fuck is going on, but I have a bad feeling about this.

"For the last time... I was in class during the day. I met up with Professor Khan, who gallantly offered to walk me to the dorm so I could give him a paper for the other Professor Khan. We went to my dorm and when we turned on the lights, there was someone in my fucking bed like Goldilocks. I went over to wake them up and get them the hell out of my bed, and that's when I knew she was dead. Professor Khan called for a crew and Head-mistress Shirdal. The. End."

The huge polar bear glares at me through his ridiculously huge mutton chop beard, his eyes dark with anger. I've never met him before and kind of hoped I never would. He hasn't been on campus since I arrived and I suppose flighty fucking Henrietta called him back after she dealt with Kinsley's parents. Headmaster Bathalzar Slechtsrijven obviously prefers not to be on campus and, based on his behavior, I can see why. I came here willingly and I've made my statement, but they keep hammering at me.

Why? What are they aiming at?

"I find it very suspicious that a girl so heavily involved in every negative incident at Apex last year is innocent when the trouble follows her to a new school," he booms as he advances on me. His enormous frame doesn't intimidate me—hello, I fucked a dragon —but I don't know his motives, so I definitely don't trust him. The past year has taught me to be smarter than that. Even people who should have your best interest at heart will sell you out for a dime.

The door busts open, splinters flying as the intruder decimates the locks with sheer brute force. I whip my head around to see Renard with a badger who looks like he could give Aubrey a run for his money in the ring. My gargoyle is smirking as he strolls in, half-shifted and menacing, but the badger looks like he's going to massacre everyone in the room and ask questions later. Head-master Balthazar huffs, puffing up his chest to compete with the bigger shifters, but it doesn't work.

"Who the devil are you chaps? This is a *private* office and a *private* meeting." He looks at the grizzlies. "Security will escort you out and off our campus *immediately*."

Rennie drops into a big chair lazily, clearly unruffled. The badger, however, cracks his knuckles loud enough to sound like he broke his fingers and advances into the Headmaster's space. I swallow hard as the massive shifter growls into Balthazar's face. "My name is Goliath McCoy. I am a representative of Miss Drew's attorney, Farley McCoy. You will cease interrogating her immediately by his demand."

Holy shit, it's a Postman!

"I don't know what you've been told or how you got on campus, but you have no right to demand anything. Every student signs an agreement to comply with all Capital Prep regulations and Council laws—"

"I don't believe you heard me." Goliath gets in the bear's face, so close they could kiss. "I *said* you will cease questioning my client. Under the Shifter Constitution of 1791 and the knuckles on my hands, you *will* comply or I will force the issue."

"Fucking epic," Rennie mutters as he drapes his legs over the arm of the chair, his tail swishing back and forth in glee. "I'm going to buy the gangster a new basket of toys for his triplets."

So many images flit through my head that I almost short circuits and I hiss at him, "Stop that!"

"And *I* asked how you got onto my property, young man!"

The badger rolls his eyes, cracking his neck just as loudly as he holds up an envelope. "I am legally obligated to deliver this notice from the courts. It is for a Carina Rockland and the court order granted me permission to enter. However, once here, I received a call from my employer to prevent an illegal interrogation. I promise I will do anything necessary to accomplish my directive, including summoning my brother from the car to assist."

The polar bear pales this time, moving away to stand behind his desk. "I'm calling out legal counsel. You can't just—"

"Feel free, but you'll find this is legally binding. Until now, our quibble was not with the school, but Farley will be happy to amend that. He believes you've breached your contract regarding standard of care, discrimination, and unlawful detention. However, he's also researching other charges to levy as we speak."

"Miss Drew is not being detained," Henrietta says with a terrified squawk. "We merely asked her to give her account because the security team found a blond hair matching her description on the body, but she claimed not to have touched the body."

Who the fuck is trying to goddamn frame me? This is out of control. At least at Apex, I knew who the fucking enemies were—mostly.

Goliath gives her a toothy grin, clearly pleased with himself. He pulls out a cellular phone, hitting a button, then putting it on speaker. "Boss, they called her in because they found a blond hair on the corpse."

"Pray tell, Goalie, what color is our lovely, *innocent* client sporting at the moment?" The voice sounds eerily like Rufus, inflection and all, but has a soft twang to it.

"Uh, like a rainbow sherbet looking thing, Boss."

The laugh that echoes out of the phone is *much* darker than my BFF. "So blond hair means absolutely dogshit in a spittoon. Is that all they have?"

"*Excuse me*, but I—"

"If I have to fly up there to handle this, I'm going to knock your teeth so far down your throat you'll spit them out one by one, you pompous prat." Farley pauses and I watch Balthazar swallow hard. "Put your listening ears on and keep it sharp because I won't say this again: Delores Drew did not kill this student. She is innocent and if I have not made it crystal clear, she invoked."

"But…" Henrietta starts and a dangerous snarl comes out of the phone.

"I *said* listen, which means mouths shut. In the spirit of cooperation, I will have forensic reports sent to your office to prove our claim and identify the *true* killer. Will that suffice?" The smugness coming over the line is damn near oozing, but my eyes cut to Rennie in panic.

We don't have that evidence… Do we? We definitely can't fake evidence!

"We can't just accept third party, non-official evidence because you say so, Mr. McCoy."

Farley sighs in annoyance, clearly ready to strangle the shitty bear from thousands of miles away. "Of course not, you boob. Our evidence was obtained by Professor Khan, documented by your clean-up team, and sent to the Head of Forensic Sciences at the Smithsonian. Chain of custody was maintained and she will testify in legal proceedings if necessary. No one can claim bias because, as you know, Dr. Bones is human and has no idea who we are."

Mother of Zeus, what the hell did Aubrey do? And why didn't they tell me this shit yet?

"The report just came through an hour ago," Rennie supplies when I give him a dirty look. "That's why we hadn't brought it to Security's attention yet. However, you will see they ran it against the Council's birth record DNA database and a positive match was made."

"This is highly unorthodox," Balthazar blusters. "Are you saying a student at this academy is a murderer?"

I give him a reproachful look. "You mean, a student besides *me*? Is it so hard to believe? Fucking hell, Rennie, tell us who it is, so they let me go home."

My gargoyle winks, rising to his feet to hold his hand out to me. "They have linked the killer with the killings at Apex and the one here, so there's nothing to dispute. Her name is Heather MacLachlan."

I'll be a three-legged wolf in a four-legged race—for once, the Universe is smiling at me.

Legends Are Made

Delores

"It thrilled me at first, you know?" I sigh as I look at Fitz through my legs while I'm in downward dog. "I thought I'd finally had some good luck. Besides you guys and my friends, I mean."

He looks pleased when I amend my statement, despite being upside down in a backbend. "Well, the Pouty Poet knew the second the report hit the big guy's email it was bullshit. The science isn't faked, but those hairs were definitely planted. That chick wasn't even on campus when the Halloween murder happened and she's been MIA from her little squad of dummies since the beginning of the year. Either someone else killed that chick and left the hairs, *or* someone found the body first and took advantage."

I watch him kick his feet up and walk over, grinning. "You're getting good at this, Fitzy. You couldn't do that a week ago."

Bobbing his brows, he grabs my waist and bumps his hips against mine until I feel his dick take notice. "If I get to teach you things, it's only fair you get to teach me shit, too. Plus, with six of us, more flexibility will be an asset."

"Good planning, baby."

My head whips up to look at who just arrived and I grin when I see Chessie. "You should see his cartwheel. It's getting way better. He doesn't look like someone has electrocuted him anymore."

"That was pretty damn funny," Chess says. "I thought Aubrey was going to bust at the seams."

"He can suck it, the big cheating fuck knuckle!" Fitz yells as he does a quick run and tumbles through a clunky, but improving round-off. "I'm a fucking baller gymnast and I didn't break the damn library."

"Fiiiiiitz," I groan as Chess snickers into his hand. "You guys have to let that go sometime, right? He loses his mind when you tease him."

"Don't do the crime if you can't do the time," Fitz sing-songs as he comes up to us. He leans in and kisses Chess like he's been away for a week, then does the same to me. "He's been riding us for *years* about that shit and I'm *never* letting it go."

I give my cheetah a pleading expression, but he just grins. "He's right, angel. It's the dragon's turn to get heckled, and he has to take it like a pred. Speaking of preds, are you two done stretching for the match tonight? I want to get some fuel in Dolly before it gets too late in the day."

"The match against *U&M* worries me a little," I admit. "I read online their players are ringers. They recruit to compete and they do nothing but practice. The university fixes their grades and shit so they don't have to focus on anything else. It seems like a recipe for my first loss."

"Honestly? They probably do, angel. That school is full of pale-faced techies and it's not against any rules to entice people to come and play. The Leonidas league rules are pretty lax in terms of team recruiting and bribery."

Awesome. I'm going to get matched with some giant bruiser with five brain cells and fists like hammers.

"Next time I say anything about the Universe giving me good luck? Smack me in the back of the head."

"Noted, Baby Girl. Spank you for hubris."

THE CROWD FOR THIS MATCH IS EVEN MORE PACKED THAN THE last one and Coach Z keeps muttering they might have to move the girls' matches to the big stadium. I agree; it's bullshit that we're stuck in the practice arena when the boys' Games are held in the giant Leonidas monstrosity. You'd think she'd have a little sway, but apparently not enough to commandeer the real arena. I shake out my hands as the entrance music plays, trying not to let the camera flashes and lights wig me out.

You've got this, Dolly. Your friends and men are in the stands. You beat the frame job assholes. Tonight is your night.

"I heard she's going to choke," Selene's voice carries from the middle of the line. She's been pissed since Zhenga announced the line-up for the field run. Her crew had mixed results in the last match and they've all missed at least three practices for various bullshit since then. Her tantrum wasn't pretty, especially since Zhenga doesn't give a single fuck about who their parents are.

The python hisses softly—her version of laughing, I've learned—and Kyaw glances at me derisively. "That was a fluke, Selene. No lowly prey animal could ever beat you in the ring. They're using her for the media attention."

"That's what happens when you're fucking a bunch of losers and gangsters like the Khans," Jaiyana says with a fake giggle. "You get plastered all over the Preynet like a tramp."

My brows furrow as I step out of line, intent on heading over to set those bitches straight. It's bad enough I had the Heathers spouting this shit, but I'm sure as hell not letting some dipshit kids of pop stars and washed up athletes insult my men. "Look…"

A hand appears in front of me, and I stop. It's Coach Z, and she winks at me, nodding towards my spot in line. When I comply, she turns to stride over to the Plastics. "Listen up, ladies. You don't have to like each other; this is a team sport but we're individual contributors. So I don't give a rat's ass if you have sleepovers and braid one another's hair. But no members of *my team* will *ever* use another woman's sexuality as a putdown. It's classless and immature—we're animals and have needs, especially after we do battle in the ring."

"But she—"

"Delores is committed to *three* kings, one enforcer, and the child of diplomats—three of which are *Khans*. Do you want to find out what happens to stupid girls who bad mouth the Khans in public? I'd be happy to let the ones who fight in the clubs know, so it gets back to Bloodstone."

Holy fuck, Coach Z!

Selene's face goes white, even under her makeup. "No, I…"

"Mmmhmm. I thought not. Now get back in line and focus on your matches, ladies."

The bell rings at the entrance and everyone gets ready to run out when their name is called. I give Zhenga a grateful look and she smiles.

I'll be damned. Maybe we are friends?

I'M UP NEXT AND COACH Z IS STILL YELLING AT THE LAST GIRL who lost. Roswitha is fighting now, and she's likely going to win. She and Charlotte will be the only two members of Selene's group to be victorious tonight. Our team is struggling and the rumor that they are field ringers has been proven true without question. Every single competitor has been outrageously huge for their species and fights like mercenaries trained them. The Cappie team isn't pro-level or anything, but these fuckers could fight people of that caliber.

My bunny is both angry and worried. We don't like cheaters; we hate being called a slut, and we're still pissed about the fucking Headmaster's shit. If it hadn't been for Farley's quick thinking, I might have been stuck there getting grilled forever, or worse, suspended until they investigated. We were supposed to clear things off the board by solving mysteries, not by discovering bodies and accepting obvious frame jobs because we don't like the person being framed.

"And who the hell names their daughter Malevolena, anyway?" I mutter as I search the crowd for my guys again.

They're waving little pastel rainbow pom-poms on sticks Rufus made to match the jerseys, despite Aubrey turning purple at all the cuteness. Felix's eyes meet mine, his gaze as steady as if to say he believes in me. Fitz and Chess are sitting on the other side of two of Rufus' Sphinx twins, and Coco is with the Captain's crew. Having them close enough to meet their eyes helps a lot. I can't figure out which of the behemoths on the other sideline is my opponent, but with their support behind me, I'm staying cool.

"Next up, the nubile newcomer, the surprising sophomore, the bad ass bunny of Capital Prep... *Deeeeeloooooresssssss Dreeeeeeewwwwwwww!*"

Oh, sweet baby Hermes, that intro is going to get me squashed.

Taking a deep breath, I stride into the ring without looking back at the roaring crowds surrounding us. My gaze focuses on the ref as they call Malevolena up and she stomps over like a goddamn mutant experiment gone wrong. I know her size will be her downfall and I'm fast, but she's also got tree trunks for arms and legs. As she comes closer, the faint smell of something sickly sweet wafts across the dirt and I frown. I recognize the scent, but I can't place it. It's not like the dickface hoods, but it's something I've smelled before. When I look at her face, suddenly I know. Her eyes are filled with malice and a hazy film that reminds me of the rave.

U&M sent this enormous chick out here to fight me high as a kite.

While it's not a violation at the college level, especially if it's not steroids or growth hormones, it's frowned upon. Different species react to various strains of the pred drugs in completely unpredictable ways. This girl is not only large and well trained, she might not be capable of higher brain function decisions. That's dangerous in so many ways that I—

"Annnnnd fight!"

The ref backs out of the ring, and I drop into a defensive stance on instinct. Our dance begins as we circle one another, watching for weaknesses and targets. Malevolena is moving more quickly than I would have expected, so I note that as I strategize. She's favoring one side and I don't know if that's an injury or just her dominant side. While I'm plotting, the hulking fighter darts across the center, forcing me to scramble backwards along the edge of the ring. I don't step out, but I come close.

Willing to win dirty—good to know.

"I'm going to clobber you, little rabbit, and then pick my teeth with your bones."

I snort as I leap past her next volley of fists, giving her a cheeky smirk. "Yes, yes. The big ogre is going to grind my bones if I don't get out of his swamp."

"What?" she asks as she lumbers towards me.

"Also not culturally aware, good to know," I mutter to myself. Using her confusion to land a hard jab to her right ribcage, I grunt at the sting. "And apparently made of fucking adamantium."

"You babble too much and don't fight enough." Ham-sized fists come towards me, and I barely avoid taking the full brunt of them.

I growl softly, shifting my claws and fangs first. Ducking the next swing, I whirl around and kick her hard in the stomach. When she barely moves, my eyes widen. Somehow, I have the Sherman Tank of their team and it doesn't feel random. I might not be bad, but she's well over my weight limit. *How did she get paired with me?* My legs flex as I hop out of range again, my eyes scanning the stadium quickly as I regroup. There has to be an explanation.

Heavy footsteps bring me back to reality, and I see the freight train roaring at me again. I swallow hard, running towards her and at the last second, I dive under her and skid away on my knees. It hurts like a bitch and I'm going to be hobbling all week, but at least I'm not rabbit pate. I get to my feet shakily, panting as I get myself together. A flash catches my eye—I don't know how in this mess—and I see my old friends, the Heathers, taking pictures from the sideline with satisfied smirks on their faces.

Oh, come on! They fixed my motherfucking Pred Games match?!

Now I can't lose or it'll be everywhere. Lucille will freak and I'll have people up my ass about it despite this girl being out of my league. I don't think I can win, but if I can fight to a draw, the ref will end it. I square my shoulders, dropping my center of gravity again. Gritting my teeth, I run towards the giant shifter at full speed. "Oi, Macarena! Let's rumble."

Her eyes darken and she heads for me, her head down like she's going to ram me. When we meet in the middle, I throw all of my bunny's strength and my body weight into her middle while sweeping my legs around hers. The move throws us both off balance and I squirm to make sure she hits the ground first to cushion our fall. Grinning at my clever move, I sit on her as she moans, turning to look at the ref to make sure he's counting.

And that's when a skull so hard it could cut diamonds smashes into mine and we both go limp.

Alive

Delores

My head feels like it's going to explode.

I fight to open my eyes, and the throbbing intensifies, making my stomach roll. *Fuck me.* Not that I'm in any shape for that kind of activity, but damn. Swallowing the trepidation, I squint at the decor surrounding me. It's fuzzy, but recognizable. I'm in my room in the annex, though I don't have a clue how I got here. The last thing I remember is a rock hard skull crashing into mine and a lot of yelling.

That bitch must have knocked my block off good.

"She's awake!"

The panicked voice isn't Fitz's, though I would have expected it to be. I can't imagine he's taking this well; people looking at me wrong sends him into a fit of rage. I turn my head slightly and blink when I see Felix looking like absolute death warmed over in the chair next to the bed. He's still watching the door, so I try to assess myself before everyone gets here.

Head? Fuzzy. Back? Achy, but okay. Legs? Probably bruised.

Arms? Sore as hell, especially my left shoulder. That might be an issue for later. Fingers and toes? Mobile.

Well, I'm not crippled or dead, so that's a relief.

I run my tongue through my mouth, relieved when I don't find any missing teeth. Sighing, I prepare myself to move. It should be safe given my little system check, so I grunt and use my palms to push upward. A gasp leaves my lips as a shooting pain runs up that arm and I have grit my teeth until I'm sitting upright against the pillows.

"Princess, stop that! What are you doing?" Felix hisses as he whips around to look at me. "You need to rest."

"I'm okay," I lie as I catch my breath. My shoulder is *definitely* fucked up, so it can't have been that long since the match. If it was more than a week later, I'd be fully healed. That's good information to have because our exams are the week after next and none of my professors will give a fucking inch on my work. Correction: the guys would, but their stuff wouldn't be my problem, anyway.

"You *will* be okay, but right now, you're recovering. Don't think I missed you almost keeling over when you put weight on that shoulder." The Raj gives me a stern look and I wrinkle my nose.

Damn know-it-all man.

"I didn't say I was healed, I said—"

The stampede into my room cuts off my retort and I have to laugh as they almost get stuck in the doorframe trying to push each other out of the way. Even the taciturn big guy is shouldering Fitz out of the way as they vie for a position at my bedside. Chess darts around to the other side and beams when he gets the seat next to me on the bed. I let him settle my injured limb against him carefully while Fitz and Rennie argue about who gets the opposite seat.

"It's good to see you awake, Angel," Chessie says softly. "I think I get why you were so upset this summer."

"How long have I been out? 'Cuz you were out for a week and we were about to commit Fitz. I had sparkly grippy socks picked out and everything." I give him a wan smile, hoping to ease the tension in the room.

Fitz shoves the gargoyle and darts under his arms, plopping on my good side with a cheesy smirk. "I would have rocked those, Baby Girl. But I pity the mental health professional who has to probe this mess." He points to his head and everyone bursts out laughing. "My brain isn't exactly a cuddly place."

I lean in to kiss his jaw, rubbing my nose along it. "I love your brain. If people don't like it, they can get fucked."

"If you're offering, it's been—"

Felix growls, smacking him in the back of the head. "Behave. She's still healing, you animal."

"Maybe once I have two functioning arms, baby?" I ruffle his hair, letting the long strands sift through my fingers. "But I still want to know how long I was out because you interrupted Chess."

"Four days, Angel," Chess says as his fingers trace over the back of my hand. "But they declared the match a tie because your opponent tested positive for predstasty and wolfsbane."

"How did they know to test? I mean, I saw it in her eyes, but clearly, I wasn't awake when you guys got me out of the ring." I frown, thinking back to how crazed my opponent looked when she was coming at me the last time.

"I *smelled* it in her blood," Fitz says proudly. "The scratches you got in were bleeding and I told the infirmary to do a tox scan. I went up against enough juicers in the pro leagues to recognize it. You're lucky it didn't send her into a mindless frenzy—wolfsbane is a sedative for canines, but for felines, it's like PCP in humans. That fucking cougar was so high it was amazing she could find the damn ring."

My eyes widen, and I blurt out the first thing that comes to mind. "I think the Heathers arranged it. I saw them looking all pleased on the sidelines before the last strike. They probably paid her or something."

The dragon at the end of my bed shoots to his feet, wings popping free as he paces across the room. "First a poisoner at your prom, and now this shit? Perhaps your friends were in it with the dead girl, lunchable."

I shake my head, then pause as the room spins a little. "No. Those girls would never chance vomit pics getting online and ruining their prom. They might have done this, but the prom is something else. Besides, the prom was scattershot—all the heirs got sick except me, so it was like the person didn't know who they were aiming at."

"Hmm," Rennie says as he leans against my desk. "That means the poisoner might have been looking for someone who didn't get sick. Perhaps by not drinking that night, you ended up becoming a target? That would explain the escalation of things once you arrived at Apex, *non*?"

"No. They didn't attempt to kidnap her until this year. They started with other small fry students and the one they killed on Halloween was a nobody. It felt like the dead kid was a message, though how they knew we'd find him, I'm unsure. I feel certain the deaths and the kidnappings are being orchestrated by two *different* factions." Feliz strokes his scruff, looking thoughtful before he continues. "Perhaps in direct opposition to one another."

I chew on my thumbnail, trying to sort through things in my cotton ball-filled mind. "Then the Heathers are acting on their own, or maybe being encouraged by their parents and, by extension, possibly Lucille. She'd enjoy making me miserable for no other reason than to see me in pain. But the kidnappers are doing *something* with the students who have never returned or been found. Is it possible they deemed the dead ones not useful, so they killed them rather than kidnap them?"

"Maybe," Aubrey says. "It's also possible whoever is killing students is trying to send the abductors a warning. The victims have gone from a lowest tier kid in your class to this Kinsley girl. Her family isn't huge, but each one of the murdered students has a little more powerful connections. They might work their way to the heirs and big wig children."

"I don't believe you were the target of the frame job, either," Chess interjects. "You change clothes in several buildings, you practice in the ring—it wouldn't have been hard for someone to get one of your hairs specifically. They had to know someone would test the hair and that all births have DNA registered for legacy purposes. Maclachlan was definitely their target, but I have no idea why."

Groaning, I put my face in my hands. "So she's off the board, but we don't know who did it or why. That seems important because we all suspected she was a spy for your dad, Felix."

The older twin snarls. "He still has Rakoto, so if she displeased him, that could be why she was set up. None of my contacts knew her, though. Her family is part of the American wing of business and most of them have been off Bloodstone for a century. They could play for more than one team, so to speak."

"Double crossing old Pops is a dangerous plan," Fitz says, as he rests his head on my stomach. "He's as vicious as Baby Girl's mother and much less concerned about public appearances. I think he would have sent the Brotherhood to make a very messy display if he was teaching one of the lieutenants a lesson."

"Is everyone in the hierarchy of power employing scary ass special forces? I mean, Rufus' family, your dad, my mother… This feels so surreal. Even without the knock to my noggin, I'd think you guys were screwing with me if I didn't know better. How does this shit stay secret?"

"Power."

"Fear."

"Money."

The three Khan brothers answer at the same time, and I look at Rennie and Aubrey for confirmation. Aubrey shrugs. "They're all correct."

"But somehow, this involves the magic users or there wouldn't have been a battle at Apex last year." I frown and give Rennie a pleading look. "Tell us more about the magic users. Anything you know would help."

He looks torn, but he finally sighs. "I can tell you some basic information about magic users, but nothing that relates to me. Will that satisfy you?"

It's a start; I'll take it.

"For now," I say. Giving him an encouraging smile, I go back to running my fingers through Fitz's hair. "What kind of magic users are there? I guess I saw… mages? Witches? I don't know which, but they had different colored magic depending on their powers when they attacked us on the way to Cappie."

Rennie looks around for a moment, then drops onto Felix's lap. The tiger looks surprised, but he lets it go as the gargoyle taps his fingers on his lap nervously. "So there are casters—those who work with elements, spells, and the like. They can be mages, witches, wizards, or elementals. The ones who have the colored energy could be several of those options, but they're likely elementals. There are also demis, which are supes with mixed backgrounds in magic, usually descended from deity lines. Unless they tell you, you won't have a clue what they can or can't do. Anyone who can warp time or reality or minds is likely one of those."

"There was *definitely* one of those along for the ride. The fucker hit me and it was not pretty," I mutter. Fitz slips his other hand in mine and squeezes as the memory ripples over me. "What else?"

The air changes and I can feel the tension amp up as Rennie looks anywhere but at us. "The last group is the most powerful and the most secretive of all the magic users. They can have vast skill sets and are highly intelligent. Fae blend into every community seamlessly and can come in and out of the Faerie at access points all over the world. After the Treaty, they scattered to the winds and no one could track them because they can shapeshift, wield magics, and are connected to nature in a way that only they understand. Many royal families in the shifter world hunted them for profit after that dark period. They were terrified Fae would work their way into our societies like shifters did to humans. With their powers, shifters would be in a great deal of trouble if they did so."

"Do you think this Society might have something to do with that?" Chess asks. "Perhaps it's some crusty old group of high born shifter families set on eliminating the Fae left on this side of the…portal?"

"Veil. They say veil," Renard says quietly. "And yes, it's possible. Many large shifter empires were eager to hire bounty hunters and magical mercenaries to exterminate them during that time."

"Maybe that's why there're tunnels?" Fitz says. "Maybe the tunnels were used for smuggling them in for sacrifices or something."

"It could just as easily have been a rebel faction who opposed that kind of genocide, using them to smuggle Fae to their access points to go home," Aubrey says. "There's always good people who don't want to commit atrocities. The tunnels being under a school make, and me think it's more likely a relic of a resistance. Scholars are usually in the ranks of the rebellions."

"What else do you know about the Fae, Rennie?"

His eyes widen at my words and he shoots to his feet, backing away from us. "Nothing. Well, nothing important to this conversation. I've told you what I can."

"I don't believe you," Felix says, giving him a suspicious glare. "You're acting like you've been burned. I don't know what you're hiding, Monsieur Laveaux, but I'd wager it has to do with those special necklaces. Don't think any of us have missed that detail."

The gargoyle's face pales, and he backs towards the door. "I can't. I can't talk about it. I-I have to go."

My jaw drops when he damn near runs out the door and we hear slams as he leaves. Aubrey shakes his head, rubbing his temples as he lets out a breath. I push up a little more on the bed, frowning at my men. "That did not go well."

"Not at all, bento bunny. Not at all. Now he'll be brooding for days." The dragon looks worried for a second before he eyes me. "Don't you dare try to go after him. We all have to deal with our trauma at some point, and he's refusing to allow us to help. He needs to come to that realization on his own or he'll never heal."

Fitz snorts. "It's been fucking centuries, Saucy Sauron. Do you really think he's gonna clue in *now*?"

"In fact, I do," Aubrey says as he looks at me. "He has many reasons to do so now, including protecting our girl. And if the Fae are tied to this fucking bullshit threatening her, he has to come to terms with it so he can help us keep her safe. It might be the kick in the tail he needs."

I sure as hell hope so. No one in this room has the knowledge he does and we're going to run out of time, eventually.

ARSONIST'S LULLABYE

RENARD

I'VE BEEN AVOIDING EVERYONE FOR THE PAST TWO DAYS AND I know it's frustrating my family. However, when I left *ma petite*'s room, I was so overwhelmed I couldn't bear to be around anyone. My guilt about the past is as fresh as the day it happened and despite knowing I have information they need, I'm unable to face it. Aubrey's tried to help me address it for centuries, but it's not in my nature to accept what happened and move on. The choices I made led to consequences I should have expected, but I was too young and arrogant to believe it would come to pass.

The egos of young princes are stroked so often we lose perspective and I paid the price—though she paid more dearly.

The car is quiet as we head to Apex to do another search, and I let the silence hang in the air like the sword of Damocles. My dragon and bunny desperately want to bring it up again; I can practically taste their desire to drag me into a conversation. They won't, though, because we have a mission tonight and anyone being off their game could cause grievous harm. We didn't run into any traps or enemies last time, but we have no idea if that will be the case again.

"I like all of Raina's men. They're great escorts and very kind. I think they like me, too, except Holliday. I can't figure him out. He says nothing, but I see him watching me when I talk to him."

I blink. *She doesn't know?* Raina usually tells people, but I guess our girl didn't get to meet him in a group setting. "*Mon amie*, Holliday is deaf. He's watching you because he's an extremely skilled lip reader."

"Oh, shit!" Dolly gasps and smacks her head. "Goddess, how stupid am I? I thought he was just shy. Now I feel like a complete asshat babbling at him."

Aubrey chuckles. "You didn't know, and no one told you. Would you like us to teach you sign language? Our broody friend taught me a long time ago. We can make sure you get the basics pretty quickly."

"Yes. Yes, of course." Our girl beams excitedly as she claps her hands. "I love learning new things, but also, I want to communicate with him. I'd hate for him to have to adapt to me—that's lazy."

"Fitz can help, too," I say casually. "He made me teach him the basics a couple years ago when he was trying to nail—" I pause and flush as I realize what I was going to say.

"Trying to nail some chick? It's okay, big guy. I know no one in our group was a virgin when we started dating. There's no reason to act like a crazy ass unless someone tries you now." Her eyes narrow and the looks on her face reminds me of the tiger in question. "Now, they'd better step off or they'll regret it."

A deep, dragon chuckle echoes out of Aubrey, and it almost makes me feel better for a moment. He was so fucking serious before our bunny showed up. Every little thing set him off and he had to constantly work to keep from flaming out. Since Dolly joined us, he's still cranky and ill-tempered, but he laughs more. He even makes more jokes and tolerates the students more easily. She's changing all of us for the better, and it's much more visible from my perches.

"No need to get growly, snack size. We're well aware you're not willing to share outside of our family—that's true of us all. But you don't have much to worry about with Rennie and I. We stayed fairly solitary most of our lives and definitely since moving to Apex." He winks at her playfully. "Only the tigers have bed posts that look like scratching posts; Chess has kept to himself the entire time I've known him as well."

She pauses, then grins. "Did I tell you guys about Coach Z before the match? I don't think I did because we had so much to discuss about all this nonsense. I think she might actually like me now. So I'm not growly about her anymore. That's growth, as Fitz would say."

That gets a laugh out of me and it feels like a weight lifts. "If you're gauging your mental health on Fitzgerald Khan's scale, we're all in trouble. But tell us the story, *ma petite*. I'm interested."

"Well, that witch Selene…"

***

Once we arrive at the secret tunnel entrance, I feel the pulse of magic again. It's getting stronger, which explains why the construction is taking so long to complete. Using all prey animals who aren't affected will exponentially increase the time needed to finish it, but the preds are likely getting weaker faster. The Captain's crew are walking ahead of us, but he stayed with me, so I look at him seriously. "Your group needs to watch all the predators except Dolly. If they fade, get the radio and check-in so we can convince them to go back to the car. I'm worried the source of this power has been back to add more magic so people will stay away. It will certainly affect them more now."

"Aye, aye Admiral!"

Shaking my head, I watch him rush ahead to communicate with the other members of his little family. It's an odd group we've formed, but I find it immensely satisfying. I've always enjoyed the company of all species—even to my detriment and shame in the past—so seeing preds, prey, and whatever our girl is working together takes me back to a happier time. *Sigh.* I can't slide back into moping about what happened so long ago when we have important things to find. *Nostalgia will have to wait.*

"Team Alphahole is at the entrance. We're going in and heading down the same path as before. Will check in at the half hour mark," Dolly chirps into the mic. "Be careful or I'll kick all your asses."

"Baby Girl," Fitz whines. "I'm still peeved you're not on my team. Your fancy mobster is picking on me."

"Delta is headed in," Aubrey interrupts. "Quit screwing around outside and let's get this done. The air here is worse tonight; I can feel it. We don't need anyone harmed by this outing."

"Fine, spoilsports. Badass, over and out!" the hyper tiger crows as his mic clicks off.

This is going to be a long night; I can tell.

THE DEEPER WE GO INTO THE TUNNELS UNDER THE FOREST, THE stronger the traces of the magic linger. My amulet pulses with the beat, making my gargoyle itch to be free. Obviously, that's not possible in this space—at least, not fully—but he's antsy and that's unusual. Chess is scouring the walls looking for the next Council room and until we find it, we can't leave. On the last trip, they found the Leonidas vault, and we found Erickson. Combined with Shirdal from the night of explosions, it's not even a quarter of the highest ranking families. They all have one; I'm certain of it.

"Over here!"

Hurrying along, I join the Captain and Chess as they stare at another door embedded in the rock walls. This one has designs that look like they belong to a temple for Demeter. "This is probably the Charles room," I murmur. "Their business is all agriculture, right?"

"Yes. They went from small farms to Agro-giant over the decades. But I don't see what we need to do to get in," Chess replies as he bends down to examine the bottom edges. "It doesn't have a puzzle that I can see, just some indents."

"What would the rich farmers use to keep their treasures hidden?" The question is rhetorical, but we all need to think in order to figure this out. "Crops need water."

"And light," the Captain adds, holding up his flashlight. "Perhaps ye need to make something grow?"

Brilliant.

"Chess, start shining that light into all the places that have depressions. I'm going to check in since it's time." Turning, I press my button and call out. "Check-in teams! We've found the Charles vault and are trying to open it. Chess seems okay still."

The silence freaks me out for a moment, but then my grump's voice comes over the line. "East of the library, we've run into a door we believe may belong to the Barringtons. We're also working on a puzzle. Cori and I are doing okay for the moment."

"Team Badass ain't found shit," Fitz snickers. "But we are getting pretty far into the west tunnel, and that might be where the treasure is hidden. The punk is fine and I'm dandy."

It takes another moment before the last response, and I want to throttle Felix. "Team Alpha…hole… is fine. We're almost under the lake now and we've run into a large chamber with a ton of art on the walls, another altar, and some crazy shit. Princess is documenting and the crew are gathering anything they carry in a big sack. We saw a door on the way in, but ignored it to follow the sliver of light to this. We'll look at the door on our way out."

"Felix, you don't sound good," I respond. "That room must have more magic in it than other places. Get what you can, try the room, and get out. I'm not arguing with you."

"He's grumbling, but I have it under control, big guy." Dolly's voice echoes into the speaker, and I realize the chamber must be quite large. "See you suckers in a half hour."

"I've got it!"

Blinking, I turn around, flicking my mic off and looking at Chess in surprise. He's beaming as a vine crawls through grooves in the door, then disappears into a hole and the sound of a lock clicking fills the silence.

I'll be damned. Looks like we're going to get the dirt on the farmers after all.

The door swings open, and I hold my hand out to keep the other two from entering. My amulet stays at a level hum, so I walk inside the oddly cozy room kept by the Charles family. There are dozens of blueprints on the wall depicting molecular structures and pots filled with dirt, but no plants. An archive of ledgers fill one book-case and a table full of what appears to be a chemistry lab sit in another corner. My eyes catch on a hanging tapestry and I walk over to it, squinting as I examine it.

It's not that old and doesn't look valuable. Pulling it aside, I grin as I uncover a walk-in wall vault. I grip the handle, betting that something hidden this well probably doesn't have a high tech safe. It's protected by all the secrecy, so they probably didn't bother to get anything reinforced against shifter strength. Yanking hard, I tear the door off the hinge to look inside.

"Uh, thanks?" Chess says as he joins me. The Captain follows, but heads over to the trunks in the last corner.

I shrug. "No problem. Does it feel colder to you now?"

He shivers. "They've got something cooling this hidden thing. Let's go in and see what is so important."

Nodding, I walk in, looking at the neatly organized and labeled shelves running from floor to ceiling. It's obvious this is being used as a seed vault—where they store their branded, modified seeds for their farms to keep the genetic codes secret. "Lot of seeds and probably half of them were hijacked from small prey farmers. But I don't think that helps us."

"It's good info if we need a public campaign, but it's not going to get the killers or hoods off our backs." Chess pauses and picks up one of the sealed tubes. "Do you recognize this plant? You're the botany guy, right?"

It can't be.

I swallow a curse before I answer. "I do. These plants haven't existed here since the Treaty. Chess, they've got Faerie plant seeds in here. That's how they've grown their business over the years. They're splicing regular shit with Faerie shit."

"You said the Fae are all but gone, right?"

"Perhaps, but flora from their lands would call to them. Hell, it might even reactivate the fucking gateways. No one's ever studied it. We didn't have the tech back then and everyone thinks that it's extinct, like magic now." Hundreds of thoughts fly through my head, making possibilities race through my mind like dogs on the track. The smell, the plants, the magic, the timing... something is definitely coming. Fae never forgive and they never forget—and they live to ages even shifters look upon as immortal like gargoyles and dragons. Turning to my friend, I ask despite not wanting the answer. "Have you heard about any spikes in the more reclusive mythical shifters recently?"

"Nope. But Fitz can run checks, man. He's the best at really digging into the dark nets for both species." The cheetah frowns and tilts his head. "Why?"

"I don't enjoy finding this. It's dangerous and we have no idea how widespread those Council idiots have let it get. If magic is coming out of the dark, Fae plant hybrids are growing, and two sides seem to be in a battle over shit no one knows about? There's a war brewing, and it's been headed in this direction for over a decade at least. The first sprouts of those plants would have taken at least twelve years to flower so they could be modified and spliced."

"Ren? You know an awful fucking lot about this shit. My angel is right; we need you to deal with your past so you can talk about whatever it is." Chess reaches out and squeezes my shoulder. "We'll all be here for you, but we're out of our depth on this topic. If a shifter/magic war has been in the making for a decade or two, we're not ready because no one but these Council twats knows."

"And they're hiding it," I sigh. "I get it. Let's get whatever paperwork and samples we can. We'll fill the others in when we get home. This, combined with whatever Felix's team found, is enough for tonight."

"We'll come back—it seems like we will never quite get away from Apex."

"That's what I'm afraid of."

Keep Your Head Up

Delores

"So Renard believes the Charles family made their fortunes off stealing Fae plants and cross-breeding them to make better produce and stuff?" Cori takes a bite out of a big licorice whip, propping her face in her hands. "How would they even *get* that if fair folk have been exterminated or whatever?"

I shrug, leaning back so I can stretch my lower back. We've been studying for exams since after my piano lesson and everything is cramping. "No one has a clue. You heard him saying even a Fae hiding in this part of the veil would give that up to shifters—even for a hefty sum. But they have a lot of different types and research that he and Aubrey have been sifting through since we came home on Saturday. Chess has Fitz burrowing through the dark web to see if anyone has said anything about the Fae, artifacts, plants, magic—like so many keywords, he had to hack into the government servers to keep it running. Felix is worried it will draw attention, but Fitz swears he's covered his tracks."

"Dollypop, it doesn't make sense," Rufus complains as he stares at his book.

Arching a brow, I snort. "Diplomacy? No shit. They fill their curriculum with lies at my level; it can't be any better at yours. And no one is going to negotiate anything if they start in a pit of false assumptions."

He throws his highlighter at me, laughing when I duck. "I meant the whole 'magic/shifter war' thing. They have conditioned preds to hate and fear magic. They wouldn't be mad if we were smiting them. Why the big secret? The Council here—or anywhere else—would look like heroes for fighting off an invasion."

I consider that for a moment, snatching one of Cori's treats and chomping on it. "Maybe they're afraid the balance has tipped and they won't win."

Cori blinks. "Oh!"

"Did you finally think of the answer to that essay question?" I tease.

"No, dummy. I know why—maybe." Cori grabs my Shifter History book and starts flipping through it. When she makes a 'eureka' noise, I look at her pointedly until she spins it to face me, putting her finger on a paragraph. "This. The Treaty was forced because *all* shifters won the war, D."

"Holy cartwheeling Kali," I mutter. "You got it, Coco. Back then, it wasn't like now. The prey shifters fought and armed and supplied the war. But the atmosphere is so bad now that the Councils are afraid the prey will take up the resistance. They think they'll *lose*."

Rufus scoffs, shaking his head. "I don't think so. I mean, it's possible a few sects or clans or whatever might join the magical misfits, but not all. Why would they *all* take that risk?"

"Freedom," I shrug. "The prey friends I have here and at Luc's have good lives and are treated well. That's probably an anomaly, Ru-Ru. Think about how some kids here or at Apex talk about prey—even when they found out their friend was a prey animal. You can't tell me the asshole Charles has good working conditions on their farms or that the Ericksons don't run tech factories with shit that would probably make our blood run cold. "

"Totally," Cori says, her curls bouncing as she agrees. "I've seen exposés on that kind of stuff. Also, remember that Dolly told us a lot of her summer friends are terrified of being out at night because preds do whatever they want without being disciplined. The promise of not living in fear is an excellent motivator."

"So you're telling me we have two groups of bitch bullies chasing Dolly because she exists, but also two groups of uber-powerful people making war for the entire shifter world who seem very interested in her being in the middle, too? Like… did you take a ruby out of a temple as a child, girl?" Rufus looks frustrated as he works out the details. "That's not even mentioning her shitty mom, the thieving counselor, and whatever is behind door number six that we haven't found yet."

Flopping on my back, I cover my face with my hands again. "I know; I know. It's insane how people keep making me part of their master plan. I don't know *why* everyone is so damn obsessed with destroying me. I promise I'm not *trying* to attract it!"

Cori sighs and joins me, then Rufus follows. As they flank me on the floor, I feel a little of the anxiety drain from my body. It's hard to live when you have this many people watching you and even harder when you know that number keeps growing. "Can we talk about something else for just a little bit? *Please?*"

"Of course we can, Dollybear. Tell us about—"

"No, Rufus," Cori says with an eye roll. "Not sexy talk right now. How about… what the hell are we going to do for Halloween? It's two weeks from today and we don't have a spare second to do what we did last year. No one is getting anything homemade."

"What does it matter? We're not going into town on Samhain night for sure. The guys would flip their shit about safety."

Rufus gives me a cagey grin. "We don't have to. There's a huge ass party in the cemetery on the other side of the fence. I heard about it from the girls in my Diplomacy class."

"Ugh, those witches," Cori grumbles. "I hate when you cozy up to them."

"It's for gossip, dahling Coco. You know I have to keep my ear to the ground so we can help head off bullshit," Rufus chides. "I don't *like* them one bit, but you know how wired in foxes are."

"But the guys' townhouse is on that side… not a cemetery," I interject.

"On the *other* side, silly rabbit!" I roll my eyes and the badger laughs. "Everyone is invited, so I'm sure your overprotective body-guard men can escort you. The triplets are meeting me there, but they won't tell me what they're coming as. It's very annoying."

I see the look on Cori's face darken, so I grab her hand. "Maybe you could arrange everyone's costume? Like order them? You have measurements from last year and we can all be a group— you, Rufus, me, and the guys. Your choice—I'll square it with them. Okay?"

The polar bear's face lights up and she squeals, pulling me into a koala bear hug. "Ooooooooh, I can't *wait*! Thank you, thank you, thank you, Dolly!"

Rufus hisses as her squeal echoes in the room. "Yikes, Coco. You are *far* too screamy for this room. We are not cheerleaders; no one needs to yell like that when not in uniform. Ouch."

I sock him in the arm. "Don't harsh her buzz, buddy. I enjoy seeing my friend this happy. If you quit being a sourpuss, you can help her."

His lips curve, and he looks positively feral. "Oh, now you're talking."

Cori finally lets go of me, her eyes big as she looks at me. "How are you going to talk those guys into a costume party when we have no idea who really killed Kinsley and those Apex kids, especially with hooded freaks appearing everywhere?"

"I don't know. Sex, maybe?" My eyes dance as I shrug. "It seems to work most of the time."

"Aw, Coco, our little girl is growing up! She realized men will do *anything* if you touch the trouser snake."

"Shut *up*, Rufus!" Cori and I smack him at the same time, and he howls in indignation.

He rolls away, pretending to nurse his arms, and I chuckle. "You are *such* a big baby."

"I am not. Just for that, I won't tell you what Farley found out." The badger sticks his tongue out at me and I glare.

"Tell me or I'm going to beat you up." I grab a pillow, holding it up threateningly.

"Whooooooooa. I've imagined this scene a million times, but never *once* was the gangster in my dream. No fair, Baby Girl." Cori giggles as Fitz swaggers in with a tray full of snacks, grinning like the tiger who ate a canary. "Chessie thought you might be hungry since you've been in for hours, but he's gonna lose it when he finds out he missed you getting ready to pillow fight."

"Oh my god, Fitzy, there's so much cheese on this tray," I groan happily. "I'm going to give him a present, I fucking swear."

"Did she just ignore me for… cheese?" he asks Cori and Rufus.

I did and I'm not apologizing—cheesy goodness is a food orgasm and I won't stand for any backtalk.

"Think so, Psycho," Rufus says as he swipes some nachos. "Your job is done here. Take your mental snapshot to keep you company and tootle-loo."

"Rufus, be nice!" Cori sighs and turns back to my tiger. "Thank you for bringing this, Professor. We're obviously pretty hangry."

"No sweat, Coco-cabana." He turns to Rufus and glares. "You're on my list, jackass." Before I can say anything, he comes over and lifts me off the ground, swinging me into the air so I'm looking down at him. "And you, Baby Girl, remember that being bratty makes Felix horny. Also, I think the winged weenies like it, but probably because you let them chase you. Or so I heard."

My face turns bright red as I hear Rufus choke and Cori dissolve into giggles again. Fitz winks at me and I wrinkle my nose. He did that on *purpose* and he knows they'll grill me like I'm a murder suspect now. "Fitz Khan, I'll get you back. Just you wait."

"Oh, I'm counting on it, Baby Girl," he says as he lowers me to the ground and swats my ass. "Now go eat and study. These fucking exams are cutting into my naked time and it makes me snarly."

That makes two of us, Fitzy.

HERE FOR YOU

AUBREY

HE'S BROODING AGAIN, AND IT MAKES ME CRAZY. SINCE WE brought back the files from the Charles vault, Renard has been poring over them, making notes until he can't see straight, then going to his bell tower to stare at that stupid orchid. In hundreds of years, he's never explained to me why it doesn't die, but I guess I've got a bloody clue now. I don't know the story behind it, either, but it seems like he's trying to figure out how to deal with this. At least, I hope he is, otherwise it's going to get ugly.

Sighing, I look at the historical records of family trees Fitz's team found in the Hopewell room. It traces families back far enough that I can tell when their clans came to this country from the rest of the world. I assume the ones with the longest lineage are all Council members and perhaps even part of this 'Society' we can't find more information about. Looking at my list, I rub my templates and groan. It's so many families and most of them have enormous trees worth of ancestors to research. I may have to get Fitz to run some computer doohickey to help weed out the unimportant ones.

Shifter Councils
Possible Members & Society Members

Hopewell
Erickson
Drew
Barrington
Maclachlan
Leonidas
Rostoff
Khan
Draconis
Charles
Shirdal
Dupree
Kavrit
Aung
Bruce
Hanson
Morinaka
Rakoto
Li
Brandenburg
O'Leary
Bruce
Faust
Birkshire
Alexandré
Bouvier
LaPorte

Blitzen
Jameson
Janssen

Hell I don't even know if this is the entire list or just the ones the Hopewells were keeping track of. All I know is this makes our board enormous and we just got two of our worries off the damn thing. Convincing Henny to let Dolly bunk with us officially and allowing the frame job on the Maclachlan girl was supposed to be the start of getting rid of our problems one by one. Instead, we've uncovered a whole list of possible suspects, many of whom have relatives at this fucking school.

"By the fires of Hephaestus, I don't know how we're going to unravel all the shit. It's too fucking much, even with our team expanding." I take off my glasses, sitting them on the table as I rub my eyes. We're only a quarter into the damn school year and everything is a mess—and I *hate* messes.

My phone buzzes and I curse again, pulling it out to check the screen. When I see the message in the group chat and no one else responds, I push to my feet and slide my glasses back on. Obviously the others are occupied and no way am I leaving this situation to burn on its own. Striding out the back door of the library, I let the dragon loose enough to half-shift and take flight. This is the fastest way to get to that stupid academic building and I need to be there immediately.

I really liked this goddamn shirt, too.

I can hear the sounds of fighting and women screaming from the elevator when I get off. That's never a good sign and I grit my teeth as I stomp towards it angrily. I don't know what the fuck this history moron is thinking, but someone should have prevented this shit. It's four o' clock in the afternoon on a goddamned *Thursday*, not Friday Night Fight Night. Our girl has to go sit through that damn woman's session after this and I don't even want to imagine what that will look like.

Flinging open the door with a loud growl, I eye the scene in front of me. Bite size is standing with her back to the corner to keep anyone from approaching from behind. She looks angry enough to spit tacks and I don't blame her. The so-called professor is sitting at his desk with his feet up, pretending to read the paper while the odious gaggle of dimwits Dolly used to be friends are leading a crowd of unruly preds towards her.

"*You* are the one who killed that science geek, *not* Heather M. They should have carted *you* off in handcuffs, you freak. Now Heather H's parents are making her marry *Todd* because the Maclachlans can't fulfill their contract. You ruin *everything* and have since the moment you popped your cherry at Prom!"

That's... a lot of dumbshit assumptions for one screeching speech.

"I didn't kill *anyone*, E. They ran tests—two separate, independent ones—and found out the hairs on Kinsley's body were that new Heather's. I don't know shit about contracts except mine was voided when that douche...," she snarls, pointing at a wimpy looking canine in a double popped collar polo and salmon shorts, "...tried to *eat me* instead of *mate* with me!"

The leader of the pack tosses her hair over her shoulder as she lets out a dark laugh. "Wouldn't we all have been better off if he had, little bunny?"

My dragon roars inside of me and I shove my way through the crowd. My wings and tail knock students over until I get into the middle of their semi-circle, facing the mob with iridescent eyes. "I wouldn't be better off, nor would quite a few others who aren't present. It's interesting how you chose to pick this fight in a place where Dolly wouldn't have any support, little Erickson. Cowardice is a family trait, I hear."

"Just like being a pathetic loser who destroys historical treasure shit runs in yours, I'd imagine," the twit shoots back.

The stupidity of youth never ceases to amaze me.

Before I can correct the girl, Dolly steps forward and gives her a knowing look. "He was a child, E. You remember that, right? Doing stupid stuff because you don't know better? I mean, I know you do because you tried to French kiss a wall socket when we were in kindergarten. Your hair looked like something out of Dragonball for months."

I can't help it; I burst into laughter. The image is priceless and she's turning an amazing shade of purple. The other girls move into place behind her and my humor screeches to halt. This is prep for an offensive and I'm not going to allow it. Stretching my wings above me until I'm filling the space menacingly, I blow two smoke rings from my nose as I smirk at them. "You have *two minutes to vacate* this room before I show you why dragons aren't allowed in the Games. I'll give you a hint: it has to do with fire."

The crowd scrambles, leaving the four blond girls looking at me with angry glares. When I don't move, the three minions scatter to grab their things, leaving their leader to pretend she's holding her ground. Dolly walks around me, heading to her desk to get her things, but I keep my eyes on Erickson. She's the truly dangerous one because she has no fear—no one has ever successfully told this girl 'no' and meant it. That means she's fine with staring down an angry dragon because she has no idea what I'll do if she doesn't stop threatening my mate.

"Let's go, Aubrey." The soft hand on my arm gets my attention and I fold my wings in as I look at her. "She's not worth it and I'm not giving her the satisfaction. Being left to stand here alone should be enough of a message."

No, it's not, my dragon argues.

"The animal inside me doesn't agree, but if you think it's time to go, we will." I hold my arm out, intending to walk her to the ridiculous 'therapy' appointment to ensure no one messes with her on the way. "But I'd be happy to fricassee this nuisance anytime, lunchable."

"Excuse me, but who gave you permission to dismiss my class?"

My head turns slowly as the professor up front finally seems to check-in. "I don't need permission from the likes of you, Blitzen. Your students were almost in a brawl when I came in and you were reading the fucking newspaper!"

The bearded man looks confused, his eyes darting around the classroom in confusion. "They were? Are you sure? I didn't see a thing."

This is not good.

Dolly and I share a glance, then I look at the bear shifter. "Yes. That student had an entire mob of preds surrounding Miss Drew and they were ready to attack. You really don't remember that?"

"Absolutely not! You're out of your mind. Of course I would know if the students were that unruly. I do not permit shenanigans in my classroom!" The professor huffs and slams his briefcase on his desk, shoving papers into it as he gives me a dirty look. "I am offended by your insinuation and will be speaking with the Heads about it. Good day!"

I watch in shock as he bustles out, followed by the bully herself, and then I turn to Dolly. "What the hell just happened, nibblet?"

Her expression changes to a frown as she shakes her head. "I don't know, Aubrey. But it was really fucking weird and we need to talk to Rennie soon. There is literally no other explanation for that shit if it isn't magic and if it is? They're not just kidnapping people on their way on and off campus—they've found a way to bespell people."

Not the way I saw my day going today at all and I am not *happy.*

It's time to talk to my family about mating again.

Don't Blame Me

Delores

The last appointment of the week with Rockland was a nightmare. The Heathers obviously told her about the fight before I got there because she spent half the time chastising me about anger management and the rest of the time not-so-subtly grilling me about sex with a dragon. It took an enormous amount of self-control not to lose my temper with her, but I knew that was what she wanted. If I flew off the handle after getting into a public fight in my history class, she could suggest I need more therapy or even something worse. I refuse to give the bitch that satisfaction.

But I did text Farley about her behavior, including a few audio clips for his files.

I spent the next two days buried in studying for the upcoming exams with Rufus and Cori to stay distracted. The guys plied me with food and snuggles, allowing me to stew in my unabated fury while I processed. But by Saturday, I knew it was time to get out of the house and do something *not* related to my shitty ex-friends and snotty counselor. Otherwise, I'd sink into frustration and not come out—a luxury I can't afford with exams next week and mysteries to solve.

"Maybe we could go out tonight?" I look over at Aubrey and Rennie sprawled out in their tasty weekend sweats with a small smile. "It's probably time for me to quit sulking."

The dragon looks amused as he pauses, sifting through another pile of old records. "The rumpled, angry college student look was *just* starting to suit you."

Renard chuckles, his eyes sparkling with mischief I haven't seen for a while. "The rat's nest bun really tops off the look. We should send your designer friend pictures."

Luc would die on the spot, and I'd never be able to face him again.

"I haven't showered since Thursday, so that's going to be a 'no' from me. Don't even think about it. I know I'm a mess." Narrowing my eyes at the gargoyle, I make sure he knows I'm not joking. "But I can't hole up forever, even if I need to study. Brooding this long is not a healthy way to cope."

"Ouch, *ma cherie.*" Rennie clutches his chest and falls back dramatically. "Right in the heart."

"You've both been ridiculous and you're lucky everyone puts up with you," Aubrey says, as he stacks his paperwork neatly.

"This from the man I learned *sign language* for because I thought he was *deaf?*"

Our grumpy mate rolls his eyes. "It was useful once Holliday came around. Don't whine; it's unbecoming."

"At least someone would come in this house," Fitz grumbles as he strolls in. He winks at me before walking over to drop a kiss on my head. "Good to hear you sounding normal again, Baby Girl."

"Where did you go this morning?" I ask as he heads for the fridge to grab a soda, then pour himself a scotch. "You left *way* early."

My crazy tiger gives me a sly expression as he brings my soda over, hopping over the back of the couch to sit next to me. "Being sneaky. I broke into the admin building again and rifled through the bitch's office. Farley wasn't joking, by the way. He's sent those giants to her publisher and agent, too. She's scrambling to prove her book is worth going to court for freedom of speech rights. His shit is tight—he's also fighting her false copyright claim to the manuscript she has so far."

"Dear god, there's a manuscript?" I groan and bury my face against his shoulder. "I'm going to die of embarrassment when I have to be associated with this nut job. Everyone is going to read her tripe and think I willingly helped her write it. I'll never live it down."

A snort makes me lift my head and Rennie shakes his head. "It's almost illiterate and everything in it screams 'I write about things I've never seen or done outside of porn.' We're *all* going to be humiliated if she gets to publish our story in her early 2000s MySpace style. The last one I read was so plotless and full of gross, inaccurate smut that I had to force myself to finish it. I imagine teenagers write better sex than this woman does."

"That does it." Aubrey rises to his feet, looking at Renard and me with a pained expression. "Rather than sit here and shrivel everyone's sex drive for months, we're going hunting. Snack size, go get cleaned up; as much as I adore you, you're smelly."

"Hey!" I protest as I lean in to smell my armpit. When the scent hits me, I turn bright red and hide behind my hair as I climb over the couch. "Nevermind. I'm going."

Fitz grabs my hand, pressing a kiss to my wrist with a cartoonish grin. "Baby Girl, don't listen to these prissy pants old farts. I'd fuck you upside in the sewer if you wanted. Needing to shower will *never* stop me."

"Thanks for sharing, you whacko," Aubrey mutters. "However, if we're going at dusk, she needs to get a move on."

"Who's getting a move on?" Chess comes in with Felix, both of them looking deliciously sweaty from what I think was a run.

"Zeus' toga, let the girl shower!" Rennie says playfully. "We'll fill you in while she's gone."

Winking at him, I sashay over to the cheetah and the king, giving them each a light kiss before I head for my room. I may not get away from my problems for long, but I haven't been hunting with my flying men for quite some time. I'm looking forward to watching them devour their dinner now that maybe I'll get to do more than rub my thighs together when I get worked up.

That shit is definitely *the pred in me—the blood makes me horny as hell.*

THE NIGHT AIR IS BRACING—WINTER IS COMING FASTER THAN expected and the closer we get to Halloween, the more apparent that becomes. I didn't dress for this chill, but AubreyDragon's scales are keeping me warm. He's literally a built-in furnace in dragon form and I absolutely love it. Rennie's been taunting him as we fly far from campus into the less populated area where they'll be less noticeable. That makes me smile, too, because I know he's been brooding as much as I have since we made our second trip to Apex.

It's like he knows the time for facing his demons is coming and there's no way to stop it.

"Stop squirming up there, appetizer. You know the rules." Aubrey's voice in full shift is dark, rumbly and full of menace. If he wanted me *not* to wriggle around on his back, talking probably wasn't the right move.

Renard darts in close, his electric blue eyes flashing as he makes a show of sniffing the air. "You're making her wet, love. I can smell it from here."

"Good. Behaving the past few times we did this was painful," the dragon growls.

Squeezing my arms around his thick neck, I lean in to whisper next to his tympanum as I grab his short horns. His hearing is even sharper in this form, but I'm purposefully teasing him. "No one is behaving tonight, big man."

His head rears back, and he lets out a bone-jarring roar followed by a quick burst of flame that Rennie barely ducks. The gargoyle swoops in close again, giving me a reproachful look. "Bad girl, *ma petite lapin*. Flames has almost no self control when he's in full dragon mode. That's why he doesn't let the lizard loose in front of most people."

I shrug at him, smiling wickedly. "I don't know if I'm ready for both of you in just fed, huge ass dude mode, but I'm sure as fuck going to find out." He groans and a sound that is suspiciously like a half-chuckle, half-snarl comes from my ride. "See? DragonMan agrees."

"DragonMan would agree to racing the capital if he'd get what he wants. He's got a two-track mind when he's scaly, *cherie*, and food is only one of them."

"Here," Aubrey says, ignoring our banter. "We land here. I smell campfires."

I can't smell from this height, but Rennie nods in agreement. Learning about their fully shifted capabilities is a slow process, given they're both reticent as hell, but I'm picking it up. My other men are apex predators and they enjoy hunting—especially Fitz—but Aubrey and Rennie are on another level. I don't know if all the mythical preds are like them or if their species are at the top of the food chain, but it's terrifying and sexy at the same time.

Maybe that's why I'm eager to allow them to control this evening; I want to experience all of it.

"Almost time, bite size."

The gravelly voice of Aubrey's dragon makes me clench my thighs and I know he's talking more than normal because he figured out what it does to me. Rennie is holding one of the creepy guys who were watching the camping college kids. He's still crouched over him as his life fades away, but my dragon finished his meal a few moments ago. I laughed as his fiery belches burned down two trees and a copse of berry bushes and he gave me the most reproachful lizard look I've ever seen.

I sniff the air, tilting my head as the coppery tang permeates my senses. My eyes burn for a moment and I growl low as my bunny pushes at my skin. Aubrey's vision is enhanced in full shift, and he can see things much more clearly than when he's wearing glasses as a human. My ears pop loose, twitching as I feel my body move towards the hulking gargoyle unbidden. It's like I'm in a trance and I can't stop myself from getting closer.

"Snacklet, I don't think you should—"

Before I can respond, the animal inside of me snaps and I fully shift. My tail pops free, fur covers my limbs, my nose wiggles, and I'm bouncing towards Rennie on enormous feet eagerly. A huff of frustration comes from behind me, but I ignore to approach my poetic onyx warrior. "What's happening to me?"

Rennie turns, looking at me with fearsome fangs and rock hard obsidian skin that shines in the moonlight. His mouth is full of blood and his eyes flashing such a bright blue that it's hypnotizing. "I knew it."

"You knew what?" I ask. My voice isn't as steady as theirs in a full shift. I don't do it often enough, I suppose, and my body isn't used to this. "What did you know?"

His lips curve into a satisfied smirk, and he picks up the body he was feeding as he rises to his feet. "Flames owes me a grand. Thank you, *ma petite.*"

Stomping my thumper, I stalk closer, trying to make my brain focus on his words and not on the smell. "Why? *Why* does he owe you money?"

"Because he bet me a thousand dollars you eat meat because you're not really prey." DragonAubrey shakes the ground as he lumbers towards us with his wings extended. "The first time we brought you along and you didn't vomit in disgust, he declared you're something else entirely."

Frowning, I step up to where the gargoyle is holding the almost lifeless body up with an expectant look. "What does that mean?"

"You shifted and couldn't stop it, right?" I nod at Rennie as he shakes his prize. "This is why. Whatever you are, your animal wants to feed on the life force, as I do. Dragons and other mythical shifters have… different needs than normal apex preds. Besides being hunted for various stupid reasons, we don't intermingle with regular preds so they can't figure out our secret."

I blink, clenching my clawed fists. "Is that why I can hardly make my brain work right now? I'm hungry?"

DragonAubrey's large head butts up against my back, pushing me into Renard gently. "It's also why you're having difficulty mastering some of your powers, we believe."

The scent overwhelms me and I dive in without another word. My bunny lets out a fierce roar inside of me as I gulp down the fluid that tastes like the best meal I've ever eaten in my life. I drink and drink until I can't get flow anymore, then lift my head to look at my men. My face has to be messy; I tore in like a rabid animal and I can feel the stickiness on it.

But they're looking at me with such intensity that I can fucking feel my pulse in my pussy.

"What?" I ask throatily. "You said—"

Rennie's eyes go black for a moment, then back to bright blue. "Run."

That one word makes my heart pound like it's going to escape my chest. I dart my eyes to Aubrey, seeing his rainbow pupils dilate as his big head bobs in response. Taking a deep breath, I let the bunny take over as I leap into action. I sprint into the darkness of the surrounding woods, ducking branches and obstacles with springy hops and jumps that I never could have made before. My muscles sing and I can hear every noise around me as I dodge and weave, hoping to throw them off my trail long enough to elude them.

"Come out and prey, my sexy carnivores," I whisper under my breath. I know they can hear me and I feel them fanning out, but I don't know how. It's like all of my senses are sharpened to the point of painful awareness of my surroundings. I hear bugs and crackling branches, the swish of grass on the breeze, and the sound of night animals slinking around.

Luckily for them, I'm the prey tonight, so they're safe.

MONSTERS

RENARD

I can smell her excitement and adrenaline in the air as I stalk through the woods. Flames went in the other direction once he changed back to a half-shift. It's easy for us; we've been shifting so many centuries we can transition easily even while moving. His enormous dragon would have torn through the space in a path of loud splinters and fallen trees, thus ruining the hunt.

Dolly shows an affinity for this; her trail is less obvious than I would have expected.

The bunny part of her moves with speed and skill naturally now that she has better control. As her animal became one with her human side, she stopped shifting into the small, helpless prey she described to Fitz last year. Instead, she's a lean, fierce bi-pedal rabbit that's giving me a merry chase through the darkness. I should thank Felix for that when I lord our little game over him and the other cats. They would enjoy this, too, but it would be far less intense.

My eyes scan my surroundings, night vision helping me discern the smallest movements in the surrounding foliage. Aubrey is likely in the sky, waiting to dive like a missile from the air if he finds her.

I could do that as well, but I've always enjoyed the thrill of moving on foot when I'm seeking my meals. Flying makes it much too easy and I like a challenge.

The snap of a twig close by gets my attention as I soak in the sounds of the night. Grinning, I stalk towards the noise silently, slipping through the shadows like the superhero Fitz likens me to. Those of us who hunt bigger game learn early on that slow and steady always wins their dinner—crashing about only gives your prey more time to hide.

"Here, bunny, bunny," I whisper to myself as I slink towards the noise. I know her hearing is sharper in this form, but I can't help taunting a little.

Another tiny crack guides me eastward and I scent the air again. Honeysuckle and blood are heavy on the breeze, so I know I'm getting closer. Since the others aren't here, I close my eyes, finding the mating bond within me that ties to my airborne mate. Using yet another secret we haven't shared with anyone, I reach for the dragon's mind with mine.

~She's close. Perhaps a couple hundred feet to east of me. ~

The rumbling sound of his shifted laugh in my head is familiar and I smile into the night. Other shifters do not share this ability as far as I know—only rare breeds—and even then, abilities are varied. Mind speech is a well kept secret amongst the various mythical beasts for a reason; it helps keep us alive and out of auctions.

As I creep closer to our girl, I remember how surprised I was to find out dragons are limited to speaking with mates. Gargoyles have always been able to put thoughts wherever they choose. That information sent him down a black hole of research that never panned out, but the question has always niggled at the back of my brain. I may not use my skill often, but I wish I knew why my clutch is so different from the likes of griffins, dragons, and the rest.

My head whips to the side as I sense movement again and I duck low, folding my wings close as I continue following her scent. It's getting stronger, so I know our game is getting her ready. She'll need to be aroused to handle us together, and I'm eager to taste the sweetness perfuming the air.

~Above you. Watching, ~ he says.

Smirking, I sniff the air again and stop when I come to a small rock face. She went up, which would be a sensible move if she wasn't being hunted by preds with wings. I dig my clawed hands into the stone, climbing up it with ease. My tail flicks back and forth in agitation until I reach the top, crawling over the ground as I blend into the darkness.

A few feet away, a heartbeat thumping like a bass drum calls to me. I slither closer, barely disturbing the patchy grass as I close the distance. Flames will join us once I have her captured and the feats will begin. The gargoyle inside practically purrs with pleasure at the thought and when I get within striking range, I leap forward, tackling the crouched bunny to the ground.

"Uh-oh, *petite lapin.* You've been caught."

Dolly doesn't shriek; instead she wraps her limbs around me, eyes dancing as she presses close. "Only one of you got me. It's a tie."

I look up, cocking my head at the half-shifted dragon slowly rising above the edge of her hiding spot. He's hovering with a hungry expression and she pouts. "I think not."

"Flying is cheating," she rasps. "No fair."

"There were no rules against it," Aubrey says as he lands. "Be specific, lunchable. You lost and now you're ours."

Her eyes are bright as she bats her lashes at me, then looks over her shoulder at my mate. "What do you get for winning?"

"Dessert," he replies as he spins her around. His grin is wicked as he sandwiches her between us and I feel my cock jump against her plump ass. "I want you to listen carefully and do exactly as I say. Can you do that? No bratting… just obey or it will be dangerous."

Fuck, I love it when he's in top mode.

"Yes," she breathes. Her skin is warm against the cold of my stone and I have to bite my lip to keep from groaning. "I can behave, Aubrey."

"Good. Now make the clothes go away."

Without that layer, she's even hotter, and I rumble darkly. "Sweet Aed, Flames. She's already an inferno."

"I like it when you chase me," Dolly admits softly. "I don't know if that's the prey in me or it's just my thing, but it made my entire body throb."

Aubrey reaches up to cup her face, gazing at her. "Chasing you makes my dragon want things you aren't ready for—but tonight, we'll try something he wants." He turns to me, a knowing expression on his face. "Do you have it in your coat?"

Oh, fuck. I know part of what he's planning now.

The coat I shed while we hunted re-appears and I dig in the inner pocket to pull out a bottle of lube. Before we started bringing Dolly along, our dinners always ended in fucking, so I carried it religiously. "Yes."

"Get her ready, love. She's soaked as it is, but we know that's not enough, especially for us." He dips his head and kisses her deeply as I fumble with the bottle like a damn teenager. When their lips break, I'm warming the liquid in my palms and he murmurs, "Did Chess and Fitz do this with you, little one?"

The minute my fingers slip through her folds then back to her ass again, her breath hitches and she lets her head fall back on my shoulder. "Yes. They did, and I fucking *loved* it."

Turning into her face as I slip one digit inside of her, I nuzzle along her jaw, pressing soft kisses there. She writhes as I work to stretch her and I swear to hell, feel my cock dripping in my pants. "Flames, I need to feel her."

He arches a brow, looking amused. While Dolly and I have the amulets to adjust our clothes to shifting, he does not. His large, sculpted body is pressed against the heat of her skin now that she's bare and I'm still clothed. Being half-shifted means she's rubbing on skin and scales, her cunt brushing along the extra features his dragon dick sports. I'd be jealous, but I'll get to bury my cock in her tight little ass. Even when I'm shifted, gargoyles aren't as ridiculously huge as a dragon—which means I go first. I'll take that win without complaint.

"Strip, but add more fingers. I want her stretched well and quickly. You'll like what I have planned, my love." He drops to his knees, grabbing one of her ankles to prop her foot on his shoulder. Dolly whimpers as he leans in close to her pussy and I slide a second finger, scissoring gently. "I'm going to make you come while Rennie is stretching your tight ass, snack size. You need to be dripping to take the two of us at once. Once you're ready, we'll fill you so full it will feel you're going to burst and then… comes the surprise."

"Please, Aubrey. I need more."

Damn, he's good—almost as good as Felix is at getting her to behave.

The minute his mouth touches her, I feel the shivers ripple over her soft fur. I let my clothes melt away and when the cool stone touches her, she gasps and arches into me. One wiggling ear brushes my horn and I chuckle softly. I'm not used to such a sweet, soft little body to fuck when I'm this much gargoyle. Her fluffy tail is brushing my stomach when she wiggles and my dick is pulsing so hard I can barely hold back.

"You need to hurry, love," I growl at my dragon. "Send her over and put this plan into motion before I accidentally explode on her ass instead of in it."

~Patience…~ he mumbles in my mind.

I know the second he transforms his tongue because her body shudders hard and her ass clenches. I grin, pushing in a third finger as she spasms, enjoying how she rocks back into my head as the orgasm crashes into her. "That's it, *ma petite*. Feel that long, forked dragon tongue stroking the perfect spot? I've felt it, too. He's so fucking good at using the perfect amount of pressure, mmm?"

Dolly's eyes pop open and she pants for a moment before turning her head to kiss me roughly. I'm surprised by the fangs on my lip and more surprised by the hard suckle on the split she caused. I break the kiss and lick away the rest of the blood before the gargoyle takes control, but she growls. "No. Need more. Want more. Again, big guy. Another finger, Rennie. Harder, boys."

Holy Freya on ice skates. Her eyes are so red that could be rubies.

"As you wish, *ma petite*," I reply. I push a fourth finger inside of her and she lets out an odd, rumbling hiss as she pushes into my hand. Aubrey has ducked lower and I feel his own hand brush mine as he grips her hip to comply with her request. Our girl wants it rougher, and neither of us will deny her.

Moving tandem, my mate and I work Dolly into another frenzy quickly. I wasn't lying when I said I was on the edge and before I can stop it, my dick quivers then shoots cum on her curvy ass. The moan that escapes my lips is raw and dark—I haven't come this quickly in many years. "Fuck, fuck, fuck."

~You'll be hard again soon, my love. Don't worry. ~

I pant softly as I let the waves of pleasure roll through me while my fingers slam into Dolly. I can feel that she's almost there, but not quite falling over. That is, until my dirty mate lets go of her hip to run his hand between her legs to the mess I left and pulls his face back. Aubrey looks up at both of us with a fangy smirk before he shoves the cum inside of her roughly, then dives back to her pussy. The shriek our bunny lets out pierces my ear drums and within moments of him working his magic on her g-spot, her entire body tenses, then she explodes.

That's when my dick perks right back up and I thank the fucking gods for shifter refractory periods.

When Dolly stops shivering and bucking like a bronco, I slow my hand to allow her to relax. I can tell her throat is getting raw as she rasps, "Motherfucking shit, Aubrey. That was so goddamn *hot* I almost died."

"Agreed," I murmur as I nip the point of her bunny ear. "He's so buttoned up during the day, but he's a freak in the sheets, *non?*"

"*Fuck*, yes." Her breath evens out finally, and I feel her melting against me. "But I haven't gotten any dick tonight, which is a tragedy."

Our sexy librarian lifts her foot off of his shoulder, putting it on the ground stands. Half-shifted, we both dwarf her and the smile on his face when he looks down at her tells me he's got something very special in mind. "Come here, tasty girl."

I let go of Dolly, and she wobbles forward into his arms. As soon as she's close enough, Aubrey grips her hips and hauls her up to wrap her legs around him. His wings extend upward, he huffs a small smoke ring. That tells me the dragon is riding him hard, and he's going to move fast. Walking closer, I press my body to our girl's and rumble with happiness as my dick nestles against her ass. "What now, baby?"

"First this," he says as he lets go of a hip and adjusts his cock to thrust inside of her. They both moan, and I have to clench my teeth at the sound. "Now, you take her."

Hell. Yes.

I grip my dick, rubbing the head against her spread cheeks for a second. She's slick as hell from the lube and cum, so I push forward, filling her until I can feel her squeezing my entire length.

Aubrey's so damn big that he's pressing against me hard through the layer of skin and it makes my eyes roll back. "And now?"

"Someone needs to move *now*," Dolly whines. "Goddess, I feel him in my fucking *stomach*. Do they get *bigger* or something? Holy fuck."

"They do," Aubrey chuckles. "I need you to hold on to my neck and waist—do not let go, no matter what. Do you understand, Dolly?"

She nods and her ass squeezes me as she does what he said. "Flames, this is… I'm not going to…It's too much."

"Not yet; it's not. Take my arms." He lets go of her hips, his arms circling her to grip my sides and pull us together more tightly.

Suddenly, I have a clue what he's going to do and I panic a little. We've done this, but not with someone else and certainly not… "Are you sure? This is…"

He winks at me then looks at the girl we're buried inside of, cocks being warmed as she throbs. "What's the word, nibblet? Say it for me so I know you understand you can opt out."

"Beetlejuice," she breathes huskily. "But I won't need it. You'd never hurt me."

"True, but you always have the power to use that word if it's too much. Understand?"

I tighten my hold on his forearms when she nods and my wings flare out to match his. He counts down in my mind and when he hits three, we're thrust into the air as he takes off. Dolly lets out a squeal of surprise and I feel her gripping my dick, but once Aubrey is flying steady, her body relaxes. The high of this will blow her mind—I should know. I just didn't know he could carry both of us at the same time. His dragon is even stronger than I realized.

"No one will ever believe me," she mutters.

Flames chuckles and looks at her shoulder. "Locomotion, please. I'm doing the heavy lifting."

Thrusting my hips upward, I draw myself in and out of her ass, slowly at first. It pushes her into him and I hear her gasp and him grunt. It takes a few strokes before her natural fear of falling fades with the pleasure and then her body rocks back and forth with my dick. The sensation is so intense, especially with my gargoyle and his dragon out, that I slide my tail between us and use it to flick her clit. I know when it brushes his shaft, too, because Aubrey curses, but doesn't let go.

His huge wings flap cool air over our fevered bodies as we gently rock together, and I can't help leaning in to kiss him over her head. He pulls back with a growl and I look down to see our girl grinning wickedly, blood on her lips again.

"She bit me again!" he snarls. "How the fuck am I supposed to…?"

We can't discuss that now. Whatever has awakened inside of our bunny is a family discussion for tomorrow.

"No breaking skin, *ma petite*. We don't want him to drop us, right?" She pouts, so I slam my hips against her harder. My tail flicks her bud more quickly, knowing another climax will distract her. "Just let us fuck you until you explode."

"Ooooooh…kay…" she half-groans as the sounds of our hips slapping gets louder.

I close my eyes and bury my face in her hair as Aubrey and I take her. The motions are fluid and rhythmic as we all move as one and when she finally peaks, I can barely hold it in any longer. Raising my head, my eyes meet his rainbow ones, and he nods. "Shit. Hold on tight," I mutter. "This may be a stretch."

We swell and lock into place, both smashing her between us as our bodies do exactly what we were afraid of last year. Dolly's pussy trembles and her ass grips me hard enough to almost be painful, but she stays in place like Aubrey instructed. Harsh pants and breaths fill the air as the heat cools from our bodies, and I look around us, completely unaware of where my dragon has been taking us.

The car is sitting in the spot we left it in and his wings are dipping to lower us to the ground very gently. When our feet touch grass, I lick my lips. "I still don't know how the actual fuck you navigate while you fuck, Flames."

His lips curve as I let go of his arms and slip out of Dolly. Letting her legs down carefully as he shifts her off his cock, my dragon leans her limp body against mine, then heads for the trunk. He shrugs when he returns with a pile of clothes and a package of wipes. "In my DNA, I suppose. Dragons are meant to fly while doing other things."

"Like a homing pigeon," Dolly mumbles in a sleepy, slurry voice.

"*Not* like a pigeon," he growls.

Oh, wait until Fitz hears about this.

Bad Things

Delores

I'm still limping a little and it's Tuesday.

Aubrey may have been right that I'm not ready to take them on when they're fully shifted—though I'd cut my tongue out before telling him so. I spent much of Sunday and Monday propped in the giant couch nest studying and mainlining caffeine. The guys came in and out as they prepared things for their exams or worked on the crap we brought back from Apex. Chess made sure I always had food and plumped pillows while I nursed the minor side effects of running through dark woods while being hunted and then be fucked within an inch of my life in mid-air.

By the time I had to put on my uniform and head to my first midterm in for Speech, I feel ready for whatever the assholes at Cappie are going to throw at me this week. I even had an extra day to study because the short #Viral play counts as the Acting mid-term and History's exam is on Thursday. All I have to do today is pass the dialect test in Speech, then sing my solo and play my piano piece for Madame Bouvier. I'm not worried about any of those because I have them dead to rights.

It's going to be a good day.

"Good morning, Dolly," Kirby says with a smile.

I hand him a small travel mug of the fancy coffee Chess made for as I sip the hot brew in my own. "I think it might be, which is unusual."

He laughs as we head down the lane to the Cappie's Shird, and I shrug. "It won't cause the sky to fall if you're happy for a day. You have so many things on your shoulders."

My lips curve and I sigh as we approach the stairs. "Well, we'll see. I have many hours left before the day ends. Thanks for meeting me before these exams. Will you be the one here when I'm done at 2?"

Kirby shakes his head. "I have duties in House Lupine in the afternoon. I think we're stretched a little thin with preparing for both the big match this weekend and All Hallows Eve. Raina said Holliday might be here, so keep your eyes peeled."

"Okay. Good luck with the dogs," I wink and wave at him.

"I'll need it."

"*Merci*, Madame Bouvier!" I call over my shoulder as I head out of the building. As promised, the armadillo is waiting for me outside. I smile brightly at him, making the sign for hello as I walk towards him.

He signs his greeting slowly because he knows Renard has only been teaching me for a week. I have to watch him do it more than once, but I eventually figure out he's signed, "Good afternoon, Miss Dolly. How were your exams?"

I press my lips together because I don't know all the signs I need for my answer. Holliday signs the letters 'y' and 'n' for me, his eyes dancing merrily. I finger spell the word 'good,' then finally give in and speak. His lipreading is excellent, but I want so badly to learn.

"Sorry. Too many words for spelling and I don't know enough signs yet. But the exams were good and I'm ready to go home so I can prop my sore ass up."

Before he can unleash another set of signs for me to puzzle through, my phone buzzes in my pocket. I pull it out and work screen lock crap Fitz put on it, only to find an email from the evil counselor witch. Despite it being mid-term week and our schedules being jumbled like a fucking jigsaw, she still expects me to put my obligatory hours in. Just like that, the decent day I was having slides downhill and I kick a rock across the path.

Turning to Holliday, I sign 'sorry,' before I talk. "Change of plans. I have to go to the Admin building for this stupid appointment. Can you come?"

The armadillo nods and I follow him to the airlock, texting the guys as we go.

> BabyGirl: Change of plans. Rockland emailed that I still have my appointments this week.

> CSpot: That nasty witch needs to go.

> TigerWoody: None of you will let me kill her, so it's not my fault.

> EmoBatman: You have to go, ma petite. She will cause trouble if not.

> BabyGirl: No shit. I know she's just waiting for me to give her something she can use to get me in trouble. Since Farley sent the Postman, she's been more subdued but compliant.

> TigerKing: You're sending him everything, right? You'll need it to ensure you have proof of the crap she's putting you through.

BabyGirl: I am. Every tiny detail goes to him so he can keep it in his files. He said one day we'll have enough to take her to court.

LustyLibrarian: And when you do, we'll make sure she regrets it. But for now, stay alert. We still don't know if she's playing only for herself or at the behest of others.

TigerWoody: Baby Girl, tell that cowboy armadillo I'm picking you up. I don't care if I have to sit in the waiting room the whole time. You're not seeing that woman without backup.

Baby Girl: Okay, Fitzy. I'll see you all soon.

CSpot: Don't get worked up, angel. I'm making tomahawks and cheesy potatoes tonight.

EmoBatman: Cheese is the only actual competition we have for our girl, Chester.

Smiling at the screen, I watch them banter as Holliday and I head down the long tube to the main part of the campus. I know they want to protect me, but Rockland is one of the few people their threats haven't deterred. The only thing that makes sense about her dismissal is that she's backed by someone powerful enough to keep her safe, but I don't know who that would be. A credited book would infuriate my mother, despite it detailing my high society connections. Lucille only likes publicity she's orchestrated and I don't believe she'd use a loose cannon like my fake ass counselor.

No, someone else is pulling Rockland's strings, but the question is who? What does humiliating me get them?

When we arrive at the building, Holliday opens the door and follows me inside. The crew doesn't normally do so, so I give him a questioning look as we get in the elevator. Signing the letter 'y' at him, I wait as the carriage heads up to Rockland's floor. He looks thoughtful for a moment, then shakes his head and shows me the screen on his phone instead of trying to sign his answer.

There's a message from the Captain telling him to stick with me no matter where I go and I turn red. The armadillo can't hear, but he'll read Rockland's lips and then he'll know what kind of shit she puts me through. I was hoping to keep that information secret so none of my guys goes off the rails and tries to murder her. Farley is the only person I'm giving all the info to, and I wanted to keep it that way. Biting my lip, I gesture at his phone, hoping he'll let me type on it. He nods and I type out 'Session info secret. Please do not repeat what she says to me. Someone will die and it will make everything worse.'

His eyes widen and he gives me an uncertain look before signing 'okay.' I let out a breath, relief filling me as the doors open. *At least he's willing to play along for now.* I stride down the hall with the armadillo on my heels, determined to get through this so I can go home in a mood conducive to studying. I have my dance final nailed, but I also have Music Theory and Diplomacy tomorrow. I'm sure Rakoto will throw me curveballs to be a bitch and I want Rennie to quiz me while we eat Chessie's dinner and veg out. I *can't* be teetering on the edge right now.

The door to Rockland's office opens, revealing the vulture herself. She frowns when she sees Holliday, but allows us to walk into the waiting area. "I'm afraid your little friend will have to wait out here. Sessions are confidential."

Sure they are, you story stealing corpse licker.

Smiling innocently, I shake my head, making sure I'm not looking at him when I answer. I won't be able to keep my face straight if I do. "No can do, ma'am. Holliday has been assigned to escort me by my mother, and Lucille gets very upset when her edicts are ignored. Besides, he's deaf, so confidentiality isn't a worry."

"Oh!" she says with a plastered-on smile. "Then it will be fine. Your privacy won't be compromised if he can't hear. How silly of me."

I blink for a second, letting her idiotic lack of knowledge about deaf shifters sink in. As usual, I cannot *believe* anyone lets this dumbass chick handle students with genuine issues. She's about as sensitive as a cactus shoved up your ass. Turning to my companion, I have to stifle a chuckle when he shrugs. I suppose he's used to people being morons, even if I'm not.

"Come, come!" Rockland calls from her office. "No time to waste. Deadlines and all."

Holding in a snarl at her comment, I head into the room and throw myself into the armchair farthest from her desk. This is a game we play every time, because I don't like to give her the upper hand. This time, however, she settles in her chair and doesn't comment on my seating choice. Holliday meanders over to the chaise on the back wall, giving himself a clear view of her face without looking interested.

The Captain's crew are very smart and very loyal prey.

"Now, where were we?" Rockland pretends to shuffle some papers around, then bends to look in a drawer. She does this often and I've wondered if she's got the remote to whatever she uses to record me down there. "Ah, yes. Last we spoke, we were discussing the merits of having more than one lover. I'd asked about feeling excluded when a bonded pair is intimate without you."

I don't even have to look at Holliday to know he's probably trying not to gape at her. Her intrusive bullshit is well over the line and I don't have a choice but to indulge her until we have enough evidence. "And I told you my relationships are none of your business. I have no concerns in that area."

"I sincerely doubt that. The information I have is that you were a virgin until the boy you thought was your mate deflowered you, then tried to eat you when you emerged as a rabbit. The trauma from that alone would cause serious sexual dysfunction, not to mention emotional issues. Those who chose polyamorous groups have complex dynamics to navigate, even when the people involved aren't abusing their authority and the many years of experience they have on you."

Closing my eyes, I push the red rage of my bunny back as she suggests I'm unstable. Rockland often pushes me this way, just hoping I'll lose my temper and she'll be able to discredit my claims. Unfortunately for her, I have a lifetime of hiding my emotions from a bigger psychopath than her. So I slip into the blank space, letting my features go slack with indifference. "I'm not crazy, nor do I have dysfunction. My sex life is fabulous and still none of your damn business."

"I see. You seem very sure those men won't get bored with an inexperienced shifter. In fact, you act as though they'll be around to stand by you forever," she comments. "That's an awfully naïve expectation for someone with your… shortcomings. Novelty wears off, Miss Drew. You need to be healthy enough to stand on your own."

I look up from my nails, arching a brow lazily. "I think the Games are proving I'm capable of exactly that."

She snorts and shakes her head. "Being able to beat lower preds in a supervised match is not the same as surviving on your own. Your victory was followed by a draw, I believe. Obviously, when the opponent is worthy, you aren't able to prevail."

"My opponent was a ringer pumped full of PEDs, you nitwit," I shoot back. My temper fires again and I have to rein it in, leaning back in my chair again. "Otherwise, the fight would have been a fair pairing. Fighting someone who has been fed speed and enhancers to a draw is the best outcome that was possible."

"Perhaps," she murmurs. "Or perhaps that's just the latest in your line of excuses for your failures. You always seem to point the finger at other preds, even those who are your betters. Why is that, Delores?”

Here we go. She's digging for what I know.

“Probably because my emotionally challenged ex-friends are obsessed with their vendetta and people are being kidnapped and murdered at my schools. It sort of feels like the old saying about being paranoid, not meaning people aren't out to get you. The guy was pretty insightful for a human, don't you think?”

“This level of paranoia isn't a colorful quote, Miss Drew. It indicates several mental disorders and I'm merely trying to—”

“Get me to admit I'm crazy? Good luck.” I roll my eyes and sigh before I continue. These sessions get worse every time and my patience is shot. “I'd have to be wrong for that to hold water. I have solid proof and witnesses to show the Heathers have stalked, harassed, bullied and abused me for two years now. I don't use it because I don't need to—they simply aren't smart enough to beat me. And as for the kidnapping and murders? There was a dead body on campus mere weeks ago. The missing students from last year haven't turned up, nor have the ones Cappie is trying to hide the disappearances of from our first week. I'm *not* imagining anything.”

Her eyes widen when I drop the bomb about the students who didn't show up when school started. Fitz turned it up in one of his ‘sneaky missions’ to the admin building and I've been saving it for the right moment. Rockland recovers quickly, though, and shakes her shoulders like she's trying to unruffle feathers. “I don't know where you got that information, Delores, but it's private. I won't discuss other students' statuses with you.”

“Mmmm,” I reply as I smirk. “I didn't expect you to. I just wanted you to know I won't fall into your trap.”

“We'll see about that,” she says as she straightens in her chair. “Now let's discuss what happened the night of your prom.”

RENEGADES

FELIX

EXAMS ARE FINALLY OVER AND THE LAST BIG EVENT THIS WEEK IS the Pred Games match tonight. The Princess is exhausted from all the studying and practices, but the Games wait for no shifter. Matches are scheduled by the Leonidas pride based on some ridiculous formula devised years ago and until we found their hidey-hole at Apex, I wondered if it was susceptible to bribery like everything else in our world. As I thought, it is, which I think is why we have a match the weekend after exams.

No sane league president would place games during midterms for any school, but no surprise we're up against Shifter U during ours.

Shifter U is the public university for preds. It has a sister school more commonly called 'Victim U' where prey who don't have means attend. Matches between the public school and the private ones are the ugliest, dirtiest ones of the season and frequently end in ambulances speeding away from the school hosting. The prey animals should be the angriest of our society, but they aren't. They have their own ecosystem and hierarchies within their species.

The most bitter families sit between the highest prey tiers and the lowest pred tiers. They're barely able to stay above the wealthy prey by their pred status, but they're also looked down upon by the elite preds. It doesn't matter if it's because of money or specific species limitations—they hate both sides and often stir up the most trouble. Of course, humans are below all shifters, but unless the need arises, most shifters keep the hell away from them. Preds might not be perfect, but the sheer lunacy of humans has made it an unwritten rule to stay as far away from them as possible. It's not illegal to interact, of course, but it definitely is to reveal our nature or attempt to 'turn' one.

That shit is a myth, and it's straight up murder, but some idiots try it, anyway.

Resting my chin on my clasped hands, I look at the list of female opponents Zhenga slipped me. None of the names are familiar, which isn't surprising, but their stats are slightly concerning. According to the roster, none of the Shifter U are apex preds and they don't have impressive win-loss ratios. They seem to be newcomers to the Games with little records except the past three league matches. Conversely, the male team has a couple preds who might get recruited for a scholarship to one of the private schools if they perform this well for the rest of the year.

"Awfully suspicious if you ask me," I mutter as I click my mouse and start a Prednet search. Fitz installed a more intensive search function based on his… shit, some fucking computer code thing he described in great detail that I've now forgotten entirely. Regardless, he swore it would help me find things regular engines couldn't, so I'm going to use it. I type in 'Erica Krandall' and hit the button to start the web crawler.

Beyond her public stats for the Shifter U team, I find absolutely nothing—not even on social media. Frowning, I plug in the next ten names one by one, running the same parameters and come up short each time. This can't be a coincidence, though I'm unsure whether it is *our* crop of enemies or if it's simply the coach at Shifter pulling a fast one. Before we found the evidence on Z's brother, I would have been dead certain it was someone looking to fuck with my Princess.

Now, I don't know, and it pisses me off.

Dolly is in the library archives with Chess, Aubrey, and Renard, so it will be safe to corral Fitz into doing something risky. He won't want D to go into a fix blind, either, so I know he'll break the fucking internet to find what we need. Swiping to open my phone, I shoot him a text and settle in to wait. We have to find out what these idiots are hiding before the match tonight and I don't care who I have to squeeze to do it.

"This is fucking crazy, bro," Fitz says as he types on the keyboard so fast his fingers are like blurs. "Like who the hell puts this kind of security up in a public college? There's fuck-all to steal and no one here is important enough to warrant the money it would take to have someone build this shit."

Rubbing my hand over my face, I sigh, gathering my patience. Fitz was eager to help as predicted, but his worry about our girl has made him manic. I'm trying to summon the wherewithal to deal with him without shouting, but it's difficult. "This isn't something that the Ericksons could have purchased or donated?"

"Fuck *no*," my twin says indignantly. "This isn't prepackaged garbage. Someone hand coded this, and they did it with the Erickson tech limitations in mind. Like, it's designed to keep those kinds of user out because it's not rooted in their operating system."

I understood about every other word of that.

"So… you think they had a rogue programmer not affiliated with the tech industry to code their base shit to make it hard to get into? But why? What the hell could they be hiding?" I shake my head, not comprehending why the university with the least amount of sensitive information would have this kind of shit when Cappie's system is beyond hackable, according to my brother.

"They sure as fuck did. I mean, I haven't seen this signature on the Pred-net or the dark web before. Whoever it was didn't want other chipheads to I.D. them. I don't know if it's a pred or prey; hell, I don't even know if it's a goddamn robot. What I know is that they've made this a multi-day, energy drink fueled manic hack, and that's *if* people leave me alone for a few days. We aren't getting into their stuff today, man."

Fitz rakes his hand through his hair and growls in frustration. I clap my hand on his shoulder, thinking for a moment while he seethes. We only have six hours until the matches start. Dolly goes closer to the end since the first night, and I have no reason to think that will change. *Perhaps...* I look at my twin with a slow grin, tilting my head. "What if we get the others to distract Princess and we go suss this out in person? Would you be able to get around this if you were physically at the servers?"

"That could work. I can..." he stops talking and I can almost see the things whizzing around in his head as he stares into space.

I close the computer, breaking his focus so he looks at me. "Gather what you need and I'll go talk to Chess. He can relay the plan to the others. Hopefully, Dolly won't be too upset when she figures it out, but she needs to stay here to get ready. Plus, without her there, you won't be distracted."

He looks like he's going to argue, but my twin finally shakes his head. "You're right. I won't be worried about her and I can wrangle the shit firing off in my head like fireworks. Do it."

THE DRIVE TO SHIFTER U WAS FAIRLY QUIET. I COULD TELL MY twin was completely caught in his head as he worked through the possibilities for cracking the insane security at our destination. When he was younger, he used to get like this when he was planning to break into some big game or illegally sneak into websites he should never be in. He'd wandered around, silent as a tomb until he figured it out, then he'd get so excited he'd damn near cripple poor Chess. After that, he'd do whatever it was and walk around smugly for days. I suppose I should have noticed his patterns and how he was struggling to hogtie the threads in his head, but what the hell did I know about how to work with ADHD? It's not like our father kept shrinks at Bloodstone. The one we saw as children after a few of the rougher incidents was promptly fed to the prisoners.

But I think I'm getting it now, thanks to the Princess. She has a knack for understanding and accepting us exactly how we are without question.

"Do you want to bounce anything off me?" I ask cautiously. "I won't be able to understand a lot, but I'll try to help you corral the ideas."

Fitz looks at me in surprise, but nods eagerly. "That'd be fucking excellent, bro. I have a lot of... unformed thoughts, and maybe you can nudge me in the right direction or something."

"Okay, so what's the first step?" I don't look at him as I pull off the exit we need for the college. Dolly said eye contact can send his brain spiraling into another path, so I'm using her advice to give this shit a chance. "What do we do when we get there?"

His fingers tap in a rhythm on his leg as he stares out the window at the houses as we head towards campus. "I'll need to re-configure their door signals or pick the lock to get us in. Once we're in, the schematics for the Science building showed the servers are in the basement. We head there and figure out which room we need."

Nodding as I pull into the lot and choose a space concealed among other cars, I let that sink in. It sounds simple enough for the beginning. "Okay, then what?"

"Depends. I'll get into the server and try to run some of my programs to find a back door or loophole in the code that I couldn't find remotely. It could take five minutes or hours. I won't know until I'm in it. While I do that, you'll need to watch the other laptop I have hacked into their cameras. *That* I managed because it's not in the more secure partitions of their network."

I pause while we gather up his backpacks full of equipment. He packed things, so we'd look like fairly normal figures as we walked on campus, but it made them heavy as hell. "Let's head for the Science building and get started then. I'll try to help when I can and if I need to handle someone, I'll leave you to it while I take care of them."

Fitz gives me a grateful look and then holds his fist out for a bump. "Thanks, man. I was spinning out, and I needed someone to let me walk through it slowly. Too many variables and my brain wanted me to compute all of them, you know?"

"I don't know, but Princess has been teaching us what to do when you're having trouble, so I followed her instructions." I shrug, not ashamed to admit that I don't know everything, particularly in this case. "She's a miracle worker, it seems, because I didn't even have the urge to shout at you."

"That *is* a goddamn miracle." He laughs as we set across the green towards the big shiny building that houses their science and tech programs. "We'll have to give her a nice reward."

"Indeed."

"HOW MUCH LONGER, FITZ?"

His fingers stop flying over the keys, and he gives me an irritated look. "I'm supposed to be the impatient one, Felix."

My eyes dart back to the camera feeds, making sure the rotating guards aren't coming any closer to our little corner of the building. It's hard for me to stay this still without actually doing anything for this long. I prefer action and it amazes me that my hyperactive twin is happily clicking away without so much as a twitch. Computers really help him focus and I didn't know how much until this moment. "This is a lot of waiting and watching the world's most boring reality show. I had no idea what kind of shit you did when you're working on this stuff for us."

"The challenge of interacting with the algorithms and reacting to its defenses then parrying again is satisfying. It's like a Pred Games match, but more brain work. I have to continually counter and block and attack while I'm working. It's fast-paced on my end and the constant input makes my spinning hamster wheel brain release happy chemicals." I blink when he looks at me with a tiny grin. "I could tell you were wondering how I stay still this long."

"Huh. I guess I didn't think of it that way."

"If you're not a tech person, you wouldn't. This is Whack-a-Mole on meth and I'm chasing the elusive golden mole while I smack down all the obstacles. Luckily, your idea about being on site was on point. I'm in one partition, though there's nothing here about our girl or the magic freaks." A ding makes us both jump, and he frowns at the screen. "Ah, here we go. I've got it now."

"You've got what?" I squint at the gibberish running through all the tiny windows in confusion. "I don't see shit."

Windows pop up one by one as if reacting to my disdain and as we look over them, the reason for this type of set-up becomes apparent. Shifter U's team is filled with shadow students and ringers, including quite a few players who have been banned from other schools or amateur leagues for juicing or violating rules of engagement. They're being rostered under fake names with fake I.D.s and the whole thing is being bankrolled by none other than the current heir apparent, Kehinde Leonidas.

Why the fuck is Z's twin running a match fixing scheme?

"I don't get it, bro. Kehinde doesn't need the small potatoes money this shit would bring in. Even in the pros, this is pennies compared to the dough the league, the branding, and the franchises earn. Doing it endangers their family's hold on the sport. Why?" Fitz rakes his hand through his hair, his brow furrowing as he tries to puzzle it out.

"Because he knows he's *only* the heir to that empire if their father doesn't change his mind and give it all to Z. If he reconsiders, a deathbed regret, or Kehinde pisses him off, the league and all the power will be hers. That idiot knows she deserves it and he's hedging his bets."

"College level seems like tiny gains for lots of risk, though."

"Not if you're hoping these idiots will attract pros and eventually, you'll own pro players, too. Knowing they've been cheating and living under false names while doing it would put them on the blacklist. They could end up at Bloodstone if the Council deems it. So once they ascend to real money, they still can't escape him." I sigh, trying to figure out if I want to tell Zhenga about this now or after the match.

She's going to lose the fucking plot, so later it is.

"The big question is: is our girl in trouble tonight?" Fitz's eyes turn amber and I chuckle as he flicks through screens to find what he wants. "I don't give a flying pig fart if they're cheating or what it means for the league. That's an old life. I care about making sure no psychos harm her to further Kehinde's money grab."

"Agreed. Download all the real stats for the female players and we'll take them home to coach her. That way, she's doomed to fail."

Fitz nods and I turn back to the cameras. We won't have to play Shifter U again until next semester, so I'm not worried about fixing this bullshit right now. We can cross the match fixing scheme off the boards until after the holidays and we can go back to focusing on the actual threats.

I'm tiring of juggling the crooked assholes sitting on our Council; perhaps that needs to be the focus once we get through this year.

The Greatest

Delores

 thank any deity listening as I stare up at the ceiling of my room.

Thanks to Felix and Fitz's outing to Shifter Secondary yesterday, the guys could prepare me for every opponent I could face in the ring. The information they found was terrifying and at first, I was determined to fake illness to scratch my entry. Zhenga's brother filled that team with criminals and violent girls who had no business being allowed to compete. Their actual records were full of things that made my blood run cold.

But I knew there would be even worse things waiting for me if I did.

Lucille wouldn't stand for being embarrassed by my weakness, even if it was a true medical issue. My shows in the matches have kept the smaller preds looking to make a name for themselves away, and the mean girl groups have been waiting for a crack in my armor. None of the enemies I have watching my every move would waste the opportunity to come for me if I showed even the tiniest hint of failure.

My life is being directed by those who want to hurt me even when I'm fighting like hell to wrest it back. Each step I take towards claiming my independence is met with retaliation by the factions using me as some sort of pawn in a much bigger game. Not knowing what the game is yet meant getting out of a match where my opponents might have actual weapons beyond their animals wasn't in the cards. The league officials should have kicked the cheating bitches out already, but Shifter Secondary hadn't been disqualified once this semester.

Which meant they knew what the competitors there were doing and allowed it to continue.

When I stepped into the circle in the vast arena, typically reserved for the male team, all I could see were screaming blobs and lights. They called my opponent Trace Anitram—nicknamed 'The Mistress of Pain.' As if that wasn't intimidating enough, the chick was built like a fucking brick house and smelled like canine. It didn't take me long to figure out she was a wolf because she told me Fitz killed her boyfriend last year.

None of that would have boded well, especially because he pissed on the headless corpse, but I knew by her name what she was going to do to win. The crazy bitch hides claw tips as acrylic nails and when she shifts, the metal shreds the hell out of the other person with every swipe. Her matches end in the other team member, nearly bleeding out on the way to medical and before any officials can see, she swallows the fucking things.

Anyone psycho enough to tear up their insides week after week to win would happily kill me for glory, and I knew it. I had to shift immediately, going on the offensive with speed and sheer shock to keep her from pulling her tricks. It didn't stop her, of course, but it helped me learn how she moved. Our fight lasted almost a half hour in the end and by the time I finally choked her out, I was almost spent.

The guys rushed the field again, helping me stay upright as I headed for the medical bay and the crowd lost its mind. Cappie won the night, but I had to be tucked into a pile of men to fall asleep that night. I might be getting stronger, faster, and meaner, but my inexperience is making it harder with every match. Somehow, I get assigned the worst opponent every time, and no one seems to figure out how.

I'm slightly concerned about what that means for the rest of the year.

Rolling out of bed carefully, I smile as Jinx pads over to her cat tree before I head for the door. The scent of something tasty catches my nose and my stomach rumbles. I'm going to devour whatever Chess is cooking—expending all that energy last night has me feeling wobbly as hell. As soon as I open the door, Fitz scoops me up in his arms, grinning like a madman.

"I've been waiting for you, Sleeping Beauty. They said I had to let you wake up on your own, *not* with the special kisses I wanted to wake you up with." He bobs his brows and I laugh as I wind my arms around his neck. "I think you'd be a lot more energetic right now if we didn't live in the land of cockblockers."

Darting forward, I kiss his nose. "You're probably right, but since you've got me now, feed me."

"Careful, Baby Girl. I love when you're all growly and hungry." He turns and heads for the main room with a bounce in his step. I can feel as we walk.

Having people who are always happy to see me the minute I wake up is still novel and I bask in it every day.

"I'm excited about the Halloween party, but after last year, I'm also a little worried?" I look at my tiger with a rueful expression. "Rufus and Cori won't tell me a thing about this group costume situation, so no one can blame me for what they end up with this year."

"The hillbilly gangster wouldn't dare make me look as silly as you did. I'll beat his ass," Fitz rumbles as he plops us on the sunken couch. "I don't give a red, randy fuck about being in drag if you choose it. You can dress me up as a goddamn purple dino if it makes you happy. He, however, does not get the same leniency."

"Don't be rude, Fitzy," Chess says from the kitchen. "Those two are doing all the heavy lifting for us and I don't think Cori will let him go too insane. She's got a good head on her shoulders."

I blink, suddenly remembering. "Oh! I forgot to ask and I have no idea if you can do this by Tuesday, but… Cori's lonely. Rufus says she's hiding it and I can tell she's upset when he's flitting off with the triplets. Any chance you can play matchmaker? I'm worried she's feeling very left out and unwanted, but won't tell us."

Fitz's smile turns into a proud beam. "Fuck, yeah, I can! In fact, I might know the *perfect* girl. She's in my Advanced Algorithmic Design class. I can chat her up tomorrow and see where she stands. This chick is smart, adorable, *and* she's one of those do-gooder hackers. I bet Coco-cabana will *adore* that about her."

Chess walks over with three plates balanced on his arm like a fancy waiter. "Fruity Pebbles pancakes, scrambled eggs, bacon, and fruit. Feliz is grabbing the coffee as we speak."

"I am *so* fucking spoiled," I mutter to myself as I take the plates for Fitz and me as he climbs in next to us. "Chessie, I know it seems like I love you for your cooking skills, but I promise other things matter, too."

"Like his sexy speared dick!" Fitz grins and pops a piece of bacon in his mouth with a hum of approval. "Dude, did you candy this shit? Holy fuck."

"I did, actually. It's maple bourbon flavored," the cheetah says as he flushes. "Do you like it?"

"Your dick or the bacon?" Aubrey snorts as he walks in. "You know what? Since the options have to do with maple bacon flavoring or Fitz's preferences, don't answer that."

Giggling, I chomp a piece of the bacon with a groan of approval then cover my mouth. "I vote for both."

"Both is good." Fitz nods.

Chess turns redder as Felix and Rennie come in, obviously scenting the delicious eats from their rooms. Felix arches a brow at me, looking amused at our pile in the cushions. "Room for more, Princess?"

I nod as I munch on the delicious food Chessie made. "Uh-huh."

To everyone's surprise, he bends to pick up the cheetah, sitting on my side and placing him on his lap before kissing my jaw. "Excellent. I don't want to miss your sexy food noises."

Fitz gives his twin an incredulous look, pointing at him with a fork menacingly. "Watch it, bro. You're edging in on my territory. But I agree about her food moans. They're spank-worthy."

"Chess' food is spank-worthy," I mumble around the sweet pancakes filled with Fitz's favorite cereal. "How could I keep my food-gasms quiet?" That gets a laugh out of all the guys, and when Aubrey brings me a huge mug of my special brew, they watch until I sigh with pleasure.

Rennie comes over with his plate, a devilish sparkle in his eyes as he mimics Felix, placing Fitz on his lap. The tiger beams at him and Aubery plops down in front of me, settling in with my feet in his lap. "This is *trés* cozy, *ma petite*. How do you feel this morning?"

"Eating tasty 'bad for me' shit while you're all snuggled in? Uh, fucking fantastic, thanks." I snort and shove another mouthful of pancakes in my mouth. "Take that, César."

"Well… about that…" Chess flushes again and ducks his head. "It's not that bad for you. None of it is, really."

I frown, looking at my half-empty plate, then back at him. "What?"

"Based on César's and Zhenga's advice, I've changed how I cook. I use a lot of raw sugar versus processed, whole grain or home-made pasta not store bought. I add a lot of hidden veggies and fruit to everything, and I sneak protein powders and supplemental nutrients into most of the food. It's tricky to get taste right at first, but I've been making sure it all works for your training requirements."

Felix chews his pancakes, then his brows furrow. "But it tastes fucking great, bro. We wouldn't have known if you didn't say anything."

Chess grins and his chest puffs a bit. "I watch a lot of YouTube videos and tutorials. I thought you'd all figure it out, but no one ever did. The cereal is garbage but Fitzy and my angel like it, so it's a treat."

"Damn, Chessie, you really are my knight in shining armor. You made healthier shit, not taste like ass." I dart forward, kissing him softly before I pull back. "Thank you for taking care of me."

"Aw, it's cuddle-wovey time," my dragon snarks playfully. "Everyone get it out of your system now before we have to walk into that ridiculous fucking party. You know it's going to be filled with booby traps and assholes."

"Maybe it won't be? Maybe we'll get to dance and drink and wear silly costumes?" Even Chess gives me a baleful expression, and I cross my arms over my chest as I pout. "Ugh, fine. It's probably going to be a pain in the ass and everyone will ruin it, but let me have a sliver of hope. I won't know how my exams with everyone but you guys went until Friday and I'm stressed enough. Plus, I'm sore as hell from fighting that nasty dog last night."

"Which is why you got special pancakes," Chess supplies helpfully. "And why we're going to veg out here today and not talk about—"

The sound of a phone vibrating in someone's pocket stops him and I roll my eyes at the ceiling in supplication. Aubrey fishes out his DiePhone, scrolling quietly. I watch the rainbow flicker through his eyes and the brief sensation of his dragon ripples over my legs as he fights back fury. When he's finally done, we're all watching him expectantly and he snarls.

"That was Aloysius at the Smithsonian texting. He's warning me about the email he sent to me that was also CC'd to the Council, Apex admins, Cappie admins, and your lawyer. His tests on the samples from the prom, the clothing from her room, her body, and her equipment in the school labs confirm Kinsley was behind the poisoning at Apex. Samples taken at Cappie show she was working on something else they couldn't identify as well. It had ingredients and DNA they don't recognize, as well as some engineering techniques known to be used by humans."

My voice is a whisper as I ask the question we're all wondering. "What does that mean?"

"He doesn't know. They're going to continue testing and possibly loop in contacts in the human world without providing context. The Smithy is shared space, so they often rope in well-known human scientists for research under NDAs that keep them quiet. But if you'd never met the girl, the target at the prom was all the heirs, not you specifically, which means this wasn't the Council. They wouldn't kill their own heirs in such a ridiculously public way." Aubrey pinches the bridge of his nose as he thinks for a moment.

"The heirs were supposed to die, which would weaken the Council. That didn't work because the alcohol and drugs accidentally countermanded the poison." Chess pauses, then frowns. "Which means they have several things we didn't know about: families or students in the shifter community on their side, knowledge that simple things could thwart their poison, and some other lab created bullshit that may or may not be finished."

"Fucking great," Fitz groans. "So we have the Council and their cronies on one side, the magic people with shifters and humans on the other, and a gaggle of randos with vendettas against our girl all working at the same time? How the hell are we going to fight all of it, man? Maybe we should head for Tahiti—it's a wonderful place, I hear."

Leaning over, I look at my worried tiger, seeing the frustration in his gaze. He'd rather just kill everyone and be done with it, but he knows that won't solve the problem forever. Whoever killed Kinsley did us and the Council a favor, but since none of this was known back then, her death must have served another purpose. There's so many strings tying things together, binding us in a tight space that it's feeling like a silken prison. And Fitz is *not* someone who does well in a cage.

"Is anyone else wondering if the mysterious ingredients have something to do with the plants we found in the Charles' room?" Chess holds up a bite of my eggs, obviously intent on making sure I finish my entire plate despite the topic.

A deep sigh from my gargoyle makes me turn to see him pressing his face into Fitz's back to hide. "I'm sure they are, Chester."

"Aloysius doesn't have reference samples for that, especially if they've been changing it all for years. But he said Kinsley must have been doing some of her work in labs other than the one at Cappie—much higher end ones. It makes sense because she had to have been working there to create the poison she slipped into the punch at the dance." Aubrey looks troubled as he scans the email again. "She had powerful and wealthy friends—not just the magic rebels."

"We're going to need more boards," I mutter as I look around. "Lots more boards."

Bad Omen

Chess

I spent Monday focused on two things: trying to snoop through Rockland's files for intel and ordering more sleuthing supplies for the Dojo. Despite Felix and the others hating the name, it amuses the hell out of me, so I don't mind Fitz's moniker for the library annex we live in. We got more boards and displays so we can accurately tie all the pieces together as we uncover them —a project I was happy to take on. I function best as a support player and I'm completely comfortable with that role.

Ironman needed Happy and Holmes needed Watson; I'm the logistical backup.

That doesn't mean I'm not eager to get my hands on the people hurting my angel, nor does it mean I won't join the fight. I'm simply better suited to making sure everyone is taken care of and we have all the things we need. Luckily, I also blend into the background since I'm unassuming, so my new 'boss' in the guidance office doesn't pay attention to me when she's not digging for gold about my sex life. I've flown under her radar most days and I keep hoping I'll overhear something juicy Rufus' relative can use to shut the bitch down before this stupid book of hers sees the light of day.

Afternoon classes are ending early today, so I don't have much time before I can go home to face whatever craziness Dolly's friends have inflicted on our attire for the night. They won't be as well fit or designed as the ones they handmade last year, but if I know Cori and Rufus, they probably tailored them based on the measurements they have in their design books. Their attention to detail is why I let them have their head last year, especially since they took our girl under their wings and it worked out perfectly.

I just hope I get pants this year. It's colder here than it was at Apex this time of year.

"Chester? I desire you in my office!"

I have to repress a shiver as the vulture beckons me in the most egregious manner possible. Taking a deep breath, I pause what I'm working on and walk over to the door to her inner sanctum. My smile is pasted on, but I'm not worried about looking sincere. I know she doesn't care if she squigs me out; she's made it very clear her office is run a certain way and complaints will lead to consequences I won't like. I'd have to be dense not to realize that means she'll take it out on Dolly.

"Yes, Carina? How may I assist you?" Again, I suppress a shudder of revulsion at the way I've been instructed to respond to her whims.

The scrawny woman tilts her head, the rat's nest messy bun on top of it looking as if it hasn't been brushed for a month as she studies me. She doesn't take any pains with her appearance and I can appreciate deciding to reject all the oppressive standards our society holds women to, but the dark bags under her eyes mean she's likely in a foul mood. I've learned to read her body language and tone quickly to avoid being verbally thrashed, if possible. It's bad enough for her to be a raging egomaniac that treats others like dog shit on her shoes, but when anything disrupts her life in the slightest, she takes it out on every person she comes in contact with.

Rockland is a miserable, self-centered hag who yearns for the lives she creates in her sordid tales and punishes the world around her because she doesn't like herself.

"A little slow this morning? I noticed you didn't respond to any of my emails this morning." Her gaze is bland, but I can sense the edge in her tone.

Forcing myself to keep my irritation buried lest I get screamed at, I reply evenly, "Your emails began coming in at six a.m. and I was not in the office until nine a.m. I cannot respond to your messages when I am not awake or in the office, so I waited to respond."

"Hmph. Lax of you, Chester. I should get an immediate response. Our work is too important and I have a busy schedule to attend to. I cannot wait for you to decide when you feel like replying to me simply because you do not have a work ethic as dedicated as mine. Do you not care about our students? Are you not committed to your role here?"

Blinking at the rapid escalation and her increasingly loud tone, I gather my thoughts. I don't want to inflame her ire further, but I also can't allow her to pressure me into making her whims central to my life. This guidance position is only half of my job at Cappie, and I have a very full life that I'm not giving up to appease her. Unfortunately, she also holds a great deal of sway with someone powerful we haven't discovered yet and I don't want her to make my angel's life miserable or ruin anyone I love's careers.

The urge to stomp in and rip her throat out for daring to threaten my family is stronger than I've ever felt it.

I swallow hard, calming the cheetah as best I can, then finally say, "Carina, the official contracts are very clear about work schedules and using personal devices to accomplish work tasks. I am in your office part time; therefore, I cannot complete tasks for you when I'm not on the guidance department's hours. That's a call made by the shifter resources department, not me."

The way her face reddens tells me logic wasn't the way to go. Pushing out of her chair, she stands behind her desk looking infuriated that I dared to correct her—although she was wrong and could very well be violating policies set by the administration. "How *dare* you act like you're smarter than me! You think you're untouchable because you're suckling the teats of your adoptive family, but I have far more power and influence than you ever could. Everyone knows you only get hired because the Khans throw money at places. Unlike you, I have *earned* my respect, my fans, and my place at the top. You will *never* achieve my success because no one believes you have even a modicum of talent or brains; you're just Fitz Khan's little fuck toy."

What in the actual fuck did I do? Why is she this triggered? Holy fuckbuckets.

"Carina," I begin carefully. "I didn't intend to imply anything with my statement other than I don't wish to violate the rules. If you felt I was being insulting when reminding you of the policies, I apologize. I merely—"

"*Stop acting like you did nothing wrong!* I don't *care* what you *intended.* What you said was clear enough for me to catch the implication. I won't stand for you making this about you. You were in the wrong and you're delusional if you think I'll accept that apology."

Rockland is almost vibrating with rage, and I have no idea what in the hell she wants now. My apology was normal; what could I say more than I didn't mean for her to infer I'm smarter? I *am* smarter than her; hell, a pineapple is smarter than this woman. But I definitely didn't imply that, nor have I ever hinted I believe that to be true. This flip-out is all her internalized trauma, but I also can't say that. She'll *definitely* lose her marbles if I point that out.

How in the name of Ares' fat cock are the idiots at Cappie allowing this psycho to advise impressionable minds?

"All I can do is reiterate my apology, Carina. I did not intend for my reminder to become an issue this large. I only wanted to make certain we were doing things correctly, so we aren't violating the rules."

She rounds the desk, looking even more angry as she stalks towards me menacingly. "If I want to be educated on something, I'll fucking *tell* you. Otherwise, you can gate keep someone else, you delusional twit."

"Carina, I don't understand. I'm not gatekeeping anything. I just felt like I had—"

"*Stop talking!* I won't listen to you stand here and play the victim any longer. I have far too many important things to do. I require *space*, so *get out of my office* and don't return until I instruct you to do so. You need to take a good, long look in the mirror, Chester Khan."

Shock slams into me as she literally pushes me back until she can slam the door in my face and I hear the lock click. The escalation was so rapid and so off-the-rails that I can't even process how it happened, much less why. Between her accusations and bullshit psycho-babble diagnoses, I have no idea what I could have done to slow that train wreck down, much less stop it.

And now I'll have to watch what she does with paperwork and the admin office.

There are many things due in the upcoming weeks because the end of the semester is in six weeks. We'll have appointments about poor exam performance and a shit ton of other things I have to complete to make sure we stay on track. If she isn't speaking to me or allowing me access to the office, I'll have to figure out how I can satisfy my position requirements on my own. It will double my workload and I won't get an ounce of credit or extra pay for it. She'll either sing her praises if it's done well or destroy me in private if it's not. I'm fucked if I do and fucked if I don't—all because she seems to have an inferiority complex and a severe case of narcissistic personality disorder.

I have no idea how I'm going to survive this year if she continues to behave like this. There's far too much stressful shit in my real life to let her abuse me this way for an extended period. Now I get why my angel looks like someone beat the shit out of her every time she comes home from her appointments—this must be what happens to her and she's keeping it quiet to prevent Fitz from eviscerating this cunt.

That stops now.

I won't destroy this party for Dolly, but tomorrow, I'm going to have a long talk with our family about how we'll take this bitch off the boards for good.

Chester Khan may not be the future Raj, but he has a few tricks up his sleeve.

"WHERE'S MY ANGEL?" I ASK AS I WALK INTO THE ANNEX. "IT'S been a bitch of a day."

Fitz leaps over the couch, tugging me into his arms immediately. His hand strokes over my curls and I sigh as the touch helps melt away some of my tension. I smile against his tee shirt, knowing he's holding back the urge to shred whoever upset me until I feel better. When I raise my head again, he kisses me softly before replying with his typical response. "Who am I killing? I haven't killed anyone in *weeks*. I'm itching to mete out justice."

"No one at the moment, love. You can't kill the counselor cunt for me anymore than you can for our girl." I rest my forehead on his, basking in the strength he provides. "But I don't want to ruin her chance at a normal, fun holiday party by going into it now. Can we decide how to handle it tomorrow?"

His snarl is unhappy, but he nods a little. "We can. But I swear on Apollo's shiny dick that I'm going to tear that body snatcher limb from limb once we're out of here. I'm going to take my time with it, too. I love hunting them for months, making them wonder if

I'm lurking around every corner ready to introduce them to their maker. "

"Going to give Rockland the full Fitz, eh?" Felix strides in, carrying a bunch of garment bags on one arm and an armful of boxes in the other.

Rufus, Cori, and Renard are trailing behind him with even more shit, and I almost choke when I see Aubrey bringing up the rear stacked with luggage and boxes so high that he can't see where the hell he's going. As if he just remembered, the badger yells, "Step!

"Thank Christ he didn't fall," Ren says as he dumps his load on the ground behind the couch. "He would have bitched *all* night. Dragons have the worst pride buttons I've ever seen."

"We do *not*. We are simply better equipped to exist without as many flaws as other species."

"See what I mean?" Ren hops over the back of the sofa and sprawls out lazily. "Unable to admit to failure or mistakes without blustering and a face full of fire. It's why he pouted for over a thousand years in that damn castle before he came to Apex."

"Castle?" Dolly looks at all of us in surprise. "What castle?"

"Someone's in trouuuuuuuble," Fitz sing-songs as he lets go of me to sweep her into his arms. She jumps up and wraps her legs around him, making Felix scold her when the robe she's wearing goes slack.

Aubrey looks like he's going to strangle Ren and Fitz both, but can't decide where to start. He finally sighs heavily and looks at our girl with a sheepish expression. "Dragons have hoards— usually a bunch and they vary in size. The one I started when I first crossed the Atlantic in my childhood is quite large and it lives in the castle I… commandeered when I arrived. The ones you know of at Apex are minor hoards."

"There was more than one at Apex?" Fitz glares at him as he sets my angel down. "Dude, you've been holding out on all of us *big time*. I demand to see this shit."

"Me, too! I want to see the castle," Dolly pouts as she approaches the grumpy dragon. He's puffing smoke like a stack and fiddling with the squishy in his pocket more than I've seen in months. This is pushing his dragon's boundaries something fierce, but he sighs as our girl continues to make a face worthy of a cartoon woodland creature.

"Go get dressed with your friends and perhaps we'll discuss it tomorrow if you behave," he relents and Ren snorts so hard he doubles over. "What are you laughing at, Chuckles?"

"It took me *centuries* to get that out of you! One fat lip and some enormous eyes and you fold like a lawn chair. Oh, how the mighty have fallen. Tsk." Aubrey swipes at him with a huge hand as we all start snickering and my angel claps her hands in excitement.

"He said I have to behave, but not *how* I have to behave—no take backs!" Her expression is smug as he fist bumps Rufus and they take off for her room with Cori.

Fitz turns to us with a knowing smirk. "We're *all* in trouble now, you know. She's going to be incorrigible and we can't say a fucking word. I *love* it."

"Me, too," Ren says as he rubs his hands together. "Chaos is delicious, and I'm going to take a huge bite."

"Fuck," Aubrey mutters at the same time as Felix.

Me? I'm good no matter what—I have my family and nothing else is important.

"ARE YOU READY?"

Felix arches his brow as the polar bear calls out from the bedroom. Her nest of curls has been slicked into a solid white pointy hairdo and she appears to be airbrushed purple from head to toe. Given the apparent theme of our group costumes, I can guess who she's supposed to be by the penciled eyebrows and blue shadow. The Raj waves the hook hand at her, his lips quirking under the tiny mustache. "As our resident Frenchman would say, *entrez-vous*[1]."

"Stealing my thunder. I guess I shouldn't be surprised because I've been sentenced to… you know…the Underworld!" Renard snarks. He's been in character from the moment he put on the toga and arranged his flaming hair. Aubrey may murder him before the end of the night because he's bad enough without being dressed as the most sarcastic god of death ever.

The door opens and we all hold our breath until Dolly walks out. My eyes widen as I look at the transformation from our sweet, sexy bunny into a towering shadow of imperiousness. The large black horns cover her rainbow hair and end in the mask that highlights her high cheekbones. Her friends have applied dark, sparkling smoky makeup and bright red 'fuck me' lipstick, making her haughty expression seem mysterious and sensual.

But the outfit is much less accurate, and it's making my dick twitch.

Dolly's curves are poured into a short, tight black dress with cutouts in the best places, a plunging neckline and straggling organza trailing in strips to her feet. The cape swirling around the thigh-high black boots is shiny and lined with deep purple silk, so it flows in the light when she strides towards us with a magical staff in hand. "So?"

I'm flabbergasted, so I fumble for words to answer her. Ren lacks a quip for the first time in hours and Felix is gripping the pommel of his pirate sword as if he's going to run someone through. Even Aubrey, in his half-shifted form as the demon from the magical mouse movie, is dumbstruck.

Of course, Fitz is the one who leaps over the couch in character to charge forward. "Baby Girl, tonight you're gonna find out no oneeee *fucks* like…"

"Shut up, Fitz!" The chorus from all of us makes my angel blink in surprise, then break character to giggle.

"Oh, dear. Has he been singing that song the whole time?" She grins at me and I nod, rolling my eyes. "I bet the words are hysterical. Maybe you can sing it for me later, Fitzy?"

His grin widens, and he sweeps her into a bridal carry, cape and all. "Anytime. Coco-cabana and the Moonshine Mobster made us fucking badass! I'm not even wearing heels this time."

"You rocked those heels," I murmur as I approach them. The thick lion skin and scar makeup make our girl smile as she looks me over. "But I like them on my angel much better."

"Damn right I did. We all made hot AF chicks and anyone who says differently can taste my blade." My mate pauses for a moment and adds, "The fake one, not the real one. That one's for running you and Baby Girl through."

"Fitz!" She smacks his shoulder lightly. "Put me down so Cori and Rufus can come out. We have to go."

He pouts but does as she says, wrinkling his nose. "They promised me inappropriate behavior, and it's Halloween. As long as no dead bodies appear, everyone needs to let me party."

"An interesting proposition," Felix says as he strolls over to kiss Dolly possessively, then lets her go. "Do we let him go wild? It *has* been a while."

"Let me?! I'm Fitzgerald Khan, enforcer of the Khan ambush, and second in line to—"

His tirade is cut off as Cori and Rufus emerge from the bedroom. Our costumes are gorgeous, expensive, and clearly tailored to fit us, but theirs are the *piece de resistance*. It's obvious the two of them put an enormous amount of time and effort into transforming store bought items into bespoke wonders because on Cori's dress, the goddamn tentacles *move*. She's holding a glowy trident with a smug look as she damn near floats over to us.

"Holy shit, Coco-cabana! You're smokin' hot tonight," Renard says as he finally finds his tongue. "I'd remember making a bargain with you, but hey, who knows? I'm unpredictable."

"Someone stop him, for the love of Jupiter's sweaty ballsack." Aubrey straightens, his size imposing as his eyes glow like the music wielding demon. He's barely dressed and even I have to admit, it looks seriously hot. I assume Rufus had something to do with the male choices because he winks at me as he steps out from behind the sea witch.

He's clad head to toe in a tight, snow white suit pants with random cutouts in the shape of spots. His skin is airbrushed black in the voids and he has on black shoes so shiny you could probably see up someone's skirt with them. His vest is also white with mesh spots and he's not wearing a shirt under it—probably because he has a white and black fur cape attached by a thin silver chain at his neck. They spiked his hair up, half white and half black with short flopped black ears coming out of it.

If any man alive could pull off the skinner of puppies without being morbid, he's standing in my living room with an evil grin full of fangs.

"You know, I can see him peeling puppies," Felix murmurs. "It's fitting, gangster."

"Since we've had our great reveal, we should get to the cars and head to the cemetery," he replies drolly. "I have triplets waiting for me, and I'm in the mood to get dirty tonight."

That said, he turns on his heel, taking Dolly and Cori's hands so their capes flutter in front of us as they sashay to the door.

We are in so much trouble tonight; I can feel it in my bones.

---

1. Come in

KILLER

?????

The moment my prey arrives, I can feel it shimmering in the air. I have been living in the shadows so long that even small shifts in energy ripple over me like electrical jolts. The power that has been growing within me over the centuries amplifies every sensation, and since we found the key, it's even more sensitive. We attempted to influence Fate many times over the years to start the prophecy, but it never worked—not until three decades ago, when we stumbled on the perfect solution to our waning magic.

It took almost a decade to re-fuel the dwindling magic of the community, but we started with those who were fading the most and worked our way back to the strongest species like me. Regaining my connection to myself made planning another attempt at the key much easier; in fact, it only took a few tries before we achieved the results we needed.

If we'd been able to control the vessel as we thought we could, this could have happened sooner.

But the Fates are wily and do not appreciate even beings such as me interfering with their weaving. Obstacles popped up constantly, preventing anyone in our group from taking the vengeance we so richly deserve—until now. We are getting closer with each one, and the alliances we've secured will help us continue to gather power. It will be time to rise soon and when we do, I will right the injustices of the past. That's my promise to every soul who bands together with us, and I will keep it until my last breath.

Centuries of living beyond what they assumed to be my last breath have made me somewhat cynical with my mortality. I am uncertain the Fates did not grant me immortality as they did the others of my kind after the split. It may have saved me when the royals betrayed me so long ago to join with the ancestors and leaders who rule the world not seen or heard by humans. I can still feel the dirt from the shovel hitting my face like it was yesterday, and the desire to make all the non-magical supernatural suffer has kept me hungry for almost a millennium.

Fortunately, those who stole the balance of power for their own have grown soft and vulnerable despite their wealth and fame. They may control things with money and fear, but they no longer learn to defend themselves from anything besides humans and prey. Both variables are far weaker than my enemies and they believe those are their only concerns, so they live soft, comfortable lives. They may viciously take out the weak, but they have no skills to confront their equals—not anymore.

Sighing, I cut my gaze to obnoxious groups of girls drinking and passing around drugs. The two groups are eyeing one another with disdain and I feel defeated that women are still behaving as if they are enemies rather than the system that keeps them beholden to men. It was that way in my youth and despite the claims of the media, it's still an issue bred into females from their childhood. Watching them makes my anger bubble hotly; they're happy to perpetuate the old ways, even with so many opportunities to affect change.

If they'd lived as long as me, hunted and alone, they might have learned to appreciate the variety in skills other women can lend when they band together. Instead, they draw invisible lines and destroy anything different from themselves. Narrowing my eyes, I lift one finger toward the bulkier gaggle, causing a drink from one of their rivals to spill on their giant wolf. Loud, shrill shouts fill the air and I turn away, smirking to myself. They wanted to fight and now they can do it like warriors, not children.

I slink along the shadows in my disguise, wanting to be closer to my targets as they enter the party in a large group. The one in all black and white is greeted by three affectionate Sphinxes wearing some sort of sexy matching dog outfits. I don't see the appeal, but it makes that one peel off as he heads for the bar with his odd puppies. It will be most fortuitous if they split up, though harder to track. I will move from group to group unnoticed if they do not stay together.

Intelligence is always useful and when shifters imbibe, they often have far looser tongues.

This evening was only meant to gain more sources for the balance of powers, but I could not resist attending while my acolytes gathered the tributes. The closer I come to the objects of my personal desire for vengeance, the harder it becomes not to witness the chaos I'm creating. It's difficult to stay hidden, as I know I must when I can taste the justice that has been denied for so many years. I thirst for it as if they have trapped me in the desert without water and, in many ways, I have. My inherent nature is not meant for the shadows and darkness; no, they made us for love, life, and enjoying the bounties of the world.

I did not get the option to join those who escaped to the light because they thought me dead and buried me in a remote grave as penance for my perceived sins.

Knowing others suffered over time for their decisions has not slaked my fury or brought me the peace it should have. The one who orchestrated my fate and accepted the demands of the masses who designed the Treaty is not dead, nor are any of those who allowed it happen. They may ache from the weight of their poor choices, but they have not felt dirt splash on their faces or had to use weakened powers to slowly claw their way out of an unmarked mound to obscurity and isolation. The world I found had changed so drastically in the month it took me to gather the strength to crawl out of my grave that I hardly recognized it and it has only strayed further from the path with every day since.

But my kind are patient and we know how to plan for the long game—being close to immortality makes the long game much easier to envision. I was but a child in terms of my species when they put me in that fake tomb without the dignity of our last rites, but when I emerged, that innocence was gone. And I've used every ounce of knowledge, power, and wisdom I've gained to band the races together for the good of our people. I knotted my petty revenge within my plans, but it is not the sole intent of our battle with the Fates. That's why I know we will prevail; we are here to right the wrongs done in the past, not simply to get what we are due.

They weave the tapestry, but their relatives also balance the scales and the world is not in balance since the Treaty.

My eyes catch on the group I'm monitoring again, noting there is someone new joining them. The spotted one left with his little fans, but now, a golden hued warrior princess is amongst my targets. She is talking animatedly with the tentacled friend and I can see the glee it's bringing the crazy tiger. I'm rusty in terms of interactions, but it appears he may have orchestrated this meeting. I believe the two chattering girls—the polar bear and the grizzly— may be intended to date.

I would offer my admittedly jaded opinion to them when they inevitably break from the larger group to talk, but I cannot give myself away. If even a portion of my story or advice floats back to the wrong person, I will be discovered. I am not ready for anyone to realize I didn't perish before being dumped into my grave. They will have to learn about betrayal and heartache on their own. My dedication to my fellow females is not such that I would jeopardize decades of planning and effort.

My patience is rewarded when the two of them finally give the obsidian clad leader a wave and head for the dance floor. The girl seems pleased, throwing her arms around the psycho and allowing him to grope her playfully. It's a shame she's caught up in this mess; nothing I've seen of her so far tells me she deserves to play a role, but I do not pluck the threads, I am only speeding their use.

Destiny does not play favorites, and it is rarely fair.

Moving closer so I can observe my true reason for appearing here, I close my eyes to reach out with my magic. I need to *feel* the auras and vibration of their souls to learn the information I require about their bonds. When I'm fully immersed, I open my eyes to see the cheetah dressed as a lion, looking in my direction. I know he cannot see me with the shadows pulled so tightly, but something about the way he's staring sets my teeth on edge. The Khan men do not have magical powers—I know because I had my followers test it several times to verify—so I do not understand why he is staring at me so intently.

He turns abruptly, whispering to the one person I cannot approach without feeling my spirit diminish. The fury on his face would frighten lesser beings, but I am not afraid. Even the mythical shifters do not have what it would take to defeat me—not on their own, anyway. Shifters have fallen so far from the natural order and balance that they no longer possess the knowledge or items they would need to rise against the tidal wave coming from them. They cast all the necessary things out with their leaders' Treaty and subsequent hunting of the losing side. Nothing they had from before that time is within their grasp; it has all been hidden

over the years and then long forgotten.

There is nothing to save them once the key is ready, and they only have themselves to blame.

My prey close ranks, talking amongst themselves in a small, tight cluster. The instinct of the cheetah has them on edge now, and I won't be able to stay in their proximity. It's too dangerous for me to be in a range of anyone with sensitivity to my skills. So I walk away, cloaked in the darkness, as I look for my companions to check on their progress. I gave their assignments before I deigned to accompany the team and I want to ensure they are being carried out. We will need to leave sooner than I expected, now that we have tipped him off.

~Report.~ I project the command into the minds of the scattered members.

The replies I get from them flood my mind and I have to organize and process all the voices in my head. They sound as if they are ready to act and transport. We can take what we need and return to our compound with what we need to continue. I turn to give the group I've been stalking one last glance; I came to glean more information and I despise failure. Perhaps I will stay long enough to watch how they react to our mission. Watching them fight back when my team accosted them on the way to this place taught me many things, and this may reveal more.

~Breach. Complete objectives immediately and return.~

Once I give the order, I alight the highest tomb, getting the best vantage point possible to see the chaos. My followers disappear with their assignments one by one, but the party continues on without a hitch. I frown, wondering if these spoiled children of the long lines who created the split are so self-absorbed that they will not notice what has happened. It would not change what we did, but it would confirm that greed and sloth have diluted their claims of superiority.

Suddenly, a panicked screech echoes over the graves and I see the group rush towards the sound, pushing the drunken revelers aside to get to the girl making the noise. I smile in satisfaction when I notice it is the girl from the groups I pushed to brawl earlier. She has a costume that matches three other girls on, but her sexy superheroine is purple. She's gesticulating wildly around the room and when the bunny girl approaches, she points at her, accusing her of being responsible for the disappearance of someone named Todd.

I guess one of our targets from the ancient family lines was her boyfriend. Too bad.

Chuckling to myself, I continue to observe the chaos unfolding as others scream that they are missing people as well. My team selected only six this time, but they were of a higher rank than anyone we've chosen before. I believe it will make it easier to get what we need and the effects will last longer to help the eldest gain even more of themselves in return.

But it is a bonus that this girl seems to have issues with the group I am focused on. Her baseless claims will distract everyone for quite some time and I will work without being detected for so much longer. They may even forget whatever the cheetah told them if they have to devote all of their energy to keeping the rabbit safe.

Love makes us all fools and in the end, we always pay for the privilege—I certainly did.

It took my life.

Dark Horse

Delores

IT'S BEEN FOUR DAYS SINCE THE ADMIN STORMED INTO THE cemetery to break up the off-campus bash that led to a swath of missing students. Their *laissez-faire* attitudes from last year and earlier this semester disappeared when children of much more well-connected families disappeared in plain sight. We were all herded back to the campus, and they canceled classes while they scrambled to figure out how to pacify people like the Hopewells. We're on a complete lockdown—no students are allowed off-campus unless parents pick them up. That caveat sent ripples through the rich, as most of them are nowhere near the campus their adult children attend, and sometimes, not even in the same country.

Which meant everyone, despite being over the age of adulthood, is now firmly trapped within the gates of Cappie.

It filled the atmosphere with the stench of fear and outrage. Exam results were posted automatically on Friday—I suppose someone in IT wasn't told to shut that off—and it only heightened the tension across the grounds. My exams went very well except for the Cs in Shifter History and Diplomacy I didn't deserve. My evil professors knew Aubrey would monitor the grades and scanned exams, so Blitzen and Rakoto had to be cautious about how heavy-handed they were with their bias. They hurt my average, but it won't be unrecoverable with the finals. I don't have to be fretting over my class rank, so I can focus elsewhere until they restart classes next week.

To help distract the students, they gave extracurriculars special permission to practice or rehearse to help keep people's minds off the situation, but having to be around one another made the shitty people worse and the angry outbursts more frequent.

The Plastics lost their shit on production assistants at the last rehearsals for #Viral—likely because the crowds for it next week won't be worth posting on social media. The lockdown means only immediate family may attend and since many of the kids here have famous parents off doing their celebrity shit, barring cameras and press means the theater won't even be filled. Their ire spilled over to the Games practice when they got into it with the obviously attention grabbing Heathers who made a scene about practicing without Purple. It devolved into a brawl before Coach Z and the Wicked Bitch of the Guidance Office pulled them apart.

I've stayed as far away from my enemies as possible because their shenanigans are serving no one but their egos.

There are real, *dangerous* things going on again and I can't be bothered with this bullshit 'pick me' crap, so I'm keeping my head down and my six covered as I move around. Rennie assigned the Captain's crew double team shifts to escort me from place to place when one of them isn't available. I'd be surprised if he changed that when classes resume, but he's not the only paranoid one. Felix insisted we start our days at five a.m. on weekdays to spar in the gym—a plan that has *everyone* irritable and grumpy.

Since it's Saturday, I got a reprieve today—lucky me.

Fitz is curled up on the couch, hacking into every camera feed he can find that might clue us in to how the kidnappers infiltrated the party and disappear with the missing kids. They obviously didn't come in their stupid mink-like hoods or someone would have noticed them—especially us. They also had to know specifically who they were looking for to identify costumed people and know they're from a higher tier of families. They didn't go for simply rich kids or even ones of super famous celebs like Selene. They targeted this at the next ring of Council kids and at least one major family. He's convinced he can find them if he keeps scanning local and private security systems via his hacker bullshit. I don't know if he can, but we all want to feel like we can do *something.*

I look over at the kitchen, sighing as I inhale the massive amount of food Chess is making. He's stress cooking; I can tell. We'll have to package a lot up for later in the week, but it's keeping his cheetah calm. Aubrey took off for the Smithsonian to visit his experts after a growling row with Rennie, who has been haunting the bell tower for days. This recent attack has made him withdraw into himself and I know he's struggling—we all know—but he won't let anyone help. Even Aubrey doesn't know what to do with him and their tiff this morning made that very clear. They snipe and spar, but I have yet to see them actually yell. It's worrisome, especially since General Felix is off battering bags at the gym as if it will somehow thrash the enemies we can't see.

I don't want to add to their problems, but I'm on the struggle bus, too.

Guilt over feeling like karma did its job punishing both Purple *and* her arranged beau, Todd, has me in an ethical quandary. I know I shouldn't feel so good about the Universe smacking them down and that she might be in real trouble but… I also remember the look in Todd's eyes when he hunted me and the cackling laughter of the Heathers when Gold instructed the rest of the crowd to help him. I remember having to delete all my accounts because of the abuse Silver encouraged random people I didn't know to come for me. The videos Pink posted for months until I left for Apex that fanned the flames. And the way Purple sat there and watched them all do it with a satisfied smirk because she was still on the inside so no one would dare cross her.

All of it runs through my brain like an audio-visual flashback when I try to talk myself out of feeling the *schadenfreude* consuming me. I've been healing slowly over the past year and a half; I even let Aubrey and Rennie hunt me without having an episode. But that doesn't mean there isn't a part of me that can't stop watching them whenever they're nearby, worried about what scheme they'll come up with to attack me next. They've spent a great deal of time since I emerged trying to punish, ruin, and even get me expelled simply because they treated me like shit and we aren't friends anymore.

It doesn't matter that I finally accepted we weren't ever truly friends and Todd never liked me, much less love me. The hurt and trauma is still inside me, rearing its head when I least expect it and making me question every inch of progress I've made.

Sometimes when I look in the mirror, I can hear the taunts and see the things they said online, and it transports me to the months I spent locked in my room while they manipulated the rest of the world to spread ugly rumors and threaten to harm me. When you add that to the bullshit that happened at Apex—like Chess almost dying—I have a host of shit that I'm working through and much of it is their doing. So, yeah. I'm shamefully happy that someone who helped abuse and batter me might get what they deserve, even if it isn't very evolved for me to feel that way.

I'm exhausted from being the bigger person and having it not count for shit.

"Baby Girl?"

Fitz's question pulls me out of my head and I give him a grateful smile. "Yeah, big bad?"

"I love it when you talk about my dick when it's not even out. Chessie, she called him '*Big Bad*.' That's even better than—"

"*Fitz,*" the cheetah says with a chuckle. "What were you going to say? I think you jumped the wheel, babe."

He rolls his eyes and grumbles for a moment, then brightens up as a ding emanates from his laptop. "Ha! There we go. I was going to say Z is having a practice today and getting sweaty might help our girl work some of that tension out. At least, until *after*, when *we* can work the rest of our tension out from watching."

I snort at the way Fitz's mind draws a direct line from watching me fight other chicks in the ring to him and Chess fucking the shit out of me. His candor always makes me laugh and if I could steal even a tenth of his 'IDGAF' attitude, my morose shit about my exes would disappear. Fitzgerald Khan is one hundred percent authentically who he is at all times and he absolutely doesn't notice—much less care—if people like him or not. I think a lot of my confidence started building just from being near him all the time last year and I didn't realize it.

Huh. I'll be damned.

Climbing across the cushions, I grab his laptop and sit it on the tabletop in the middle of our nest. He beams when I straddle his legs, looking at his face as my hand cups his cheek. "Fitzgerald Khan, you are the psycho sunshine in my world and I will never *ever* regret talking to you on prom night or letting you stalk me ever since."

"Did you hear that, Chessie?! That's as good as an 'I love you' from our girl. She *admitted* she knows. I *told* you assholes I wasn't being intrusive; she *likes* it."

Giggling as he bounces around with me on his lap in some form of victory wiggle, I lean in and press my forehead to his. "Of course I knew after the night at the club. My senses weren't as developed as they are now, but when you rubbed your tiger head on my hand, I knew what that smell meant every time it came near. I'm well aware you have many gadgets watching me all the time. In a weird way, it felt like someone finally gave a shit about whether I was safe or not. That's why I never moved or disconnected them."

"Ha ha ha!" Fitz says, as he leaps to his feet with me in his arms. "I told you fuckers so and *damn it*, none of the others are here, so they'll never believe me!"

Chess comes over, hopping into the nested couch with a cheerful smile. I owe him some credit, too, but at the moment, he's as enchanted with our lover as I am. "I heard her, baby. Don't worry. I'll back you up."

Fitz waddles us over the cushions to him and tumbles us into a mass of limbs, his hands groping us happily. "This is the best fucking day. Now I'm a little mad we have to get Baby Girl dressed and to the field. The Big Bad has plans he can't execute, and he's not happy."

"*Fitz*," we say at the same time and we all burst into laughter.

Okay, maybe if Fitz can bring me out of my funk, I can do the same for Rennie, eventually.

It just takes a little love.

Zhenga surprised us with some new opponents at practice, and it's kicking my ass. The two enormous women are from the Prey Games—a much smaller, less attended version of our games the larger prey take part in locally. Her friends, a rhino named Laurel, and a hippo called Magritte, put us through brutal matches until even Selene dropped to the ground and cried 'uncle.' Not one of our team could move them, though if we'd been allowed to use some of the more dangerous aspects of our shifts, we definitely would have evened the playing field.

The point was to show us that without the weapons we rely on, we have to work harder and get smarter about how we approach opponents. It was a lesson I believe was aimed at me specifically because she watched me like a hawk and I suspect Felix had something to do with her sudden addition to the training lineup. I narrowly missed getting gored by a fucking rhino horn a couple times because other surprises distracted me, but at the end of practice, Coach Z let us know her friends would come back to work with us more.

"Just fucking great," I mutter under my breath as I hobble to the sidelines to grab a drink. "I love bruising the hell out of myself by throwing my weight into a brick wall for hours."

"Don't worry, Dollypop! Your men will rub some nice arnica on those marks, like we told them last year."

I blink, watching Rufus and Cori stroll across the field towards me in *cheerleading uniforms*. "What in the name of Hera's thong are you two doing here dressed like that?"

"Did someone bash your brains in earlier?" Cori winks at me playfully and does a twirl in her outfit. "We're here because we joined the cheer squad. Years and years of dance made it *very* easy to convince the vulture bitch we'd help make her team look less like clowns on roller skates."

"But… you *hate* cheerleaders. Rufus' favorite part of *Bring It On* is when the fake choreographer says that cheerleaders are dancers who—"

"Yes, yes. I adore that part despite its awful, insulting language towards the disabled." He shakes his head, looking towards the sky pleadingly. "Why can't we find movies from the 90s that aren't full of jokes at the expense of every marginalized community that exists? It's a goddamn shame because I love them so much and feel so dirty afterward."

"Focus, Ru-Ru," my friend snaps as she comes closer and lowers her head to whisper in my ear. "We're also here, so there are people on the field at every game who will bum rush a mother-fucker if this cheating and scheming doesn't stop. We decided the stands are too far away and none of your men can stay on the grass, so we're here as backup."

My lips curve when I look at Rufus, and he nods in agreement. "You guys didn't have to do that. Rockland will be nasty as hell and that's *before* you get to the crap the Heathers will put you through."

The smile on my tattooed badger's face is downright vicious. "I dare them to cross me. The things I will do to ruin their lives haven't even been used in a teen movie before. I'll own their souls when I'm done and no one can stop me. You might be a good person, Dolly Drew, but I am *not*. My goodwill extends to my friends and family—that's the limit."

His declaration is so cold it almost makes me shiver. I haven't seen Rufus truly drop his jolly mask before, and now that he has, it's terrifying. I understand how he won whatever bullshit competition his family had to be the next heir and why the people from his clan seem to hop in line without question. He's got a dark side that rivals Fitz's and he's been waiting to unleash it.

"Okay. Well, thank you—both of you. I didn't consider how good it would feel to know someone's close enough to help if I get in trouble."

Cori snorts and shakes her head. "Of course not. You're trying to show everyone you're not the tiny, munchable rabbit from your prom night, D. Admitting weaknesses doesn't fit that narrative. I get it, so does Ru-Ru. Besides, we look spectacular in these, don't we?"

I run my eyes over the skimpy outfits, tilting my head. "You two have been hiding out in the townhouse, altering these for the past few days, haven't you?"

Rufus winks at me. "With an Amazon account, a little talent, and some hard work, the bullshit they provided is now worthy of our glory. The triplets can not *wait* to see my rah-rah."

My eyes dart to my other friend, watching for signs of her previous melancholy to return, but she just beams. "Giselle is eager to come, too. She's never been to a Pred Games match; sports aren't her thing. But she wants to come watch us twirl."

Hot damn, Fitz, I owe you another blowie. You did it.

"Well, the next match isn't until right before Thanksgiving, so you've got time to make that routine sparkle."

A whistle blows and they roll their eyes before Cori jerks her head towards the other end of the field. "Duty calls, Dollykins. Go home with your escorts and we'll call you after practice."

"You better!" I grin as they jog off, picking up my water bottle to head for the locker rooms.

I can't wait to hear what goes on at Rockland's stupid practices.

EMPIRES

LUCILLE

GLARING AT THE IDIOTS ON THE BIG SCREEN, I LEAN BACK IN MY chair. Matilda scurries over with a fresh martini, avoiding Bruno as he lurks in the background. He's been overseas checking in with his various vendors to make certain the shenanigans of these freaks aren't disrupting cash flow to the Council businesses. I enjoyed having him gone and I won't deny that I considered arranging for him to have an 'accident' while he was far away. It would have been convenient for several reasons, the least of which he wouldn't be stomping all over my Berber like a bumbling fool now.

I refuse to stoop to the same bullshit the men on our Council resort to when they tire of their spouses—it's so plebeian and boring.

I'll deal with my lumbering oaf when I have fewer issues that outweigh his irritating presence. For the moment, I have bigger fish to fry. The escalation of kidnappings that occurred last week was a direct challenge to our authority. It forced me to have our nitwit government puppets pull satellite footage and comb through it since the beginning of the school year in hopes we'd find clues about our enemies.

Imagine my surprise when one of the eggheads approached me with clips of useless progeny and the Khan spare fighting off a band of magic users on their way to Capital Prep. Her skills and the way she hid this from every spy I have planted at that ridiculous place briefly impressed me, but then I realized what it meant.

Not only have the magic wielding scum crawled out of their holes to challenge us, but my daughter has been fighting them without my knowledge.

In our world, such ignorance can dethrone even the most powerful leaders, and I'm no exception. Bruiser took care of the wimpy analyst—he won't be talking to anything other than Ouija boards—but that's only half the problem. The attack on our most treasured school last year was no outlier. Indoctrination from birth will not prevent the younger preds from questioning what they've been taught if the spell casting trash use the internet as a platform.

That's why I have the leaders from around the world on this wretched video call listening to them bluster about missing kids and the dopey Hopewell heir. I need to see them all to verify none of the current Council have wavered in their commitment. The history of our dominance over the other supernaturals is a legacy started by ancestors of the men and women on this call, but most of their lines have grown soft over the years. If the races of magic wielded have banded together to reveal themselves, this plan has been in motion for much longer than the past year.

I won't stand for weakness and anyone who refuses to stomp them out as our families intended will be dealt with severely.

"And no one at this party saw a thing! How is that possible? Why wasn't there security?" Hannah Hopewell booms her question like the brainless bear she is while her figurehead husband cowers behind her.

Her tone is unacceptable and I rise from my chair, crossing to stand in front of the screen. "Are you suggesting the Council are mind readers? I thought that sort of thing offended your deep faith."

"Well, no, I don't think magical scum tainted any of our members, but—"

"Perhaps you believe I knowingly put my heir in danger by not protecting a silly college party?" I arch a brow at them as I sip my drink, waiting to see how they respond.

"Come off it, Lucille," Erickson snorts. "You sent that girl to the wolves after declaring her persona non grata last year. We all know you don't give a rat's ass about her."

Look who thinks their techie toys are a substitute for a pair of balls.

"It is a tradition in the Rostoff empire to teach our offspring to learn to defend themselves. We don't coddle our young like *some* families do. That's why Delores isn't busy waging war on a lost cause, like your daughter is."

"No, she's busy screwing half the fucking staff," Barrington snarls dismissively. "Though I suppose we're focusing on the wrong issue with your defective progeny. She's *prey*, so it's no surprise she's a whore."

My hand pauses on its way to bringing my martini to my lips. A slow, cruel smile spreads over my face as I meet his gaze. "You'd prefer she was pretending to be Bruno's wife instead, Oliver? Your bumbling bimbo has achieved little to nothing in her brief life, save failing to quash the rumors that you replaced your mysteriously departed wife with your teenage daughter."

My strike hits as he turns pale as a ghost; I always knew that old pervert wasn't trustworthy around young girls.

"I have *never…*"

Bruno snorts, letting me know Barrington might not have fooled around with his dimwitted offspring, but I'm close to the mark. It's guaranteed he's been screwing high school girls and his daughter likely provided the buffet. My lip curls in disgust, but I'm not surprised by the lechery of old rich men. My father makes his fortune off of the weakness of men like him and that trade has been our family's staple crops for generations. It will be a pressure point for all future negotiations. And… he handed me the gun to hold to his head on his own.

"We've gotten off-topic," Septimus Charles says. He looks bored, but that's the norm for the fifth-in-line moron the Charles family had to resort to naming an heir in his generation. Like the others, he's weak willed and lazy, living off the profits from formulas developed by his more ruthless predecessors. "The real reason for this meeting is deciding how we are going to respond to this nonsense."

"It didn't matter when the missing students were lower tier preds," Hannah sniffs. "Now that we know they tried to poison the heirs and have kidnapped one of them, we must act."

"Why didn't *I* think of that?" I snort at the cowering fools. "Hannah, your mental prowess is *astounding.*"

"This bullshit has broken a *third* contract with Birkshire. I am *owed* recompense by the Council for their refusal to deal with this last year after the disaster at Apex!"

"And what recompense would you like, Bram? You've been granted new contracts for your useless son twice now. He wasted his opportunity with Delores by acting like a half-witted stray and you cannot possibly blame us for Maclachlan's girl killing a random student. She was stupid enough to *get caught.* Is that the stock you want to breed?"

This kind of shortsighted blister is why I prefer meetings to be in person. They all feel powerful enough to question me from afar, but in person, I would destroy anyone who dared demand anything from me. Berkshire is a minor member and certainly not high enough to question the Society members. But he forgets himself on video—a mistake I'll make certain he regrets later.

"Your daughter is damaged goods, just as Ollie said!"

That was his ultimate mistake.

"I'll pass on your thoughts to the Raj when I'm negotiating her marriage to three of his sons. I'm sure the Khans will appreciate your perspective." I snap at Matilda, who runs up with a stack of folders fearfully. "Likewise, I'll mention it to the dragon king and the gargoyle queen."

"You can't possibly be serious. They won't agree to—"

"Oh, I think they will. Exiled offspring are rarely financially viable and their errant children have value now. Partnership with the Council will only strengthen their kingdoms, and I intend to make the best out of an unpleasant situation. That's something none of you seem capable of comprehending."

"Since you're so *cozy* with the Khan thugs," Seamus O'Leary drawls in his whimsical brogue, "perhaps you can arrange for some of their stateside enforcers to patrol the campus. It would prevent more incidents without involving the S.B.E. Morrigan knows we don't want them writing reports that might get to the human liaison's desk."

Turning away from the spineless wastes on my conference call, I pinch the bridge of my nose. I hate to admit Seamus is correct for once in his whiskey soaked life, but we don't want anyone to panic and go to the fat-footed clods our sham government in D.C. pretends to police shifters with. Part of the Treaty involved keeping the humans informed of all pertinent shifter related developments via a liaison whose family has served that purpose secretly for centuries. The Council avoids giving their dull-eyed representative anything useful, but if the Sibbies get involved, no one will control the flow of information that could escape to our less evolved cousins.

I'll have to bargain with that randy old bastard on Bloodstone so my colleagues on the Council will shut up about their precious heirs' safety.

"Fine, Seamus. I'll work with the Raj to have the borders guarded, but..." I spin back to them all, half-shifted so they know I mean what I say. "I am warning every one of you: *keep your mouths shut.* Do not speak to your staff, your children, your spouses, your fuck toys—*no one*—about our theories about the magical riff-raff re-emerging. There is no need for leaks to cause a panic. We will handle this if I have to contract every bounty hunter in North America to slay anyone with a whiff of magic in their family lines —human and shifter alike. Understood?"

They don't speak and I didn't expect them to. When I show what a true Rostoff is capable of, they remember what will happen when I am displeased quickly. I make no bones about my willing-ness to cause a transfer of power in any of their families for any reason. Showing them the claws often brings that threat back in vivid color.

"Now go back to making us money and making the public think everything is fine." I motion at Matilda and the screen cuts out when she ends the call. Irritated beyond measure, I look over at my useless spouse. "Leave me. I will debrief you about your travels tomorrow. I have no patience left for stupidity today."

Bruno looks like he's going to argue, but Bruiser is already holding the door to my office open. "I'll have your car waiting, boss. You should visit the club."

As if I didn't figure out 'the club' was code for whatever mistress he's banging long ago.

"Yes, go relax at your club. I'm sure your swing won't be too short for a hole in one." I smirk at my humor, enjoying the angry stomping of my husband as he leaves the room. I sink into my expensive chair, leaning back as I contemplate how I will approach the churlish leader of Death Island. "Matilda!"

She practically leaps to bring me a fresh drink, her small features creased in concern. "Madame..."

Before she can sputter some nonsense about my daughter, a loud ring comes from the video screen and the face of my father appears. My gaze cuts to the hawk, promising pain for forgetting to disconnect that function when she ended my Council conference. Now Dmitri is three feet tall on my wall, glaring at me from under his thick brows as he did when I was a child and I can't stop him.

"*Dobryy den*[1], papa," I say dutifully.

His gaze intensifies, and I can almost feel the fury radiating through the feed. "I will be in Cambridge in three days' time. *Bud'te gotovy ob"yasnit'sya*[2]."

To say this is not optimal would be like calling Mount Everest a hill.

"Why are you troubling yourself with travel, papa? You hate to—"

"What did I say, *razocharovyvayushchaya doch*[3]? Make ready for me."

The screen goes black without another word and fury fills my veins. A loud feline roar of frustration echoes off the marble as I throw my glass, smashing it against the fireplace below my conference screen.

This is most unfortuitous and I need to find someone to slake my anger on before I can focus on strategizing.

"Matilda, get me my daughter on the phone. *Now.*"

Her look of horror almost makes me feel better, but I know talking to Delores will be even better.

Do svidaniya[4], *papa.*

---

1. Good afternoon
2. Be prepared to explain yourself.
3. disappointing daughter
4. until next time

Sanctuary

Delores

After a week and a half of being locked on campus, the tension has amped up considerably. This past Sunday, a bunch of enormous skeevy looking men and women showed up in Cappie security uniforms to patrol the perimeter and gates. Rufus and Cori almost had panic attacks because they might have to move back into their dorms, but Fitz pulled up videos of the typical routes of the old guards to study so they'd have a vague idea of when they could come and go. The additional guards are definitely *not* law enforcement nor are they Capital Prep employees, so I can only assume the Council has sent them.

They stay out of camera range, so we haven't identified them by Fitz's tapping into the Sibbies' facial rec system, but Felix says they look like mercenaries based on their build and demeanor. None of us have run into one yet, but that's probably a good thing. The last thing I need is for them to figure out who I am and focus on sucking up to Lucille by shadowing me.

One stalker is all I consent to, thank you very much.

"You seem pensive, Dolly. What is going through your head?" Raina says as we walk towards the tunnel.

I just finished Acting and of course, the Plastics bemoaned that people won't be allowed on campus for the performance this weekend. Cori, Rufus, and I have done great work on the sets and such, so I'm disappointed my improvement in those areas won't be seen by many people, but I also don't want another fucking body dropping like the Phantom's chandelier, either. The guys can take some pictures and maybe this awful choice of productions can be filed as 'thank fuck this got little attention.' She's right, though. I *am* pensive, though not because of the play.

"There are so many things going on at once. I keep worrying that even with all our notes and plans, we're missing something big. I hate that feeling, especially since my mother has been quiet and Rockland is pushing me enough that I might have to let Farley know it's time to send round two." I swipe my card, frowning as I shrug. "Plus, now we're locked in here like fish in a barrel. Keeping us in one place probably won't stop the people who can appear in places without using traditional doors."

Raina nods, then gives me a hesitant expression. "You asked me once how the prey species view the Treaty and what differs in how we're taught history at home. We never got back to it. Would you like me to tell you now?"

I blink. "Holy shit, yes! It could rattle something loose. Tell me, Raina."

"The treaty was centuries ago, but it was the start of the new age for everyone but the predators, Dolly. Humans have their views on how the world changed because they think it was their war, but it wasn't. You probably realize that much of their history has been glossed over but directly relates to supernatural history."

"Well, yeah. A shifter having to hide rather than heal caused their World War. But that was seven hundred years after the Treaty." I wrinkle my nose, trying to remember. "So the Treaty corresponds with what they call the Hundred Years War?"

"Exactly. It was not simply the English versus the French, as they thought. It was shifters versus magic wielders." She pauses for a moment and dips her head. "The stories are passed down through the years, but a lot of prey died because they were conscripted to fight with the preds. When the sorcerers were defeated, the Treaty forced them into the shadows if they stayed on this side of the Veil. Many took refuge in the Faerie with the Fae because their lands have magic whereas here it was forbidden."

I ponder that as we cross the green to head to the Scholastic building. "I guess things were bad long before the war broke out, right? Probably a lot of conflicts on both sides and it amped up."

"The stories we're taught say so." Raina pauses for a second then says softly, "They also say the prey animals were promised equal positions of power and after the pred banished magic, they reneged on their promises. So… it's likely many old prey families regret their ancestors' decisions, especially mythicals. Magic users would find many allies in our community if they were looking."

She's trying to tell me our hooded friends probably built an entire rebellion over the years and their plans aren't new.

"I don't blame them. Hell, even the preds are living in a caste system now. It makes sense they'd find allies among the weaker preds and prey alike," I say as we approach the building. "Have you and the crew found out where the tunnels are here? I have a feeling that's what we'll need to investigate to find new pieces of this puzzle."

"Not yet, but I have Holliday and Percy on it. People ignore Holli because he's deaf, not even considering that he reads lips. It's rude, but he says he's used to it. But in the case of doing surreptitious sleuthing, it's very useful." The raccoon beams at me and adds, "He believes he has a lead on the longest working prey who might be susceptible to coaxing after a few drinks."

Nodding, I open the door for her, and we head inside. "I hate they treat him that way, but I also see how it would be advantageous. I appreciate you poking around for us, though. I know it wouldn't be well received if any of us went tromping in to ask."

"Always, Dolly. You and your family are the kindest preds any of us have ever known." She tilts her head as we get in the elevator, her eyes serious. "You look less worried than before, but still heavy. Is something else bothering you?"

"Besides the kidnappers, murderers, my sociopath mother, and evil girls trailing me?" We both chuckle and I shrug. "This class is one of my least favorites. Rakoto and Blitzen are jerks for no reason. At least I can identify that los Feliz simply wants to kiss the Plastics' asses. These two hate me because I'm breathing and it makes it hard not to feel resigned when I have to go."

"That makes sense. But their bias is *their* problem, not yours. Prey learn that from a very young age and we have to arm ourselves with the knowledge that despite what preds say or do, their hang-ups do not change who we are. It's an unfortunate adaptation, but they did not teach you how to reject the opinions of others because you grew up in the powerful majority."

Oh, man. I know she didn't mean it that way, but now I feel like a whiny baby.

"You're right, Raina. I've had to let go of what my family and all the hateful people gathered by my ex-friends think. I need to throw out the opinions of these chuckleheads, too. It doesn't matter if they're professors; I don't exist for their approval."

She smiles as we get to my classroom, holding out a tiny fist to bump. "Exactly. You have many who love you for you and those who don't like you should raise their standards."

"Truth," I reply as I open the door. "See you in a couple of hours, Raina. And thank you."

"Anytime, Dolly. You're my friend."

By the time class is over, I'm thoroughly wiped. Rakoto was in top form, picking me to grill on every other question. Interestingly, we seem to skip a section of the text and heading into the very Treaty Raina and I were discussing this morning. Someone asked why we were moving to the middle ages and she barked at the poor alligator like he was a dog that piddled on the rug. We didn't get an answer, but she assigned a fifteen page paper on the Treaty and its effects on pred society due right after Thanksgiving.

The worst part is that I'm not sure if that was a punishment or something she was told to do.

"How was class?" Raina is waiting for me just outside of the room and I head over quickly so no one hassles her. There are too many of my obsessed chicks around for me to leave her alone.

"It was weird, Raina. We skipped a bunch of stuff and started talking about the damn magic treaty out of nowhere!" I walk towards the staircase with her, not wanting to be where others might overhear. "Talk about making me paranoid; we were just talking about it and then my entire class is about it. And I have to write a huge paper about how it affected society and international diplomacy, which I have a feeling will need to be slanted just so in order to get a good grade."

"That is very troubling," she says softly. "The stories our elders passed down talked about a period before the Treaty where things shifted. Preds and prey were told lots of bad things about magic users—my Nonna has old school books that have been in our family for many generations. You should ask Monsieur Renard and Master Aubrey to accompany you to the prey exhibits in the Smithsonian. Look at the texts from before and after the Treaty, then…"

"Then what, Raina?" I frown as she stops me, scooting close and gesturing for me to lean down.

Her voice is barely a whisper as she says, "Then look at the texts from the land near the Witch Trials. Nonna said it was an uprising that was covered up and the oldest books will have information on the group who squashed if you can find them."

Holy shit, is this the Society we keep hearing about? Are they the ones who make sure magical folk don't resurface?

When I straighten, I blink at the raccoon. "How do you know this?"

"I've been talking to many people on the preynet in my spare time, Dolly. I'm hoping to help you stay safe. If this is truly the moment that the fight is coming back, I'm afraid for you. Even the Captain is, because you are an anomaly in our world—prey born to preds—and that sort of thing is always a sign of things to come."

"Why are you telling me now?" I frown. "Have you thought about this since last year?"

She shakes her head as we head into the underground. "No. When the campus got destroyed, I wondered, but it has been very difficult to get people to talk about the old days. If we're discovered disputing the accepted history, they could wipe families out. So it's taken me a while to catch even whispers of theories. When you asked me about the tunnels, I realized you definitely need to know before you go into underground spaces none of us are familiar with."

Rubbing my hands over my face, I groan softly. How in the fuck am I caught up in some ancient battle all our ancestors started? It's so fucking stupid, too. Why can't shifters and magic folks live together? Sure, greed has to be part of it, and I don't put it past any of the families on Aubrey's list to be part of this to preserve their legacies. But seriously, it's 2023. What backwards dumbass shit requires us to subjugate a bunch of races just to stay relevant?

Ugh. I swear to Aphrodite's brassiere, I hate rich people shit.

"Dolly?"

The questions flying through my head stop when Raina says my name again and I look around. We're at the library and I've been walking along in a damn trance. I look like a total spaz today. "Sorry. I was just lamenting all the problems a bunch of species-ist old money bags are causing. It seems like we should just let the wizards come out of hiding and take part."

"Money is a great motivator, Dolly. Preds have been at the top for centuries now. Who knows how that balance would shift when they had true competition? It is very hard to change centuries of beliefs without bloodshed."

That's what I'm worried about.

Walls Could Talk

Felix

"Who is this woman? I've never heard of her, but she clearly feels superior enough to throw her weight around. Did you send her?"

I took this call in the stadium office since no one would be around on the Wednesday before the holiday. It's only three p.m. here, but it's near to midnight at Bloodstone. My father is known for his insomnia—a fact I used to make certain I'd get him when I reached out. As long as he wasn't drunk and passed out or fucking some courtesan, I knew he'd answer if I waited out the court sycophants. But calling him from this location was also to keep him from speaking to Fitz or asking to meet our girl. I don't need his bullshit, making everyone angry.

We have enough shit bothering us without adding the casual cruelty of the Raj.

"What do you mean, son? Who do you think I sent and why? I'm thousands of miles away."

Rolling my eyes, I try to rein in my irritation. My father has always claimed you're less than fifty feet from a Khan loyalist no matter where in the world you go. That's likely an exaggeration, but it's close to the truth. There are ambush enclaves every-where because his businesses—both legitimate and illegitimate—are all over the world. He's fond of infiltrating cities important to various leaders and crime syndicates, so he certainly has several locations in D.C. outside of the fights beneath *Inky Depths*.

"Your reach is felt much closer and you know it. Who is this Kamara Rakoto women positioned at Capital Prep? She's a tiger and a rare one, so I'm not so foolish as to assume you didn't place her here. What I want to know is, was it a normal strategic move or are you spying on me?"

His laugh is low, rumbling, and full of pleasure. "You can't think I'd be stupid enough to reveal my spies to you, Felix. You'd tell Fitzgerald, just as you did when you were a cub, and he'll tell that scraggly cheetah he drags around like a security blanket. I might as well broadcast it on the internet."

I count to ten in my head, hoping to keep my temper in check. My father loves to play mind games and his disdain for Chess is one button he pushes to get a rise out of me. When we were small, he often got his way by having various flunkies threaten our adopted brother any time our grandmother did not protect him. No one ever said a word out loud, but they'd make it very clear how they were going to hurt him, and I knew it was my father flexing his muscles.

Fitz has no idea how close he came to ordering Chess killed to convince me to marry his choice of bride before my exile—and he never will.

"I'm not asking for you to reveal anything other than her alle-giance, Father. She's overreaching with her behavior and as your proxy, I need to address the way she's drawing attention to herself. A normal professor would not thumb their nose at kings and heirs, even if they were exiled. It's making people wonder." My lips curve as I press one of his buttons. "You wouldn't want people to think you cannot control our ambush, even those from far-flung enclaves."

The brief pause before he responds tells me my shot hit the mark. "You gave up the right to question my orders when you chose that ridiculous girl over your intended. That's why you're stuck at those snooty schools in the first place, Felix. Unfortunately, your choices of late are as dubious as the ones in the past."

Breathe, Felix. Don't let him know insulting the Princess is going to get him killed.

"If I have no right to question the business of our family, then what concern of yours are my unfortunate escapades? It seems you are confused who I answer to—you, myself, or no one."

"*Felix Ivan Nestor Khan*, I will not allow you to take that *tone* with your *King*!"

As if he gives a randy red fuck what I'm doing other to flex his power and spread misery to anyone he can. "Again, Father, if I'm no longer part of—"

"You will go back to the fight club tonight and prove your worth." I can almost hear his salacious grin when he adds, "Bring your brothers and that girl you've had dripping off your arm. Her mother had an interesting proposal, and I'd like to see what happens if we consider it."

"Proposal? Since when do you chat with the likes of Lucille Drew?" I don't like the sound of this one bit and it will ruin Dolly's holiday if she has to go home unaware of her mother scheming behind her back again.

"That's for later, son. Do as I said. Go to the club and fight. The rest you can earn by drenching our name in victory."

Fuck. I have a bad feeling about this.

"We're almost there. I don't think I need to remind you that this bar is owned by the Princess' family and my father runs the fights. Nothing we do or say is private, and no one goes off alone." I look at the others in my backseat, hoping like hell Chess is giving the same speech in the car behind us.

I knew I'd never convince the others to stay behind, but I didn't know we'd be hauling her friends as well.

"How did you get me an off-campus pass?" Dolly asks from her place squished between Fitz and Aubrey.

Fitz bobs his brows. "He didn't. I 'arranged' it in the system. The dipshits patrolling the grounds don't question why something pops up for them, so they didn't question why five professors and a student are making an educational trip the night before break. It's what happens when you hire muscle trained not to think; they don't."

"Hopefully, the mouthy mobster doesn't get himself in trouble," Aubrey mutters. "I think Cori will behave, but I worry about the other one."

"Rufus can be vicious, you guys. I know he's silly and shit when he's with me, but I saw the giants he must have fought to keep his place as the McCoy heir. If he gets into a scrap, he'll finish it." Princess gives me a serious look and since she knows what the cage looks like under *Inky Depths*, I have to trust her.

"Truthfully, I have no idea why he wanted me to come fight tonight. The only reasons that make sense are he's trying to kill me with some asshole ringer or he's putting money on the fights. I'd be a wildcard, and he'd have the knowledge to hedge how he bets until I show."

Ren stops the car in the parking lot as I muse, waiting for the other vehicle before he turns off the engine. "*Mon ami,* there are likely multiple motives behind this demand. We are all prepared to help if it warranted, but our primary concern should be why he insisted you bring *ma petite.* With the lockdown, it would have been infinitely easier for you and Fitz to go on your own. No, I do not believe betting is the only answer."

We all step out of the car, and I gaze at the motley crew. Everyone but Fitz and I were dressed to the nines to appear as spectators. Just in case our asshole father throws a curveball, my twin came ready to change for a fight as well. Neither of us like being here on command and definitely not with our father's explicit directive. We cannot trust the Raj in normal times, but now that he's colluding with Lucille Drew and fuck knows who else, he's even more dangerous.

"Ren's right," I say as I look at them all. "The Raj is sneaky and only out for himself. We're going to get in, do this, and leave before any other bullshit rains down on us. As I said in our car, no one goes anywhere alone, and think about every word that leaves your mouth. Who knows who is listening and what their allegiance is? Understand?"

Aubrey huffs a smoke ring, squeezing the squishy in his pocket as he shifts. "Okay, General Patton. You've made your speech. Let's go in and attempt to comply without my dragon deciding to decimate this hellhole."

Not an auspicious start at all.

Fitz positions himself on one side of the Princess and I take the other, leading her inside as the rest of our group follows. We don't meet resistance upstairs this time—no, we've waved to the elevator to head downstairs immediately. I don't enjoy feeling as though we've been pre-announced and my gut is telling me to be prepared for something worse than expected. The door dings and we step out into the cavernous underground full of sin and vice.

"There's a regular shifter Vegas down here," Chess murmurs. "That asshole probably makes a fortune on the vig and the take."

I snort. "Definitely. He's got loan sharks down here, no question. Players are getting taken for a ride no matter what they do."

Fitz shakes his head. "Let's get to the ring and get out of here. I've got a bad feeling now, too."

"Starting to feel like *Star Wars* and I don't *like* it," Dolly grumbles. "Everyone needs to calm down before the big guy singes someone's suit coat."

"She's not wrong."

Whipping my head around to glare at the dragon, I convey what I hope is a plea for restraint. He and Ren are high-value, rare shifters. The less attention they attract to themselves, the better chance we have of *not* having to kick the ass of some rogue hunter watching the fights. "Everyone, just keep it cool."

"This place is terrifying," Cori whispers, and I hear Rufus laugh.

He seems unperturbed as we approach the smell of blood, sweat, and fear that saturates the area around the ring. I realize Dolly may have been right—the badger has some experience with this. He might be useful if we get into trouble. Before I can say anything to him, I see Z running up in her skimpy fight clothes, already stained with blood.

"No, no, no!" she yells as she sees us. "Damnit, Felix, why the *fuck* are you here?"

I blink. "What the hell is with you, Z? You're covered in blood and shouting like a lunatic."

"Take a Xanax, woman. No one's here to mess up your little Leonidas bullshit." Fitz rolls his eyes at her, but tension rolls off him. He knows something is wrong.

Zhenga pulls the towel off of her neck, blotting the blood spatter off of her face before she grits her teeth and grinds out, "I asked why you're here *tonight* because it's a *special night*. We have planned it since I got here and no, I didn't mention it because why the hell would I? You never showed an ounce of interest in underground fighting until the one night you showed, and it was clear that was a stunt. But you shouldn't be here *tonight*."

"Zhenga, please tell us why the hell you're having a panic attack in full view of everyone in this cave?" Aubrey looks like he's being polite, but you can tell by the timbre of his voice that his dragon is not happy.

"Tonight is Pred Games night, you idiots! Any former or current competitor mus*t* fight if they attend. Didn't anyone tell you when you came in upstairs? They're supposed to inform people."

And there it is… my father's gambit all along. They will force both Fitz and me to fight, which should net him a small fortune.

"Wait a tick," Rufus says, interrupting my thought process. "Did she just say current *and* former?"

"*That son of a bitch!*" My eyes widen as Dolly's eyes turn crimson and her hand squeezes mine hard enough to crack bones. "He sent you here to win him money, but that motherfucker and my cunt mother made you bring me, hoping to take me out. They knew the rules and that I'd be forced to fight, too."

"This is a joke, right?" Ren says as he looks around. "No one can actually *force* any of you to fight. Since they did not inform us before we came in, we'll turn around and go back the way we came. No harm, no foul."

"You won't get past the elevator. It's the rules and trust me, they have ways of enforcing them. She's right, Laveaux. The tigers and the rabbit have no choice." Zhenga sighs regretfully and crooks her finger at us. "Follow me to the locker room. The rest of you should find a seat and stay together. I have a feeling it's going to get rowdy."

Centuries

Delores

As much as I'd like to say I can't believe this shit is going on, it's not surprising at all. That cagey old fuck who fathered my tigers got together with my bitchy mother to arrange a test—or an execution—on the sly. I've only been competing in this stupid sport for a couple months and I didn't even *want* to do it. We thought it would keep people from screwing with me, which it has *not*. Now I'm required to fight in an underground club where it might as well be to the death because our sadist families tricked us into showing. Fucking Iago—the dude, not the bird—has nothing on the people who contributed to our DNA.

Calm down, Dolly. You can survive this.

I lean my head on the locker room door, closing my eyes. Fitz and Felix are being corralled by Zhenga and Chess, so I can get dressed and focus. Their angry, nervous energy was making my bunny nuts and I can't operate solely on rage in this fight. It might work in the college rings, but it won't work here. These people do this for big money and notoriety—they aren't bound by any of the rules the league puts on competitors. Nothing is off the table; I'm on my own and I have to do this without a ref who gives a shit.

"What the hell am I going to do if they put me with some giant dickweasel? They don't even keep women and men separate. I am so dead," I groan softly as I kick off my heels. Zhenga lent me some of her shit and it should fit okay. I only need enough to cover myself until I shift and then someone will robe me after. "Good thing she's not tiny, or I'd be getting boob strangled while I get neck strangled."

"That's not very positive thinking," the voice behind me is amused, and I turn to see Rufus watching me dress.

"Fitz will murder you if he finds you in here. They're being kept out for a reason," I say as I hop from one foot to the other while putting on the shorts. "Plus, I'm half-naked."

"Pffft, as if I fucking care about that. You're lovely, Dollybear, but you don't put the tension in my spring." He pushes off the doorframe and walks over, sitting on the bench opposite me as I wrap my hands. "I am, however, an expert at doing this level of shit with people who are out for blood, not trophies. And I'm not nearly as big as my opponents were, so I have insight to offer."

I blink. "You're coming in to coach me?"

"No, I'm here to tell you how to play dirty, so you win. They have trained you to play fair and use legal moves, babe. That's not what these guys will do."

Shit. He's right. Z and the guys know how to fight dirty, but they sure as fuck haven't been teaching me that for the Games.

"Okay. We don't have long." I pull my hair into a tight bun and look at my friend seriously. "Talk to me about being a cheating bastard."

His grin is feral as I sit down. "Gladly."

By the time Rufus is finished, I think I'm as ready as I can be. Squaring my shoulders, I head out the door of the locker room with my bunny lurking under my skin and my head held high. I've got Lucille's 'off-the-chain' look on my face—the one she's always wearing when I know it's going to hurt. It took me a few minutes of making faces in the mirror until I got it just right. The combination of a smirk and a feral grin isn't my usual look, but even Rufus approved.

I doubt it will work, but here the fuck we go.

The guys rush over as we exit, and I hold my hand up to stop them. Without a word, I want them to understand that if they fawn over me, it will make me look weak. They have to follow as if they have every confidence in the world that I can do this. Fitz and Felix catch it first, of course, and turn to the others with hushed whispers. I've let the smallest bit of my shifter powers out, so I can smell the blood and sweat in the room more distinctly. It should be intimidating, but it isn't. Even the ring isn't scary as I walk towards it.

The unknown is terrifying and when Zhenga clears me to wait for my round, the slight tinge of fear I get from her almost breaks me. She's worried, and it means it should scare me shitless. But I can't be, especially outwardly. I crack my neck as I look around, feigning boredom as I scope out the current match and the people waiting. As I suspected, I don't see another girl, so they're definitely going to pair me with someone who should be in a goddamn prison.

Fucking Lucille and that assclown Raj—they're moving up the list. I'm over this bullshit.

"Princess," Felix says as he moves closer to me. He and Fitz won't go until later because of their standing, but he's down here watching. "Do what you have to, no matter what."

I nod, leaning back as he nips my ear, then I feel him pull away. Chess sidles up next and one by one, my guys give me their encouragement until the last one appears. Fitz rumbles a dark growl against my ear and I shiver. He's already amped up beyond belief and as long as I don't die, he'll enjoy the hell out of watching me fight.

"Baby Girl, show them you're the Queen of that fucking school and our ambush. If you don't, they'll come for us all, especially my father. You know what you need to do in there. That's why I sent the badger."

"*You* sent Rufus?" I breathe in surprise.

He shrugs and licks the shell of my ear. "I'm an excellent judge of character. He's as dirty as them come and I knew he'd say what needed to be said."

"Which is?"

"Kill the motherfucker and pick your teeth with his spine. No holding back."

"Not a direct quote, but I get it."

The loudspeaker crackles, and I look at the stretcher being carried out of the ring. The last match has ended; I'm up. Zhenga nods at me and I wait for the announcer to yell the intro.

"Next up, the surprise contender from Capital Prep, the bad ass bunny beating the odds, the heir who's a hare, Deloreeeeeeeeessssss Dreeeeeeeeeeew!"

I take a deep breath and straighten again, stalking into the brightly lit ring as I eyeball the crowd. Money is exchanging hands, and the noise has risen to raucous levels. My eyes bleed red with the bunny as I notice the scads of men leering at the tiny fight outfit, and I hope they stay in their place. One of the guys will *kill* them and tonight, I couldn't possibly predict which one. They're all hopped up on pissed off punch and all it would take is someone to give them an excuse to beat the snot out of them.

Standing on my side of the caged-in ring, I wait for my opponent to be called. The crowd finally dies down a little and the speaker crackles before the voice comes on again. "And on this side of the ring, one of our frequent champions, the girl who puts the 'fall' in Fallon, the gore in manticore, Fallon O'Learrrryyyyyy!"

I'm sorry, she's a what?!!

Screams and hoots fill the air as my brain scrambles to remember what the actual fuck a manticore is. Suddenly, a picture of a lion's head with the tail of a scorpion comes into my mind. *But they're supposed to be male. WTF is this shit?* I pretend to be ignoring her strut around the ring, cracking my knuckles and shaking my limbs, but I am *not* ready for this. This is a mythical shifter, one who's likely been alive as long as Ren or Aubrey and has centuries of fighting experience under her belt. Not to mention she was born with a goddamn poisoned weapon on her ass—how am I going to combat that shit?

My eyes narrow as she passes by with a smirk, looking as though she's extremely pleased to introduce me to my maker. Within seconds, my bunny bursts through the surface, half-shifting me so I have claws and fangs to flash at the cocky bitch. I hear some asshole comment on my fluffy tail, but seconds later, a crunch says someone I know just broke something important. I can't get distracted by that, though. I have to focus only on this mythical oddity and staying alive.

Speed—the only thing that will save me is speed.

The ref calls us into the center while I adjust my starting strategy to lean on my speed and jumps to keep out of her tail range. If I can duck that nightmare, I know how to handle the lion part; it's like fighting Coach Z and I bet she's way better than this chick. I hold my hand up to bump fists with her, still wearing my psycho Lucille look as I back away slowly. Something in my gut twitches and before I know it, my hand flies up and I blow her a kiss.

Oh, Dolly, what the fuck *are you doing?*

My bunny snarls happily, and I realize she pushed that through. She wants to taunt my opponent because she's hungry, angry, and kept in a cage since the night of the explosions at Apex. Even in the Games fights, I never let her *all* the way out. I remembered the severed head and the piles of mushy professor; a picture that kept me from opening the doors too wide for fear of killing someone. I don't have that worry tonight, and I can feel her excitement buzzing in my veins like fine wine.

"You're dead, little bunny foo-foo," the manticore snarls in a deep voice.

"Get fucked, O'Leary," I shoot back as I drop into a fighting stance and start circling. The gravelly laugh echoes in the ring and I'm surprised to see her shift immediately. The stinger on her tail and mouthful of lion fangs are intimidating—not gonna lie. Darting out of the way when the tail comes at me, I wink at the shifted mythical as I leap out of range.

Another stab comes too close, and she speaks, so I know she should be a damn leader of her people, not fighting in an underground hellhole. "Too bad I'm not into *prey* like your pathetic teachers."

"Too bad I'm not into arthropod va-jay-jays." Hopping around from behind, I drop onto the lion's back, putting a tight forearm around its neck and start squeezing. "I have enough dicks to keep me busy for a couple centuries, anyway."

The crossed pressure from my arms makes her choke and gasp, but she rears up, throwing me off by using her tail to threaten me. I fly over her head and tuck into a roll as I hit the mats. Kipping to my feet, I bounce a little to test all my limbs. Everything seems okay, so I circle again, looking for an opening. I haven't had any opponents trash talk this much, but then, I haven't been dodging scorpion stingers, either.

Fallon rushes forward, catching me as I pass, and knocks me flat. Her bulk is massive in this form, and I use all my strength to dodge the dangerous tail as I try to get free. I can see the malice in her eyes as spittle drips onto me from her maw and I make a face. "Gross, woman! Get control of yourself."

Her answer is to throw her head back in a roar and I wiggle an arm free to stab her in the neck with two sharp claws, like Rufus showed me. The scent of copper fills the air as she stumbles backward. I roll away, getting up as fast as I can so I can take advantage of her pain. Running at her, I push off the ground hard with my fist curled in a video game worthy power punch that lands right between her eyes. It hurts like a motherfucker and I've probably broken a few bones, but it dazes the beast again.

Now's your chance, Dolly. Aim for the belly.

Ducking as the tail flails wildly, I slide across the mat on my knees and thrust both sets of claws into her side hard. Her hide is tough, but I put enough force into my move that they sink in. Rufus told me to aim for kidneys and rip upward, but I'll be damned if I know where the hell a lion beast's kidneys are. I just push up as hard as I can, winging a prayer to Ares that I've hit something important. When bone stops me, I yank my hands free and roll away again.

"Now you've pissed me off," Fallon snarls, stalking forward despite the blood dripping from her face, neck, and side. "I'm going to tear your pretty head off."

"Just fucking give in," I mutter as I eye her, looking for more weak spots. She's moving damn good for someone filled with holes, but mythicals are strong and hard to kill. That much I know from Ren and Aubrey. My gaze flicks to the stands and I see worried faces looking into the ring from the front row. I can't disappoint them; I have to be worthy of *something* for once.

I want it to be them.

The bunny pushes at me inside, and I know it's time. I'm going to let her finish this bullshit. The second that decision is made, my limbs crack and stretch more, making me taller and broader. The ears on my head twitch as fur sprouts over every inch of my exposed skin and I grin around the lengthening fangs. I hate for everyone in the universe to see this, but it's necessary. I take a deep breath as the need to hunt this bitch down and take my spoils fills me. It's easily as dark and alluring as it was when the guys took me hunting, but much more wild. She knows we're going to kill our enemy, and it's making every pore in my body tingle with anticipation.

I move so quickly I barely register it, slamming into the manticore hard enough to propel both of us into the side of the ring. Fallon's head slams into the side, her eyes filled with fear when she realizes I was fighting with one hand tied behind my back before. Claws slash over her arms as I grab her, lifting her up in the air like a wrestler and then throw her to the other side of the circle like a rag doll. The power in my rabbit is so intense right now that it's almost like being outside of my body watching someone else stalk over to the girl on the ground wheezing around what has to be broken ribs.

Giving her a macabre smirk, I lift my large bunny foot over her chest and peer down at her. "I gave you a chance to throw this shit. Don't blame me for doing what I have to."

A look almost like acceptance flits over her face, but she spits at me, anyway. "Fuck off, *freak.*"

Stomping on her until I hear the satisfying crunch of bones over and over, I wait until she stops moving and drop to the ground, looking at the crowd before I lean down and rip her throat out. The fresh blood splashes over me, but I revel in the sensation. The animal in me is victorious and when I'm done finishing her, I push to my feet, spinning in a circle with my hands in the air. I know I have to look like a gorey mess of fur, blood, and gross, but this image will be everywhere on social media.

I want to shove my win so far up the asses of my mother and my enemies that they taste it for months.

"If you come for me, I'll hit back twice as hard and leave you bloody in the dirt like her," I shout as the audience goes wild. "Nobody puts this bunny in a fucking corner again!"

The words echo in the room as my men come leaping over the ring, smashing me between them as I pant. Fitz grabs me around the waist and hauls me up on his shoulders, whooping like he's headed into battle with the fucking infantry. His voice carries as he winks at me, and Aubrey shoots a ring of fire around us.

"All hail, Delores Drew, queen of the Pred Games!"

Oh, shit. He just had *to scream that, didn't he?*

Now I'm definitely going to get killed.

Glory & Gore

Delores

The trip home was a blur and to no one's surprise, I was out before I got there. My body seems to drop into a healing stasis after fights and when I woke the next day, Felix assured me it was normal for a shifter who's only been emerged for a year, especially a powerful one. The guys all swear it's my body and my animal trying to protect me, but it makes me feel like a weak little girl who has to be carried out every time she does something big.

I was *supposed* to go home for the holiday—Lucille's text decree—but given I didn't wake until late in the day, it didn't happen. Chess made us all a big spread, and we lounged in our huge couch nest, ignoring the internet and my phone's constant buzzing as my mother tried in vain to reach me via text or calls. I knew it wasn't the best way to handle her, but I just did *not* have the spoons to let her screech at me for not getting killed at the fight night like she planned. Whatever plans she and the Raj cooked up, the Khans and I were unwilling to allow either parent to ruin the comfy family day we were all enjoying.

We'll pay for it later, but fuck them and the stick up their ass, too.

The decision to stay at Cappie seemed even more prudent when the Captain and his crew rushed into our home late in the evening on Thanksgiving night, eyes glittering with excitement. Holliday witnessed a conversation between some of the prey staff in their quarters, discussing the tunnels they would use to leave campus without being seen by any remaining students. They weren't being careful about their chat because, as expected, people vastly under-estimate anyone they consider disabled. He memorized the markers on campus they mentioned, and the crew went out to check as soon as the staff left for the break.

Today, we're going to explore those damn passages, even without Cori and Rufus. If possible, I might be more excited about the prospect of finding more clues about the maelstrom of bullshit being thrown at us in this war than I was about beating Fallon. I'm still a bit of a mess of bruises, knitting bones, and scrapes, but I'll hobble through with everyone to find out what the fucking shit is going on and why everyone seems determined to make me the center.

Pain heals, psychos dig scars, but preventing a civil war is glory that lasts forever, right?

I give Jinx a last pat on the head, then walk over to the dresser to make sure my braids are tight. I'm wearing clothes that are easy to move in because we don't know what the hell is *in* Cappie's tunnels, be it residents or booby traps. I smell like arnica and oint-ment under all the bandages Argyle re-applied this morning. It's stifling to be bound by gauze, butterfly clamps, and braces under Fitz's hoodie and my skinny jeans, but Chess insisted. His worried eyes were more effective than any of the blustering and commands the rest threw at me.

Fitz shrugged them off as usual, vowing to 'unwrap me' when we return and despite myself, I let them have the skunk bind me up like a fucking mummy. He stayed with me while the nurse fussed, regaling me with tales of his fight victories and gross 'finish him' moves, while the others printed the maps and gathered supplies. It occurred to me while he babbled excitedly that just like I know how to soothe their fury and fears, the guys have learned which one of their special touches are needed to make me agree.

It's sweet and I kind of love it.

"Hey, Baby Girl, you ready to go?" Fitz pokes his head in, clad all in black and ready to drive Aubrey nuts with his secret agent playlist humming.

"I am. I was just making sure everything's secure so I don't get caught on something." I pick up my crossbody with my phone and the supplies, chuckling to myself. Someone bought us fucking spy gear after the last outing to Apex and I'd love to know who it was. Anymore, I can't figure out where *anything* comes from because they've all started randomly buying shit. "Who did this?"

"Not I," he sing-songs. "It appeared and hell if I'm not gonna play with the new toys, though."

"Okay, Indiana Fitz. Let's go spelunk some caves."

THE ENTRANCE HOLLIDAY SUSSED OUT WAS UNDER HOUSE AVIAN. Their dorm was deserted—birds definitely like to migrate home to friendlier climes in the winter—so we could take the elevators down to the basement and enter without being seen. Fitz jammed the security feed with some whizbang he found in the spy gear and we ducked into the secret opening behind the drying racks in the laundry. The tunnels here feel a lot more like servant paths than passages to protect the prey staff; it's creepy as hell.

It makes me thankful I had Mattie as a kid; she kept me from buying into Lucille and Bruno's rich people's bullshit.

"Since we're missing a few people, we're going to stick together in a single group, but as we find rooms, we can cover them in small clusters. We don't have to worry about the magic toxins here as far as we know, but we also have no idea if there are traps. Stay focused and don't let your guard down," Felix says as he peers down the darkened walkway.

"Should we use the flashlights, or are we worried we'll tip someone off?" I ask as I put my earpiece in. As people peel off to examine family vaults, we need to keep in contact.

Rennie tugs on a braid, giving me a small smile. "Just shift your eyes, *ma petite*. Chester has excellent night vision and the prey animals will be fine. We'll save torches for when they are necessary."

I nod, looking at him earnestly. "No matter what we find, none of us is to blame for this bullshit. Not me, not the cats, or you—even if our parents or our pasts are tied to what's going on. We cannot be held responsible for what others do. None of us are clairvoyant, nor are we omniscient, so don't look so worried."

His lips curve up, and he grabs my hand, kissing my knuckles gently. "The fiercest warriors can have the souls of poets, *cherie*. Your compassion does all our hearts good."

"Amen to that, Stony Sulker," Fitz says with a toothy grin. "Baby Girl makes all of us assholes feel like kings."

I blush and swat at him playfully. "Okay, okay. Stop blowing sunshine at me and let's get moving. You're going to give the Captain and his crew cavities."

"I think it's lovely, Dolly," Raina pipes up and I give her a pretend glare. She laughs softly, but I see her men gathered around her protectively, so maybe she understands.

Felix clears his throat, chuckling as he and Aubrey start down the hallway. Chess and Fitz flank me, then the crew walks behind us with Rennie at the back. I feel like I'm being escorted by my personal squadron, but since I'm moving slowly, I let it go. I could defend myself if I had to, but it would exacerbate my injuries. I'm not stubborn enough to risk all our lives just to feel like a big girl.

"Why did you have to hunt for info about these tunnels?" I ask Raina. "At Apex, all the prey knew about them. Is there a reason they're cutting you and the nurses out?"

"Sometimes when groups of prey bond over time, they get as territorial as preds. They forced us into their ranks without preamble, and I believe they fear our connection to your family."

"Bunch of lollygagging cowards," the Captain mutters. "None of them maintain good order in their crews."

Rennie chuckles, the sound echoing a little on the stone walls. "You are a consummate disciplinarian, Captain. None of the prey under your banner could ever be accused of shirking their responsibilities."

"We take pride in our work," Kirby chirps. "The prey staff at Apex may have been terrified of half the campus, but they were a tight ship with standards. Half the departments at Cappie are filled with personal servants from higher tier families. They only work hard for their actual employers and skate through everything else. Raina says it's some sort of tax scam."

"Shhhh!" Aubrey interrupts as he and Felix pause. "Do you hear that?"

I frown, tilting my head. The sound of water trickling becomes obvious quickly. "A fountain?"

"I don't know," Felix replies as he squints. "It's a little further down, but we wanted to quiet everything down before we come up to it."

Oops. I'm not only injured, but distracting.

We creep down the passage silently, everyone on guard as the sound gets closer and closer. The tunnel opens up into a larger antechamber flooded with water on the floor. Everything is covered in moss and swamp flora, including a large door to the left that has several different sized water wheels on it. They're covered in greenery, looking as though they haven't been touched for years. Each wheel has a pipe made of a different metal over it, and the scent of swamp fills my nose.

"Shit. It's Bruno's family vault," I mutter. "Who the fuck knows what will be in there?"

"The Captain and I will stay here and figure this out," Renard says as he looks over the room. "It's some sort of water puzzle, and I believe it will open the door. The rest of you should keep moving while we focus here."

"Be careful. My father is clownish in his villainy, but Grandmére is not." I look at my broody boyfriend seriously, then at the Captain. "I've only met her twice, but she's scary as hell. I had 'accidents' both times she visited when I was a kid. No one ever told me how I ended up in the hospital—or why."

Aubrey huffs smoke rings that float up towards the ceiling before he looks at Chess. "Add her to the boards when we get home."

Walking over to the big man, I put my hand on his cheek and smile. "You realize we can't kill everyone who was ever mean to me, right?"

"Not true, Baby Girl. I'll happily hunt down every motherfucker who ever made you frown with Hot Sauce. Hell, we can make it a game. You like games, right?" Fitz tugs me back, his expression full of the crazy I love.

"Focus," Chess says to us as I wrap my arms around his neck. "We don't want to be down here all day."

I pout as I pull back, turning to our leader. "Alright, General Khan, let's move out. Chess is right; we have more to explore while they work on whatever my cranky croc relatives have in store for them."

We leave Rennie and the Captain to work on the weird water riddle, heading out of the alcove to the hallway on the other side. It seems appropriate that the rooms here are fancier than at Apex; Cappie boasts a celebrity student body, but finding my father's family storage here is odd. I wasn't aware the Drews had this kind of notoriety, but then, neither of my parents has given me much information about their heritage. I've barely met Bruno's mother and, to my knowledge, never met Lucille's father. They kept me as insulated and naïve as possible my entire life—to the point of threatening everyone around me to keep their secrets safe, I suppose.

It only takes a few more minutes before we happen upon another round atrium, this one cold and sterile, like an operating theater. It's fairly empty, only sporting light green tiled walls and a metal door with an odd stone in the center. Chess squints at it for a moment, then looks around the space. He walks around, touching shiny surfaces here and there, then looks at us with a satisfied expression.

"This is some kind of light puzzle, I believe. Given the sparse decor and cleanliness, I think it might belong to our incarcerated Heather's family. The Maclachlans are loosely affiliated with the Khans in a legitimate business venture that runs the medical industry. I can stay here with one of the triplets and work on getting the door open while you guys press on."

I hate separating, but I know we have to do it.

We need as much information as we can get in the shortest time. Our mission is to gather it before anyone knows we've been down here, so dividing resources is the only logical choice. "Okay, but be careful. You have the earwigs and we should check in like we did at Apex now that we've started breaking off."

He comes over and presses a kiss to my temple. "Don't worry, Angel. We won't do anything stupid."

Sighing, I look at Felix and nod. "Let's keep going."

His gaze cuts to my cheetah, exchanging a wordless conversation before he turns to lead us across the circle into the passage on the other side. The path is getting darker, and the temperature has dropped, which makes me think we may twist along or under the river that split the campus. Our maps are fairly useless given the lack of lighting and basic sketches of the tunnels. They're more like original architectural drawings and they've obviously upgraded and added to this system since they made the drawings. Every time we come across a room that seems to correlate to it, I become more certain that *all* the drawings we've been trying to identify are underground tunnels under the five private pred academies across the world. It makes sense that all the ruling families would hide their dirty secrets in them and that means we'll find one for all or most of them eventually—including my guys' families.

No way the Khan vault is anywhere but that hellhole they rule over, though.

"Wait." Felix's voice cuts through the darkness as we approach a brightly lit opening that is definitely the next alcove. Everyone stops as he creeps toward the light carefully, his animal instincts clearly telling him something is wrong with the place we're approaching.

"What do you see, Felix?" I murmur as I edge closer to the front.

Aubrey puts his arm in front of me, holding me back. "There's something in there, but it feels wrong. Let him investigate."

It feels like I hold my breath forever as I wait for our royal leader to come back, but I know it's not that long. When Felix emerges, his lips are quirked in amusement. "This is definitely the Kavarit area. Draconis, you and Holliday should work on this one. There are several… robot Sphinxes guarding three doors and they seem eager to play games."

Blowing out a breath pf air as I roll my eyes to the ceiling, I groan. "What the fuck kind of *National Treasure* bullshit did these fuckers think they were doing? I feel like we're excavating for Tutankhamen, not digging through sketchy business records and family archives."

"Secret societies are basically cults, snack size. They operate the same way and use the same methods of keeping their members in line. Everything we find in these places could bring down some of the oldest, wealthiest, and most powerful lines in shifter society. Tradition dictates they use the same places their ancestors always have rather than update to more advanced security, especially since no one has ever found them before us."

A thought skitters through my mind, and my eyes widen. "Except maybe we aren't."

"What do you mean, Baby Girl? This shit is locked down," Fitz says, as he scratches his head. "None of the shit we've gone through looks tossed."

"No, but think about this for a moment. Apex is the *only* school we know of where a student like me was told how to use the tunnels. I was *only* told by the prey staff because I'm prey and I attended there. The minute I started using them, weird shit started happening, culminating in everything getting blown up. That meant construction crews and people running around recovering anything they could from the underground archives and shit. The magic doesn't affect the prey, only the preds."

Aubrey looks like I have smacked him in the face with a brick as it dawns on him. "They blew everything up on purpose. The blue lightning fuckers *wanted* someone to discover the family vaults under Apex and the room with the painted over maps for the other schools. Preventing Apex from being re-built with magic meant students would be sent to other schools."

"Allowing His Grace to bring his crew meant you'd eventually figure out how to get into the prey tunnels wherever you went," Raina says. "That's why he could get us on so easily."

"We're playing right into their hands by raiding this shit," I murmur under my breath. "The hoods want the dirty secrets of the founding families of the Treaty known. But why?"

Felix's gaze lands on me, his eyes dark as he replies. "I don't know, except that it definitely has something to do with you, Princess."

And the hits keep on coming.

Secrets

Delores

Our trip to the tunnels led to one more room, and it was a doozy. They protected the Barrington room with a gauntlet of codes and ciphers that took the rest of us hours to unravel. When we got inside, it was as damning as the Charles room—filled with file cabinets from floor to ceiling with massive amounts of research on every pred and prey family that's ever been anywhere near the media, even ones who aren't wealthy or influential. Every person who works for their empire must have contributed since they formed their very first newspaper centuries ago. Their horde of knowledge is how they stay relevant and on top, no matter what anyone in their family does, even the youngest Heather.

No shifter would ever want this shit to go public.

Felix pulled out his phone, and we started searching for every family on Aubrey's list of possible Society members. Not a single branch on any of their trees, no matter how small, was left in their cabinets when we finished piling up the folders and files. I have no idea how we're going to make time to go through all of it, but there have to be answers here. Some boxes we pulled can't even be opened unless Aubrey takes them down to his archives—a fact that made him shudder with glee once he finished his tasks at the Kavarit vault.

"The breadth of shit we found on those names is so enormous. There's no way they weren't involved in the Treaty and the war that preceded it. The Barringtons have been using this gold mine to blackmail and bribe people ever since," Chess says as he flips through a file on a lesser branch of the Janssen tree.

My dragon snorts from his table, looking up from where we're working on two ancient ass books with gloves and tweezers. "Obviously. That little snot acts as though no one can touch her and her Riptok audience isn't that much protection. She's been told she's immune her entire life. I'd guarantee it."

As much as I enjoy dunking on my ex-friends, it doesn't hold the same satisfaction as it did before.

"She's harmless on her own. The lot of them have been obnoxious this year, but the moment they weren't saturated in glory like at Apex, their antics became pathetic, you know? Even hiring that doper for the Games backfired on them. Plus, Selene and the Plastics are eating them alive." I set my tools down, pondering for a moment before I continue. "I actually don't think I've thought of them as a genuine threat since."

Rennie looks down at me from the top of the shelf he's perched on while he reads his files. "It is the way of life, *ma petite*. Small people focus on small things—your old friends have nothing more significant in their lives than their petty rivalry. You, however, have moved on. Our family and solving this mystery before a bloody war begins are higher callings than they can comprehend. They cannot hurt you like they did last year because you evolved while they remained petulant children."

"Agreed," Felix mutters from behind a box of files on the Leonidas family. "Your escorts in the crew are not because of them, though you probably assumed they were."

"Hell yes, I did. Those girls and the Plastics seemed dangerous," I grumble. "Why wouldn't you make sure they can't shave my head or some shit?"

"Because your hair would grow back, Baby Girl. Doesn't mean I wouldn't have scalped the person responsible, but the bigger concern was hooded freaks, murderers, and unknown spies." He walks over to me, lifting me out of my chair and places me on top of a set of shorter shelves. "We can't get put in check or we'll lose the whole game."

My face turns red as he moves closer, standing between my legs and resting his hands on my thighs. "You need to quit calling me a queen. People will think I'm conceited and snooty."

"Angel, three of your fated mates were kings. It's accurate, despite Felix's insistence on calling you 'princess', because it aggravates you." Chess leans back, pulling off the glasses that make him look adorably nerdy and rubbing his eyes. "These codenames are infuriating, by the way. Every file has last names that correspond, but figuring out what reference they used to create the codename for the first moniker is making my eyes bleed."

"Fuck, yes," Fitz groans as he leans his forehead against my sternum. "I love a good nickname and watching mysteries with our sweet little cottontail, but this is ridiculous. There has to be some sort of master list so we can figure out which stupid ass Bruce is in which file. Their second tier Council members aren't as familiar as the big ones."

Aubrey sighs and looks up from his tome. His gaze narrows as he looks at us. "You're all very distracting suddenly. I am trying to translate this while making certain the pages don't crumble. Perhaps you could focus?"

I push Fitz back, hopping off the shelf to walk over to my grumpy book dragon. Standing behind him, I put my hands on his shoulders and dig my thumbs in, hoping to release some of the tension making him rigid. "I know you're worried, big guy, but we all are. Everyone is doing their best and we're not going to figure everything out today. It's going to take time, even if we don't want it to."

"Guys?"

Chess interrupts us before Aubrey can grumble his answer. He's holding up a handful of scrolls that look as old as the book my dragon is working on. "They feel like someone has misfiled them. And since this is all more recent stuff, I'd say they probably did it on purpose."

"Wait. Do not unroll them," Rennie says as he leaps off the tall shelf. He walks over casually, but I sense the tension in him. He takes the scrolls from Chess gingerly, placing them on the table and gesturing for Aubrey to come over. Once he gets the gloves and tweezers from him, the gargoyle unrolls the first leathery scroll slowly. "These are not to be trifled with, *mes amis*. I recognize the way they are crafted."

Aubrey huffs a few smoke rings as they unfurl. "That's the ancient shifter language. We used it before the Treaty. Afterward, the various groups reverted to their species' language or that of the region they lived in. Schools stopped teaching the universal tongue, and it went the way of Sanskrit. But I do not know what the other markings are."

"High Fae," Rennie whispers softly. "The other writing is in High Fae."

We all look at him, and he ducks his head in shame. My eyes cut to Aubrey, asking the question the rest of us are wondering. "Do you speak the old shifter language, Aubrey? Is it something the mythicals still know?"

His jaw grits, and he nods. "When I was young, it was still in use. I'm uncertain if the rare breeds still use it now, though."

"They taught it in my childhood," Rennie says with a sigh. "I suspect it still is. Remember, shifters like Aubrey and I are not usually found outside closed groups. The manticore you killed was also an exception."

Fitz growls under his breath, stomping over to the gargoyle with an angry expression. "Do you speak High Fae, fucker? Because I've been really sensitive about your moping, but the longer you wait to tell us, the more danger Baby Girl is in. And I'm just about at the end of my rope with you pretending to be a giant chicken instead of a fucking gargoyle."

"I do."

The room fills with growls and snarls of fury, but I can't let frustration break us apart or eclipse the actual problems we're facing. As angry words are flying, I climb onto the chair, standing above them slightly before I put my fingers to my lips and let out a whistle that pierces my own ears. All five of my men stop where they are, their mouths hanging open as they look at me.

"Yes, he's been holding back and yes, we could be further along. It doesn't matter now because it's done. We need to use Rennie to read every single thing we find with this writing, and maybe we'll find clues. If the hoods planted old shit in one box, they probably did in others. We have a day and a half to go through what we have here and go back for more if we don't get it all. After that, people will be back at the school and we'll lose our chance. Spending this time fighting is dumb and it won't solve shit, so put them away."

They're all silent for a moment before Felix starts a slow clap and within seconds, they all follow him. I give him a dirty look as I hop down, my face so red I feel like a damn tomato. How I became the grown up in a family full of men twice to a bazillion times my age, I don't know. Huffing, I stomp over to my table and flop into my chair, not looking at any of them as they chuckle.

"Shut up," I mutter as I pull on the gloves. "Someone had to tell you assholes to stop waving your dicks around or we'd get nothing done."

"As opposed to when she *wants* us to wave our dicks around so *she* gets done," Fitz amends with a lecherous grin. "And if we don't get this shit done, none of us will get done, either."

"Thin ice." I point at him, trying to stay serious as he pulls his usual pervy jokes to make me crack a smile.

Chess comes over and bends down, brushing my hair out of my face. "How about I go get some snacks ready? Maybe we're all a little hangry and it'll help keep our minds on the task."

"Thank you," I whisper as I lean my forehead on his. "That sounds perfect."

When he pulls away and heads for the door, Aubrey picks up another box, smacking it on an empty table. "Everyone, get to work. We're on a tight timeline before the school re-opens and from what we've found so far, we're being given bread crumbs to help us solve this mystery. If we sit around, we might miss the next set."

What he didn't say was: who knows what they'll do if we don't play their game the way they want us to?

Look At What You Made Me Do

Renard

According to the email Henrietta sent to the staff, thirty-five more students failed to get to their homes or back to school so far. Included in that number are several high-profile kids like her dickless ex-boyfriend, Heather Charles, Jaiyana Faiz, and the O'Leary heir. The Council is up in arms as all their children were accompanied by what sounds like security battalions and they've disappeared as well.

It's hard not to feel responsible—a guilt I share with *ma petite*. The email came in during breakfast and a bit of quick math told us the number of kidnapped students now tops a hundred. I watched her rub her battered arms as emotions warred on her beautiful face. And I knew. She's blaming herself for being their prime target and feeling awful because she wished the Heathers and Todd would get what they deserved.

I didn't tell her whatever the hoods are doing is likely more than anyone deserves; it would only make her feel worse.

"The things we translated yesterday show the birth rate for mythicals dipped after the Treaty. They weren't rare before it, and that means magic *had* to contribute." She looks at Aubrey and me, her eyes questioning. "And suddenly, we have the hoods and a public mythical fighting in underground rings despite death being on the table."

"I haven't seen a manticore in so long," I reply as I think about it. "I don't know if they're usually that bulky or not. There used to be nests in Europe and South America."

"Perhaps we should tell her what the most common mythicals were in our youth?" Aubrey sips his coffee, frowning at the table. "If births have secretly been on the rise because of a partnership with the magical folk, we could encounter far more than a single manticore in the coming months."

"Unicorns were my favorite," I say with a smile. "They're so beautiful and majestic." My lover glares at me and I duck my head, amending my statement. "That is, after dragons and their awe-inspiring flames."

Our quibble gets a small giggle from our girl. "Uh-huh. Their big old dicks are probably part of it, too."

Now Aubrey turns red in the face, blustering as Fitz fist bumps her gleefully. "Hell yeah, Baby Girl. Make them uncomfortable; it's hysterical."

"Chimera, krakens, griffins, gorgons, phoenixes, gargoyles, dragons, unicorns, cockatrices, sirens, mer-folk… all of those are on the table now," Felix drawls, trying not snicker. "We have no idea what we'll run into if you're right, Princess. But how do the missing students fit in?"

We all look at one another, hoping the immediate thought that leaps to mind isn't correct. They're kidnapping young, fertile students, and who knows what they're doing with them? Incubators or donors—neither is an appealing possibility.

"*Cherie,* we cannot do more for them than we are. Every spare moment is spent figuring out whatever we can. You can't blame yourself if you hoped some of the missing students got what they deserved for torturing you."

She blinks, looking at me in surprise. "How did you know?"

I give her a small, sad smile. "Because I have been struggling with similar emotions over not being able to talk about the past that damaged me and why it's important to what's going on now."

"For fuck's sake," Felix growls as he stands. The Raj rakes his hand through his growing hair, then puts his palms on the table, leaning in to look each one of us in the eyes. "We keep having to remind one another we're not the bad guy and it's a waste of time. From now on, unless you kill someone yourself, no one may feel guilty about this shit. Understand?"

We all look sheepish as we mumble agreement, but I don't feel the words.

Chess rises, picking up a few of the plates to clear the table, and Fitz joins him. Felix rolls his eyes at me as I stay still, but he heads for the kitchen with his brothers. I'm still picking at my waffles when my mate rounds the table and leans in to whisper in my ear. His husky voice makes me flush with pleasure and I catch *ma petite* watching us with interest.

"You might start by telling bite size and me first, love. It would be easier and we'll make sure you feel safe," Aubrey murmurs. "We can even help you tell the others."

"We're fighting too many enemies with blindfolds on. The things you know about the magic users are what we need to figure out what their game is. Aubrey wasn't around his clash when the Treaty happened, but you were with your clan. You were old enough to overhear important information." Dolly reaches over the table and takes my hand, squeezing it. "We need you."

"I know." My voice is low as I duck my head. "Cradling the pain of those days has become so ingrained that I don't know where to start. I was young and foolish, but my destiny was to be greater and I squandered it."

Her lips curve as she looks at me in amusement. "Did you? I'm not sure finding a home, a mate, and a family of your own is squandering anything, Rennie. It might not have been what you were told was your path, but you made a new one on your own. Do you regret anything since you came to Apex?"

I shake my head. "No. Unless you count not listening to Fitz after he met you, but all of us were guilty of thinking he'd lost what little sanity he had chasing after a freshman prospect."

Dolly chuckles and shrugs. "I wasn't ready when he met me. The hurt and pain were so raw—my entire world collapsed in a single moment and I lost everything I thought I knew. You may empathize with me now, but I needed that summer to figure out who I was when others didn't define me anymore."

"You're better off without them."

"Mmmm. Has it occurred to you that you're also better off without the people who hurt you so badly?" She gets up and comes closer, making me scoot so she can sit on my lap. "All of you were cast out by people who betrayed you—regardless of the reason—and therefore don't deserve you. The sage wisdom you guys gave me about my friends and family applies just as easy to you as it does to me. It might be why we work so well."

She's fucking got me there.

"We need to talk about that, *ma petite*." I cup her cheek, looking into her eyes seriously. "The time for cementing the bond that scared you so much last year is drawing near. Since you are accepting your animal in the ring, she's been pushing you to behave like a female that's found her mate."

Her nose wrinkles, and she turns bright pink. "Noticed that, did you?"

"It'd be fucking impossible not to," Aubrey interjects as he returns. "You come closer to breaking skin every time and we're all afraid to let you make a choice you haven't voiced your desire to make."

I roll my eyes at him. We all agreed I could handle this topic, and I finally found a good time, but here he is stomping in like the damn dragon he is. "Flames is correct, *chérie*. We can't allow you to draw blood until we know you understand and accept the gravity of the deed."

"Guys, Coach Z had a *long* conversation with me privately about mating during a gym session. I don't need you to teach me what it means." Dolly pauses and looks at both of us for a moment before she mumbles, "But I need to know if people are going to be pissed when it happens. I mean, you know. It won't all be at the same time and Z said there's like a pecking order? I don't know shit about that because—"

Dragon belly laughs ring out as Aubrey throws his head back in mirth. "Oh, for the love of Hera's girdle, bite size! Do what feels right. If one of us gets a little butt hurt about not being first, you can work your girly wiles on them. As men, *we* might have hang-ups on what we can do in what order, but you can do whatever you want."

"You can fight over what order you get to go in, but if I choose, you all have to suck it up?" She squints at him curiously, then looks at me. "Really?"

"Really," I say with a rueful grin. "Your mates will not complain their woman chose them nor ruin their chance at being next. At least, that's what I assume."

Dolly crosses her arms over her chest, rolling her eyes as she grumbles, "Again, *why are men*? Ugh!"

The tigers finally return with Chess, watching our girl as she glares daggers at them. Fitz frowns at Aubrey and me, raising a hand to point accusingly. "What the hell did you morose mother-fuckers do to my Baby Girl? You made her pissy and I won't have it. Felix, where's that damn sword from Halloween? I want to challenge them to a duel."

That stops everyone and we all just stare at the hyper twin incredulously. Felix cracks first, putting his hands on his knees and damn near crumbling with laughter. Chess snickers next and before long, we're all hooting with amusement as Fitz shoots us glares of disapproval. He jumps on a chair, looking down as he poses.

"I'm not joking, assholes. If you make our girl pissy, I'll pull out some D'Artagnian and go revolution on your asses."

When she catches her breath, Dolly pops out of my lap, wiping her eyes as she walks over to him. "Fitzy, people just do *not* give you enough credit for making everything lighter. Get down here and give me a kiss, you loon."

He hops down with a goofy grin, putting his arms around her and dipping her almost to the floor before kissing her. They straighten after a few polite coughs, and he winks at us. "Make her laugh, make her come, and bring her body parts—that's why I'm the favorite."

Felix elbows him, stealing Dolly away to dip her next. "Train her, fuck her, and wear the dress she made you—that's why I'm the favorite."

A squeak escapes as Chess grabs her, twirling her before he imitates his brothers. "No, no. Feed her, fuck her, and treat her wounds—that's why I'm the favorite."

I look at Aubrey with a devilish grin, leaping from my seat at the same time as him. He dips her, then spins her back to me, her blue eyes glazed as she looks at us. I shake my head at the others. "*Non, mes amis.* Hunt her, fuck her mid-air, and then take her to a library. That's why we're the favorites."

"Guys…" Dolly groans as she tries to hide her face in her hands.

"Wait. *Fuck her mid-air?!*" Fitz roars as he stomps his foot. "You sons of *bitches!*"

"Now look at what you did," Dolly hisses at me. "We're never hearing the end of this."

As long as she's smiling like she is now, I don't think I care.

Best Friend

Delores

In the wake of the missing students, Cappie has gone on full lockdown again.

They have brought in another contingent of beefy guards to patrol the grounds and it's feeling like a damn police state. The past week has been a flurry of rushed coursework and professors getting flustered as their lesson plans seem to drift further from our actual courses to focusing on things related to the Treaty. Rakoto and Blitzen are shoving enough work at us to float a barge of whale sharks and I almost have to hold my nose to complete it. It's obvious the Council is pushing the academies to get the students to drink the tasty juice before an all-out skirmish begins.

"Do you think they'll cancel Yule Break?" Cori asks as she snatches a vegan egg roll from the special plate Chess left her. "I'm supposed to go skiing with Giselle's family in the Alps. I haven't been to Europe since I was a kid and I'm going to be pissed if we miss it."

Shrugging, I nibble on my taco potato skin. "I don't know. Aubrey said some of his friends at the museum are being told visas to leave the country for research are getting held up. For all we know, there could be a total travel ban by New Year's."

"Anyone else *really* uncomfortable that no one has brought in the Sibbies yet?" Rufus yawns and scratches Jinx's head. "It's fucking weird, even Farley says so. He's convinced there's a conspiracy to take away our freedom or something, but I haven't told him about all our magical shit, so… Conspiracy theories are all the normal folks have at the moment."

"The Council is keeping this shit locked down until they feel like they have the upper hand. Not publicizing all the missing people is part of their massive cover-up. That's why we're all suddenly learning a bunch of lies about the time before the War and the Treaty." I grumble as I hold up my tablet with a presentation on it. "I mean, who the fuck believes the Fae were murdering shifters in the middle of the street unprovoked? No one, that's who. You'd have to be an idiot to believe this shit."

My polar bear friend turns bright red. "Giselle's family is very Council oriented. She's really buying this stuff, and it's hard not to tell her what I know."

"Oh shit, Coco!" Rufus rolls over and gives her a hug. "Damn, girl, a Loyalist? What the hell are you gonna do if this all goes boom?"

"I don't know," she admits. "I can't stay with her if she spouts false news and random bullshit the Council feeds us from the media. I just thought she was different; those people aren't usually the kind that date shifters like me and…"

I hand her a cupcake off the dessert plate with a sympathetic smile. "If it makes you feel better, my parents and all my enemies will be screaming that shit. So will the twins' dad."

"For sure, a lot of my family members will latch onto it," Rufus says with a sigh. "It'll be up to me and Memaw to set them straight, which is something I'm never a fan of."

"Rufus!" I smack him with a pillow, groaning at his terrible joke. "Behave. Cori's upset."

He sighs, raking a hand through his hair. "Look, Coco. In times like this, we find out who people really are. Maybe Giselle will figure out it's all crap, and maybe she won't. The only thing you can do is decide what you'll tolerate and what you won't. That's really the important thing because if she's presented with the truth and refuses to see it, you won't have a choice but to accept her as is or cut bait."

"Agreed." I scroll through the text on my presentation, wrinkling my nose at the rhetoric I'll have to agree with to keep my grades where they have to be. "For now, I'm playing the game by pretending to accept the Council's version of events. It sucks, but given the more dangerous things on my plate, I don't want to battle with professors over marks."

Cori looks worried, but she nods. She's about to add something when my phone walks across our pile of materials as it vibrates. Her eyes widen when she sees the name on the screen, covering her mouth as she points at it. I peer at the device, groaning loudly when I see Lucille's picture glaring at me.

"Just fucking perfect," I mutter as I reach for it. I look at my friends, putting a finger to my lips as I swipe to answer. My finger hits 'speaker' so they can hear, then I speak. "Good evening, Lucille."

"Delores Drew, I have been trying to reach you since that wretched video got plastered all over the Prednet!"

And I've been trying to ignore you, but here we are.

"I'm sorry, Lucille. It took some time to heal from my injuries and afterward, the school was in a panic over the kids who didn't make it back." My friends give me a *look*, but I think it's time to bait my mother about this shit. She doesn't know they're here, and I want to find out exactly what she and her cronies are saying about the hundreds of disappearances.

"Piffle, Delores. There are missing students at every school. The moron at Capital Prep should have been handling it. Why would it affect your ability to return *my* phone call and texts? Don't lie to me or I'll…"

I pinch the bridge of my nose and grit my teeth as I finish her sentence. "Yes, you'll send Bruiser to teach me my place. I understand, Lucille."

"Exactly." Her smug confidence bleeds through even with one simple word, and Rufus' eyes flash in anger.

Holding up my hand to keep him from butting in, I consider how to use the information she let slip. None of us knew the other academies had missing kids, which means the number is far higher than estimated. Whatever the hoods are using the shifters for, it's on a global scale. That they've kept it quiet is astounding. I bite my bottom lip, unsure if I should push more, until Lucille interrupts my thoughts.

"Since I've rendered you speechless, you should know why I've been trying to reach you. You have duties to fulfill in the upcoming days that I expect to be honored to the letter. If you do not, your suffering will be far worse than ever before and I'll make sure it extends to all the ragamuffins you're associating with."

Irritation at her threats gets the best of me and I mutter, "Of course, it wasn't to make sure they did not permanently injure me or to congratulate me on my nearly impossible victory."

Her laugh is full of malice. "Obviously not, my chunky little brawler. You didn't embarrass me for once, but that buys you very little leeway."

I want to put my thumbs in her eyes and push.

"What do I need to do, Lucille?"

"That's better," she practically purrs into the receiver. "The Council has kept all students and staff at the academies during the holidays to prevent any further mishaps. You cannot repeat this as we have not informed the public yet. Barrington's people are working on the press release as we speak."

"But…"

"I didn't ask for your input, Delores! Shut up and listen to me. In lieu of holiday celebrations at home, each academy will hold a Yule Eve masked ball. Parents and age-appropriate siblings will get invited to attend, which means your father and I will be at Capital Prep to show the world our schools are safe."

My friends both cover their mouths before curses slip out and I flop onto my back, staring at the ceiling blankly. I wouldn't have the slightest issue staying at Cappie instead of heading home to the empty mansion, but having Bruno and Lucille *here* showing me off like a pony? Fucking kill me now. I'd rather swim through a pool of acid naked. I can't even fathom how horrible that's going to be, especially if I have to meet the parents of all these snooty celebrity kids.

"A ball?" I choke out. "It seems unsafe to… gather… such important people in one place."

Damn, that was pretty good, Dolly.

Lucille sniffs, and I can almost hear her rolling her eyes at me. "Delores, the Council is never without guards and security measures. We've already flooded the campus with protection. Surely you're not dim enough to have missed the Khan guards?"

"N-No, I didn't miss them. I thought it was because of the deaths."

"Ha. Not hardly, you little fool. We're slowly building up the precautions for this event." The line muffles for a moment and when she comes back, her voice is even sharper. "Figure something out to wear and you'd better look like the heir to the Drew seat, even if you're not. I will not tolerate being made a fool at the biggest event of the year."

"Yes, Lucille," I murmur as I continue looking at the colorful patterns on the walls. "I understand."

"You'd better."

She hangs up, and I let out a long, heavy breath. Talking to my mother is always difficult, but allowing my friend to hear her and see how I have to behave is worse. I feel angry and numb, but I can't process it because I'm still reeling from all the information we just learned.

Did she tell me on purpose to test me or is she really rattled enough to have dropped a secret?

"Your mother is a see-you-next-Tuesday," Cori finally says. "And she's *definitely* up to something. With all the shit going on, why the hell would they risk putting all the leaders in one place?"

"Not just here, but at all the functioning schools," Rufus points out. "I hate to say it, but I think those old fuckers are setting a trap for the hoods using the kids as bait."

I swipe my hands over my face, letting out a brief shriek of frustration before I respond. "Unfortunately, I agree with you, Ru-Ru. I think the assholes who run everything are offering sacrifices to catch the bad guys. And fuck knows none of them will get harmed, so we're all cannon fodder."

"Who's cannon fodder?" I look over to see Felix prowling into my room, the others hot on his tail. He must have heard my shriek from the living room.

"We are," I say dejectedly as I point to everyone. "All of us. Lucille just dropped a few bombs on us."

"Then we'll handle it like we handle everything else—together," Aubrey says as he stomps over to liberate Jinx from Rufus' hold. "Whatever they are cooking up can't be that complex."

"It's not." Rufus smirks. "But it's going to require a *lot* of planning on our part just the same."

Fitz frowns and hops on the bed, pulling me onto his lap. "Why's that Cotton-Eyed Bro?"

"Because we have to go to a goddamn ball as bait." The guys look at me, blinking in surprise, so I add, "Where my parents will be in attendance."

"Shit."

I nod at Chess, then sigh again. "Which begs the question…"

Cori's eyes dance as she leaps to her feet, bouncing on my bed. "What are we gonna wear?"

I think we fixed her Giselle moping.

Born For This

Felix

WHILE THE PRINCESS AND HER FRIEND FOCUS ON EXAMS, IT LEFT the rest of us to finish going through the shit from the vaults and come up with a plan for the night of the ball. I don't trust the mercs from my father's security for a second—and the Council shouldn't either—so I'm busy working with Fitz on the map of the school. We believe the only entrance to the tunnels is in the spot Holliday located, so that will need guards. There are several other ingress and egress points beside the primary route that sneaky infiltrators could use, so Zhenga is contacting as many of the Pred Games people she knows are trustworthy to help us smuggle in protection we can actually depend on.

My twin is hacking like a madman, consuming everything from energy drinks to narcotics to stay awake. He's hoping to find more information on the other academies' missing and whispers about the event on the dark web. I had to take his exam drives to his classes for him so he didn't have to stop working. His computer nerds shrugged and went to work at their stations while I sat at the front drawing diagram after diagram of the campus. My goal is to cover the gaps in physical coverage and camera blind spots, but this is pretty last minute. Every time I try to do it with the amount of people we have so far, it fails, and a group of invaders can slink through the spaces I can't fill.

My phone buzzes and I pick it up, seeing the group chat light up.

TigerWoody: How's the exam going, bro? I'm striking out big time on the academies, but I think I found some breadcrumbs about the event.

TigerKing: Tell me.

CSpot: Spill it, Fitzy. And I can hear your teeth chattering from here.

TigerWoody: Okay, okay! Chillax guys. So I found this thread on a message board talking about the full moon.

EmoBatman: Fitz, that could be magic users planning normal things. Moon phases are—

LustyLibrarian: The full moon in December is on Yule Eve. That is not a coincidence.

TigerWoody: That's what I thought!

TigerKing: Fitz, for the love of Jupiter's sandals...

TigerWoody: Alright, alright. I found this group of weirdos talking about the full moon and ceremonies. They had a couple separate forums—more than five, so don't ask. I don't know if our magic assholes are hiding among normie magic peeps, if that's even a thing.

EmoBatman: It would be brilliant to hide in plain sight and speak in codes.

LustyLibrarian: How the fuck is the dark web plain sight?

TigerWoody: Look, Pepper Pants, not everyone hates tech as much as you. And people who have to live in hiding definitely take refuge there. I'm pretty sure the crap they're blathering on about with opening doors and harnessing the moon and blessing the waters is about the ball. But I could use some help of the poetic variety, if you know what I mean.

EmoBatman: I'll come assist once my Victorian Lit exam is over.

LustyLibrarian: Fuck that. I'll come cover the stupid exam and you go to Fitz.

TigerKing: I still can't figure out how to close the gaps in security, FYI.

TigerWoody: Is there a nerdy looking little fuck that smells like Funyuns?

Arching my brow, I rise from the chair to walk around the room. When I hit the scent, I almost recoil, but pull back before the kid sees me. He's greasy as hell and looks like he might be from one of the vulpine families.

TigerKing: Found him.

TigerWoody: Show him the map and say it's from a MMORPG I'm designing. He'll believe you because that's all the douche thinks about. Ask him to find the holes and calculate how to close the net with finite resources.

TigerKing: Can we trust him?

TigerWoody: Fuck, no. That's what the ruse is for, big bro. Do that and I bet he gives you enough bullshit to either fix it or know what we need to fix it. The kid's a savant with this shit.

LustyLibrarian: Good call, Fitzgerald.
Rennie, I'm on my way to your classroom.

EmoBatman: I'll be waiting.

TigerWoody: Over and out, Snowman.

Hopefully, Chess is having better luck wrangling all the ordering the Princess' friends demanded.

After all, it wouldn't be a ball if we showed up wearing sweatpants and hoodies.

"DID YOU GET IT FIXED?"

The second I walk through the arch to the spacious living area, Fitz yells over his shoulder. He's been mainlining so much shit to stay focused and awake that Chess is right—he's almost vibrating. Heading to the sideboard, I pour myself a bourbon and join him in the plush cushions. "You were right. The kid finished his exam in a blink and snatched the paper like a golem with a ring. It was fucking hysterical."

"What did he come up with?"

My brother isn't even turning his head as he watches lines of move on several black windows on his screen. I'd worry about him, but Fitz does his best work when he's utterly obsessed with things. Dolly is the deepest obsession I've ever seen him juggle, and figuring out how to keep her safe is fueling this marathon of hacking. I don't think I could pull him away if I wanted to. Perhaps the Princess could, but she's probably shuttered in her room with her friends hoping she won't get flunked in her classes. They only have three days of exams left before the weekend, so it's crunch time.

"He said we need five more people, or it's a bust." I sigh, rolling my head back to look at the ceiling. "Z's tapped out because of the holidays. You've already conscripted César. The winged fuckers don't have other friends besides the crew, and Dolly's friends don't want to reveal the magic secrets yet. The badger is afraid his cagey old grandmother will try to take advantage of it. Where are we going to get the five we need?"

A throat clears and I look over my head to see Aubrey standing at the edge of the sofa. "Perhaps we're not thinking broadly enough, Raj. Every person we place doesn't have to be a fighter; they need to defend. Correct?"

I nod. "Yeah. But…"

"If our friends in the armory were to 'borrow' some distance weaponry that would at least slow down the invaders, we could use less beefy sentinels in some of the less likely target areas." The dragon scratches his chin, then gives me a mischievous smile that's very unlike him. "Some of my research friends spend quite a bit of time in dangerous war zones and climates. They are not built for hand-to-hand combat, but they can definitely throw grenades or shoot bows like Raina's."

Ohhhhh.

"Are these the same people being prevented from leaving the country for their projects?" He nods and I chuckle. "And they're pretty pissed, I assume."

"Cornelius Bathwaite is one angry goddamn walrus at the moment. He's huge when not shifted and lethal in the water. It would be a perfect fit for one end of the river. Plus, his sister Amelia is twice his size, and the restriction has kept her from studying Antarctic migration during the high season. If they have the right equipment, they'll hold up both ends."

"I could move two of the stronger preds from those positions…" I pull out the map that the greasy vulpine helped me configure, snapping my fingers when I don't have a pen. Fitz throws one at me from his nest, once again not taking his eyes off the display. "Yes, that could work. Who else do you have?"

"Who else does he have for what?"

My eyes connect with Dolly's the minute she stumbles into the room. Her hair is secured away from her face in two adorable ponytails and she's wearing an enormous pair of sweatpants that must be the dragon's. Her shirt is torn and ripped to make a crop top, but I recognize it as one of Fitz's league shirts. She looks tired, but absolutely adorable. "We're strategizing, Princess. You don't have to worry about anything besides exams and primping for the ball at the moment."

"Ugh, that damn thing," she grumbles as she throws herself over the back of the sofa. "I can't believe I have to be dressed to impress my parents and a bunch of pretentious jackwads, *plus* I have to be ready for something bad to happen. It feels very unfair, and I'd like to register a complaint."

Rufus and Cori appear in the doorway, skirting around Aubrey to hop into the spots they've been claiming on the other side of our sunken nest. The badger wraps his arm around the bear, laughing as she yawns big enough to swallow the Captain whole. Dolly reaches into her pocket and tosses a wrapped candy at her, snickering when it bonks her friend in the forehead.

"Easy, children," I scold, pretending to frown. "It's all fun and games until someone gets hurt. None of you look as if you've slept in days. You're as bad as my brother."

Fitz finally looks up from the computer, his eyes bloodshot and his expression petulant. "Fuck off, Felix, I'm gonna make sure our girl is safe if it kills me."

"For fuck's sake, baby." Princess crawls over me, narrowly missing the soft bits, as she clambers to steal the laptop from his lap. He yells in protest, but she puts her fingers to his lips. "You're recording the logs. We can review it tomorrow. For now, you're going to eat actual food and put this aside."

"But…"

"We're about studied out for History," Cori says with another yawn. "I think everyone needs a break. What do you say, Ru-Ru?"

He nods, catching yawn and releasing one of his own. "Agreed. Mexican? I could seriously ravage some tacos."

"Only if there're margaritas," Fitz mumbles. "Margaritas and tacos are like me and my Baby Girl—inseparable."

Aubrey snorts, pulling out his phone. "I'll text Chess and Rennie for their orders, then we can have it brought in. I hate the idea of those muscle bound twits at the gates touching our food to inspect it, but I don't think any of us need to cook tonight."

Exhaustion creeps in as I flick through the menus on the Pred-Dash app. "We're all tapped out. It's been a long seven days and the next seven won't be any better."

At least we're safe here, curled together and getting ready to face the music together.

Just Like Fire

Delores

Letting out a loud war whoop, I boogie my way down the steps to greet Kirby. He gives me his happy quokka smile, waving his hands excitedly. This was my last exam of the semester and even with gloom lurking over the horizon, I'm stoked. "It's *done!*"

"You made it, Dolly. We knew you would." Kirby reaches into his belt bag and pulls out a plastic container with a single red velvet cupcake. "Raina wanted to make certain you could celebrate immediately. She figured out these were your favorites through Mister Chester."

My eyes light up and I snatch it, opening it to peel the paper and shovel it into my mouth eagerly. I caught the bunny shaped sprinkles and that he called Chess by his full name, but I'm too busy moaning with delight to comment on either. Raina makes amazing food and I don't get enough chances to sample it in the dining hall because I'm a spoiled brat with a live-in chef. "Mmmmphh mmmmmmmmmMMMMM!"

Kirby laughs as Bowser comes running up to join us, his expression full of amusement at the icing and crumbs on my face. "Raina will be so pleased that you like it."

I close my eyes as I chew, nodding my pleasure at the unexpected treat. The prospect of ugliness coming within the next couple of days has me trying to enjoy every second of happiness as it comes. I don't think I'm going to die or anything, but I also don't want to miss out on good shit because I'm worried about the bad. The past few months have shown me I can't predict what's coming around the corner—not with two powerful factions preparing for war with all of us as pawns in the middle. It would be foolish not to bask while I can.

Maybe I'm getting wiser, maybe I'm just letting go of the past and what I can't control—either way, I'm not letting manipulative twatmuffins live rent-free in my head anymore.

"That was delicious," I mumble as I dig in my bag for a tissue to wipe my face. "Man, Raina can bribe me with baked goods *any day*. No wonder you guys always look so damn cheerful."

Bowser snorts and mutters, "She's good at a lot of things worth grinning about."

My eyes pop open, and I cover my mouth as I giggle. Once I stop, I pretend to give him a stern look. "*Bowser*. You cad."

"She's going to murder you, mate," Kirby says with a sigh. "Don't mind him, Dolly. He and Percy can be absolutely filthy once they get comfortable with people."

Winking at the admonished quokka, I shrug. "I've got a few of those myself. I won't be nearly as flustered when the dirty jokes don't revolve around me."

"Raina agrees with you." Bowser winks at me and jerks his head toward the tunnel. "Shall we get you back to your suitors before they come looking?"

I squint as I look over the campus green. More students are pouring out of buildings, but most of them look depressed rather than gleeful. "Yeah. I don't know how people are going to behave after getting the news that they're trapped here for the break. Let's hit the bricks."

We head for the tunnel, my eyes on the flying preds as usual. I know they're not supposed to do anything to other students, but the circling has bothered me from day one. Avians at Apex had their own areas for stretching their wings to fly, but here, the winged are given far more freedom. Kirby tugs on my blazer sleeve, knocking me out of my head.

"Why do they worry you, Dolly?"

I frown, shaking my head. "I don't know, Kirby. Something about the way there's always some of them up there feels wrong. It could be the rabbit in me, but I have this very perturbed feeling when I see them."

"I agree that it's unusual for there to be preds in the air so consistently, but the rules are different here—not always in good ways," Bowser grumbles as he waves his smaller badge at the tunnel door. "The Captain hates the lax standards here as much as he hated the occasionally overbearing rules at Apex."

"The Captain is an exacting shifter. I like that he refuses to compromise simply because others disagree," I reply as we walk down the echoing tube. "Your crew has become indispensable to my family, you know."

Kirby gives me a pleased look, his smiley face tinting with color as Bowser huffs a bit. "Thank you, Dolly. Outside of His Grace, we never expected to find a pred who treats us as well, and you and yours. I think even Percy's cousin Argyle has taken a shine to you. She's a tough nut to crack."

It's my turn to blush. "The ladies in the infirmary saved my life when I first got to Apex and I've been trying to pay them back ever since. They knew Cori and Rufus before me and took their word that I wouldn't harm them. I don't leave anyone behind if they've been a good friend, and neither does Rennie, it seems."

"Yes, you are very similar that way. He has a body of stone, but his heart is as soft as cotton." Kirby swipes his card so we can exit the tube, following me up the stairs. "Raina says he harbors a great wound that has never healed. She's convinced you can help."

Help my boyfriend heal his centuries old broken heart, save the shifters from war… the Fates aren't asking much of me this year, are they?

"I hope I can, too. Rennie deserves to be happy without the past holding him back."

Bowser arches a brow as we approach the back door. "We all do, Dolly."

I think I was just schooled by a shifter named after a pixelated lizard who kidnaps princesses.

"Do you think we can get the triplets a pass onto campus for the ball? I'd hate to waste looking that fine without the proper amount of adoration." Rufus bows his brows and I throw one of Chess's parmesan garlic fries at him. "What?"

"You aren't the only one hoping the fancy shit I'm creating will get them laid," Cori says with an impish grin. "I mean, I know none of you have seen what Ru-Ru and I have up our sleeves, but *trust me*, it's going to turn some heads. I emailed Luc to help with the designs and…"

"Wait a minute!" I mock glare at my bestie, wagging a finger. "Since when are you emailing Luc?"

Her face turns bright red and she mumbles, "Since I showed him some of my stuff when he came to your first match. He's been really supportive… like, I think he might let me do a work study at his place in the summer."

"Coco, that's fucking amazing!" I launch myself across the cushions, displacing the cheetah lying with his head in my lap. Chess only grumbles a little, stealing my spot next to Fitz as I hug my bubbly friend tightly. "You're so good at design and costuming; high fashion would be lucky to have you."

Rufus snorts, huffing in feigned affront. "I help."

"Of course you do, but you have a criminal empire to run while banjos play or something," I shoot back. "Coco is free to take the runaways by storm."

Felix clears his throat, looking at me practically sitting in Rufus' lap so I could hug Cori. "I take it we should say we're wearing a Cori..." He frowns, looking at the polar bear for a moment. "I feel like an absolute ass, but I don't think you've ever told me your last name."

Cori's face gets even redder, and she ducks her head. It occurs to me I don't think *I've* ever heard her say it, either. *What in the actual hell?* Rufus doesn't look at me when I swing my gaze to him, suddenly very interested in his phone and a chat window. "Okay, what is going on with you two? Why is Cori's last name such a big deal?"

"Because... because..." Cori fumbles a little and worry takes root in my gut.

"Holy shit!" Fitz yells, waving his phone in the air.

My body tenses and I leap off of Rufus, crouching as I look around the room for danger. When it doesn't come, I glare at him in annoyance. "Not funny, Fitzy. I was ready to mighty morph."

He grins cheekily. "Not my intent, Baby Girl, but you can mighty morph anytime. I *love* stroking your fur."

His twin sighs heavily and looks at Chess, who whacks Fitz in the back of the head for him. "*Why* did you just shout, Fitz?"

"I know why she hasn't told you yet," he sing-songs with a mischievous smirk. "And what it is."

"Easy, Khan," Rufus growls through his pointy teeth. "I won't let you—"

"Oh, take a hit, gangster. I'm no threat to Coco-cabana. We love her here, even if her family doesn't."

My brows furrow. Cori always acted like her mother was a normal, loving one versus my nightmare in Leopartins. "Cori? What are they talking about?"

She swallows hard and gives me a sorrowful expression. "My actual mother was amazing. She died right before I came to Apex. When I talk about my mother, I definitely mean her. But, um, my father? Not so much, especially since he married into my step-mother."

"Well, that's okay. Lucille's awful, the Raj is a cocksucker, their parents disowned them…" I point to each of the guys and shrug. "We will not judge you by your parents."

"You might once I tell you I'm a Bouvier," she mutters.

I blink. "Bouvier, as in *Le Maison de Bouvier*? Bouvier as in the fashion designer who went missing climbing Mt. Everest with her husband, Bouvier? The heiress everyone thought was…"

Cori nods miserably. "That's the one. We never found her, but my dad held a funeral and everything. People who die that far up aren't usually found, and he had to… declare her dead for the business to move on. I don't tell people because it makes them treat me differently."

"No *wonder* you're so fucking good at this shit. You were probably born with a needle in your paw," I marvel as I remember how skilled she was at teaching me to do complicated stitches. "Luc would be stupid not to scoop you up if your family doesn't want you. Good for him."

"Told you she wouldn't care," Rufus drawls as he tosses his phone down. "Dolly is the least pre-possessing girl I've ever met. She wouldn't have cared if you revealed your parents were ax murderers or, worse, humans."

I roll my eyes at him, then give my embarrassed friend another hug. "He's right. I don't give a shit if your family is full of snooty French designers."

"They're on the European Council—at least, her father is," Aubrey says. "But so is someone from my clash and Rennie's clutch and lots of others. That doesn't mean they're all privy to the crooked shit going on now."

"So… we should tell any media people they let in that we're wearing a Bouvier original?" Felix says, bringing us back to the original topic.

Cori snorts and shakes her head. "Fuck, no. I don't want to be associated with them. Say it's a 'Coco' original. That's what I'm gonna call my brand."

Despite the exhaustion of the past week and worry over what's coming, I feel a genuine smile come over my face. Knowing my guys trust my friends and they all get along is a boon. Everyone in this room is important to me, and I know I'm going to need them to get through the bullshit coming. Hearing Cori talk about her brand like we actually *have* a future after we do all this crap gives me hope. I'm not sure when I started worrying that we might not have one, but now… I'm good.

"Then we'd better be ready to work the room, so you get lots of press before it all goes to shit." I wink at her, then crawl back over the cushions to squeeze between Rennie and Aubrey this time. As if on command, Rennie's wings pop free and wrap around, hiding me from view. Laughing, I poke my head out. "Not yet, silly. We're fine for the moment."

"*Ma petite*, our inner beasts will get more protective as we get closer to danger. The gargoyle is not happy. We don't know what will happen at the ball. I suspect the others are having the same problem, but my reaction is harder to hide."

I look at the rest of my guys, and they're studiously *not* looking at me. *Big scaredy cats… some literally.* I lean in and kiss Ren's nose, then move to Aubrey. Once I do that, I crawl over to the ambush of cats, sprawling across them with a grin.

"Annnnnd that's our cue to make like a tree," Rufus says as he tugs Cori up. "Lovely food, Chess, and good time had by all. We'll hunker down in the reading room in the library for the night. It has excellent couches and pillows."

I lift my hand, waving at them as they tromp off, unable to take my eyes off the dark look in Felix's eyes. "Good night!"

"Oh, it's going to be, Princess. You've been a very good girl this week."

Fuck yeah, I have.

Feeling Good

Chess

I look down at my angel with the hunger of my cat shining in my eyes. The twins' tigers are similarly shimmering just under their skin and I know whatever happens tonight is only going to cement Dolly's bond to our family even deeper. Felix rises, winking at me as he leans down to scoop our girl up and turns to the winged shifters.

"To the Bunnycave, gentlemen."

They laugh, joining Fitz and I as we leap to follow our exiled royal. The playfulness is not new, but since he and my angel got together, it's returned from the dead. Felix has stopped punishing himself for the past and it makes my heart happy to see it. I look over at Aubrey and Ren as they smile like idiots—something very unlike them until last year—and a sense of fulfillment sparkles through me like champagne.

This is what we're meant to be, and Dolly gave it to us.

"Chessie, get a move on!"

My Angel's voice calls to me from the hallway to her room and I chuckle as Felix boots the door open with a grunt. Her delighted laugh echoes off the high ceilings of her chamber, and I watch her bounce as the tiger tosses her on the bed with a smirk. She sprawls out on the mess of tangled black satin sheets, her pastel rainbow hair a stark contrast to the inky color. Fitz is already rummaging through her toy chest, muttering to himself excitedly, but Felix is eyeing her with a wicked gleam in his amber eyes. He's plotting something and I'm going to wait until he works it out in his head.

Strategy is one of his gifts, after all.

"Fitz," he barks suddenly. "I think the dragon needs his ropes."

Aubrey's face lights up as he runs to join the tiger in rummaging through the trunk. I arch a brow at Felix, but he doesn't seem worried at all; in fact, he looks extremely pleased. He peels his shirt off, jerking his head at Ren and me to do the same. Once we're bared, he walks over to my angel, looking down at her with love shining in his eyes. She hasn't moved, and she doesn't look concerned, which is a good sign.

"Princess, have they tied you yet?"

Dolly shakes her head as he leans over her to brush his lips over her temple. "No, Sir. Not beyond wrists."

"Then I want you to pay close attention. You need to understand everything so you're safe—something we will ensure as long as you do as you're told. Understand?"

"Yes, Sir," she breathes as he helps her to a sitting position and sits down next to her.

The Raj smiles gently. "Good girl. Now, Aubrey is going to tie you into a harness that will feel intensely tight, but not cut off circulation. You must stay still so he can focus the knots on the right places and not damage nerves. Once he's done, we'll get you ready. What's the word again, Princess?"

"Beetlejuice. I say it and everything stops."

Rennie grins at her, his eyes dark as they cut between her and the others as they pull out the equipment. "It doesn't matter why, *ma petite*. If it hurts, if you're scared, if you don't like it… none of that will get you in trouble. *Oui?*"

"*Oui, mon chere*[1]," she whispers and all three of us groan.

What is it about French that makes you horny? Fuck if I know, but hearing it from my angel just made my cock turn to iron.

"Teach her more of that, Broody Bi-lingual," Fitz yells. "My dick could drive nails right now."

"*Votre souhait est mon ordre*[2], *Fitzgerald.*" This time Aubrey rumbles and smoke rings drift over towards us as he mutters to himself. "Flames likes it, too."

"Who the hell *wouldn't?*" I ask as I lean in to kiss Dolly softly. "You're going to look beautiful, Angel. Once you're ready, Felix will tell us all what to do."

"Should I call him—"

"*No*," we all say in unison, and she dissolves into giggles at our horror.

"Oh, that's going in my pocket for later. Just when you least expect it." Her eyes are full of bratty promise and Felix huffs a curse. We just gave her the perfect way to set all of us off at once without meaning to.

Aubrey gives her a dark glare as he comes over with the jute ropes. "Get all the sass out now, little one. Then you're ours for tonight."

"Fitzy," she wrinkles her nose and pretends to pout, but no one takes it seriously, least of all my hyper mate.

He bounces over happily with his arms full of lube and a harness that makes me choke on a couch. *Is he serious? I thought he was fucking joking.* "No take backs, Baby Girl. But I promise you'll have fun."

I'd say so; he's taking this pretty seriously when he breaks out that stuff.

"Stay still," Felix reminds her as Aubrey wraps the rope in slow, careful lines around her ribs.

It's fascinating from an artistic standpoint, and I'm almost entranced until Fitz grabs me, tugging me over to the bed to watch. His arms band around me as he leans back against the huge dragon headboard, nuzzling my ear. "She looks beautiful, mmm, love? See how he's binding around her pretty tits?"

I nod, sucking in a shuddering breath as his hands wander past the waistband of my sweats to grip my cock. "Yes… gorgeous."

Felix winks at me as he moves closer to Dolly. "Are you okay, Princess?"

Her answer is a low moan as Aubrey adjusts the jute criss-crossing over her shoulders to her back. He's focused as hell, which is impressive given the scents now permeating the room. Ren takes one of the ropes from him and pulls the chair from her vanity over, leaping onto it and pulling a thick ring out of the ceiling. I blink, looking up at Fitz over my head, and he laughs softly.

"Use your words, Baby Girl. Chessie wants to see you dangle and Felix won't let them pull until you say it." His hand squeezes my dick at the base and my hips arch up. "I promise you're going to like my part of this, so be good for the hard asses."

"Yessss. Good. All good." Dolly hisses. Her body wants to move as Aubrey finishes tying the knots between her shoulder blades and it shows, but she's fighting every instinct because Felix said so. She's watching us, occasionally licking her lips as Fitz teases her by almost pulling the cloth away from his hand.

If they aren't impressed, I am and I'm not ashamed to admit it.

"Are you ready, *ma petite*? He's used the shinju so you'll be facing the cats and we're only going to pull you up a little the first time so you get used to it. I'll be right here to adjust after the tatu hitch."

My Angel nods, still watching us hungrily. A flush creeps up her body as the dragon clips the line, and she's pulled upward to hang about a foot off the bed. The scent of arousal gets heavier, making me squirm against the tiger behind me. She's definitely flooded now, and my cheetah wants more. As if he can sense it, Fitz pulls my joggers down, exposing my cock to the air and cups my balls.

"Be good, Chessie. You're going to get filled up soon. Red Hot and I have a plan," he whispers into my ear. "For now, enjoy the show."

My hips buck and I nod, panting a little as Felix comes up behind our girl, giving her a light smack on the ass. She whimpers, making the ropes swing a bit as she wiggles helplessly. He winks at me before giving the same treatment to the other cheek, then dips his fingers between her legs. The rumble of his cat calls to mine when he draws them back coated in shiny fluids, then licks them clean.

"More, pleaseeeee…" Dolly whines. She can't reach out because of her bindings, but her toes are scraping the sheets, trying to find purchase to move closer to Ren.

The gargoyle smirks, looking over at his lover with a smug expression. "I *like* when she begs, Flames. Should I get the harness now?"

His question is to Aubrey, but they both look at Fitz with arched brows. I saw what they picked and suddenly, I get why my mate had three bottles of lube when he came back from the trunk. My mind races as I imagine what they've got planned and how I fit into that diagram. The pictures make pre cum bead on my cock— however I'm positioned, I'm ready for this.

"Do it, Dark Flight," Fitz says as he lets go of my dick and sits us up. He looks like he's going to clap with glee when he grabs the bottle off the bed, handing it to me. "I can't wait to see her face."

Dolly's eyes flit from me to Aubrey to Ren, seeing the bottles of lube being passed around. The older twin strips off his clothes, prowling over to our bunny and sitting on the bed. He pulls her closer, kissing her hungrily while he plays with her nipples. The soft growls from them distract me until I smell the cherry scent of Fitz's favorite lube. While Felix has my angel writhing, Renard approaches from behind to buckle the harness around her thighs.

"Holy fuck," she gasps as her lips break from the tiger's. Her eyes get round as saucers when the smirking Frenchman slides the slicked vibrator inside of her, then reaches around to adjust the dildo positioned on the front of it. "I have a dick!"

Everything stops for a moment and we all look at one another, then burst out laughing as she squirms on the rope, making it flop a bit. Fitz scrambles onto the bed in delight, grabbing her face to kiss her before he turns back to us. "All we had to do to get her to smile was tie her up and give her a cock. Someone make a note of that."

Aubrey rolls his eyes, but I can see his mirth. The dragon tugs his clothes off and this time, I gape. *How the* fuck *do Ren and my angel take that goddamn thing?* Renard catches my gaze and bobs his brows before he flicks the remote on Dolly's vibe. She moans and curses, swinging a bit more from her hook.

"Do not cum, *ma petite*. Felix will tell you when it's time." Ren pulls off the rest of his clothes and walks over to the end of the bed, his hand rubbing over where Felix spanked her. He looks over at Aubrey and crooks his finger. "Come, *mon ami*. I'm ready."

I look at them for a moment, then back at Fitz. "Someone tell me where to go."

My mate practically beams as he crawls over to sit on his haunches, facing my angel. "Chessie, get me ready, then I'll do you. Those assholes can take care of themselves."

Oh, shit. Did Aubrey and Fitz plan a fucking dick chain?

Nodding as he hands me the bottle of lube, I move to sit behind him. I drizzle the lube in my hand, warming it for a moment. "You need to relax, baby. Scoot forward a bit and lean forward on your hands."

A low moan comes from the winged duo, and I assume they're already prepping. Dolly is watching me as I slip a finger into Fitz, licking her lips hungrily as she pants. I don't know how she's holding on in that position, but our girl is stubborn when she wants to be. She won't give in if Felix told her not to—she can't.

"Fitzy, is he getting you ready for me?" she asks as her tongue darts over her lip.

"You know it, Baby Girl. You're going to fuck the shit out of me while I take him." Fitz grins wickedly, grunting as I continue stretching his ass. "And if you think that's hot, wait until you hear the rest."

Her gasp echoes off the walls when the gargoyle comes up behind her, slipping fingers in her ass as he murmurs, "I'm going to take you here and Flames will take me. The more he pushes, the further I'll go and the harder you'll take Fitz. Chess may want to be ready to walk funny."

My eyes narrow as I reach out to slick the lube along the dildo. "I can take it."

"What… What about Felix?" she pants as he continues to work her. "Where is he?"

"In your mouth, Princess." He nods at Ren and Aubrey, watching with a dark expression as the gargoyle lines up his cock behind her. "Now be a good girl and take Ren in."

His hands come around her, holding onto her breasts as he thrusts into her. "*Mon Dieu*, petite. You're so… hot and tight. Flames, you must hurry."

I look at Fitz, amused beyond belief that he's bottoming for our girl. "Time for you to get in position."

"Give me the lube, Chessie. I have a feeling no one will last long once the chain's in place." Fitz kisses me lightly, then gets into position in front of our girl.

Another shriek fills the air and I know the big ass dragon just pounded his way into the gargoyle. I look at her with a soft expression, still amazed she's okay with all this, then grab the dildo to position it against my mate's ass. Aubrey thrusts again and her hips propel forward, burying the strap-on in Fitz all the way to the hilt. He lets out a roar of pleasure, his eyes golden as he looks at me.

"Get. Over. Here. Now."

Scrambling into position, I wait for him, my body trembling with anticipation. By the time he has me ready, I'm almost incoherent with the need to be filled. The smells, the sight of him being split by Dolly and the sounds coming from the others are killing me. I don't know how the actual fuck Felix is sitting there so calmly, watching as he strokes his cock like we're putting on a show just for him.

Maybe we are.

"Fitz, take him. I want to feel her scream around me."

I'd look at the growling Raj, but that's when my lover buries himself in my ass and I can't do anything but bury my face in the satin. My voice is muffled, but when the next thrust ripples from Aubrey down the line to me, I damn near feel my eyes cross. The bed dips, and I assume Felix is getting into position. The muffled moan that comes from our girl tells me I'm right.

"Go," Felix commands.

His order must be for the dragon because that's when the pace picks up and the slap of skin gets louder. My eyes roll back in my head as Fitz spears me harder and faster, propelled by the chain behind him. Dolly's garbled moans and cries make me throb and I grit my teeth against the orgasm that's building so fast I can barely keep a hold of myself. "I… holy fuck, Fitz… Not gonna last… long…"

I've been teased and tortured while they got our girl ready and the force of this fucking is too goddamn much.

"Hold it until I say." The bark from my king is tinged with his power, and the shudder that runs through me is almost violent.

A low whine emanates from Dolly and growls fill the air as we all scent how close she is. The force of the thrusts increases again and I know for a fact every one of us in this hot AF chain is going to be walking funny. My head jerks up as I smell blood—my eyes bleed amber with the cheetah, sniffing until I realize it's Felix. She's nicked his cock. A burst of energy fills the air as Felix loses control of power he rarely uses and it makes my entire body wobble in submission.

"Felix… you're…"

There's a pop, then a low, husky voice chuckles darkly. "He's *mine.*"

My cheetah bursts free and I let out a yowl that makes my throat protest in pain. It's followed by the sound of the others' join in, roars echoing off the walls as their animals emerge unbidden.

Something tells me we're about to find out what happens when our bunny levels up.

The last thing I see before it goes dark is a rainfall of sparkles and blue lightning zinging around the room.

---

1. Yes, my dear.
2. Your wish is my command.

TEENAGERS

Aubrey

NONE OF US ARE REALLY SURE EXACTLY WHAT MY LUNCHABLE DID last week. She didn't mate with Felix—that requires a reciprocal action—but whatever makes her special inside definitely reared its head to leave a mark. Chess and Fitz were out like a light, just like her. The rest of us were dazed, but not unconscious, so we untied our precious bunny first, then cleaned everyone up. Rennie seemed baffled by the whole thing, so I didn't press him to see if it was some bullshit magic thing he could have warned us about.

But I think it was, and that raises some very specific questions that we've all studiously ignored in our pursuit of the warring factions.

There are far too many blank spaces in our understanding of snack size. She's not a pred, but was born to them according to everything on record. One could say it's nature versus nurture, but the emergence of her claws, fangs, and dominance says otherwise. She's hungry for life force like Ren and I—something I've only known mythical shifters to crave during my vast lifetime. Her emergence went into hyper-drive quickly and, despite having a few of the new shifter quirks, she learned to control various shifts easily. Hell, Dolly can even shift pieces like Rennie and no two-year-old shifter, even an alpha type, should gain control that quickly.

Her use of the lightning the night Apex exploded and the light show last week proves whatever forces are within her aren't just offensive toys. There's something different about her on a cellular level and I guarantee the reason why is a secret so closely guarded there may be less than a handful of people alive who know it. Snack size may occasionally pull on the persona of her wretched bio-donors, but she's not like them at all. I simply don't believe that's because she had a lovely nanny who taught her things as a child.

Delores Drew is a riddle wrapped in an enigma, and if we're going to figure out why she's been targeted, we need to explore her shrouded history.

"Hidey-ho, screamers. I've come to make you all acceptable in not-so-polite society." The badger has a cunning look on his face and I approve.

I don't know what he and the adorable polar bear did to get the multiple garment bags ready in time, but I'm grateful. Tonight is important on so many levels that I can hardly wrap my wings around them. We have to present a strong united front in this shark tank while still being on our guard against whatever might be coming. I've felt like we're gearing up for battle as I arranged all the players around the campus via video conferences throughout the week. I'm glad we have people on our side, but if this goes poorly, we're going to need more than a few friends to deal with the future.

There hasn't been an all-out shifter war on a global scale since the 1950s and I have no idea how it's going to play out now, especially against magic users.

"I hope to hell you didn't forget we need to be armed," Felix grumbles as he strides in behind him. "I don't trust ninety-eight percent of the assholes who will attend this godforsaken thing."

Rufus smirks. "Don't worry, Prof. Coco made sure you all have a few hidey-holes for the special gear you ordered."

Rolling my eyes, I walk over to Rennie, leaning to whisper, "Who the hell needs knives and shit when they have a dragon? It's like giving plain old guns to those Avengers guys."

"Are you insinuating you're our Hulk, Flames? I admit, green would look good on you." My mate gives me a fond smile and I shrug.

"You're not so bad yourself when you're full sized. The likelihood of anyone in the room coming close to the two of us is minimal." I take the bag from the badger as he comes over to us, nodding my thanks. He and the bubbly designer have been good friends for our bunny and they're becoming invaluable as team members. Even a solitary shifter like me recognizes that as a group, we're much stronger and more prepared to handle all the shit being thrown our way. "Thank you, Rufus."

He blinks, looking surprised, then gives me a genuine smile. "Anything for Dollypop, Professor D. Cori and I have been Team-Bunny from day one, you know."

"And we appreciate it, though not all of us show it," Rennie adds as he cuts his eyes to Fitz. "Though I suppose his teasing has always been an indicator that he's fond of someone."

"I've got cousins like that. Don't worry your pretty wings about me, gentlemen. I'm a survivor."

That, I am certain, is true.

Ren and I exit our room first, dressed in sharp three-piece tuxedos and shiny shoes. I can't quite figure out what the wacky sewing duo was thinking as I look at my mate in lavender with a white bow tie and myself in a similar get-up in spring green. Each piece is bespoke and fits perfectly—from the pants to the vest to the jacket— so I can't complain about that, only the odd Easter egg colors. Felix and Fitz come out next, followed by Chess, sporting matching tuxes in light blue, peach, and soft yellow. I still don't know if the assholes at this thing will accept our non-traditional, non-black tie attire, but I have to admit we're even coordinated down to our skin tones.

The youngest Bouvier takes her shit seriously.

"Anyone know why I look like something out of the 70s?" Felix mutters as he sweeps his hair out of his face. "I feel like a scoop of sorbet."

"Patience, boys," Cori says as she carefully exits the room. She and Rufus have Dolly squirreled away in again. She's got a mermaid-style getup with a train of ruffles three feet long trailing behind her and a glittery white bow in her sea green hair. "Did you find all the little pocketses for your shit?"

Fitz grins and walks over to give her a bear hug. "Sure did, Coco-cabana! You and the Country Consigliere did a good job. And you look hot AF, by the way. Your girl is gonna flip her ponytail."

She blushes and swats Fitz playfully before turning to us with her hands on her hips. "You all have to look hot and unbothered when you enter, like models, you know? Someone will *definitely* ask who you're wearing and *that* is my bonus for making all the spiffy adjustments to the gown you're about to see."

"Are you ready?" Rufus pokes his head out the door, rainbow hair color covering his usual white streaks. Cori nods and I arch a brow as he steps out in a shining pastel sharkskin suit that matches our tuxes. He has a white bow tie as well and suddenly, the theme smacks me in the face. "Behold, Thee Dress of the Season, worn by Miss Delores Drew, Queen of the Pred Games."

"Ruuuufuuuuuss!"

We laugh as we hear her groan at the moniker before she walks through the door. My eyes widen and I know my jaw hits the floor at the same time as the others when snack size floats across the floor.

"Son of a bitch," Chess whispers.

Her long unicorn hair is half pinned up, decorated with the one item I insisted her friend work into the outfit—a sparkling rose gold crown with baby pink diamonds. It's something I came into possession of many, many years ago, and I had to sneak out to my main horde with Rennie at night to fetch it. Her dress is the same hue as the diamonds, strapless, and has an enormous tulle bottom like a damn princess. There's a white faux wrap around her shoulders, making her look even more like royalty.

"Our damn tuxes match her hair," Fitz says with a grin. He bounces on his toes for a second, clapping his hands. "Our tuxes match her hair! It's brilliant!"

Dolly flushes and looks at all of us, her big blue eyes unsure. "Is this okay? I mean, I know, I'm like a fucking walking marshmallow, but… it has *pockets*!"

I grin with evil glee as she pulls her phone out of a mass of material in one hand and a folded knife in her other. Rennie coughs, then snorts, and before I know it, we're all laughing. Of all the things she could be happy about, the pockets are definitely the most 'Dolly' of them all. "Good thing. The food may be inedible at this thing. Chess should slip you a few treats to hide in that giant mess."

"Good idea!" she says, reaching down to lift the big skirt so she can scurry to the kitchen. "Come on, Chessie. Aubrey's plan is brilliant."

Cori groans, stomping her foot. "She'd better not spill anything on that. I want perfect pictures before shit goes to hell, and it's covered in blood. Perfect. Do you clowns hear me?"

Felix holds his hand up, his expression amused. "Relax, Cori. I promise we'll all pose so your excellent work gets seen by important people. Fitz and I know how important it is to stick it to your shitty parents in the most spectacular manner possible."

"Amen, Prof. Coco deserves to show them she's not defective."

I hold up my phone, hoping to calm frayed nerves. "How about Rennie takes one of you and Cori, then we'll set up a few more before we go? I believe we have a few minutes before the Captain and his crew arrive to escort us to the main building. At least those will flit off to the cloud thingy before anything gets ruined."

Ren leans in, grabbing my phone and snapping a selfie with it before I can even protest. "Great idea, Flames. Very unlike you to admit tech might save the day. Everyone, add this to your calendar."

"Shut up," I grumble. "Let's do this and get our asses to the big fancy trap—I mean, the ball."

"Word," Fitz says as he fist bumps me. "I can't wait to piss people off."

Excellent.

BY THE TIME RUFUS AND CHESS GOT ALL THE SHOTS THEY WANTED pushed into the air, the Captain showed up with his entire motley crew. Raina spent the entire walk 'oohing' and 'ahhing' over the girls' dresses, which made the lunchable blush as pink as her giant dress. Not one of them would tell us how she's supposed to do anything but look beautiful if the shit hits the fan, but I trust Dolly's friends wouldn't leave her stranded in yards of tulle.

At least, I don't think so.

The trip through the tunnel gave me pause because I've long thought of it as a choke point. Having to walk under the river to classes in an enclosed space with locks on either end was a major factor in getting the crew to stay with Dolly all semester. Both Felix and I were uncomfortable with her being trapped under-water with someone who wanted to do her harm and I have no fewer concerns about it now. The damn thing is a menace if you have bad actors on campus and I wonder how many times smaller preds have suffered a terrible fate in this monstrosity.

I flick my badge at the scanner, waiting for something to go wrong, but it doesn't. The Captain and Bowser lead the way onto the campus green, followed by Felix, then Dolly on the arms of Chess and Fitz. Kirby and Banjo form the next layer in front of Rufus and Cori, then Percy and Holliday, while Rennie and I bring up the rear. We're taking zero chances that some nefarious motherfucker can ambush us and get to our girl tonight.

"Look at how the Student Center is lit up!" Dolly gasps as we cross the quad. "It's twinkling like the stars."

"Too bad they didn't spend more money on security rather than these fucking lights," Rennie mutters and I hum my agreement.

It's not surprising the Council and the school have gone all out for this event, especially because the students are fancy hostages during the break. But it pisses me off they haven't considered inviting all these outsiders and goddamn press onto campus completely negates the effect of the stupid lockdown. Certainly, many of the big names will be recognizable, but dozens of small families and staff for the event will be unknown. The whole thing begs for bad juju to come knocking and my dragon wants to lock everyone in my family up where it's safe.

I can't, though. This is a chance to do a great deal of sleuthing and all the players are in the house.

"Anyone else feel like we're in a rich people's version of *Murder on the Orient Express* tonight?" Fitz asks. "I know they were all rich, but you know what I mean. All these scheming dicklickers and their rancid kids, plus the droves of outsiders? The damn ball is bait and the Council or Society or who the fuck ever is hoping to shut down the magic twats when they attack."

Dolly sighs, patting his hand. "Yes, baby. We're all being used as bait and it sucks, but what can we do? If nothing happens, we eat crappy food, do some snooping with the suspects, and go home tipsy. Conversely, if the hoods attack and everything goes off the rails, we'll do what we have to."

Felix holds his hand up as we approach the building. "No discussing secret shit inside. Make notes on your phone or whatever you have to do, but say nothing that could be picked up with spells or good hearing. The crew will change into server gear so they can circulate in the crowd. No one goes off alone—period. Not to the bathroom, not to peek up the Princess' petticoats, nothing. Understood?"

"I am *not* wearing petti—"

"Not the point, Baby Girl." Fitz grins and tweaks her nose. "Felix is right on this one. We have to be smart. Divided is how everyone gets picked off one by one."

"Fine. But if any of you guys think you're not dancing with me tonight, you'd better sack up and get your Prince Charming on. No fucking way I'm dressed like Cinderella and I don't get the full experience." She looks at each one of us, then turns back to the open door to the Dupree Center. "Why is everyone standing in the rotunda like a bunch of lemmings?"

"Because, *ma petite*, you are right. This is a real ball and they will not let anyone in until they're announced." Rennie looks almost gleeful, and I roll my eyes.

Aphrodite save us from the hopeless romantic having a moment.

Canon in D

Delores

This is such utter horseshit.

They packed the antechamber to the gills with students, families, and visiting dignitaries like a poorly planned festival. If someone wanted to attack right now, they'd all be well-dressed fish in a damn barrel. I told the guys to hold back so we could huddle just outside the doors in the shadows—not inside where it smells like the perfume counter at Bergdorf's. It feels like we've been waiting for ages, but luckily, Fitz has been keeping me entertained. People have been passing us by as we stay out of the limelight, and it makes me chuckle that they've written us off as unimportant.

Suddenly, speakers above my head play *Canon in D* by Pachelbel, and I huff. Anyone with a hint of taste wouldn't bring in their fancy guests to the world's most overused wedding march. "Handel's *Queen of Sheba* or Holst's *Jupiter* would have been better," I grumble as the crowd moves into a line without even being told.

"Agreed, *ma petite*," Rennie whispers as we head for the back of the newly formed line. "But, alas, the people making these decisions are not so musically inclined."

Felix and Fitz take my arms and Chess walks between my winged warriors behind us. Fitz shrugs, giving me a crazy smirk. "With the way tonight's likely to turn out, I think we should enter to the fucking *Ironman* theme song.

Of course, he'd think we should rock up to this old world ball backed by AC/DC.

"For once, I don't even have the urge to smack him in the back of the head, Princess. It's not a bad idea."

Turning to Felix, I wrinkle my nose at him, hissing low. "What did I say about this being a *Cinderella experience* until it isn't? I will *murder* you all if you ruin this."

"Baby Girl, I would never, ever deprive you of your little girl fairy tale ball daydream. The shitheads in hoods might, but we're gonna Prince Charming the *fuck* out of you until then. Got it?" My hyper tiger squeezes the hand on my arm, then leans in to put his lips to my ear. "Besides, all fucking five of us are rocking the magic tattoos you accidentally gave us when you scratched big bro's dick—which I still think was a bad ass move, little bunny."

"Fitz!" I grind out. "What did Felix say about *secrets* in *public*?"

He grins roguishly, avoiding his brother's glare. "You've always known I'm a bad boy, Baby Girl. You'll just have to continue keeping me in line."

A muffled snort from behind us makes me chuckle and I nod at the line. "It's moving. We should stop for the cameras as a group when we enter the ballroom. If they want a spectacle, we'll give them one."

"Ooh. Feisty lunchable," Aubrey says. "Looks we're in for an interesting evening."

We sure as hell are.

Everyone shuffles forward and the anticipation of entering a room with all my bullies, my parents, and every crooked asshole in the

Northeast claws at my gut. I know I will never measure up to any of their scrutiny, but with my friends just ahead of us and my guys around me, it will be okay. They can stare at me disdainfully all they like; I know better now.

"Angel, you look like you're getting ready to run." My sensitive cheetah probably noticed how tense I'm getting as we step forward every time the crier guy inside announces another name. "It's okay. None of them matter; you know that."

"I do. But I'd rather some beer swilling jackass in the underground ring be calling my name right now than this. At least those people are honest about wanting to kill me."

Felix snickers, but whatever he planned on saying is cut off by the loudmouth in the room, saying Cori and Rufus' names. That means we're next, so I take a deep breath, straightening my spine and putting on my Lucille face. She'd never be dressed as softly as I am, but using her attitude against her kin has worked for me so far. No use fixing something that isn't broken.

"*The Honorable Delores Diamond Drew, daughter of Lucille Rostoff and Bruno Drew, escorted by…*" he pauses for a moment and I snarl under my breath. "*… escorted by Prince Felix Khan, Royal Enforcer Fitzgerald Khan, Chester Khan, His Highness Aubrey Draconis, and Le Roi de Laveaux, Renard Laveaux.*"

"That's a fucking mouthful," Fitz mutters. "I don't know how our girl does it, honestly."

I pinch his arm hard as we walk into the room, pausing at the top of the stairs. My eyes skate over the crowd, immediately zeroing in on the gaggle of Council members that include Lucille and Bruno ensconced at a table surrounded by goons. The ghost of a smirk dances across my face as my mother takes me in, surrounded by my men, clad in couture, and sporting a crown straight from a dragon's hoard. When I feel like we've made a big enough statement, I nudge Felix and the twins lead me down the stairs. I'm surprised when Renard and Aubrey deal with the giant pouf of my dress without being asked, but by the time I get to the bottom, I know why. They lived through a time where this kind of shit was normal.

Way to make yourself feel like a kid, Dolly. No more history bullshit tonight.

When we reach the bottom, the music resumes, but I can hear whispers around the room. My hearing has been much better since I emerged, especially when I shift, but this is crazy. It's like I can hear people across the crowded room despite the small orchestra playing a light waltz in the background. Whispers of all our names assault me and I shake my head slightly, trying to dispel the weird auditory effects.

"You okay, Princess?" Felix rumbles under his breath as we walk past older shifters that have mixed expressions of scorn, fear, and uncertainty.

"My hearing just got markedly better as we walked down into this snake pit. Like… questionably so. I'm having a hard time adjusting," I murmur, then smile at some sparkling old bat who raises a glass at me.

His brows raise, but the regal smile doesn't leave his face. "We knew after the… oddity the other night you might have effects. Less than optimal time for one to show up, but concentrate on your bunny. Get her to focus on controlling her strengths."

"Great. The Universe is having a grand old time with Dolly again, granting me powers I don't know how to work in a room full of people who'd like to kill me." I hold on to both of my tigers tightly, praying something I can't control won't send this evening spiraling into the abyss.

If it's my fault, they'll have a perfect scapegoat—the disgraced mutant ex-heiress.

"You're not a mutant, Angel."

I stop in place, turning my head to look over my shoulder at Chess. "What did you just say?"

He frowns, tilting his head at me. "I said you're not a mutant."

My body stiffens, and Feliz leans in to whisper in my ear. "Not here, Princess. Turn around and keep moving to our table."

Giving him a fake flirtatious smile, I pretend we're having a normal conversation in case someone's watching. "Of course, dear."

We're almost to the goal line—a table near the front that would befit the guys' professor status and their backgrounds. It doesn't escape my notice that our spot is located off to one side of the stage where the musicians are playing Bach, almost in the shadows. While no one in my group is excluded from wealthy or well-known families, we're definitely being seated like the blackest sheep possible. I snicker under my breath as I sweep my eyes over the sheeple watching us descend on our table. To my delight, the triplets appear to greet Rufus, and Giselle follows their lead to sit by Cori.

I was worried she'd chicken out after our entrance, but it looks like Cori's maybe girlfriend has a stronger spine than my friend thinks.

Fitz pulls my chair out, making sure I'm settled before he grabs the chair to my left. Aubrey and Ren sit next to the triplets, facing the room with suspicious gazes. I blow a kiss at them when Felix takes the open chair between Aubrey and me. Then Chess finally sits between Fitz and Giselle. Our table is packed, more so than most, and I wonder how we got everyone together.

"The Captain," Rennie says absently as he strains to look at the three head tables full of Council members, the Headmaster, and somehow, my nemesis, Rockland, weaseled an invitation to one of them.

"Again… there it went again," I murmur to Felix and he frowns.

"What again?"

Licking my lips nervously, I close my eyes, turning away as I think about my answer without saying it. If I'm right about what is going on, I won't need to repeat myself out loud.

"Oh." When I turn to face him, my Tiger King is beaming broadly like I just gave him winning lottery numbers. "Perfect timing. It really altered something, just not like a normal shifter."

His words catch Aubrey's attention and he stares at us, arching a brow. Felix winks, then taps his temple once, making my dragon blink. He nudges Rennie, tilting his head to me and mimicking the move he saw. They both grin broadly, obviously happy with this turn of events. A small piece of bread flies across the table to hit Fitz in the nose, then they repeat the charade.

Can they not do this with each other?

"Of course *some* of us can, Angel, but…"

Fitz snorts and leans in to kiss Chess' temple when it finally hits him. "Welcome to the conversation, baby."

"Ahem." We all look over at Rufus, Cori, and their guests when the badger clears his throat. "It's adorable that you're all figuring some big secret out, but I should warn you we've got a problem."

Following his discreet pointing, I see Lucille and Bruno rising from their table. Bruiser rushes forward, immediately hovering nearby, and I groan. "Here it comes."

"We knew the crazy bitch was going to accost us, Dollykins," Cori says. "Stand your ground. Own your power."

"Thank you for that YouTube worthy pep talk, Coco," Rufus chuckles. "My advice is to do that, but make sure the bitch knows who she's fucking with. You don't need to look like someone's going to skin you if her name comes up on your phone."

"I hate to agree with the Cornbread Mafia, but…" Fitz puts his hands on my cheeks, pulling me close so his forehead rests on mine. "… that woman doesn't get to treat our girl like shit in front of us. We're Khans and they're ill-tempered flying assholes. If you don't handle them, we will. Capiche, Baby Girl?"

Talk about your Catch-22: hot protective boyfriends or victory over my mother? How the hell do I choose?

"Just do what you feel is right, Princess," Felix says. "But you need to stand before she gets here or you'll lose ground."

Nodding, I rise from my chair, straightening my spine as I lock eyes with the woman who's tortured me most of my life.

Time to put her in her place, Dolly.

KINGS & QUEENS

DELORES

MY EYES LOCK ON MY MOTHER'S AS SHE AND BRUNO SLINK through the crowd. They don't watch where they're going; no, it parts for them like some mythical figures moving through the sea. I feel the support of my family from behind me, but they can't do this for me. It may not be time to take Lucille off the board, but I know in my gut that I have to stand my ground with her tonight.

I don't move when they reach me—not even to dip my head in acknowledgement, as I would have in the past. The silence is deafening as I hold my ground, staring back at Lucille without flinching. Knowing her, this could have gone on forever, but one of the triplets speaks before either of us breaks.

"Who are these people?" Chisisi asks innocently.

His lack of knowledge hits Lucille right where it was intended and she whips her head around to give him her patented death glare. The anger at someone feigning ignorance of her station radiates off of her in waves and Bruno smirks a little at her back. "Just who are *you* to interrupt a private conversation?"

The soft chuckle from behind me almost makes me smile. "I am Chisisi Kavarit, one of the three princes of Kavarit, and guardian of ancient knowledge. Pardon my ignorance, madam, but our kind do not focus on the passing fancies of current leaders so much as history."

"Though conversation is stretching the term a bit," Ramses adds drily. "I've been in tombs less quiet than this stand-off."

Lucille's face contorts with rage and this time, Bruno does laugh. That draws her ire to him, and my mother whirls to hiss at him. "Be gone, you useless sack of purse leather. It's *your* fault we're in this situation. Go pretend you're relevant elsewhere or I'll inform Dmitri."

What the fuck?

I've seen Lucille treat Bruno like an accessory unworthy of her airspace before, but *this* is much more pointed. Something has changed, and she's cagey enough to keep me far from the information I'd need, even if it would help me survive. A single brow quirks as I watch Bruno shrink and scurry off without a word—though Bruiser stays put. I suspected his real loyalty was to my mother and now it's confirmed. At least one question has been ticked off my list so far, though it brought a new one as Bruno's cowering.

"It appears you have made quite a few acquaintances since I sent you to Apex, Delores. I would have expected you to keep me in the loop about your life. Apparently, I was misguided." Lucille's eyes have shifted golden, but the rest of her is human. It's a warning I recognize, but I can't allow her to dominate me this time. "I'm disappointed."

My expression is placid but tempered with ice as I respond. "I'm a grown woman, Lucille. Surely you realized it was time for me to manage my own affairs?"

Her gaze narrows as she rakes it over my table of friends and lovers. "It appears your judgment has improved since your prom night. That's a relief. I was concerned you'd continue chasing those vapid ninnies and your whimpering dog forever."

Bullshit. She was furious at the loss of my connection to the other Council families.

"I don't choose my friends and family to use their connections or wealth, Lucille. That's *your* bailiwick—not mine." I paste an even faker smile on as I look in their direction, feeling the strength emanating from my guys. Of course, there's a barely contained vein of rage there as well, but they know as well as I do that I have to do this on my own.

Lucille snorts, waving her jewel encrusted hand. "Highly doubtful. Kings, princes, enforcers, heirs… you have the combined GDP of South America at this table—both legal and illegal incomes. Your ability to sniff out those who can elevate your pathetic abilities is unparalleled."

A growl echoes from behind me, and I know it's Fitz. His cup is overflowing with the need to torture my mother until her screams fade into the abyss. I lift my hand, waving at him as my mother did with Bruno. The only show of power she respects is the kind she knows, and dismissing his concern will show her I'm in charge.

I'm absolutely fucking not, *but she doesn't need to know that.*

"Why are you here, Lucille?" I stand straighter, lifting my chin to make the crown on my head seem more appropriate.

Her lips curve, eyes dancing with evil intent when she notices the glittering dragon crown—just as I intended. "Excellent. I see you're already reaping the benefits of your associations. Perhaps I'll make a Rostoff out of you yet."

Felix slams his fist on the table, and I turn to touch his head lightly to calm him. "I am who I am, Mother. You no longer have the ability to mold me in your image, and I no longer wish to pretend

I'm allowing you to do so. So I'll ask again. What. Do. You. Want?"

"I want to know exactly what I'm dealing with, Delores. If we're going to stop pretending, you know the Council is here to put a stop to the missing heirs before someone important is taken. No more, no less. Inspecting my merchandise is only a side benefit."

My temper flares when she refers to me as *merchandise*, but I don't let her see my fury. "I don't see how holding an event destined to draw attention and therefore, harm, to a large swath of the elite achieves that goal."

"Most of them are expendable, Delores; you've never paid attention to my lessons the way you should have. Those who aren't know what to do should the worst come to pass."

The people she thinks are important know a way out of this nightmare scenario and everyone else will be left to fend for themselves.

"By your estimation of expendability, of course." I turn for a moment, looking at the crowds of shifters dancing, my gut twisting at the idea of sacrificing an entire room of people to prove a point. "This is low, even for you, Lucille. It feels… over your paygrade."

Her left eye twitches—just once and almost small enough that it's barely noticeable—but she shrugs languidly. "Nothing is above my paygrade, daughter. You'd do well to remember that."

"Enough!"

The voice startles me and I turn to see Aubrey standing in his place, the rainbow of his dragon bleeding into his eyes. His fire is burning hot inside—that much is apparent—but his temper is even more volatile. I dip my chin at him, hoping to show that I'm okay and he doesn't have to do this. In fact, it may make things worse in the end. But his expression doesn't change and I know I won't be able to back him off from across the table.

"Did you have something to say, Draconis?" Lucille smirks, pleased that she's gotten a rise out of someone.

Aubrey crosses his arms over his broad chest, not backing down an inch. "If a single hair on Dolly's head is harmed tonight, it will nullify all treaties. Renard and I will make certain the news travels to the right individuals. Your power will be diminished if every one of the remaining groups of old withdraws support for your side."

Excuse me, what? What the fuck is he talking about?

My eyes drift to Rennie briefly and the twinkle I see there, even briefly, tells me what I need to know. Aubrey is purposely baiting her with our suspicions. They're all watching to see how Lucille reacts, hoping to guide us where to look for answers next. This is a gambit—a dangerous one—but a gambit, just the same. When I look at my mother again, there's another twitch in that eye. A smile curves my lips as I realize I've found one of her tells.

"You risk much, dragon. We're all aware of how long you've been in exile, no matter how short your time at Apex has been in contrast." Lucille looks at him carefully, studying him like a big under a jar. "The influence you think you wield is vastly overblown."

Aubrey smiles, his expression crafty and taunting. "We're a secretive lot, mythicals. Who are you to determine I'm not a plant? I've been on this continent watching for longer than most of the families who now pretend to rule all of shifterdom have existed."

That gets her attention. My mother stiffens and I can tell she's fighting the urge to do something rash because she's uncertain if he's bluffing. To be fair, I wouldn't know, either, if it weren't for Rennie giving me the heads up.

I'm never playing poker with my lust librarian, that's for certain.

"Fine. You can deal with my erstwhile progeny—for now." Her sniff is one of absolute disdain and I shoot her a haughty glare.

"Delores, you will continue focusing on bringing positive attention to our family through academic excellence and your performance in the Games. Otherwise, I—"

Her command is cut off by a strangled scream echoing across the ballroom. I whip my head around to look at the guys. "It's happening."

Another shout, followed by a roar, accompanies the first, and the noise level in the crowd increases as people move. Felix stands, removing his jacket and rolling up the sleeves of his shirt—hot as fuck and I have to shake my head a bit to clear. He winks at me, draping the suit coat on the chair before looking at Lucille in amusement. "I believe the chaos you hoped to lure has arrived. Do you plan on fighting or running?"

Lucille scoffs, half-shifting in a blink as she turns to Bruiser. "Make a hole. We must adjourn to our positions."

"Of course you must," I mutter as I watch the ballroom descend into panic as people realize there's a problem. "You've never been one to sacrifice for anyone but yourself."

"Dollypop, it's time," Rufus says as he and the triplets mimic Felix. The rest of the guys do the same, their eyes alight with their animals in anticipation of a fight. "You and Coco need to join us."

I smirk, giving my mother the finger up close and personal before I reach down to yank the giant ball of tulle from my waist. The velcro gives just as Cori intended, leaving me in the special skintight leggings and knee-high, heeled combat boots that match the top of my ball gown. I'd kept the guys out from under my fancy getup for a reason—I needed everyone to underestimate me in case something like this happened. Cracking my neck, I half-shift, letting my ears and tail break free before turning to check that Cori had similarly ditched her gorgeous gown for snowy white fur.

"Let's go save the day," I say as I flex my claws.

Fitz smacks my ass, looking delighted as he takes in my change. "That's it. I'm hiring Coco-cabana to recreate your entire fucking wardrobe, Baby Girl. I don't know if I'm hard because we're going to kill shit or because you look like Badass Barbie, but I am *here for it.*"

That said, he jumps on to the table, looking at the room for a moment before he lets out an ear-splitting roar. It gets the attention of the people fighting across the room and he winks at me before yelling, "*Cowabunga!*"

Did he just yell 'Cowabunga' as a battle cry? I swear to Hera, I love that fucking tiger.

My eyes pop open at the revelation, but I know we don't have time for it. "You heard the man—time to kick some ass."

With that, my family explodes away from our table into the growing fray of scrambling shifters and screams, leaving Lucille behind without another word.

REVOLUTION
RENARD

EVERYONE MOVES AT *MA PETITE*'S COMMAND AND I SMILE PROUDLY. She's gained so much confidence this year and despite wanting to rip her mother limb from limb, watching her stand up for herself was satisfying, too. Dolly needed to know she could do it and her mother deserved to be knocked back for once.

But now we have mass chaos and I honestly can't see who's actually caus-ing it.

Using my wings as a shield, I let the gargoyle harden me from head to toe so I can push through the knot of people yelling and flailing about. There are a lot of shifted students and family members, but I can't find the source of their fear. It's like there's something invisible that's—

"Mind benders," I mutter to myself. "Mages, perhaps, but also…" I touch the shining amulet at my neck, then jump on a table, using it to see over the crowd. It makes a creaking sound, but I only need it briefly until I can see her. Dolly is stalking the perimeter, using the shadows at the edges to get the lay of the land. My chest tightens as I realize that's a skill she learned hunting with Flames and I. "Good girl."

Leaping off my perch before it buckles under my weight, I return to stalk through the hysteria. I listen for the original scream—the one that sounded as if it was preceded by someone being harmed. If there are mindbenders of any kind here causing the group to fight demons only they can see, they'll be hidden, blending in to avoid detection.

~I can't find any hoods. This assault is different magical users. ~

Hearing his voice in my head, I have to stop myself from nodding in response. I know he likely can't see me, but we need to tell the others we won't be able to stop this unless we find those who are wielding the illusory powers. I'm about to reply when a light flashes and a horde of hooded figures pour into the room from the shadows. *~Fuck. We have to let the others know some people are fighting illusions—mages or Fae. But now we have actual physical magicians as well. Ones who could be anything under those goddamn hoods. ~*

~I see Felix. I'll start with him. Keep your eyes peeled, love. And watch for the lunchable. ~

~She's on the hunt. I saw her. ~

His presence in my head fades, leaving me to ponder how we're going to find the illusionists. Suddenly, it occurs to me they would need a perch to see their destruction and control the puppets. They won't be among the rioting academy shifters; no, they'll be hiding in plain sight somewhere strategic. Pushing my way through until I reach a wall, I shift more, whipping my tail out for balance as my claws dig into the drywall for purchase. I climb and climb until I hit the high ceiling, then turn to look out over the scene carefully.

TigerFitz is ripping through as many groups of struggling people as possible, separating them from hoods and invisible attackers alike. I'm not sure if he can see them in his full form or if he's going on instinct, but he's trying to herd the innocents towards the main stairs as he does it. It's a good plan—his focus work with Dolly is paying off. Close to him, I see Rufus and his triplets; the latter lifting people as they hover on large wings so the badger can beat the snot out of them with…brass knuckles?

But of course he is.

A loud roar gets my attention and I swivel to see Flames zipping across the room in a low dive, taking out three hoods creeping up on our girl as she fights a tall one spurting red magic. His appearance scared the piss out of a bunch of nearby shifters, so BearCori is busy pushing them to the exits like Fitz. So far, I haven't found my targets, but I also don't see Felix or Chess. My brow furrows and crab crawl across the wall to get to the balcony above. *Perhaps if I…*

Blue lightning shoots across the room, getting everyone's eyes as it zips to a corner where Chess is being pinned to the wall by two hooded figures. TigerFelix is fighting his way there, but he's getting stopped by invisible shit as he snarls in fury. I have to find these magical fuckwits before people realize *ma petite* is the one shooting power; otherwise, she might get labeled as part of the rebels, not someone fighting to free our students.

As soon as the bolts hit the hoods holding Chess, Dolly darts back to the shadows and I breathe easier. Checking the area, I leap over the balcony railing to mingle with the people hiding above the fray downstairs. The mage has to be up here; the view is perfect for an area of effect attack—it allows them to see but not engage directly. Knowing that tidbit makes me think our conjurer is *not* Fae, but likely one of the other varieties of spellcasters. Fae know how to defend both magically and physically; they were trained warriors from the beginning of time.

That doesn't mean they're not involved in this group, though. I've smelled proof of things that cannot be without their presence.

A dull throb emits from my amulet, and my eyes widen. It hasn't done that in many years. Shaking my head, I mutter to myself, "They are here. But how is the question, even if why seems more prudent."

Pressing against the wall for a moment, I close my eyes, remembering the last time I saw any of the Fair Folk in person. I know what happened then—which is why they cannot be here. It's possible some enclaves remained afterward, but not a single whisper of their existence has made it through the world since. Unless they have been biding their time… No. Despite their immortality and penchant for grudges, I do not believe they'd risk their secret lives to attack shifters with random magic users.

Unless…

I swallow hard, knowing if my wild supposition is true, the world is not ready for the violence that will be unleashed. If magic users and Fae who were not forced into the portals after the Treaty have been gathering forces, biding their time over centuries of development in the non-magical world have decided it is time to make themselves known… This results from a long planned out endgame and they have knowledge about the outcome. The Fates will have foretold this and there's a prophecy *somewhere* being hidden by our crooked leaders.

The room fills with arcing colored lights and I shake myself out of it. It's getting out of hand; a battle like this cannot continue inside or many people will die. The stone at my neck pulses again and I turn to see a very regal-looking woman dressed in designer clothes watching the mess. Her aura is far too calm and I don't recognize her as one of the founding families of the Council.

She has to be the mage—and a powerful one at that, because she's using no amplification tools.

I stride through the crowd, keeping my eyes on her as I reach for Flames. *~I think I found the illusionist. Keep your eyes on the team while I try to force her to leave. ~*

He doesn't respond, but I feel his agreement as I make my way through the milling dignitaries, who are too stupid to get the hell out of here. None of them are Council members—those assholes disappeared once we entered the fray, along with Dolly's mother.

They must have had a bolt hole planned for the inevitable attack and it wouldn't surprise me if they're watching this with glee. If you cut the footage just right, it will look as though magic users are all dangerous and traitors to their rule.

They might be, but I get the sense more is going on here and I'm going to find out what.

"*Cease*," I say when I get close enough to the woman for her to hear me above the din. I push my royal command into the words, something I rarely do. Her head turns, and she gives me a knowing smirk when she sees the amulet dangling from my neck.

"The poor exiled King. Yes, we were warned you might be trouble. Unfortunately for you, that trinket holds minor magic, and you've weakened it by splintering a piece off." Her eyes glow a brilliant green, then fade to black as she chuckles menacingly. "You are the wrong shifter to come for me, child of the Earth."

I don't have time to respond when her hand flicks at me and my feet are surrounded by rocks. They hold me in place as firmly as any bondage I've ever felt except they're melding into my obsidian outer layer to prevent me from breaking free without shattering my skin. Panic floods me as I gaze at the woman, the touch of her magic on me breaking whatever illusion she'd cast over herself.

The real illusionist is a five foot tall earth pixie glowing with power much stronger than pixies have ever contained. She grins with a mouthful of razor-sharp teeth as her cage crawls up to my waist, pinning me. "Aye, *Monsieur*. We have so many new tricks up our sleeves from resting for so long and drawing in the power of those who would force us into the shadows. Your merry band of misfits is no match for what is coming."

My eyes narrow, catching something in her words. The exact phrasing used by *any* of the Fair Folk is extremely important and a long time ago, I was well-versed in diplomacy with their kind. "What you aren't saying is that you don't have permission to kill me, only stop me from helping."

"Perhaps, gargoyle. But your time will come—*all* of your times will come. The shifters with their lust for domination, the sheep who followed without questions, and the betrayers who sided with them. None of you will escape The Reckoning. It has been foretold."

A mighty growl that shakes the wall comes from below and we both turn to see my girl standing on a table, her hands clutched around a knife as she fights a hood with the purple magic she warned us about. My pixie captor laughs crazily when she sees me growl, slapping her leg in mirth. I flex my wings, determined to break free even if I'm in the infirmary for weeks afterward.

I won't let them hurt her.

"Oh, punished Prince! We won't harm your precious little rabbit. No, we have plans for her, and this is only the beginning." She watches for another moment, grinning as blue lightning arcs around the room wildly. "There it is. Another level. Excellent. She will be pleased."

I blink, confused by her babbling. The pixie winks at me, waving her hand at the battle downstairs casually. The invisible enemies seem to disappear, because injured shifters fall to the ground in a heap. The hooded figures mixed in go up in smoke, leaving behind their wounded and the people fighting them off. Those who don't get up dissolve into dust that flies towards the exits as the pixie points. Her smug expression only gets more so as she laughs again and snaps her fingers. The rocks holding me disappear, but I still can't move.

"Know this, Renard Laveaux. We will continue to take what we need to defend ourselves and win back what was lost. Your band of misfits have the choice to help or hinder—for now. Soon enough, we will not give them a choice. The girl is key and you cannot prevent our path, nor can you escape the payment long due for your own sins."

"My sins?" I growl. "I didn't—"

"You are not responsible for the larger war, young gargoyle. However, you have shaped our destiny since you were exiled. She will not be denied."

A clap of thunder rents the air and I'm no longer frozen in place as she poofs. Running to the railing, I see everyone below knocked out cold, thrown to the ground with the force of her magic. Jumping the rail to hit the ground hard, I ignore the building shaking as I make my way to Dolly. Unlike the others, she's awake, just dazed as fuck. I can almost *see* the birdies flying around her head as she mumbles to herself.

"*Ma petite*, are you okay?" I ask as I drop to look at her carefully.

"Did you get the number on that fucking bus? The driver's a lunatic," she mutters. "Knocked me clear into a fucking duck pond."

"No, *mon amour*. I didn't see the license plate." Her crazy head smacked babble hits me and I laugh, holding my sides as I look around the unlikely scene. I can't stop and even the dark rumble I recognize as my mate doesn't make the gallows humor flowing over me subside.

When he finally dusts himself off and comes over to us, he gives me a heavy sigh. "The three of us are the only ones awake, Rennie."

"I know." I keep laughing, despite catching the meaning behind his words.

"You know what it means."

"Yep."

Aubrey rolls his eyes and looks down at our girl, grabbing the phone out of her reinforced pockets. "Thank fuck it survives this shit. I'm calling all our reinforcements in. If they survived, we need to triage the wounded and get the dead to the dining hall until funeral homes arrive."

"Fuck," I whisper.

"What?" he says as he stabs at the screen to text the Captain and our auxiliary friends.

"They're going to throw away all the ice cream to cool the corpses. I could really use some double chocolate chip right now."

The dragon blinks, then shakes his head as Dolly sits up to mumble. "I like ice cream. Let's have some."

"Ra save me from my fucking family and the paperwork this mess is going to generate," he grumbles.

"I don't think anyone will be exempt from this old friend. This was the start of war and we're the only ones standing."

Dolly squints at me, her hair a mess, crown askew, and blood and gore painted over her skin and pink outfit. "If war is what those assholes want, then it's what they'll get. Once I sort these fucking ducks out, this bunny is done running. From now on, we take the fight to them."

Delores Drew, Council Heir, Mate to Royalty, and Queen of the Pred Games, has spoken.

Long live the Queen.

Preorder Eat. Prey. Love (Book 4) in the Apex Academy Capers series now!

Want to know what happens next? Flip to the bonus scene!

REVIEWS, PRINT, AND MERCHANDISE

If you have enjoyed this book, please leave reviews! It helps other
readers find my work,
which helps me as an indie author.

Thank you!

**Reviews for In Prey We Trust are appreciated
on the following platforms:**

Amazon
Goodreads
Bookbub
StoryGraph
TikTok
Instagram
Facebook

To purchase print copies or merchandise, go to The Worlds of
Cassandra Featherstone

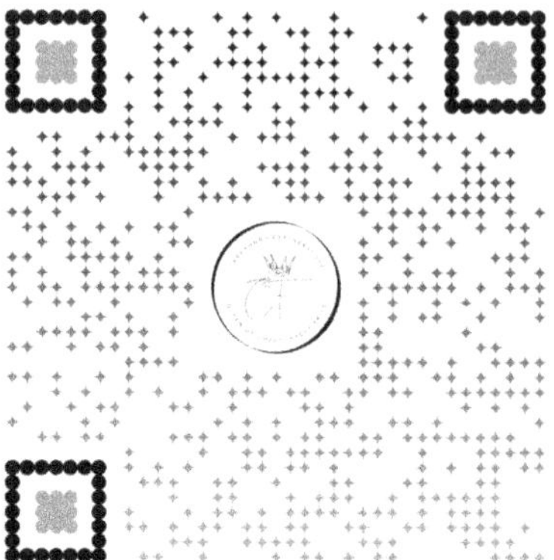

World Guide & Pronunciation

CHARACTERS

DELORES DIAMOND DREW (DUH LOR ES DIE MOND DROO)

Lucille Rostoff Drew (lou SEAL ross TOV Droo) leopard, evil genius, Dolly's mother

Bruno Drew (Brew noh Droo)- crocodile, Dolly's father

Matilda/Mattie (mahTILduh/ mahTEE) Lucille's assistant, former nanny to Dolly, hawk shifter

Bruiser (Brew ZER)- komodo dragon, bodyguard for Drews

Heather Erickson (heh THUR AIR ick sun) aka Gold, bitchy ex-BFF, wolf

Heather Barrington (heh THUR BEAR ing tun) aka Pink, bitchy ex-BFF, jackal

Heather Honeywell (heh THUR hun EE wel) aka Silver, bitchy ex-BFF, coyote

Heather Charles (heh THUR ch ARRL zuh) aka Purple, bitchy ex-BFF, African dog

Heather MacLachlan (heh THUR mac LOCK lan) aka Yellow, newcomer Heather at Apex, tiger

Todd Birkshire (doosh BAHG)- hyena, former fiance to Dolly, asswad who took her v-card

Fitzgerald Khan/Fitz (FIH TZ jair uhl duh/ FIH TZ KAH N)- comp sci, Pred Games, tiger

Felix Khan (FEE licks KAH N)- professor Shifter Studies 200, tiger, twin of Fitz, exiled heir

Chess Khan (CHeh SS KAH N)- Apex Student Liaison, Guidance Assistant, cheetah, Fitz's consort and mate

Aubrey Draconis (AW BREE Drah CON iss)- Librarian and Archivist, National Library, exiled King, dragon

Renard Laveaux (Rey NAR d LA Voh)- Guest Lecturer at Capital and the Smithsonian, exiled King, gargoyle

Rufus McCoy (Roo fuss MICK OY)- honey badger, gangster, heir to drug empire, Dolly's BFF

Cori Bouvier (kor E boo VEE ay) polar bear, Dolly's BFF

Henrietta Shirdal (hen REE ett UH SHEER dahl) former Headmistress at Apex, Apex advisor and assistant Headmistress of Capital Prep

Raina (REY nuh) part of Captain's crew, has her own harem, works in cafeteria

The Captain- pirate raccoon, heads crew, loyal to Renard

Banjo, Kirby, and Bowser (Ban JOE, Kir BEE, BOE zuhr) triplet quokkas, part of Captain's crew, in Raina's harem

Holliday (Hohl IH day) armadillo, works in armory, part of Captain's crew and Raina's harem, deaf

Percy (Purr see) skunk, works in laundry, part of Captain's crew and Raina's harem, related to Argyle

Luc Growlvinchy (looKUH GR owl VAHN she) Dolly's boss at design firm, (tiger)

Emile (ee MEAL) pangolin, head of pangolins who work for Growlvinchy

Bettina (BEH tee nuh) school nurse, hedgehog

Clarice (Claire ees) school nurse, opossum

Argyle (ar-guy-ul) school nurse, skunk

Zhenga Leonidas (zen GUH lee oh nEYE diss)- shifter biology and Pred Games

Chisisi, Ramses, Asim Kavarit (ch IH see see, Rahm zen, aH seem Kah bah riht) owners of *Riddles & Rituals*

Madame Solange de Bouvier (MAH dahm SOlahnjuh deh BOO vee yay)- new Vocal teacher (orca)

Herr Helmut Blitzen (HAIR Hell MOOT Bleet ZEN)- Shifter History (shark)

Professor Natasha Blutarsky (Nah tah shah BlOO tar ski)- new dance instructor (Python)

Adriatica los Feliz (AH dree AH tick UH lohs Feh leez)- Theater Director and Studies (jaguar)

Kamara Rakoto (Kah MARR uh RACK oh toe)- Human Diplomacy & International Shifter Relations (Tiger)

Carina Raquel Rockland (CAH reenuh RAH kell Rahk land) Capital Preparatory Guidance Counselor & Cheer Squad Coach (jackal)

Headmaster Balthazar Slechtschrijven (BAHL thuh zahr Sle CHT sreye VEN) Headmaster of Cappie (hippo)

Selene (SehLEAN) Pred Games team, daughter of Hecate the pop star panther and rapper FangZ (jaguar)

Charlotte Bruce (SHARlet Broose) Pred Games team, parents diplomats from Australia (great white shark)

Jaiyana Faez (JAY AhNUH FIE eez) Pred Games team, parents a fashion designer and Hercules the ex-Pred Games World Champion (saltwater crocodile)at

Roswitha Faust (ROW ZWiya THaa Fow ST) Pred Games team, mother second heir to Ursa clan in Germany, father polar bear and famous mystery author (grizzly bear)

Kyaw Aung (CHAW Ung) Pred Games team, father President of Prey Games League and mother model (Burmese python)

Headmaster Bathalzar Slechtsrijven (Hehd Mahstir BAHL thuh ZAHR Sl EH ckt SRIH V ehn) Cappie Headmaster (polar bear)

Titus Maclachlan (TIE-tuhs MACK-lock-lahn) father of Heather M. aka Yellow, Council member, tied to Khans tangentially, runs health care and hospital systems

Hannah Hopewell (HaN uh Hoh P weh l) mother of Heather H. aka Purple, Council member, tied to ministry and sketchy church with husband

Lief Erickson (Leaf AIR ik suhn) father of Heather E. aka Gold, Tech wizard, Council member

Oliver Barrington (AH-live-er Bear-ing-tuhn) father of Heather B. aka Pink, Council member, head of all media and social platforms

Kehinde Leonidas (Keh IN day Lee O nye duss) wastrel spare heir twin of Zhenga, runs all sports leagues for their father, involved in match fixing and cheating

Septimus Charles (SEHP tih muss CH-arl-zu) father of Heather C aka Silver, Council member, controls agro giant food industry

Bram Birkshire (Brahm Bur-K-shur) father of Todd, lower Council member, family runs low end banking for prey banks

LOCATIONS

Apex Academy - college being repaired from magical bomb incident

Drew Mansion- Delores' home

House of Growvinchy- designer fashion house she worked at

Capital Prep- College they are doing an exchange program with while Apex is being rebuilt

Shirdal Arts Compex- arts building at Capital Prep

Erickson Scholastic Complex- classroom buildings

Leonidas Capital Prep Pred Games Arena- official Pred Games Arena

Khan Battle & Training Arena- training arena

Dupree Student Center & Admissions- main admission center

Savananda Kavrit International Library and Diplomatic Archives- Capital Prep Library

Washington D.C.- nearby city, human capital, and location of secret Council Capital HQ

Bloodstone Isle- Khans rule this island and reform school

Council Capital Headquarters- location of the Council formal business HQ and human liaison services

Underground Tunnels- prey staff use these below the school just like at Apex

National Library- the Library of Congress equivalent

House Lupine- dorm for all canine/adjacent species

House Feline- dorm for all feline/adjacent species

House Aquatic- dorm for all aquatic shifters

House Avian- dorm for all bird/ flying shifters

House Reptilian- dorm for all reptile/amphibious shifters

National Theater- Kennedy Center equivalent

Smithsonian- museum in the capital

Inky Depths- dive bar owned by the Rostoff syndicate in the red light district where illegal fights happen

Feathered Quill- subversive bookstore

Diamond Delights- a strip club owned by Rostoff syndicate

Riddles & Rituals- bookstore used by Cappie students in D.C. owned by Kavarits

Dungeons, Dragons, & Daddies- sex shop in the red light district

Happy Kitsune- Chinese buffet in the arts district

GET A SECRET BONUS SCENE!

For a secret bonus scene that follows *Eat. Prey. Love.* click the link below, sign up for my newsletter, and get your freebie.

Get your bonus scene from EPL here!

SNEAK PEEK: BLOODTHIRSTY

QUEEN BEE

They dim the lights in the club, and the spots click on as the curtain slides open.

It's a full house tonight in the little burlesque club off the Rue Pierre Montaine.

Chez Arc En Ciel is not well known compared to the *Moulin Rouge* or *Le Lido*, but the wealthy from both sides of the Seine gather here for shows four nights a week. If you pass the various layers of security checks to even be permitted to book a reservation, you also have to be able to afford the two thousand Euro per guest cover charge. If you don't eat or drink anything, that's all it will cost; however, that would get you blacklisted.

Intro music pumps through the speakers and I stand on my mark in the opening position. My cane is resting on the wooden boards of the stage by my front foot as I pretend to lean on it. Roars of applause echo through the room as our troupe of dancers catch the lights, sequins sparkling like diamonds when the stage lights rise. We're dressed in pinstriped black pant suits and fedoras to match the big band style opening to the song. As soon as the horn-filled intro finishes, the dance begins.

I follow the routine with precision, snapping and popping my hips to the beat as we spread out across the stage. You wouldn't know by the fake smile on my face that I'm scanning the crowd. Two fan kicks later, I've rotated past the proscenium, and I think I've found my mark. Twirling, I stop in the place I need to be for the bridge, singing along as if my life depends on it. It might, to be honest, because I need to sell my cover tonight, so no one notices me.

The Guillotine moves in the shadows, but tonight, she's in the spotlight.

My ass shakes as I dance my way through the song, swinging the prop cane I'd replaced with one of my design. You wouldn't know by looking at it, but it's not the painted balsa the other dancers have for a very specific reason. I need it to complete the mission that forced me to spend two months in Paris working my way into this job at *Chez Arc En Ciel*. If I can't strike tonight, the surveillance, counterintelligence, and time spent building this cover are wasted because my mark is leaving for Asia tomorrow.

Tonight, the Cobra dies for his sins.

The break of the song slows the music and the dancers pour into the crowd to wiggle around the rich assholes. It's choreographed, but it's also to advertise each girl for private dances in the lounges upstairs. We're not strippers—not that there's a damned thing wrong with a woman using her body to support herself—but we do bare more skin in the closed rooms. The *laissez-faire* attitude of the owners means as long as we kick them thirty percent of the fees for those dances, they don't care what any of the girls do in the rooms. I'd find it sleazy, but the girls who work here are highly skilled performers who choose to make thousands of dollars a night rather than peanuts in some ballet troupe or chorus line.

By the time I've flirted my way to the VIP tables, the Cobra is staring intently at all of us. Spotlights pin each one of us on the floor at the bass hits, and I swivel my hips as my free hand slides down to the secret spot on my jacket. In unison, we tear the jackets off to reveal rhinestone studded bras with straps criss-crossing our waists like shibari ropes. A lift of the fedora and pop of my hip, along with the beat, draws the fierce-looking brawler's eyes directly to me. I pout prettily and stalk towards his table with the swagger of a tiny dicked asshole that owns a monster truck.

His thin lips pull back over the famed curving fangs he had implanted. Dark, glittering eyes follow every move I make as I approach, and I pretend to whip my hair from side to side as I check for his guards. They're here somewhere, but I need them to be far away so I can beat my escape before they notice. When I get within inches, I tap his leg with my cane and spin around to shake my ass in his face. The grunt of approval makes me want to heave, but I turn, holding onto the prop with both hands. My feet click on the floor in a soft shoe step as I make 'fuck me' eyes at the dirty bastard. He leans back, his pants tented as he gestures towards his lap.

Fucking gross.

I don't care about his weapons trade or what happens when people get the shit he moves. I have no clue why I have to take him out. The reason they have sentenced him to death isn't part of my contract, and I'm nothing if not a dispassionate observer of the darkest parts of human desires. Twelve years at *l'Académie* ensured I care very little about anything that isn't directly related to my ability to complete my jobs.

Sighing, I dance closer and drop onto his rather unimpressive erection and wiggle. There's plenty of cloth between us to prevent him from doing anything I'd make a scene over, so I focus on the task at hand. I slip the cane behind his head, resting the wood against his neck as I tug him forward. The move reads as playfully bringing his face to my breasts, but at the last second, I click the release built into the custom weapon. One end slides open to reveal the razor sharp garotte and before he can say a word, I yank it through.

Faint gurgling is the only noise besides the end of the song, and I carefully slide the sides of the cane together. Climbing off the nasty fucker, I put my hands on his cheeks so I can pretend to flirt with him while I arrange the head so it looks as if he's leaning back in the booth. It needs to look realistic to allow me to return to the stage with the others. When I have it settled, I back away from the booth, blowing fake kisses as I walk backwards through the crowd. I almost collide with a dark-haired guy with his collar pulled high as I head for the stage, and I roll my eyes. Whatever celeb that is trying to keep their face away from the paps is doing a shitty job of it.

The entire troupe takes a few bows and shuffles off of stage left to the wings. I exhale a sigh of relief when the next group enters on the opposite side. I haven't heard shouting yet, so I don't think the Cobra's men realize he's down. Now I take this emetic pill, have a vomiting episode, and I'll get sent home.

That's when Arabella Montaigne, the burlesque dancer, will cease to exist, and Remy Arsine Benoit will re-emerge.

I smile to myself as I chew on the tablet that will have me retching my guts out in a few moments. This is a more complex extermination than I usually prefer, and I can't leave my normal calling card behind. The Cobra's head had to remain in the booth rather than get delivered to his home in a basket.

Such a shame, that. I quite enjoy the reactions my little gifts engender when they're discovered.

Walking into the dressing room, I carefully strip my costume off, putting all the pieces in my bag. Every item in the locker room that belongs to gets placed in the duffel carefully as I wait for the effects to hit me. It won't do to leave loose ends, even if my prints have never touched a single surface in this place. My gut roils and I turn, facing one of the other dancers as the vomit finally comes. Gracelia screams like she's being skinned when I hurl on her and it's everything I can do *not* to smirk through the chunks.

"C'est la merde!" she shouts, running for the showers as if she's on fire.

It takes less than a minute for the owner to send me home for the night. I walk out the back door of the building with everything just as the sirens scream.

Perfect timing, as always.

I jump into the first cab I can hail, directing him to the *Hôtel de Crillon*. Their suites are the ritziest in Paris, and it's my go-to hideout when I'm here. I used to only stay in the Bernstein Suite, but some rich fuckwad purchased it six months ago. If I could track them down and beat the hell out of them, I would, but I booked my schedule until late 2025. Assassins with my skill set and accuracy are getting harder to find. They forced the old guard into retirement because they refuse to adapt to the digital age. Too many cameras, crime labs, and hackers running about to do everything Cold War style.

The future of murder for hire is millennial, people. We're old enough to be stable, but young enough to be agile with new technology. Plus, most of them are broke AF from crooked ass student loans.

It's not an issue I have, but I've been in the business since I hit double digits. You don't survive *l'Academie des Invisibles* if you haven't killed someone before the end of primary school. It's unheard of.

I was eight the first time I used the weapon that would become my signature.

Shivering, I tap on the window of the cab and bitch the driver out. He's taking a longer route than necessary to raise my fare, and I'll have his guts for garters if he doesn't knock it the fuck off. A string of curses in French erupt from him when I voice the accusation, and I slam my palm on the window with enough force to crack the plexiglass barrier. He almost drives into another car, but when he regains control, he makes the requested adjustments to our route.

We arrived at the front entrance after a few more arguments and a traffic jam around the *Champs*. I throw the euros at him in disgust, memorizing the medallion number for later. He's not worth my time, but I have quite a few contacts who might be interested in blackmailing a cabbie in town. Getaway cars are cliche in the crime world now. Most ne'er-do-wells like myself find greater comfort in anonymous taxis or ride-share accounts hacked through the deep web accessed on burner phones. If your ride doesn't know you're a villain, there's no one to flip if law enforcement comes looking.

I never look the same for any job—ever.

I will not use Arabella Montaigne as a cover in the future, and once I move to the location of my next job, I'll ensure that she meets with a terrible fate. It's a lot more work to slowly kill off my alters once I've used them, but it's also why I've never even come close to being caught. The dancer with long wavy red hair, freckles, and big green eyes will never grace the streets of Paris again after I hop a plane. She will, however, get a minor story in the paper and an obituary when I decide how she tragically dies.

The Guillotine will rise from her ashes and be reborn.

Sneak Peek: Veiled Flame

Loser

Kat

The little blue icon on my app has been glaring at me all day, but I'm too damn nervous to open it. Everyone at Woodlawn High has been buzzing all day with their notifications and the squeals of joy and moans of despair were too much for me to take. My anxiety is through the roof—this is the moment I've been waiting for since middle school, but I can't seem to force myself to bite the billet and check.

Maybe it's because I don't have the support system most of my classmates have?

That's probably true, given I've always been a loner and I don't fit into any specific 'caste' here. It's hard to make friends when you get shuffled from foster home to foster home over the years. I've rarely stayed anywhere long enough to make a friend, much less a group of them.

I'm not delinquent or anything—the families I've been placed with just return me like a pair of pants that doesn't fit after a year or so. The caseworkers click their tongues sympathetically and hunt down a new placement, but I've never been given a reason *why* people don't want me around. One lady said I must be born under a bad sign and hell if I knew what that meant other than I'm not good enough to keep around.

It would be different, almost understandable, if I misbehaved or got bad grades. But I don't—I'm always in the top five percent of my class and I do everything I'm asked. I don't even lord my smarts over the other kids or adults. Being presentable and unassuming was something I adapted long ago to improve my probability of staying in a home long term.

Unfortunately, it never worked and though I should be a shoo-in for scholarships and acceptances galore, I can't bring myself to be rejected yet again.

So I wait for the last bell of the day, slinging my bag over my shoulder and trudging home to the latest in my temporary housing. I can't even contemplate looking at the possible heartache waiting for me in the college application system WHS insisted we use. The fear is too great and despite knowing I'll be on my own for good at the end of this year, I'm unable to risk the pain.

I hate being this way.

My court mandated therapist says it's some sort of attachment disorder that's common in foster kids, but I think that's bullshit. The problem isn't *me* not forming attachments; it's asshole adults not forming one to me. Being left at a safe haven in a fucking basket as a baby wasn't because *I* did anything wrong—again, fucking adults couldn't handle their commitments.

As usual, I arrive home to an empty house. There are two other kids who live here—Bryce and Blake—but they're at football practice. Of course, the Jamesons *love* them; they get to strut around at games because their strays are the stars of the team. I'm not mistreated, but I'm definitely an afterthought. Both of my 'parents' are still at work, so I drop my bag on the couch and head for the kitchen to get a snack.

Don't get me wrong. I *could* have been placed in far worse homes than any of the seven I've been in since elementary school. None of the ex-fosters starved, beat, molested, or abused me. They were all decent folks with jobs and houses that weren't hellholes, but they never liked me.

I have no idea why. I tried to be everything they wanted.

But when the end of each school year came, I was handed in like a textbook and off I went to some group home until the next contestant stepped up. It baffled everyone, not just me, but that's what happened every single time.

Sighing, I pull some fruit out of the fridge and grab a soda. I have homework to do and if I want to have time to work on my stories, I'll need to get it done before the house is full of people at dinner time. Bryce and Blake will have gotten messages about their applications, too, and I'd bet my pinkie toe those idiots got into some big sports school. Brett and Allison will be oozing happiness for them and I don't know if I'll be able to keep food down if I have to admit my failure when they ask.

Being eighteen sucks ass.

After I grab my books and tablet, I head down to the den. I have to give my current parents credit; they set up a very nice workspace for us to study in the converted basement. By the time they took me in, the Jamesons created a cozy room down here where the three of us could relax and do our work for school without being interrupted. It might have been more for the boys than me, but I appreciated it all the same. Desks, a couch, big chairs, and bookshelves fill the space, making it almost seem like our mini-library. They even put a small fridge for drinks and snacks in case we had to be up late to cram.

It's my favorite place in the entire house and I spend most of my time here.

I sink into the huge armchair, putting my drink and snack on the side table. It only takes a few minutes to arrange myself in the soft cushions and I pause to tug my headphones out of my pocket. Music always soothes my jagged edges and I need it to stay focused on the bullshit AP Calculus I need to keep my average up in. My course load is heavy, but I applied to tough colleges. I wouldn't have a chance to get in, especially on a scholarship, if I wasn't taking equally challenging classes in comparison to all the prep school kids.

As always, the sounds of Vivaldi carry me away as I scrawl equations on my screen and before long, thoughts of the blue notification completely fade away.

"Kat!"

The shouts barely register as I continue working on the problem set, gnawing on my lower lip in concentration.

"Jesus fuck, where is she? I could eat a hippo!"

"Kat!"

Thumping followed by what could pass for a stampede of elephants jerks me out of my math filled trance when Bryce and Blake come down the stairs. They smell as bad as the aforementioned pachyderm's cage, so they must have rushed home right after practice. The blond twins glare at me as if I'm the offending element despite being sweaty and covered in dirt and grass stains.

This doesn't bode well.

Usually, they're tired and hungry after practices so I'm used to cranky ass boys, but tonight, there's a light to their faces. That had to mean they've gotten their letters and dinner will be a gush fest in honor of their perfection. I'm going to need all of my strength to fake smile and nod as Brett and Allison fawn over them.

I don't begrudge them their success—not really. They work hard and play even harder on the field. It's not their fault they're the American dream teens and I'm the nerdy basement troll no one wants. But it's awfully hard living in the shadow of their bright light, especially when I'm no less intelligent or talented.

"I'm finishing the AP Calc, guys. What do you want?"

They roll their eyes at me before Blake scoffs. "It's not due until Monday. You're so hyper."

Duh. I take anxiety meds, douchebag; of course I'm 'hyper.'

"I can only be who I am, Blake." That earns me a snort from Bryce and I know it's because he thinks that's the problem. "Is dinner ready?"

"Almost. Get upstairs and set the table so we can shower—Brett's orders." Blake grins smugly.

The two of them seem to always arrange it so chores get passed to me for some half-assed reason and this is no exception. Sighing, I put my stuff aside, fully intending to hide down here after the dinner mess is cleaned up. Likely by me, but like I said, I could definitely live in worse foster homes so I let it go. Doing some chores isn't worth risking the group home for the last few months of my high school career.

They take off running up the stairs and I wait for them to disappear before I follow suit. My phone is tucked in my pocket and I feel like it's a stone of shame I have to bear. I know once the adults make over the twins' success, they will remember me, and I'll be forced to find out what disappointment lies in wait for me. The dread weighs on me, but I head into the sunny kitchen and pick up the pre-prepared pile of plates, silverware, and napkins on the counter.

Allison looks up from the stove and gives me a half-smile, nodding as I take the dishes into the dining room. Like I said, no one is mean or horrid, they just seem…obligated. After a while, it makes it hard to waste time trying to be bright and sunny. Being reserved makes it a hell of a lot easier not to feel rebuffed when they don't pay attention to you regardless.

"Make sure you include champagne glasses for your dad and I!" she calls from the other room.

The twins definitely got acceptance somewhere big. Brett must have gotten the bubbly on the way home.

Once I set the table, I return to help Allison bring out the roast and sides. I'm a little amazed at her efficiency when it comes to getting the housework done while working full time, but I suppose it's something people with real parents get taught as they grow up. My home life has been so fractured that I haven't learned how to cook more than very basic shit from YouTube videos. That may be a problem after graduation, but I've never felt comfortable enough to ask Allison if she'd teach me. I'm sure she would try, but it doesn't feel right.

"How was school, Kat?"

I look over my shoulder, seeing Brett in the entry to the dining room. He's already changed from work and smiling, but I see the distraction in his eyes. He's waiting for the boys to come down. "It was fine. I've got a Calc test at the end of the week. I'll be studying a lot to get ready."

"Good, good. No matter what happens with applications, keeping your grades up will ensure no one pulls any offers," he says.

Those words aren't for me. They are for the two wet haired boys who just appeared behind him.

"Kat's too much of a geek to ever let her grades slip, Dad," Blake says as he pushes past his brother and drops into his usual chair at the table. "Grab me a Powerade since you're in the kitchen, mouse!"

Both Brett and Bryce stare at me and I turn around, heading to the fridge despite the fact that I was *not* closer than the other twin. Out of habit, I take two of the drinks and a soda for myself. I've been here long enough to know Bryce will send me back to get him one as well. It would feel like typical sibling stuff, but for some reason, I just *know* they do it to fuck with me. I have no idea why I feel that way, but trusting my gut has been the one thing that helped me get through all the upheaval in my life over the years. It's a good gauge for knowing when I'll get booted or if people are being earnest in their reactions.

The therapist says that's some sort of trauma induced early trigger warning shit, by the way.

After I hand out the drinks, I sit down on my side of the table and we wait for Allison to come out. Brett is at his seat at the far end of the table and the twins are punching each other as they look at something on their phones. I know where this is all going but I drop my gaze to the table, swallowing the coppery taste of fear as it courses through my body.

I'm going to be exposed and there's nothing I can do to stop it.

Read the first three episodes free on Kindle Vella: https://www.amazon.com/kindle-vella/story/B0BSTMB1X3

Sneak Peek: Failed State

Every Day is Monday

Sydney

"Jesus fucking Christ," I mutter as I slog through the streets of Tempest Seven. "Just because they locked us up like animals doesn't mean we have to live like them."

Pausing in my walk to the education center, I look around myself in abject disgust. The inhabitants of this end of Tempest Seven aren't the bottom of the proverbial barrel, but outside of the 'lockdown losers', people stuck here never seem to get out of the cycle of poverty and despair. I don't think it means we have to throw garbage everywhere and give the drones nice shots to prove to the humans that we're as unworthy as the leaders of this stupid country say we are.

What would it hurt to tidy up, even if we don't have much?

Honestly, I believe it's only a third rooted in laziness. I think the other parts are exhaustion and hopelessness. Since the First Infected Being Sweep of 2020, supernaturals all over this country were tracked, catalogued, reassigned, and declared property of the government. By the time they ran the second through fourth sweeps, the population of some supernatural species dropped by fifty percent. The rules on how to track us down and receive your bounty were infuriatingly vague, which gave the most violent psychopaths in the world a free license to kill, maim, rape, and disappear anyone caught on the 'Non-Human Watchlist'.

I was a baby when my mother left, but my father taught me everything I needed to know about being a shifter. Unfortunately, he was one of the people who ended up on that list and was killed in the Second Infected Being Sweep of 2020. That sweep was brutal, and since I was a 'half-breed' orphan, I was placed in the orphanage in Tempest Seven. From the moment every child and teen arrived, they were forced to attend the Federal Enrichment Assimilation & Re-Education Center.

Our human professors taught us that being born this way is a punishment from their God, especially if you were a mixed type. At first, we tried to tell them about our various species, but it became clear very quickly what would happen if we didn't fall in line. You either learned to smile and nod, providing the rote answers and scripts they gave you when tested or interrogated, or you died.

Now, in 2024, there are no rebellions against the Federated Human States of America, nor are there any aid workers from other countries left to help or try to get us out. The world has given up on the former United States—it's been ruled a failed state by the United Nations and cordoned off at every border on land and sea.

We're on our own in the former land of the free and home of the brave.

"As if anyone would want to come here anyway. Shit went downhill fast after that baboon was elected," I mutter to myself. I realize I've spoken louder than I thought and I look around carefully, making certain I'm not near a Confession Enforcement zone or any other beings. My breath releases slowly when I confirm that I'm totally alone and not in a hot zone.

No one watches out for others now; the temptation to gain things your family or group needs is too high. A random person would dime me out for a week's supply of crackers and I can't blame them. Food and drink are rationed, our clothes are drab and provided, and the world is dimmer since the Sweeps. They force us to stay small so they're in control, and we have to live with it because of the fucking Markers.

My hand flies to the back of my neck, grunting in irritation as I scratch at the tattoo that covers the skin where the implant is located. These were the second step on the path to the current tyranny of our 'benevolent' government. That spray tanned fuck won the election because the humans here were that goddamn stupid, and then the virus hit. COVID brought America to its knees and like all good con artists, President Taterman used the distraction to funnel money into secret programs under DARPA.

Men who stare at goats my skinny ass.

They released a widely contested study that blamed the virus on the 'infected'. Unfortunately, they defined that as beings living in our country that had paranormal capabilities. The rest of the world laughed at the senile old fuck until the media hype was so huge that the various species around the world convened a leadership meeting. With so many cameras and videos everywhere, it was only a matter of time until a random human caught one of us doing something and bam! A viral TikTok would expose all of us whether we were ready or not. The vote was close, but the supernatural community decided to come out of hiding to protest their innocence.

'The Unveiling' was the most watched TV event in decades, and the consensus was our leaders had done the right thing. At least, until the next study was released. This one made Taterman damn near salivate as he screamed into the TV cameras about the 'unclean' liars and thieves who have been hiding in plain sight, taking our jobs, and stealing the lives humans should have. It quickly devolved into a mass panic and our kind were left scrambling.

We'd told them who and where we were, like a bunch of fools.

Thus, the evil assholes at the top started their mission to protect the humans from us and reclaim their country. Supernaturals in other nations were fine, but the atmosphere here became dangerous within the blink of an eye. Taterman stacked his own deck in the courts and the legislature by fear-mongering, especially since the world was still reeling from a pandemic. Eventually, he was able to get the support he needed for the first Sweep.

Secret Supernatural Enforcement Agents used databases, social media, DNA websites, immigration records, and everything they could to gather the biggest dragnet of personal information ever assembled. Civil rights advocates and other world leaders were vocally opposed to such violations, but nothing could stop the juggernaut of hatred. Once they identified every supe in the nation—to the best of their ability—that's when they stripped our citizenship, robbed us blind, and re-assigned every single one to the sectors they'd been building in secret.

Let's be honest—they're supe prison camps.

But the humans felt safe once more because while we were all being shuffled all over like cattle, the rest of the scientific community worldwide started to get COVID under control. Taterman crowed about the United States' involvement, taking credit for slowing the spread by locking up the infected beings. No one but his nutty followers believed him, but at that point, it didn't matter.

So when they came to implant the Markers, no one spoke up.

We all have them, and depending on what you are and how powerful you are, they are different. But resting above the spot where they cut us open to shove in the controller, there's a matching tattoo of the logo that is now on the flag of the Feder ated Human States of America… but that came much, much later.

Democracy dies in the dark, the old slogan said… and here lies her rotted corpse.

"Hey, Syd. It's a beautiful day in the neighborhood, huh?"

My brooding gets interrupted by the arrival of Thad, my friend since we got placed here four years ago. He's a bear shifter and the size of a small SUV, but it doesn't bother me. I survived the sector version of high school partially because we stuck together. My brains and his bulk were a good match and it kept us from getting cornered by the gangs and cliques.

Okay, fine, it kept me from getting cornered. Obviously, Thad held his own without me.

"That sentiment hasn't been applicable for half a decade, man." I toss my braid over my shoulder and wait for him to catch up. It's our second week at the F.E.A.R. Academy's college level program and being late is more than frowned upon. I have to give us extra time every morning because Thad lumbers out of bed like his animal—slow and grumpy. "We gotta get moving."

The dark haired shifter looks at me, scratching the piratical scruff he's usually sporting. "You're ridiculously concerned about rules for someone with such a rebel spirit."

"Rebels die, Thad. I'm very aware of that." Turning on my heel, I head toward the huge building at the end of the main drag with a heavy heart. Losing Dad was hard and I'll never forgive him for assuming humans are anything but ignorant beasts that barely rise above their simian relatives.

We continue walking in silence until we reach the steps. The line is stretched down them as the guards run the wand over each student to check for weapons. After that, we put our bags on the conveyor belt for the magical detection while the security mages in government issued loyalty collars scan us for anything the wands wouldn't catch. It's not quick, but it keeps fights in the schools non-lethal most of the time.

That's the official reason, but the real purpose is to allow the staff to abuse students if they step out of line. The Markers not only brand and track us, but they siphon energy and power in small bits to keep us all weak enough to be controlled. Weapons would even the score and the humans who run these stupid ass brain-washing cults would be at risk.

"Look who's last at the trough again." The wry voice of the only demon in Tempest Seven gets my attention. Huck Monroe saunters up, tilting his worn black cowboy hat back as he smirks at me. "Y'all are just cruisin' for a bruisin'. I swear, you don't have the sense that the Devil gave a goose."

My eyes narrow at him briefly, then I turn forward and shuffle along as the line moves. "You don't have to hang out with us, Huck. In fact, it'd be great if you fucked off and stayed there."

Thad laughs, bumping his shoulder against the annoying fear demon's and I sigh. Huck was sent here during the First Sweep, like us, and he's been a Southern bramble in my side ever since.

It's my bad luck that Thad enjoys his folksy charm and it means he sticks to us like glue during school hours.

"Sometimes you're meaner than a wet panther shifter, Sydney Jolie. I should take you at your word and mosey off, but I like your boy."

Huck's pitch black eyes are hidden by his Ray-Bans, but I know they're sparkling with amusement. He finds my dislike funny, and I don't get why. But then, I don't get a fucking thing about men, especially supes, nor do I want to. Life in our sector is hard enough without having to consider birth control or babies or even finding privacy. I'll save that for the day when I get the fuck out of here.

"I heard they're bringing in a new group of students today." Thad changes the subject quickly, knowing I'll continue to needle Huck and vice versa until one of us loses their temper. "The rumors say the shipment has vamps, losers, and traitors. I'm worried this sector is turning into a dumping ground for psychos."

It wouldn't surprise me if the humans started segregating the camps by species, value, or even criminality. Even after they corralled us into the sectors, the leaders have continued to exert their influence and power over us. The Markers were first, then the lockdowns for the ones they deemed dangerous, and now they're shuffling people weekly at random. I've often wondered if all of this is covering up something like what went on in the 1940s among the humans, but I haven't seen any proof.

Our media is monitored and curated, so unless you know someone with a highly illegal device, you have no idea what's happening outside of the FHSA.

"Next! Keep it moving, you little shits," the yell from the front of the line brings me back to reality again.

"Wicker is the fucking worst," Thad mumbles as we ascend the steps to stand behind the person being inspected. "Watch his hands, Syd."

"I'm aware." Despite thinking we're the scum of the earth, some of the human staff and enforcement in the sectors are fucking creeps. Some supes are willing to trade sex for perks, but that doesn't stop the predators from being creeps to those who don't. "I'll let you go first so Bishop gets me."

"Got it," he says as he muscles in front of me. "Huck, stay behind her."

"Why, I'd be delighted, Thaddeus."

I guess he's useful sometimes, but he'd better not let it go to his head.

Get it now!

About Cassandra Featherstone

Cassandra Featherstone has channeled her lifelong passion for writing into a flourishing career, a journey that started when she first grasped a pencil as a gifted child with ADHD.

Her debut novel, born during the solitude of COVID lockdown in March 2020, draws on a tapestry of personal encounters and insights that resonate deeply with her readers.

An international bestseller, Cassandra has topped Amazon charts in categories such as LGBT Anthologies, LGBTQ+ Mystery, and Bisexual Romance, among others. Her works navigate the complexities of bullying, PTSD, body dysmorphia, mental health struggles, personal reinvention, and the empowerment of claiming one's own space. Importantly, Cassandra offers a thoughtful and respectful portrayal of LGBTQIA+ relationships, subtly reflecting her own connection with the community through her narratives.

Her literary repertoire spans sci-fi fantasy, urban fantasy, paranormal, and comedic genres in academy whychoose settings, with a strong commitment to portraying consensual, safe, and accurately depicted BDSM and kink lifestyles. Her books are an invitation to explore transformative stories that are both inclusive and engaging.

Often affectionately called 'The Muppet' for her wacky theater kid personality, she resides in the Midwest with her tech-savvy husband, their creatively inclined college student, a literary-minded dog, and four scheming cats.

READ MORE AT CASSANDRA'S WEBSITE OR HER FACEBOOK PAGE. SIGN UP FOR EXCLUSIVE CONTENT AND UPDATES HERE.

FIND HER ON ANY OF THE SOCIAL MEDIA BELOW AS SHE *LOVES* TO CHAT AND *NEVER* SLEEPS!

Prey It By Ear

AUDIO OF THE APEX ACADEMY CAPERS SERIES

Come Out & Prey

Let Us Prey

In Prey We Trust

TRANSLATIONS OF THE APEX ACADEMY CAPERS SERIES

Come Out & Prey (German)

Let Us Prey (German)

In Prey We Trust (German)

DISCORDIA UNIVERSITY

Veiled Flame (Book One)

Quiet Burn (Book Two)

Zero Spark (Book Three)

Hell for the Holidays (Crossover Holiday w/ SSU & FA)

Obsidian Inferno (Book Four)

AUDIO OF THE DISCORDIA UNIVERSITY SERIES

Veiled Flame (Book One)

Quiet Burn (Book Two)

Zero Spark (Book Three)

SECRETS OF STATE U

Blood on the Ice (Book One)

Suspicions on the Stage (Book Two)

Fatality on the Field (Book Three)

FAETAL ATTRACTION

Hell on Wheels (Book One)

Jammer in the Box (Book Two)

Ghosting the Pack (Book Three)

F.E.A.R. ACADEMY

Failed State (Book One)

Trigger Protocol (Book Two)

VILLAINS & VIXENS

Bloodthirsty (Book One)

Ruthless (Book Two)

Wicked (Book Three)

AUDIO OF THE VILLAINS & VIXENS SERIES

Bloodthirsty

Ruthless

TRIANGLES & TRIBULATIONS

Hoist the Flag (PQ)

Yo-Ho Holes (Book One)

CHILDREN OF THE MOON-
WITH SERENITY RAYNE

New Moon Rising (Book One)

Waxing Crescent (Book Two)

Waxing Gibbous (Book Three)

Samhain Secrets (Novella 3.5)

Full Moon (Book Four)

Waning Gibbous (Book Five)

Waning Crescent (Book Six)

RISE OF THE RESISTANCE

Ream Exclusive Prequels

Hooked on a Feline (Book One)

Peacock Me Like A Hurricane

Love The Way You Lion (Book Three)

Snake It Off (Book Four)

REAM SERIALS

Secrets of State U

Discordia University

Faetal Attraction

Rise of the Resistance

F.E.A.R. Academy

ANTHOLOGIES

Unwritten

Shifters Unleashed

Jingle My Balls

Love is in the Air

Silent Night

Snowed In

All Hallows Eve